E. E. Smith

The Skylark of Space & Skylark Three

e-artnow 2022

E. E. Smith
The Skylark of Space & Skylark Three

2 Sci-Fi Books in One Edition

e-artnow, 2022
Contact: info@e-artnow.org

ISBN 978-80-273-4495-6

Contents

The Skylark of Space	11
CHAPTER I: The Occurrence of the Impossible	12
CHAPTER II: Steel Becomes Interested	14
CHAPTER III: Seaton Solves the Problem of Power	20
CHAPTER IV: Steel Liberates Energy—Unexpectedly	28
CHAPTER V: Direct Action	35
CHAPTER VI: The Object-Compass at Work	41
CHAPTER VII: The Trial Voyage	48
CHAPTER VIII: Indirect Action	55
CHAPTER IX: Lost In Space	59
CHAPTER X: The Rescue	69
CHAPTER XI: Through Space Into the Carboniferous	76
CHAPTER XII: The Mastery of Mind Over Matter	86
CHAPTER XIII: Nalboon of Mardonale	91
CHAPTER XIV: Nalboon Unmasked	98
CHAPTER XV: The Escape from Mardonale	105
CHAPTER XVI: An Osnomian Marriage	113
CHAPTER XVII: Bird, Beast, or Fish?	122
CHAPTER XVIII: The Invasion	129
CHAPTER XIX: The Return to Earth	135
Skylark Three	139
CHAPTER I: DuQuesne Goes Traveling	140
CHAPTER II: Dunark Visits Earth	142
CHAPTER III: Skylark Two Sets Out	150
CHAPTER IV: The Zone of Force Is Tested	155
CHAPTER V: First Blood	163
CHAPTER VI: The Peace Conference	173
CHAPTER VII: DuQuesne's Voyage	181
CHAPTER VIII: The Porpoise-Men of Dasor	192
CHAPTER IX: The Welcome to Norlamin	201
CHAPTER X: Norlaminian Science	212
CHAPTER XI: Into a Sun	220
CHAPTER XII: Flying Visits—Via Projection	225
CHAPTER XIII: The Declaration of War	233
CHAPTER XIV: Interstellar Extermination	239
CHAPTER XV: The Extra-Galactic Duel	251
Epilogue	259

The Skylark of Space

CHAPTER I

The Occurrence of the Impossible

Petrified with astonishment, Richard Seaton stared after the copper steam-bath upon which he had been electrolyzing his solution of "X," the unknown metal. For as soon as he had removed the beaker the heavy bath had jumped endwise from under his hand as though it were alive. It had flown with terrific speed over the table, smashing apparatus and bottles of chemicals on its way, and was even now disappearing through the open window. He seized his prism binoculars and focused them upon the flying vessel, a speck in the distance. Through the glass he saw that it did not fall to the ground, but continued on in a straight line, only its rapidly diminishing size showing the enormous velocity with which it was moving. It grew smaller and smaller, and in a few moments disappeared utterly.

The chemist turned as though in a trance. How was this? The copper bath he had used for months was gone-gone like a shot, with nothing to make it go. Nothing, that is, except an electric cell and a few drops of the unknown solution. He looked at the empty space where it had stood, at the broken glass covering his laboratory table, and again stared out of the window.

He was aroused from his stunned inaction by the entrance of his colored laboratory helper, and silently motioned him to clean up the wreckage.

"What's happened, Doctah?" asked the dusky assistant.

"Search me, Dan. I wish I knew, myself," responded Seaton, absently, lost in wonder at the incredible phenomenon of which he had just been a witness.

Ferdinand Scott, a chemist employed in the next room, entered breezily.

"Hello, Dicky, thought I heard a racket in here," the newcomer remarked. Then he saw the helper busily mopping up the reeking mass of chemicals.

"Great balls of fire!" he exclaimed. "What've you been celebrating? Had an explosion? How, what, and why?"

"I can tell you the 'what,' and part of the 'how'," Seaton replied thoughtfully, "but as to the 'why,' I am completely in the dark. Here's all I know about it," and in a few words he related the foregoing incident. Scott's face showed in turn interest, amazement, and pitying alarm. He took Seaton by the arm.

"Dick, old top, I never knew you to drink or dope, but this stuff sure came out of either a bottle or a needle. Did you see a pink serpent carrying it away? Take my advice, old son, if you want to stay in Uncle Sam's service, and lay off the stuff, whatever it is. It's bad enough to come down here so far gone that you wreck most of your apparatus and lose the rest of it, but to pull a yarn like that is going too far. The Chief will have to ask for your resignation, sure. Why don't you take a couple of days of your leave and straighten up?"

Seaton paid no attention to him, and Scott returned to his own laboratory, shaking his head sadly.

Seaton, with his mind in a whirl, walked slowly to his desk, picked up his blackened and battered briar pipe, and sat down to study out what he had done, or what could possibly have happened, to result in such an unbelievable infraction of all the laws of mechanics and gravitation. He knew that he was sober and sane, that the thing had actually happened. But why? And how? All his scientific training told him that it was impossible. It was unthinkable that an inert mass of metal should fly off into space without any applied force. Since it had actually happened, there must have been applied an enormous and hitherto unknown force. What was that force? The reason for this unbelievable manifestation of energy was certainly somewhere in the solution, the electrolytic cell, or the steam-bath. Concentrating all the power of his highly-trained analytical mind upon the problem-deaf and blind to everything else, as was his wont when deeply interested-he sat motionless, with his forgotten pipe clenched between his teeth. Hour after hour he sat there, while most of his fellow-chemists finished the day's work and left the building and the room slowly darkened with the coming of night.

Finally he jumped up. Crashing his hand down upon the desk, he exclaimed:

"I have liberated the intra-atomic energy of copper! Copper, 'X,' and electric current!

"I'm sure a fool for luck!" he continued as a new thought struck him. "Suppose it had been liberated all at once? Probably blown the whole world off its hinges. But it wasn't: it was given off slowly and in a straight line. Wonder why? Talk about power! Infinite! Believe me, I'll show this whole Bureau of Chemistry something to make their eyes stick out, tomorrow. If they won't let me go ahead and develop it, I'll resign, hunt up some more 'X', and do it myself. That bath is on its way to the moon right now, and there's no reason why I can't follow it. Martin's such a fanatic on exploration, he'll fall all over himself to build us any kind of a craft we'll need ... we'll explore the whole solar system! Great Cat, what a chance! A fool for luck is right!"

He came to himself with a start. He switched on the lights and saw that it was ten o'clock. Simultaneously he recalled that he was to have had dinner with his fiancée at her home, their first dinner since their engagement. Cursing himself for an idiot he hastily left the building, and soon his motorcycle was tearing up Connecticut Avenue toward his sweetheart's home.

CHAPTER II

Steel Becomes Interested

Dr. Marc DuQuesne was in his laboratory, engaged in a research upon certain of the rare metals, particularly in regard to their electrochemical properties. He was a striking figure. Well over six feet tall, unusually broad-shouldered even for his height, he was plainly a man of enormous physical strength. His thick, slightly wavy hair was black. His eyes, only a trifle lighter in shade, were surmounted by heavy black eyebrows which grew together above his aquiline nose.

Scott strolled into the room, finding DuQuesne leaning over a delicate electrical instrument, his forbidding but handsome face strangely illuminated by the ghastly glare of his mercury-vapor arcs.

"Hello, Blackie," Scott began. "I thought it was Seaton in here at first. A fellow has to see your faces to tell you two apart. Speaking of Seaton, d'you think that he's quite right?"

"I should say, off-hand, that he was a little out of control last night and this morning," replied DuQuesne, manipulating connections with his long, muscular fingers. "I don't think that he's insane, and I don't believe that he dopes—probably overwork and nervous strain. He'll be all right in a day or two."

"I think he's a plain nut, myself. That sure was a wild yarn he sprung on us, wasn't it? His imagination was hitting on all twelve, that's sure. He seems to believe it himself, though, in spite of making a flat failure of his demonstration to us this morning. He saved that waste solution he was working on—what was left of that carboy of platinum residues after he had recovered all the values, you know—and got them to put it up at auction this noon. He resigned from the Bureau, and he and M. Reynolds Crane, that millionaire friend of his, bid it in for ten cents."

"M. Reynolds Crane?" DuQuesne concealed a start of surprise. "Where does he come in on this?"

"Oh, they're always together in everything. They've been thicker than Damon and Pythias for a long time. They play tennis together—they're doubles champions of the District, you know—and all kinds of things. Wherever you find one of them you'll usually find the other. Anyway, after they got the solution Crane took Seaton in his car, and somebody said they went out to Crane's house. Probably trying to humor him. Well, ta-ta; I've got a week's work to do yet today."

As Scott left DuQuesne dropped his work and went to his desk, with a new expression, half of chagrin, half of admiration, on his face. Picking up his telephone, he called a number.

"Brookings?" he asked, cautiously. "This is DuQuesne. I must see you immediately. There's something big started that may as well belong to us.... No, can't say anything over the telephone.... Yes, I'll be right out."

He left the laboratory and soon was in the private office of the head of the Washington or "diplomatic" branch, as it was known in certain circles, of the great World Steel Corporation. Offices and laboratories were maintained in the city, ostensibly for research work, but in reality to be near the center of political activity.

"How do you do, Doctor DuQuesne?" Brookings said as he seated his visitor. "You seem excited."

"Not excited, but in a hurry," DuQuesne replied. "The biggest thing in history has just broken, and we've got to work fast if we get in on it. Have you any doubts that I always know what I am talking about?"

"No," answered the other in surprise. "Not the slightest. You are widely known as an able man. In fact, you have helped this company several times in various deal-er, in various ways."

"Say it. Brookings. 'Deals' is the right word. This one is going to be the biggest ever. The beauty of it is that it should be easy-one simple burglary and an equally simple killing-and won't mean wholesale murder, as did that...."

"Oh, no, Doctor, not murder. Unavoidable accidents."

"Why not call things by their right names and save breath, as long as we're alone? I'm not squeamish. But to get down to business. You know Seaton, of our division, of course. He has been recovering the various rare metals from all the residues that have accumulated in the Bureau for years. After separating out all the known metals he had something left, and thought it was a new element, a metal. In one of his attempts to get it into the metallic state, a little of its solution fizzed out and over a copper steam bath or tank, which instantly flew out of the window like a bullet. It went clear out of sight, out of range of his binoculars, just that quick." He snapped his fingers under Brookings' nose. "Now that discovery means such power as the world never dreamed of. In fact, if Seaton hadn't had all the luck in the world right with him yesterday, he would have blown half of North America off the map. Chemists have known for years that all matter contains enormous stores of intra-atomic energy, but have always considered it 'bound' —that is, incapable of liberation. Seaton has liberated it."

"And that means?"

"That with the process worked out, the Corporation could furnish power to the entire world, at very little expense."

* * * * *

A look of scornful unbelief passed over Brookings' face.

"Sneer if you like," DuQuesne continued evenly. "Your ignorance doesn't change the fact in any particular. Do you know what intra-atomic energy is?"

"I'm afraid that I don't, exactly."

"Well, it's the force that exists between the ultimate component parts of matter, if you can understand that. A child ought to. Call in your chief chemist and ask him what would happen if somebody would liberate the intra-atomic energy of one hundred pounds of copper."

"Pardon me, Doctor. I didn't presume to doubt you. I will call him in."

He telephoned a request and soon a man in white appeared. In response to the question he thought for a moment, then smiled slowly.

"If it were done instantaneously it would probably blow the entire world into a vapor, and might force it clear out of its orbit. If it could be controlled it would furnish millions of horse-power for a long time. But it can't be done. The energy is bound. Its liberation is an impossibility, in the same class with perpetual motion. Is that all, Mr. Brookings?"

As the chemist left, Brookings turned again to his visitor, with an apologetic air.

"I don't know anything about these things myself, but Chambers, also an able man, says that it is impossible."

"As far as he knows, he is right. I should have said the same thing this morning. But I do know about these things-they're my business-and I tell you that Seaton has done it."

"This is getting interesting. Did you see it done?"

"No. It was rumored around the Bureau last night that Seaton was going insane, that he had wrecked a lot of his apparatus and couldn't explain what had happened. This morning he called a lot of us into his laboratory, told us what I have just told you, and poured some of his solution on a copper wire. Nothing happened, and he acted as though he didn't know what to make of it. The foolish way he acted and the apparent impossibility of the whole thing, made everybody think him crazy. I thought so until I learned this afternoon that Mr. Reynolds Crane is backing him. Then I knew that he had told us just enough of the truth to let him get away clean with the solution."

"But suppose the man *is* crazy?" asked Brookings. "He probably is a monomaniac, really insane on that one thing, from studying it so much."

"Seaton? Yes, he's crazy-like a fox. You never heard of any insanity in Crane's family, though, did you? You know that he never invests a cent in anything more risky than Government bonds. You can bet your last dollar that Seaton showed him the real goods." Then, as a look of conviction appeared upon the other's face, he continued:

"Don't you understand that the solution was Government property, and he had to do something to make everybody think it worthless, so that he could get title to it? That faked demonstration that failed was certainly a bold stroke-so bold that it was foolhardy. But it worked. It fooled even me, and I am not usually asleep. The only reason he got away with it, is, that he has always been such an open-faced talker, always telling everything he knew.

"He certainly played the fox," he continued, with undisguised admiration. "Heretofore he has never kept any of his discoveries secret or tried to make any money out of them, though some of them were worth millions. He published them as soon as he found them, and somebody else got the money. Having that reputation, he worked it to make us think him a nut. He certainly is clever. I take off my hat to him-he's a wonder!"

"And what is your idea? Where do we come in?"

"You come in by getting that solution away from Seaton and Crane, and furnishing the money to develop the stuff and to build, under my direction, such a power-plant as the world never saw before."

"Why get that particular solution? Couldn't we buy up some platinum wastes and refine them?"

"Not a chance," replied the scientist. "We have refined platinum residues for years, and never found anything like that before. It is my idea that the stuff, whatever it is, was present in some particular lot of platinum in considerable quantities as an impurity. Seaton hasn't all of it there is in the world, of course, but the chance of finding any more of it without knowing exactly what it is or how it reacts is extremely slight. Besides, we must have exclusive control. How could we make any money out of it if Crane operates a rival company and is satisfied with ten percent profit? No, we must get all of that solution. Seaton and Crane, or Seaton, at least, must be killed, for if he is left alive he can find more of the stuff and break our monopoly. I want to borrow your strong-arm squad tonight, to go and attend to it."

After a few moments' thought, his face set and expressionless, Brookings said:

"No, Doctor. I do not think that the Corporation would care to go into a matter of this kind. It is too flagrant a violation of law, and we can afford to buy it from Seaton after he proves its worth."

* * * * *

"Bah!" snorted DuQuesne. "Don't try that on me, Brookings. You think you can steal it yourself, and develop it without letting me in on it? You can't do it. Do you think I am fool enough to tell you all about it, with facts, figures, and names, if you could get away with it without me? Hardly! You can steal the solution, but that's all you can do. Your chemist or the expert you hire will begin experimenting without Seaton's lucky start, which I have already mentioned, but about which I haven't gone into any detail. He will have no information whatever, and the first attempt to do anything with the stuff will blow him and all the country around him for miles into an impalpable powder. You will lose your chemist, your solution, and all hope of getting the process. There are only two men in the United States, or in the world, for that matter, with brains enough and information enough to work it out. One is Richard B. Seaton, the other is Marc C. DuQuesne. Seaton certainly won't handle it for you. Money can't buy him and Crane, and you know it. You must come to me. If you don't believe that now, you will very shortly, after you try it alone."

Brookings, caught in his duplicity and half-convinced of the truth of DuQuesne's statements, still temporized.

"You're modest, aren't you, Doctor?" he asked, smiling.

"Modest? No," said the other calmly. "Modesty never got anybody anything but praise, and I prefer something more substantial. However, I never exaggerate or make over-statements, as you should know. What I have said is merely a statement of fact. Also, let me remind you that I am in a hurry. The difficulty of getting hold of that solution is growing greater every minute, and my price is getting higher every second."

"What is your price at the present second?"

"Ten thousand dollars per month during the experimental work; five million dollars in cash upon the successful operation of the first power unit, which shall be of not less than ten thousand horsepower; and ten percent of the profits."

"Oh, come, Doctor, let's be reasonable. You can't mean any such figures as those."

"I never say anything I don't mean. I have done a lot of dirty work with you people before, and never got much of anything out of it. You were always too strong for me; that is, I couldn't force you without exposing my own crookedness, but now I've got you right where I want you. That's my price; take it or leave it. If you don't take it now, the first two of those figures will be doubled when you do come to me. I won't go to anybody else, though others would be glad to get it on my terms, because I have a reputation to maintain and you are the only ones who know that I am crooked. I know that my reputation is safe as long as I work with you, because I know enough about you to send all you big fellows, clear down to Perkins, away for life. I also know that that knowledge will not shorten my days, as I am too valuable a man for you to kill, as you did...."

"Please, Doctor, don't use such language...."

"Why not?" interrupted DuQuesne, in his cold, level voice. "It's all true. What do a few lives amount to, as long as they're not yours and mine? As I said, I can trust you, more or less. You can trust me, because you know that I can't send you up without going with you. Therefore, I am going to let you go ahead without me as far as you can-it won't be far. Do you want me to come in now or later?"

"I'm afraid we can't do business on any such terms as that," said Brookings, shaking his head. "We can undoubtedly buy the power rights from Seaton for what you ask."

"You don't fool me for a second, Brookings. Go ahead and steal the solution, but take my advice and give your chemist only a little of it. A very little of that stuff will go a long way, and you will want to have some left when you have to call me in. Make him experiment with extremely small quantities. I would suggest that he work in the woods at least a hundred miles from his nearest neighbor, though it matters nothing to me how many people you kill. That's the only pointer I will give you —I'm giving it merely to keep you from blowing up the whole country," he concluded with a grim smile. "Good-bye."

* * * * *

As the door closed behind the cynical scientist, Brookings took a small gold instrument, very like a watch, from his pocket. He touched a button and held the machine close to his lips.

"Perkins," he said softly, "M. Reynolds Crane has in his house a bottle of solution."

"Yes, sir. Can you describe it?"

"Not exactly. It is greenish yellow in color, and I gather that it is in a small bottle, as there isn't much of the stuff in the world. I don't know what it smells or tastes like, and I wouldn't advise experimenting with it, as it seems to be a violent explosive and is probably poisonous. Any bottle of solution of that color kept in a particularly safe place would probably be the one. Let me caution you that this is the biggest thing you have ever been in, and *it must not fail*. Any effort to purchase it would be useless, however large a figure were named. But if the bottle were only partly emptied and filled up with water, I don't believe anyone would notice the difference, at least for some time, do you?"

"Probably not, sir. Good-bye."

Next morning, shortly after the office opened, Perkins, whose principal characteristic was that of absolute noiselessness, glided smoothly into Brookings' office. Taking a small bottle about half full of a greenish-yellow liquid from his pocket, he furtively placed it under some papers upon his superior's desk.

"A man found this last night, sir, and thought it might belong to you. He said this was a little less than half of it, but that you could have the rest of it any time you want it."

"Thank you, Perkins, he was right. It is ours. Here's a letter which just came," handing him an envelope, which rustled as Perkins folded it into a small compass and thrust it into his vest pocket. "Good morning."

As Perkins slid out, Brookings spoke into his telephone, and soon Chambers, his chief chemist, appeared.

"Doctor Chambers," Brookings began, showing him the bottle, "I have here a solution which in some way is capable of liberating the intra-atomic energy of matter, about which I asked you yesterday. It works on copper. I would like to have you work out the process for us, if you will."

"What about the man who discovered the process?" asked Chambers, as he touched the bottle gingerly.

"He is not available. Surely what one chemist can do, others can? You will not have to work alone. You can hire the biggest men in the line to help you-expense is no object."

"No, it wouldn't be, if such a process could be worked out. Let me see, whom can we get? Doctor Seaton is probably the best man in the country for such a research, but I don't think that we can get him. I tried to get him to work on the iridium-osmium problem, but he refused. "

"We might make an offer big enough to get him."

"No. Don't mention it to him," with a significant look. "He's to know nothing about it."

"Well, then, how about DuQuesne, who was in here yesterday? He's probably next to Seaton."

"I took it up with him yesterday. We can't get him, his figures are entirely out of reason. Aren't there any other men in the country who know anything? You are a good man, why don't you tackle it yourself?"

"Because I don't know anything about that particular line of research, and I want to keep on living awhile longer," the chemist replied bluntly. "There are other good men whom I can get, however. Van Schravendyck, of our own laboratory, is nearly as good as either Seaton or DuQuesne. He has done a lot of work on radio-activity and that sort of thing, and I think he would like to work on it."

"All right. Please get it started without delay. Give him about a quarter of the solution and have the rest put in the vault. Be sure that his laboratory is set up far enough away from everything else to avoid trouble in case of an explosion, and caution him not to work on too much copper at once. I gather that an ounce or so will be plenty."

* * * * *

The chemist went back to his laboratory and sought his first assistant.

"Van," he began, "Mr. Brookings has been listening to some lunatic who claims to have solved the mystery of liberating intra-atomic energy."

"That's old stuff," the assistant said, laughing. "That and perpetual motion are always with us. What did you tell him?"

"I didn't get a chance to tell him anything-he told me. Yesterday, you know, he asked me what would happen if it could be liberated, and I answered truthfully that lots of things would happen, and volunteered the information that it was impossible. Just now he called me in, gave me this bottle of solution, saying that it contained the answer to the puzzle, and wanted me to work it out. I told him that it was out of my line and that I was afraid of it-which I would be if I thought there was anything in it-but that it was more or less in your line, and he said to put you on it right away. He also said that expense was no object; to set up an independent laboratory a hundred miles off in the woods, to be safe in case of an explosion; and to caution you not to use too much copper at once-that an *ounce or so* would be plenty!"

"An ounce! Ten thousand tons of nitroglycerin! I'll say an ounce would be plenty, if the stuff is any good at all, which of course it isn't. Queer, isn't it, how the old man would fall for anything like that? How did he explain the failure of the discoverer to develop it himself?"

"He said the discoverer is not available," answered Chambers with a laugh. "I'll bet he isn't available-he's back in St. Elizabeth's again by this time, where he came from. I suggested that we get either Seaton or DuQuesne of Rare Metals to help us on it, and he said that they had both refused to touch it, or words to that effect. If those two turned down a chance to work on a thing as big as this would be, there probably is nothing in this particular solution that is worth a rap. But what Brookings says goes, around here, so it's you for the woods. And don't take any chances, either-it is conceivable that something might happen."

"Sure it might, but it won't. We'll set up that lab near a good trout stream, and I'll have a large and juicy vacation. I'll work on the stuff a little, too-enough to make a good report, at least. I'll analyze it, find out what is in it, deposit it on some copper, shoot an electrolytic current through it, and make a lot of wise motions generally, and have a darn good time besides."

CHAPTER III

Seaton Solves the Problem of Power

"Well, Mart," said Seaton briskly, "now that the Seaton-Crane Company, Engineers, is organized to your satisfaction, let's hop to it. I suppose I'd better beat it downtown and hunt up a place to work?"

"Why not work here?"

"Your house? You don't want this kind of experimenting going on around here, do you? Suppose a chunk of the stuff gets away from me and tears the side out of the house?"

"This house is the logical place to work. I already have a complete machine shop and testing laboratory out in the hangar, and we can easily fit up a chemical laboratory for you up in the tower room. You can have open windows on four sides there, and if you should accidentally take out the wall there will be little damage done. We will be alone here, with the few neighbors so thoroughly accustomed to my mechanical experiments that they are no longer curious."

"Fine. There's another good thing, too. Your man Shiro. He's been with you in so many tight pinches in all the unknown corners of the world on your hunting trips and explorations that we can trust him, and he'll probably come in handy."

"Yes, we can trust him implicitly. As you know, he is really my friend instead of my man."

During the next few days, while workmen were installing a complete chemical laboratory in the tower room, Seaton busied himself in purchasing the equipment necessary for the peculiar problem before him. His list was long and varied, ranging from a mighty transformer, capable of delivering thousands of kilovolts down to a potentiometer, so sensitive that it would register the difference of potential set up by two men in shaking hands.

From daylight until dark Seaton worked in the laboratory, either alone or superintending and assisting the men at work there. Every night when Crane went to bed he saw Seaton in his room in a haze of smoke, poring over blueprints or, surrounded by abstruse works upon the calculus and sub-atomic phenomena, making interminable calculations.

Less than two miles away lived Dorothy Vaneman, who had promised to be his wife. He had seen her but once since "the impossible" had happened, since his prosaic copper steam-bath had taken flight under his hand and pointed the way to a great adventure. In a car his friend was to build, moved by this stupendous power which he must learn to control, they would traverse interstellar space-visit strange planets and survey strange solar systems.

While he did not forget his sweetheart-the thought of her was often in his mind, and the fact that her future was so intimately connected with his own gave to every action a new meaning-he had such a multitude of things to do and was so eager to get them all done at once that day after day went by and he could not find time to call upon her.

Crane remonstrated in vain. His protests against Seaton's incessant work had no effect. Seaton insisted that he *must* fix firmly just a few more points before they eluded him, and stuck doggedly to his task.

Finally, Crane laid his work aside and went to call upon the girl. He found her just leaving home, and fell into step beside her. For awhile she tried to rouse herself to be entertaining, or at least friendly, but the usual ease with which she chatted had deserted her, and her false gayety did not deceive the keen-minded Crane for an instant. Soon the two were silent as they walked along together. Crane's thoughts were on the beautiful girl beside him, and on the splendid young genius under his roof, so deeply immersed in his problem that he was insensible to everything else.

* * * * *

"I have just left Dick," Crane said suddenly, and paying no attention to her startled glance. "Did you ever in your life see anyone with his singleness of purpose? With all his brilliance, one idea at a time is all that he seems capable of-though that is probably why he is such a genius. He is working himself insane. Has he told you about leaving the Bureau?"

"No. Has he? Has it anything to do with what happened that day at the laboratory? I haven't seen him since the accident, or discovery, whichever it was, happened. He came to see me at half-past ten, when he was invited for dinner-oh, Martin, I had been *so* angry! —and he told such a preposterous story, I've been wondering since if I didn't dream it."

"No, you didn't dream it, no matter how wild it sounded. He said it, and it is all true. I cannot explain it to you; Dick himself cannot explain it, even to me. But I can give you an idea of what we both think it may come to."

"Yes, do."

"Well, he has discovered something that makes copper act mighty queer-knocks it off its feet, so to speak. That day a piece went up and never did come down."

"Yes, that is what is so preposterous!"

"Just a moment, please," replied the imperturbable Crane. "You should know that nothing ordinary can account for Dick's behavior, and after what I have seen this last week I shall never again think anything preposterous. As I said, this piece of copper departed, *via* the window, for scenes unknown. As far as a pair of good binoculars could follow it, it held to a perfectly straight course toward those scenes. We intend to follow it in some suitable vehicle."

He paused, looking at his companion's face, but she did not speak.

"Building the conveyance is where I come in," he continued in his matter-of-fact voice. "As you know, I happen to have almost as much money as Dick has brains, and some day, before the summer is over, we expect to go somewhere. We do not know where, but it will be a long way from this earth."

There was a silence, then Dorothy said, helplessly:

"Well, go on....I can't understand...."

"Neither can I. All I know is that Dick wants to build a heavy steel hull, and he is going to put something inside it that will take us out into space. Only occasionally do I see a little light as he tries to explain the mechanism of the thing to me."

After enjoining upon her the strictest secrecy he repeated the story that Seaton had told him, and informed her as to the present condition of affairs.

"It's no wonder the other chemists thought he was crazy, is it, Martin?"

"No, especially after the failure of his demonstration the next morning. You see, he tried to prove to the others that he was right, and nothing happened. He has found out since that an electrical machine in another room, which was not running that morning, played a very important part. When the copper refused to act as it had the night before they all took the snap judgment that he had suffered an attack of temporary insanity, and that the solution was worthless. They called him 'Nobody Holme'."

"It almost fits, at that!" exclaimed Dorothy, laughing.

"But if he thought of that," she added, thoughtfully, "if he was brilliant enough to build up such a wonderful theory...think out such a thing as actually traveling to the stars...all on such a slight foundation of fact ...I wonder why he couldn't have told me?"

She hadn't meant to utter the last thought. Nobody must know how being left out of it had hurt her, and she would have recalled the words if she could. Crane understood, and answered loyally.

"He will tell you all about it very soon, never fear. His is the mind of a great scientist, working on a subject of which but very few men have even an inkling. I am certain that the only reason he thought of me is that he could not finance the investigation alone. Never think for an instant that his absorption implies a lack of fondness for you. You are his anchor, his only hold on known things. In fact, it was about this that I came to see you. Dick is working himself at a rate that not even a machine can stand. He eats hardly anything, and if he sleeps at all, I have never caught him at it. That idea is driving him day and night, and if he goes on the way he is going, it means a breakdown. I do not know whether you can make him listen to reason or not-certainly no one else can. If you think you can do it, that is to be your job, and it will be the biggest one of the three."

"How well you understand him," Dorothy said, after a pause. "You make me feel ashamed, Martin. I should have known without being told. Then I wouldn't have had these nasty little doubts about him."

"I should call them perfectly natural, considering the circumstances," he answered. "Men with minds like Dick's are rare. They work on only one track. Your part will be hard. He will come to you, bursting with news and aching to tell you all about his theories and facts and calculations, and you must try to take his mind off the whole thing and make him think of something else. It looks impossible to me."

* * * * *

The smile had come back to Dorothy's face. Her head, graced by its wealth of gleaming auburn hair, was borne proudly, and glancing mischief lit her violet eyes.

"Didn't you just tell me nothing is impossible? You know, Martin, that I can make Dicky forget everything, even interstellar-did I get that word right? —space itself, with my violin."

"Trying to beguile a scientist from his hobby is comparable only to luring a drug addict away from his vice ... but I would not be surprised if you could do it," he slowly replied.

For he had heard her play. She and Seaton had been caught near his home by a sudden shower while on horseback, and had dashed in for shelter. While the rain beat outside and while Shiro was preparing one of his famous suppers, Crane had suggested that she pass the time by playing his "fiddle." Dorothy realized, with the first sweep of the bow, that she was playing a Stradivarius, the like of which she had played before only in her dreams. She forgot her listeners, forgot the time and the place, and poured out in her music all the beauty and tenderness of her nature. Soft and full the tones filled the room, and in Crane's vision there rose a home filled with happy work, with laughter and companionship, with playing children who turned their faces to their mother as do flowers to the light. Sensing the girl's dreams as the music filled his ears, he realized as never before in his busy, purposeful life how beautiful a home with the right woman could be. No thought of love for Dorothy entered his mind, for he knew that the love existing between her and his friend was of the kind that nothing could alter, but he felt that she had unwittingly given him a great gift. Often thereafter in his lonely hours he had imagined that dream-home, and nothing less than its perfection would ever satisfy him.

For a time they walked on in silence. On Dorothy's face was a tender look, the reflection of her happy thoughts, and in Crane's mind floated again the vision of his ideal home, the home whose central figure he was unable to visualize. At last she turned and placed her hand on his arm.

"You have done a great deal for me-for us," she said simply. "I wish there were something I could do for you in return."

"You have already done much more than that for me, Dorothy," he answered, more slowly even than usual. "It is hard for me to express just what it is, but I want you to know that you and Dick mean much to me....You are the first real woman I have ever known, and some day, if life is good to me, I hope to have some girl as lovely care for me."

Dorothy's sensitive face flushed warmly. So unexpected and sincere was his praise that it made her feel both proud and humble. She had never realized that this quiet, apparently unimaginative man had seen all the ideals she expressed in her music. A woman expects to appear lovely to her lover, and to the men who would be her lovers if they could, but here was a man who neither sought nor expected any favors, saying that he wanted some girl as lovely for his own. Truly it was a compliment to be cherished.

After they had returned to the house and Crane had taken his departure, Dorothy heard the purr of a rapidly approaching motorcycle, and her heart leaped as she went to the door to welcome her lover.

"It seems like a month since I saw you last, sweetheart!" he exclaimed, as he lifted her clear from the floor in a passionate embrace and kissed in turn her lips, her eyes, the tip of her nose, the elusive dimple in her cheek, and the adorable curve of her neck.

"It seems longer than that to me, Dicky. I was perfectly miserable until Martin called this afternoon and explained what you have been doing."

"Yes, I met him on the way over. But honestly, Dottie, I simply couldn't get away. I wanted to, the worst way, but everything went so slow...."

"Slow? When you have a whole laboratory installed in a week? What would you call speed?"

"About two days. And then, there were a lot of little ideas that had to be nailed down before they got away from me. This is a horribly big job, Dottie, and when a fellow gets into it he can't quit. But you know that I love you just the same, even though I do appear to neglect you," he continued with fierce intensity. "I love you with everything there is in me. I love you, mind, body and spirit; love you as a man should love the one and only woman. For you are the only woman, there never was and never will be another. I love you morally, physically, intellectually, and every other way there is, for the perfect little darling that you are."

She moved in his embrace and her arms tightened about his neck.

"You are the nearest thing to absolute perfection that ever came into this imperfect world," he continued. "Just to think of a girl of your sheer beauty, your ability, your charm, your all-round perfection, being engaged to a thing like me, makes me dizzy-but I sure do love you, little girl of mine. I will love you as long as we live, and afterward, my soul will love your soul throughout eternity. You know that, sweetheart girl."

"Oh, Dick!" she whispered, her soul shaken with response to his love. "I never dreamed it possible for a woman to love as I love you. 'Whither thou goest....'"

Her voice failed in the tempest of her emotion, and they clung together in silence.

They were finally interrupted by Dorothy's stately and gracious mother, who came in to greet Seaton and invite him to have dinner with them.

"I knew that Dot would forget such an unimportant matter," she said, with a glint of Dorothy's own mischief in her eyes.

* * * * *

As they went into the dining-room Dorothy was amazed to see the changes that six days had wrought in Seaton. His face looked thin, almost haggard. Fine lines had made their appearance at the corners of his eyes and around his mouth, and faint but unmistakable blue rings encircled his eyes.

"You have been working too hard, boy," she reproved him gravely.

"Oh, no," he rejoined lightly. "I'm all right, I never felt better. Why, I could whip a rattlesnake right now, and give him the first bite!"

She laughed at his reply, but the look of concern did not leave her face. As soon as they were seated at the table she turned to her father, a clean-cut, gray-haired man of fifty, known as one of the shrewdest attorneys in the city.

"Daddy," she demanded, "what do you mean by being elected director in the Seaton-Crane Company and not telling me anything about it?"

"Daughter," he replied in the same tone, "what do you mean by asking such a question as that? Don't you know that it is a lawyer's business to get information, and to give it out only to paying clients? However, I can tell you all I know about the Seaton-Crane Company without adding to your store of knowledge at all. I was present at one meeting, gravely voted 'aye' once, and that is all."

"Didn't you draw up the articles of incorporation?"

"I am doing it, yes; but they don't mean anything. They merely empower the Company to do anything it wants to, the same as other large companies do." Then, after a quick but searching glance at Seaton's worn face and a warning glance at his daughter, he remarked:

"I read in the *Star* this evening that Enright and Stanwix will probably make the Australian Davis Cup team, and that the Hawaiian with the unpronounceable name has broken three or four more world's records. What do you think of our tennis chances this year, Dick?"

Dorothy flushed, and the conversation, steered by the lawyer into the safer channels, turned to tennis, swimming, and other sports. Seaton, whose plate was unobtrusively kept full by Mr. Vaneman, ate such a dinner as he had not eaten in weeks. After the meal was over they all went into the spacious living-room, where the men ensconced themselves in comfortable Morris chairs with long, black cigars between their teeth, and all four engaged in a spirited discussion of various topics of the day. After a time, the older couple left the room, the lawyer going into his study to work, as he always did in the evening.

"Well, Dicky, how's everything?" Dorothy asked, unthinkingly.

The result of this innocent question was astonishing. Seaton leaped to his feet. The problem, dormant for two hours, was again in complete possession of his mind.

"Rotten!" he snapped, striding back and forth and brandishing his half-smoked cigar. "My head is so thick that it takes a thousand years for an idea to filter into it. I should have the whole thing clear by this time, but I haven't. There's something, some little factor, that I can't get. I've almost had it a dozen times, but it always gets away from me. I know that the force is there and I can liberate it, but I can't work out a system of control until I can understand exactly why it acts the way it does." Then, more slowly, thinking aloud rather than addressing the girl:

"The force is attraction toward all matter, generated by the vibrations of all the constituent electrons in parallel planes. It is directed along a line perpendicular to the plane of vibration at its center, and approaches infinity as the angle theta approaches the limit of Pi divided by two. Therefore, by shifting the axis of rotation or the plane of vibration thus making theta vary between the limits of zero and Pi divided by two...."

He was interrupted by Dorothy, who, mortified by her thoughtlessness in getting him started, had sprung up and seized him by the arm.

"Sit down, Dicky!" she implored. "Sit down, you're rocking the boat! Save your mathematics for Martin. Don't you know that I could never find out why 'x' was equal to 'y' or to anything else in algebra?"

She led him back to his chair, where he drew her down to a seat on the arm beside him.

"Whom do you love?" she whispered gayly in his ear.

After a time she freed herself.

* * * * *

"I haven't practised today. Don't you want me to play for you a little?"

"Fine business, Dottie. When you play a violin, it talks."

She took down her violin and played; first his favorites, crashing selections from operas and solos by the great masters, abounding in harmonies on two strings. Then she changed to reveries and soft, plaintive melodies. Seaton listened with profound enjoyment. Under the spell of the music he relaxed, pushed out the footrest of the chair, and lay back at ease, smoking dreamily. The cigar finished and his hands at rest, his eyes closed of themselves. The music, now a crooning lullaby, grew softer and slower, until his deep and regular breathing showed that he was sound asleep. She stopped playing and sat watching him intently, her violin in readiness to play again, if he should show the least sign of waking, but there was no such sign. Freed from the tyranny of the mighty brain which had been driving it so unmercifully, his body was making up for many hours of lost sleep.

Assured that he was really asleep, Dorothy tip-toed to her father's study and quietly went in.

"Daddy, Dick is asleep out there in the chair. What shall we do with him?"

"Good work, Dottie Dimple. I heard you playing him to sleep-you almost put me to sleep as well. I'll get a blanket and we'll put him to bed right where he is."

"Dear old Dad," she said softly, sitting on the arm of his chair and rubbing her cheek against his. "You always did understand, didn't you?"

"I try to, Kitten," he answered, pulling her ear. "Seaton is too good a man to see go to pieces when it can be prevented. That is why I signalled you to keep the talk off the company and his work. One of the best lawyers I ever knew, a real genius, went to pieces that same way. He was on a big, almost an impossible, case. He couldn't think of anything else, didn't eat or sleep much for months. He won the case, but it broke him. But he wasn't in love with a big, red-headed beauty of a girl, and so didn't have her to fiddle him to sleep.

"Well, I'll go get the blanket," he concluded, with a sudden change in his tone.

In a few moments he returned and they went into the living-room together. Seaton lay in exactly the same position, only the regular lifting of his powerful chest showing that he was alive.

"I think we had better...."

"Sh...sh," interrupted the girl in an intense whisper. "You'll wake him up, Daddy."

"Bosh! You couldn't wake him up with a club. His own name might rouse him, particularly if you said it; no other ordinary sound would. I started to say that I think we had better put him to bed on the davenport. He would be more comfortable."

"But that would surely wake him. And he's so big...."

"Oh, no, it wouldn't, unless I drop him on the floor. And he doesn't weigh much over two hundred, does he?"

"About ten or eleven pounds."

"Even though I am a lawyer, and old and decrepit, I can still handle that much."

With Dorothy anxiously watching the proceeding and trying to help, Vaneman picked Seaton up out of the chair, with some effort, and carried him across the room. The sleeping man muttered as if in protest at being disturbed, but made no other sign of consciousness. The lawyer then calmly removed Seaton's shoes and collar, while the girl arranged pillows under his head and tucked the blanket around him. Vaneman bent a quizzical glance upon his daughter, under which a flaming blush spread from her throat to her hair.

"Well," she said, defiantly, "I'm going to, anyway."

"My dear, of course you are. If you didn't, I would disown you."

As her father turned away, Dorothy knelt beside her lover and pressed her lips tightly to his.

"Good night, sweetheart," she murmured.

"'Night," he muttered in his sleep, as his lips responded faintly to her caress.

Vaneman waited for his daughter, and when she appeared, the blush again suffusing her face, he put his arm around her.

"Dorothy," he said at the door of her room, using her full name, a very unusual thing for him, "the father of such a girl as you are hates to lose her, but I advise you to stick to that boy. Believe in him and trust him, no matter what happens. He is a real man."

"I know it, Dad...thank you. I had a touch of the blues today, but I never will again. I think more of his little finger than I do of all the other men I ever knew, put together. But how do you know him so well? I know him, of course, but that's different."

"I have various ways of getting information. I know Dick Seaton better than you do-better than he knows himself. I have known all about every man who ever looked at you twice. I have been afraid once or twice that I would have to take a hand, but you saw them right, just as you see Seaton right. For some time I have been afraid of the thought of your marrying, the young men in your social set are such a hopeless lot, but I am not any more. When I hand my little girl over to her husband next October I can be really happy with you, instead of anxious for you. That's how well I know Richard Seaton....Well, good night, daughter mine."

"Good night, Daddy dear," she replied, throwing her arms around his neck. "I have the finest Dad a girl ever had, and the finest...boy. Good night."

* * * * *

It was three o'clock the following afternoon when Seaton appeared in the laboratory. His long rest had removed all the signs of overwork and he was his alert, vigorous self, but when Crane saw him and called out a cheery greeting he returned it with a sheepish smile.

"Don't say anything, Martin—I'm thinking it all, and then some. I made a regular fool of myself last night. Went to sleep in a chair and slept seventeen hours without a break. I never felt so cheap in my life."

"You were worn out, Dick, and you know it. That sleep put you on your feet again, and I hope you will have sense enough to take care of yourself after this. I warn you now, Dick, that if you start any more of that midnight work I will simply call Dorothy over here and have her take charge of you."

"That's it, Mart, rub it in. Don't you see that I am flat on my back, with all four paws in the air? But I'm going to sleep every night. I promised Dottie to go to bed not later than twelve, if I have to quit right in the middle of an idea, and I told her that I was coming out to see her every other evening and every Sunday. But here's the dope. I've got that missing factor in my theory-got it while I was eating breakfast this afternoon."

"If you had eaten and slept regularly here and kept yourself fit you would have seen it before."

"Yes, I guess that's right, too. If I miss a meal or a sleep from now on I want you to sand-bag me. But never mind that. Here's the explanation. We doped out before, you know, that the force is something like magnetism, and is generated when the coil causes the electrons of this specially-treated copper to vibrate in parallel planes. The knotty point was what could be the effect of a weak electric current in liberating the power. I've got it! It shifts the plane of vibration of the electrons!"

"It is impossible to shift that plane, Dick. It is fixed by physical state, just as speed is fixed by temperature."

"No, it isn't. That is, it usually is, but in this case it may be shifted. Here's the mathematical proof."

So saying, Seaton went over to the drafting table, tacked down a huge sheet of paper, and sketched rapidly, explaining as he drew. Soon the two men were engaged in a profound mathematical argument. Sheet after sheet of paper was filled with equations and calculations, and the table was covered with reference books. After two hours of intense study and hot discussion Crane's face took on a look of dawning comprehension, which changed to amazement and then to joy. For the first time in Seaton's long acquaintance with him, his habitual calm was broken.

"By George!" he cried, shaking Seaton's hand in both of his. "I think you have it! But how under the sun did you get the idea? That calculus isn't in any of the books. Where did you get it? Dick, you're a wonder!"

"I don't know how I got the idea, it merely came to me. But that Math is right-it's *got* to be right, no other conclusion is possible. Now, if that calc. is right, and I know it is, do you see how narrow the permissible limits of shifting are? Look at equation 236. Believe me, I sure was lucky, that day in the Bureau. It's a wonder I didn't blow up the whole works. Suppose I hadn't been working with a storage cell that gave only four amperes at two volts? That's unusually low, you know, for that kind of work."

* * * * *

Crane carefully studied the equation referred to and figured for a moment.

"In that case the limit would be exactly eight watts. Anything above that means instant decomposition?"

"Yes."

Crane whistled, a long, low whistle.

26

"And that bath weighed forty pounds-enough to vaporize the whole planet. Dick, it cannot be possible."

"It doesn't seem that way, but it is. It certainly makes me turn cold all over, though, to think of what might have happened. You know now why I wouldn't touch the solution again until I had this stuff worked out?"

"I certainly do. You should be even more afraid of it now. I don't mind nitroglycerin or T.N.T., but anything like that is merely a child's plaything compared to this. Perhaps we had better drop it?"

"Not in seven thousand years. The mere fact that I was so lucky at first proves that Fate intended this thing to be my oyster. However, I'll not tempt the old lady any farther. I'm going to start with one millionth of a volt, and will use a piece of copper visible only under a microscope. But there's absolutely no danger, now that we know what it is. I can make it eat out of my hand. Look at this equation here, though. That being true, it looks as though you could get the same explosive effect by taking a piece of copper which had once been partially decomposed and subjecting it to some force, say an extremely heavy current. Again under the influence of the coil, a small current would explode it, wouldn't it?"

"It looks that way, from those figures."

"Say, wouldn't that make some bullet? Unstabilize a piece of copper in that way and put it inside a rifle bullet, arranged to make a short circuit on impact. By making the piece of copper barely visible you could have the explosive effect of only a few sticks of dynamite —a piece the size of a pea would obliterate New York City. But that's a long way from our flying-machine."

"Perhaps not so far as you think. When we explore new worlds it might be a good idea to have a liberal supply of such ammunition, of various weights, for emergencies."

"It might, at that. Here's another point in equation 249. Suppose the unstabilized copper were treated with a very weak current, not strong enough to explode it? A sort of borderline condition? The energy would be liberated, apparently, but in an entirely new way. Wonder what would happen? I can't see from the theory-have to work it out. And here's another somewhat similar condition, right here, that will need investigating. I've sure got a lot of experimental work ahead of me before I'll know anything. How're things going with you?"

"I have the drawings and blue-prints of the ship itself done, and working sketches of the commercial power-plant. I am working now on the details, such as navigating instruments, food, water, and air supplies, special motors, and all of the hundred and one little things that must be taken into consideration. Then, as soon as you get the power under control, we will have only to sketch in the details of the power-plant and its supports before we can begin construction."

"Fine, Mart, that's great. Well, let's get busy!"

CHAPTER IV

Steel Liberates Energy-Unexpectedly

DuQuesne was in his laboratory, poring over an abstruse article in a foreign journal of science, when Scott came breezily in with a newspaper in his hand, across the front page of which stretched great headlines.

"Hello, Blackie!" he called. "Come down to earth and listen to this tale of mystery from that world-renowned fount of exactitude and authority, the *Washington Clarion*. Some miscreant has piled up and touched off a few thousand tons of T.N.T. and picric acid up in the hills. Read about it, it's good."

DuQuesne read:

MYSTERIOUS EXPLOSION!

* * * * *

Mountain Village Wiped Out of Existence!
Two Hundred Dead, None Injured!

* * * * *

Force Felt All Over World. Cause Unknown.
Scientists Baffled.

* * * * *

Harper's Ferry. March 26.—At 10: 23 A.M. today, the village of Bankerville, about thirty miles north of this place, was totally destroyed by an explosion of such terrific violence that seismographs all over the world recorded the shock, and that windows were shattered even in this city. A thick pall of dust and smoke was observed in the sky and parties set out immediately. They found, instead of the little mountain village, nothing except an immense, crater-like hole in the ground, some two miles in diameter and variously estimated at from two to three thousand feet deep. No survivors have been found, no bodies have been recovered. The entire village, with its two hundred inhabitants, has been wiped out of existence. Not so much as a splinter of wood or a fragment of brick from any of the houses can be found. Scientists are unable to account for the terrific force of the explosion, which far exceeded that of the most violent explosive known.

"Hm...m. That sounds reasonable, doesn't it?" asked DuQuesne, sarcastically, as he finished reading.

"It sure does," replied Scott, grinning. "What'd'you suppose it was? Think the reporter heard a tire blow out on Pennsylvania Avenue?"

"Perhaps. Nothing to it, anyway," as he turned back to his work.

As soon as the visitor had gone a sneering smile spread over DuQuesne's face and he picked up his telephone.

"The fool did it. That will cure him of sucking eggs!" he muttered. "Operator? DuQuesne speaking. I am expecting a call this afternoon. Please ask him to call me at my house....Thank you."

"Fred," he called to his helper, "if anyone wants me, tell them that I have gone home."

He left the building and stepped into his car. In less than half an hour he arrived at his house on Park Road, overlooking beautiful Rock Creek Park. Here he lived alone save for an old colored couple who were his servants.

In the busiest part of the afternoon Chambers rushed unannounced into Brookings' private office. His face was white as chalk.

"Read that, Mr. Brookings!" he gasped, thrusting the *Clarion* extra into his hand.

Brookings read the news of the explosion, then looked at his chief chemist, his face turning gray.

"Yes, sir, that was our laboratory," said Chambers, dully.

"The fool! Didn't you tell him to work with small quantities?"

"I did. He said not to worry, that he was taking no chances, that he would never have more than a gram of copper on hand at once in the whole laboratory."

"Well ... I'll ... be ... damned!" Slowly turning to the telephone, Brookings called a number and asked for Doctor DuQuesne, then called another.

"Brookings speaking. I would like to see you this afternoon. Will you be at home?... I'll be there in about an hour. Good bye."

When Brookings arrived he was shown into DuQuesne's study. The two men shook hands perfunctorily and sat down, the scientist waiting for the other to speak.

"Well, DuQuesne, you were right. Our man couldn't handle it. But of course you didn't mean the terms you mentioned before?"

DuQuesne's lips smiled; a hard, cold smile.

"You know what I said, Brookings. Those terms are now doubled, twenty thousand and ten million. Nothing else goes."

"I expected it, since you never back down. The Corporation expects to pay for its mistakes. We accept your terms and I have contracts here for your services as research director, at a salary of two hundred and forty thousand dollars per annum, with the bonus and royalties you demand."

DuQuesne glanced over the documents and thrust them into his pocket.

"I'll go over these with my attorney to-night, and mail one back to you if he approves the contract. In the meantime, we may as well get down to business."

"What would you suggest?" asked Brookings.

"You people stole the solution, I see...."

"Don't use such harsh language, Doctor, it's...."

"Why not? I'm for direct action, first, last and all the time. This thing is too important to permit of mincing words or actions, it's a waste of time. Have you the solution here?"

"Yes, here it is," drawing the bottle from his pocket.

"Where's the rest of it?" asked DuQuesne as he noted the size of the bottle.

"All that we found is here, except about a teaspoonful which the expert had to work on," replied Brookings. "We didn't get it all, only half of it. The rest of it was diluted with water, so that it wouldn't be missed. After we get started, if you find it works out satisfactorily, we can procure the rest of it. That will certainly cause a disturbance, but it may be necessary...."

"Half of it!" interrupted DuQuesne. "You haven't one-twentieth of it here. When I saw it in the Bureau, Seaton had about five hundred milliliters-over a pint-of it. I wonder if you're double-crossing me again?"

"No, you're not," he continued, paying no attention to the other's protestations of innocence. "You're paying me too much to want to block me now. The crook you sent out to get the stuff turned in only this much. Do you suppose he is holding out on us?"

"No. You know Perkins and his methods."

"He missed the main bottle, then. That's where your methods make me tired. When I want anything done, I believe in doing it myself, then I know it's done right. As to what I suggest, that's easy. I will take three or four of Perkins' gunmen tonight. We'll go out there and raid the place. We'll shoot Seaton and anybody else who gets in the way. We'll dynamite the safe and take their solution, plans, notes, money, and anything else we want."

"No, no, Doctor, that's too crude altogether. If we have to do that, let it be only as a last resort."

"I say do it first, then we know we will get results. I tell you I'm afraid of pussyfooting and gumshoeing around Seaton and Crane. I used to think that Seaton was easy, but he seems to have developed greatly in the last few weeks, and Crane never was anybody's fool. Together they make a combination hard to beat. Brute force, applied without warning, is our best bet, and there's no danger, you know that. We've got away clean with lots worse stuff."

"It's always dangerous, and we could wink at such tactics only after everything else has failed. Why not work it out from this solution we have, and then quietly get the rest of it? After we have it worked out, Seaton might get into an accident on his motorcycle, and we could prove by the state of development of our plans that we discovered it long ago."

"Because developing the stuff is highly dangerous, as you have found out. Even Seaton wouldn't have been alive now if he hadn't had a lot of luck at the start. Then, too, it would take too much time. Seaton has already developed it-you see, I haven't been asleep and I know what he has done, just as well as you do-and why should we go through all that slow and dangerous experimental work when we can get their notes and plans as well as not? There is bound to be trouble anyway when we steal all their solution, even though they haven't missed this little bit of it yet, and it might as well come now as any other time. The Corporation is amply protected, and I am still a Government chemist. Nobody even suspects that I am in on this deal. I will never see you except after hours and in private, and will never come near your offices. We will be so cautious that, even if anyone should get suspicious, they can't possibly link us together, and until they do link us together, we are all safe. No, Brookings, a raid in force is the only sure and safe way. What is more natural than a burglary of a rich man's house? It will be a simple affair. The police will stir around for a few days, then it will all be forgotten and we can go ahead. Nobody will suspect anything except Crane, if he is alive, and he won't be able to do anything."

So the argument raged. Brookings was convinced that DuQuesne was right in wanting to get possession of all the solution, and also of the working notes and plans, but would not agree to the means suggested, holding out for quieter and more devious, but less actionable methods. Finally he ended the argument with a flat refusal to countenance the raid, and the scientist was forced to yield, although he declared that they would have to use his methods in the end, and that it would save time, money, and perhaps lives, if they were used first. Brookings then took from his pocket his wireless and called Perkins. He told him of the larger bottle of solution, instructing him to secure it and to bring back all plans, notes, and other material he could find which in any way pertained to the matter in hand. Then, after promising DuQuesne to keep him informed of developments, and giving him an instrument similar to the one he himself carried, Brookings took his leave.

Seaton had worked from early morning until late at night, but had rigorously kept his promise to Dorothy. He had slept seven or eight hours every night and had called upon her regularly, returning from the visits with ever-keener zest for his work.

Late in the afternoon, upon the day of the explosion, Seaton stepped into Crane's shop with a mass of notes in his hand.

"Well, Mart, I've got it-some of it, at least. The power is just what we figured it, so immensely large as to be beyond belief. I have found:

"First: That it is a practically irresistible *pull* along the axis of the treated wire or bar. It is apparently focused at infinity, as near-by objects are not affected.

"Second: I have studied two of the border-line regions of current we discussed. I have found that in one the power is liberated as a similar attractive force but is focused upon the first object in line with the axis of the bar. As long as the current is applied it remains focused upon that object, no matter what comes between. In the second border-line condition the power is liberated as a terrific repulsion.

"Third: That the copper is completely transformed into available energy, there being no heat whatever liberated.

"Fourth: Most important of all, that the X acts only as a catalyst for the copper and is not itself consumed, so that an infinitesimally thin coating is all that is required."

"You certainly have found out a great deal about it," replied Crane, who had been listening with the closest attention, a look of admiration upon his face. "You have all the essential facts right there. Now we can go ahead and put in the details which will finish up the plans completely. Also, one of those points solves my hardest problem, that of getting back to the earth after we lose sight of it. We can make a small bar in that border-line condition and focus it upon the earth, and we can use that repulsive property to ward off any meteorites which may come too close to us."

"That's right. I never thought of using those points for anything. I found them out incidentally, and merely mentioned them as interesting facts. I have a model of the main bar built, though, that will lift me into the air and pull me all around. Want to see it work?"

"I certainly do."

As they were going out to the landing field Shiro called to them and they turned back to the house, learning that Dorothy and her father had just arrived.

"Hello, boys!" Dorothy said, bestowing her radiant smile upon them both as Seaton seized her hand. "Dad and I came out to see that you were taking care of yourselves, and to see what you are doing. Are visitors allowed?"

"No," replied Seaton promptly. "All visitors are barred. Members of the firm and members of the family, however, are not classed as visitors."

"You came at the right time," said Crane, smiling. "Dick has just finished a model, and was about to demonstrate it to me when you arrived. Come with us and watch the...."

"I object," interrupted Seaton. "It is a highly undignified performance as yet, and...."

"Objection overruled," interposed the lawyer, decisively. "You are too young and impetuous to have any dignity; therefore, any performance not undignified would be impossible, *a priori*. The demonstration will proceed."

Laughing merrily, the four made their way to the testing shed, in front of which Seaton donned a heavy leather harness, buckled about his shoulders, body and legs; to which were attached numerous handles, switches, boxes and other pieces of apparatus. He snapped the switch which started the Tesla coil in the shed and pressed a button on an instrument in his hand, attached to his harness by a small steel cable. Instantly there was a creak of straining leather and he shot vertically into the air for perhaps a hundred feet, where he stopped and remained motionless for a few moments. Then the watchers saw him point his arm and dart in the direction in which he pointed. By merely pointing, apparently, he changed his direction at will; going up and down, forward and backward, describing circles and loops and figures of eight. After a few minutes of this display he descended, slowing up abruptly as he neared the ground and making an easy landing.

"There, oh beauteous lady and esteemed sirs," he began, with a low bow and a sweeping flourish-when there was a snap, and he was jerked sidewise off his feet. In bowing, his cumbersome harness had pressed the controlling switch and the instrument he held in his hand, which contained the power-plant, or bar, had torn itself loose from its buckle. Instead of being within easy reach of his hand it was over six feet away, and was dragging him helplessly after it, straight toward the high stone wall! But only momentarily was he helpless, his keen mind discovering a way out of the predicament even as he managed to scramble to his feet in spite of the rapid pace. Throwing his body sidewise and reaching out his long arm as far as possible toward the bar, he succeeded in swinging it around so that he was running back toward the party and the spacious landing field. Dorothy and her father were standing motionless, staring at Seaton; the former with terror in her eyes, the latter in blank amazement. Crane had darted to the switch controlling the coil, and was reaching for it when Seaton passed them.

"Don't touch that switch!" he yelled. "I'll catch that thing yet!"

At this evidence that Seaton still thought himself master of the situation, Crane began to laugh, though he still kept his hand near the controlling switch. Dorothy, relieved of her fear for her lover's safety, could not help but join him, so ludicrous were Seaton's antics. The bar was straight out in front of him, about five feet above the ground, going somewhat faster than a man could run. It turned now to the right, now to the left, as his weight was thrown to one side or the other. Seaton, dragged along like a small boy trying to hold a runaway calf by the tail, was covering the ground in prodigious leaps and bounds; at the same time pulling himself up, hand over hand, to the bar in front of him. He soon reached it, seized it in both hands, again darted into the air, and descended lightly near the others, who were rocking with laughter.

"I said it would be undignified," chuckled Seaton, rather short of breath, "but I didn't know just how much so it was going to be."

Dorothy tucked her fingers into his hand.

"Are you hurt anywhere, Dick?"

"Not a bit. He led me a great chase, though."

"I was scared to death until you told Martin to let the switch alone. But it was funny then! I hadn't noticed your resemblance to a jumping-jack before. Won't you do it again sometime and let us take a movie of it?"

"That was as good as any show in town, Dick," said the lawyer, wiping his eyes, "but you must be more careful. Next time, it might not be funny at all."

"There will be no next time for this rig," replied Seaton. "This is merely to show us that our ideas are all right. The next trip will be in a full-scale, completely-equipped boat."

"It was perfectly wonderful," declared Dorothy. "I know this first flight of yours will be a turning-point or something in history. I don't pretend to understand how you did it-the sight of you standing still up there in the air made me wonder if I really were awake, even though I knew what to expect-but we wouldn't have missed it for worlds, would we, Dad?"

"No. I am very glad that we saw the first demonstration. The world has never before seen anything like it, and you two men will rank as two of the greatest discoverers."

"Seaton will, you mean," replied Crane, uncomfortably. "You know I didn't have anything to do with it."

"It's nearly all yours," denied Seaton. "Without your ideas I would have lost myself in space in my first attempt."

"You are both wrong," said Vaneman. "You, Martin, haven't enough imagination; and you, Dick, have altogether too much, for either of you to have done this alone. The honor will be divided equally between you."

He turned to Crane as Dorothy and Seaton set out toward the house.

"What are you going to do with it, commercially? Dick, of course, hasn't thought of anything except this space-car—equally of course, you have?"

"Yes. Knowing the general nature of the power and confident that Dick would control it, I have already drawn up sketches for a power-plant installation of five hundred thousand electrical horsepower, which will enable us to sell power for less than one-tenth of a cent per kilowatt-hour and still return twenty percent annual dividends. However, the power-plant comes after the flyer."

"Why? Why not build the power-plant first, and take the pleasure trip afterward?"

"There are several reasons. The principal one is that Dick and I would rather be off exploring new worlds, while the other members of the Seaton-Crane Company, Engineers, build the power-plant."

During the talk the men had reached the house, into which the others had disappeared some time before. Upon Crane's invitation, Vaneman and his daughter stayed to dinner, and Dorothy played for awhile upon Crane's wonderful violin. The rest of the evening was spent in animated discussion of the realization of Seaton's dreams of flying without wings and beyond the supporting atmosphere. Seaton and Crane did their best to explain to the non-technical visitors how such flight was possible.

"Well, I am beginning to understand it a little," said Dorothy finally. "In plain language, it is like a big magnet or something, but different. Is that it?"

"That's it exactly," Seaton assured her.

"What are you going to call it? It isn't like anything else that ever was. Already this evening you have called it a bus, a boat, a kite, a star-hound, a wagon, an aerial flivver, a sky-chariot, a space-eating wampus, and I don't know what else. Even Martin has called it a vehicle, a ship, a bird, and a shell. What is its real name?"

"I don't know. It hasn't got any that I know of. What would you suggest, Dottie?"

"I don't know what general name should be applied to them, but for this one there is only one possible name, 'The Skylark.'"

"Exactly right, Dorothy," said Crane.

"Fine!" cried Seaton. "And you shall christen it, Dottie, with a big Florence flask full of absolute vacuum. 'I christen you "The Skylark." BANG!'"

As the guests were leaving, at a late hour, Vaneman said:

"Oh, yes. I bought an extra *Clarion* as we came out. It tells a wild tale of an explosion so violent that science cannot explain it. I don't suppose it is true, but it may make interesting reading for you two scientific sharps. Good night."

Seaton accompanied Dorothy to the car, bidding her a more intimate farewell on the way. When he returned, Crane, with an unusual expression of concern on his face, handed him the paper without a word.

"What's up, old man? Something in it?" he asked, as he took the paper. He fell silent as he read the first words, and after he had read the entire article he said slowly:

"True, beyond a doubt. Even a *Clarion* reporter couldn't imagine that. It's all intra-atomic energy, all right-some poor devil trying our stunt without my horseshoe in his pocket."

"Think, Dick! Something is wrong somewhere. You know that two people did not discover X at the same time. The answer is that somebody stole your idea, but the idea is worthless without the X. You say that the stuff is extremely rare-where did they get it?"

"That's right, Mart. I never thought of that. The stuff *is* extremely rare. I am supposed to know something about rare metals, and I never heard of it before-there isn't even a gap in the Periodic System in which it belongs. I would bet a hat that we have every milligram known to the world at present."

"Well, then," said the practical Crane. "We had better see whether or not we have all we started with."

Asking Shiro to bring the large bottle from the vault, he opened the living-room safe and brought forth the small vial. The large bottle was still nearly full, the seal upon it unbroken. The vial was apparently exactly as Seaton had left it after he had made his bars.

"Our stuff seems to be all there," said Crane. "It looks as though someone else has discovered it also."

"I don't believe it," said Seaton, their positions now reversed. "It's altogether too rare."

He scanned both bottles narrowly.

"I can tell by taking the densities," he added, and ran up to the laboratory, returning with a Westphal balance in his hand. After testing both solutions he said slowly:

"Well, the mystery is solved. The large bottle has a specific gravity of 1.80, as it had when I prepared it; that in the vial reads only 1.41. Somebody has burglarized this safe and taken almost half of the solution, filling the vial up with colored water. The stuff is so strong that I probably never would have noticed the difference."

"But who could it have been?"

"Search me! But it's nothing to worry about now, anyway, because whoever it was is gone where he'll never do it again. He's taken the solution with him, too, so that nobody else can get it."

"I wish I were sure of that, Dick. The man who tried to do the research work is undoubtedly gone-but who is back of him?"

"Nobody, probably. Who would want to be?"

"To borrow your own phrase, Dick, Scott 'chirped it' when he called you 'Nobody Holme.' For a man with your brains you have the least sense of anybody I know. You know that this thing is worth, as a power project alone, thousands of millions of dollars, and that there are dozens of big concerns who would cheerfully put us both out of the way for a thousandth of that amount. The question is not to find one concern who might be backing a thing like that, but to pick out the one who is backing it."

After thinking deeply for a few moments he went on:

"The idea was taken from your demonstration in the Bureau, either by an eye-witness or by someone who heard about it afterward, probably the former. Even though it failed, one man saw the possibilities. Who was that man? Who was there?"

"Oh, a lot of the fellows were there. Scott, Smith, Penfield, DuQuesne, Roberts-quite a bunch of them. Let's see-Scott hasn't brains enough to do anything. Smith doesn't know anything about anything except amines. Penfield is a pure scientist, who wouldn't even quote an authority without asking permission. DuQuesne is ...hm-m ...DuQuesne ...he ...I...."

"Yes. DuQuesne. I have heard of him. He's the big black fellow, about your own size? He has the brains, the ability, and the inclination, has he not?"

"Well, I wouldn't want to say that. I don't know him very well, and personal dislike is no ground at all for suspicion, you know."

"Enough to warrant investigation. Is there anyone else who might have reasoned it out as you did, and as DuQuesne possibly could?"

"Not that I remember. But we can count DuQuesne out, anyway, because he called me up this afternoon about some notes on gallium; so he is still in the Bureau. Besides, he wouldn't let anybody else investigate it if he got it. He would do it himself, and I don't think he would have blown himself up. I never did like him very well personally-he's such a cold, inhuman son of a fish-but you've got to hand it to him for ability. He's probably the best man in the world today on that kind of thing."

"No, I do not think that we will count him out yet. He may have had nothing to do with it, but we will have him investigated nevertheless, and will guard against future visitors here."

Turning to the telephone, he called the private number of a well-known detective.

"Prescott? Crane speaking. Sorry to get you out of bed, but I should like to have a complete report upon Dr. Marc C. DuQuesne, of the Rare Metals Laboratory, as soon as possible. Every detail for the last two weeks, every move and every thought if possible. Please keep a good man on him until further notice....I wish you would send two or three guards out here right away, to-night; men you can trust and who will stay awake....Thanks. Good night."

CHAPTER V

Direct Action

Seaton and Crane spent some time developing the object-compass. Crane made a number of these instruments, mounted in gymbals, so that the delicate needles were free to turn in any direction whatever. They were mounted upon jeweled bearings, but bearings made of such great strength, that Seaton protested.

"What's the use, Mart? You don't expect a watch to be treated like a stone-crusher. That needle weighs less than half a gram. Why mount it as though it weighed twenty pounds?"

"To be safe. Remember the acceleration the Lark will be capable of, and also that on some other worlds, which we hope to visit, this needle will weigh more than it does here."

"That's right, Mart, I never thought of that. Anyway, we can't be too safe to suit me."

When the compasses were done and the power through them had been adjusted to one-thousandth of a watt, the lowest they could maintain with accuracy, they focused each instrument upon one of a set of most carefully weighed glass beads, ranging in size from a pin-head up to a large marble, and had the beads taken across the country by Shiro, in order to test the sensitiveness and accuracy of the new instruments. The first test was made at a distance of one hundred miles, the last at nearly three thousand. They found, as they had expected, that from the weight of the object and the time it took the needle to come to rest after being displaced from its line by a gentle tap of the finger, they could easily calculate the distance from the compass to the object. This fact pleased Crane immensely, as it gave him a sure means of navigation in space. The only objection to its use in measuring earthly distances was its extreme delicacy, the needle focused upon the smallest bead in the lot at a distance of three thousand miles coming to rest in little more than one second.

The question of navigation solved, the two next devoted themselves to perfecting the "X-plosive bullet," as Seaton called it. From his notes and equations Seaton calculated the weight of copper necessary to exert the explosive force of one pound of nitro-glycerin, and weighed out, on the most delicate assay-balance made, various fractions and multiples of this amount of the treated copper, while Crane fitted up the bullets of automatic-pistol cartridges to receive the charges and to explode them on impact.

They placed their blueprints and working notes in the safe, as usual, taking with them only those notes dealing with the object-compass and the X-plosive bullet, upon which they were still working. No one except Shiro knew that the original tracings, from which the blue-prints had been made, and their final, classified notes were always kept in the vault. They cautioned him and the three guards to keep a close watch until they returned. Then they set out in the biplane, to try out the new weapon in a lonely place where the exploding shells could do no damage.

They found that the X-plosive came fully up to expectations. The smallest charge they had prepared, fired by Crane at a great stump a full hundred yards away from the bare, flat-topped knoll that had afforded them a landing-place, tore it bodily from the ground and reduced it to splinters, while the force of the explosion made the two men stagger.

"She sure is big medicine!" laughed Seaton. "Wonder what a real one will do?" and drawing his pistol, he inserted a cartridge carrying a much heavier charge.

"Better be careful with the big ones," cautioned Crane. "What are you going to shoot at?"

"That rock over there," pointing to a huge boulder half a mile away across the small valley. "Want to bet me a dinner I can't hit it?"

"No. You forget that I saw you win the pistol trophy of the District."

The pistol cracked, and when the bullet reached its destination the great stone was obliterated in a vast ball of flame. After a moment there was a deafening report—a crash as though the world were falling to pieces. Both men were hurled violently backward, stumbling and falling flat. Picking themselves up, they looked across the valley at the place where the boulder had stood, to see only an immense cloud of dust, which slowly blew away, revealing a huge hole in the ground. They were silent a moment, awed by the frightful power they had loosed.

"Well, Mart," Seaton broke the silence, "I'll say those one-milligram loads are plenty big enough. If that'd been something coming after us-whether any possible other-world animal, a foreign battleship, or the mythical great sea-serpent himself, it'd be a good Indian now. Yes? No?"

"Yes. When we use the heavier charges we must use long-range rifles. Have you had enough demonstration or do you want to shoot some more?"

"I've had enough, thanks. That last rock I bounced off of was no pillow, I'll tell the world. Besides, it looks as though I'd busted a leg or two off of our noble steed with my shot, and we may have to walk back home."

An examination of the plane, which had been moved many feet and almost overturned by the force of the explosion, revealed no damage that they could not repair on the spot, and dusk saw them speeding through the air toward the distant city.

In response to a summons from his chief, Perkins silently appeared in Brookings' office, without his usual complacent smile.

"Haven't you done anything yet, after all this time?" demanded the magnate. "We're getting tired of this delay."

"I can't help it, Mr. Brookings," replied the subordinate. "They've got detectives from Prescott's all over the place. Our best men have been trying ever since the day of the explosion, but can't do a thing without resorting to violence. I went out there myself and looked them over, without being seen. There isn't a man there with a record, and I haven't been able so far to get anything on any one of them that we can use as a handle."

"No, Prescott's men are hard to do anything with. But can't you...?" Brookings paused significantly.

"I was coming to that. I thought one of them might be seen, and I talked to him a little, over the phone, but I couldn't talk loud enough without consulting you. I mentioned ten, but he held out for twenty-five. Said he wouldn't consider it at all, but he wants to quit Prescott and go into business for himself."

"Go ahead on twenty-five. We want to get action," said Brookings, as he wrote an order on the cashier for twenty-five thousand dollars in small-to-medium bills. "That is cheap enough, considering what DuQuesne's rough stuff would probably cost. Report tomorrow about four, over our private phone-no, I'll come down to the café, it's safer."

The place referred to was the Perkins Café, a high-class restaurant on Pennsylvania Avenue, heavily patronized by the diplomatic, political, financial, and sporting circles of upper-class Washington. It was famous for its discreet waiters, and for the absolutely private rooms. Many of its patrons knew of its unique telephone service, in which each call went through such a devious system of relays that any attempt to trace it was hopeless; they knew that while "The Perkins" would not knowingly lend itself to any violation of law, it was an entirely safe and thoroughly satisfactory place in which to conduct business of the most secret and confidential character; a place from which one could enjoy personal conversation with persons to whom he wished to remain invisible and untraceable: a place which had never been known to "leak." For these reasons it was really the diplomatic and political center of the country, and over its secret wires had gone, in guarded language, messages that would have rocked the world had they gone astray. It was recognized that the place was occasionally, by its very nature, used for illegal purposes, but it was such a political, financial, and diplomatic necessity that it carried a "Hands Off" sign. It was never investigated by Congress and never raided by the police. Hundreds of telephone calls were handled daily. A man would come in, order something served in a private room, leave a name at the desk, and say that he was expecting a call. There the affair ended. The telephone operators were hand-picked, men of very short memories, carefully trained never to look at a face and never to remember a name or a number. Although the precaution was unnecessary, this shortness of memory was often encouraged by bills of various denominations.

No one except Perkins and the heads of the great World Steel Corporation knew that the urbane and polished proprietor of the café was a criminal of the blackest kind, whose liberty and life itself were dependent upon the will of the Corporation; or that the restaurant was especially planned and maintained as a blind for its underground activities; or that Perkins was holding a position which suited him exactly and which he would not have given up for wealth or glory-that of being the guiding genius who planned nefarious things for the men higher up, and saw to it that they were carried out by the men lower down. He was in constant personal touch with his superiors, but in order to avoid any chance of betrayal he never saw his subordinates personally. Not only were they entirely ignorant of his identity, but all possible means of their tracing him had been foreseen and guarded against. He called them on the telephone, but they never called him. The only possible way in which any of his subordinates could get in touch with him was by means of the wonderful wireless telephone already referred to, developed by a drug-crazed genius who had died shortly after it was perfected. It was a tiny instrument, no larger than a watch, but of practically unlimited range. The controlling central station of the few instruments in existence, from which any instrument could be cut out, changed in tune, or totally destroyed at will, was in Perkins' office safe. A man intrusted with an unusually important job would receive from an unknown source an instrument, with directions sufficient for its use. As soon as the job was done he would find, upon again attempting to use the telephone, that its interior was so hopelessly wrecked that not even the most skilled artisan could reproduce what it had once been.

At four o'clock Brookings was ushered into the private office of the master criminal, who was plainly ill at ease.

"I've got to report another failure, Mr. Brookings. It's nobody's fault, just one of those things that couldn't be helped. I handled this myself. Our man left the door unlocked and kept the others busy in another room. I had just started to work when Crane's Japanese servant, who was supposed to be asleep, appeared upon the scene. If I hadn't known something about jiu-jutsu myself, he'd have broken my neck. As it was, I barely got away, with the Jap and all three guards close behind me...."

"I'm not interested in excuses," broke in the magnate, angrily. "We'll have to turn it over to DuQuesne after all unless you get something done, and get it done quick. Can't you get to that Jap some way?"

"Certainly I can. I never yet saw the man who couldn't be reached, one way or another. I've had 'Silk' Humphreys, the best fixer in the business, working on him all day, and he'll be neutral before night. If the long green won't quiet him-and I never saw a Jap refuse it yet—a lead pipe will. Silk hasn't reported yet, but I expect to hear from him any minute now, through our man out there."

As he spoke, the almost inaudible buzzer in his pocket gave a signal.

"There he is now," said Perkins, as he took out his wireless instrument. "You might listen in and hear what he has to say."

Brookings took out his own telephone and held it to his ear.

"Hello," Perkins spoke gruffly into the tiny transmitter. "What've you got on your chest?"

"Your foot slipped on the Jap," the stranger replied. "He crabbed the game right. Slats and the big fellow put all the stuff into the box, told us to watch it until they get back tonight-they may be late-then went off in Slats' ship to test something-couldn't find out what. Silk tackled the yellow boy, and went up to fifty grand, but the Jap couldn't see him at all. Silk started to argue, and the Jap didn't do a thing but lay him out, cold. This afternoon, while the Jap was out in the grounds, three stick-up men jumped him. He bumped one of them off with his hands and the others with his gat-one of those big automatics that throw a slug like a cannon. None of us knew he had it. That's all, except that I am quitting Prescott right now. Anything else I can do for you, whoever you are?"

"No. Your job's done."

The conversation closed. Perkins pressed the switch which reduced the interior of the spy's wireless instrument to a fused mass of metal, and Brookings called DuQuesne on the telephone.

"I would like to talk to you," he said. "Shall I come there or would you rather come to my office?"

"I'll come there. They're watching this house. They have one man in front and one in back, a couple of detectaphones in my rooms here, and have coupled onto this telephone."

"Don't worry," he continued calmly as the other made an exclamation of dismay. "Talk ahead as loud as you please-they can't hear you. Do you think that those poor, ignorant flat feet can show me anything about electricity? I'd shoot a jolt along their wires that would burn their ears off if it weren't my cue to act the innocent and absorbed scientist. As it is, their instruments are all registering dense silence. I am deep in study right now, and can't be disturbed!"

"Can you get out?"

"Certainly. I have that same private entrance down beside the house wall and the same tunnel I used before. I'll see you in about fifteen minutes."

In Brookings' office, DuQuesne told of the constant surveillance over him.

"They suspect me on general principles, I think," he continued. "They are apparently trying to connect me with somebody. I don't think they suspect you at all, and they won't unless they get some better methods. I have devices fitted up to turn the lights off and on, raise and lower the windows, and even cast shadows at certain times. The housekeeper knows that when I go to my library after dinner, I have retired to study, and that it is as much as anyone's life is worth to disturb me. Also, I am well known to be firmly fixed in my habits, so it's easy to fool those detectives. Last night I went out and watched them. They hung around a couple of hours after my lights went out, then walked off together. I can dodge them any time and have all my nights free without their ever suspecting anything."

"Are you free tonight?"

"Yes. The time-switches are all set, and as long as I get back before daylight, so they can see me get up and go to work, it will be all right."

Brookings told him briefly of the failures to secure the solution and the plans, of the death of the three men sent to silence Shiro, and of all the other developments. DuQuesne listened, his face impassive.

"Well," he said as Brookings ceased. "I thought you would bull it, but not quite so badly. But there's no use whining now. I can't use my original plan of attack in force, as they are prepared and might be able to stand us off until the police could arrive."

He thought deeply for a time, then said, intensely:

"If I go into this thing, Brookings, I am in absolute command. Everything goes as I say. Understand?"

"Yes. It's up to you, now."

"All right, I think I've got it. Can you get me a Curtiss biplane in an hour, and a man about six feet tall who weighs about a hundred and sixty pounds? I want to drive the plane myself, and have the man, dressed in full leathers and hood, in the passenger's seat, shot so full of chloroform or dope that he will be completely unconscious for at least two hours."

"Easy. We can get you any kind of plane you want in an hour, and Perkins can find a man of that description who would be glad to have a dream at that price. But what's the idea?... Pardon me, I shouldn't have asked that," he added, as the saturnine chemist shot him a black look from beneath his heavy brows.

Well, within the hour, DuQuesne drove up to a private aviation field and found awaiting him a Curtiss biplane, whose attendant jumped into an automobile and sped away as he approached. He quickly donned a heavy leather suit, similar to the one Seaton always wore in the air, and drew the hood over his face. Then, after a searching look at the lean form of the unconscious man in the other seat, he was off, the plane climbing swiftly under his expert hand. He took a wide circle to the west and north.

Soon Shiro and the two guards, hearing the roar of an approaching airplane, looked out and saw what they supposed to be Crane's biplane coming down with terrific speed in an almost vertical nose-dive, as though the driver were in an extremity of haste. Flattening out just in time to avert destruction it taxied up the field almost to the house. The watchers saw a man recognizable as Seaton by his suit and his unmistakable physique stand up and wave both arms frantically, heard him shout hoarsely "...all of you...out here," saw him point to Crane's apparently lifeless form and slump down in his seat. All three ran out to help the unconscious aviators, but just as they reached the machine there were three silenced reports and the three men fell to the ground. DuQuesne leaped lightly out of the machine and looked narrowly at the bodies at his feet. He saw that the two detectives were dead, but found with some chagrin that the Japanese still showed faint signs of life. He half drew his pistol to finish the job, but observing that the victim was probably fatally wounded he thrust it back into its holster and went on into the house. Drawing on rubber gloves he rapidly blew the door off the safe with nitro-glycerin and took out everything it contained. He set aside a roll of blueprints, numerous notebooks, some money and other valuables, and a small vial of solution-but of the larger bottle there was no trace. He then ransacked the entire house, from cellar to attic, with no better success. So cleverly was the entrance to the vault concealed in the basement wall that he failed to discover it.

"I might have expected this of Crane," he thought, half aloud, "after all the warning that fool Brookings persisted in giving him. This is the natural result of his nonsense. The rest of the solution is probably in the safest safe-deposit vault in the United States. But I've got their plans and notes, and enough solution for the present. I'll get the rest of it when I want it-there's more than one way to kill any cat that ever lived!"

Returning to the machine, DuQuesne calmly stepped over the bodies of the detectives and the unconscious form of the dying Japanese, who was uttering an occasional groan. He started the engine and took his seat. There was an increasing roar as he opened the throttle, and soon he descended upon the field from which he had set out. He noted that there was a man in an automobile at some distance from the hangar, evidently waiting to take care of the plane and his still unconscious passenger. Rapidly resuming his ordinary clothing, he stepped into his automobile and was soon back in his own rooms, poring over the blueprints and notebooks.

Seaton and Crane both felt that something was wrong when they approached the landing field and saw that the landing-lights were not burning, as they always were kept lighted whenever the plane was abroad after dark. By the dim light of the old moon Crane made a bumpy landing and they sprang from their seats and hastened toward the house. As they neared it they heard a faint moan and turned toward the sound, Seaton whipping out his electric torch with one hand and his automatic pistol with the other. At the sight that met their eyes, however, he hastily replaced the weapon and bent over Shiro, a touch assuring him that the other two were beyond the reach of help. Silently they picked up the injured man and carried him gently into his own room, barely glancing at the wrecked safe on the way. Seaton applied first-aid treatment to the ghastly wound in Shiro's head, which both men supposed to be certainly fatal, while Crane called a noted surgeon, asking him to come at once. He then telephoned the coroner, the police, and finally Prescott, with whom he held a long conversation.

Having done all in their power for the unfortunate man, they stood at his bedside, their anger all the more terrible for the fact that it was silent. Seaton stood with every muscle tense. He was seething with rage, his face purple and his eyes almost emitting sparks, his teeth clenched until the muscles of his jaws stood out in bands and lumps. His right hand, white-knuckled, gripped the butt of his pistol, while under his left the brass rail of the bed slowly bent under the intensity of his unconscious muscular effort. Crane stood still, apparently impassive, but with his face perfectly white and with every feature stern and cold as though cut from marble. Seaton was the first to speak.

"Mart," he gritted, his voice husky with fury, "a man who would leave another man alone to die after giving him that, ain't a man-he's a thing. If Shiro dies and we can ever find out who did it I'll shoot him with the biggest explosive charge I've got. No, I won't either, that'd be too sudden. I'll take him apart with my bare hands."

"We will find him, Dick," Crane replied in a level, deadly voice entirely unlike his usual tone. "That is one thing money can do. We will get him if money, influence, and detectives can do it."

The tension was relieved by the arrival of the surgeon and his two nurses, who set to work with the machine-like rapidity and precision of their highly-specialized craft. After a few minutes, the work completed, the surgeon turned to the two men who had been watching him so intently, with a smile upon his clean-shaven face.

"Merely a scalp wound, Mr. Crane," he stated. "He should recover consciousness in an hour or so." Then, breaking in upon Seaton's exclamation, "It looks much worse than it really is. The bullet glanced off the skull instead of penetrating it, stunning him by the force of the blow. There are no indications that the brain is affected in any way, and while the affected area of the scalp is large, it is a clean wound and should heal rapidly. He will probably be up and around in a couple of days, and by the time his hair grows again, he will not be able to find a scar."

As he took his leave, the police and coroner arrived. After making a thorough investigation, in which they learned what had been stolen and shrewdly deduced the manner in which the robbery had been accomplished, they departed, taking with them the bodies. They were authorized by Crane to offer a reward of one million dollars for information leading to the arrest and conviction of the murderer. After everyone except the nurses had gone, Crane showed them the rooms they were to occupy while caring for the wounded man. As the surgeon had foretold, Shiro soon recovered consciousness. After telling his story he dropped into a deep sleep, and Seaton and Crane, after another telephonic conference with Prescott, retired for the rest of the night.

CHAPTER VI

The Object-Compass at Work

Prescott, after a sleepless night, joined Seaton and Crane at breakfast.

"What do you make of it, Mr. Prescott?" asked Crane. "Seaton here thinks it was DuQuesne, possibly acting for some foreign power, after our flying-machine to use in war. I think it was some big industrial concern after our power-plant. What is your opinion?"

"I haven't any," replied the great detective after a moment. "Either guess may be true, although I am almost positive that Dr. DuQuesne had nothing to do with it, either way. It was no ordinary burglary, that is certain from Shiro's story. It was done by someone who had exact information of your movements and habits. He chose a time when you were away, probably not so much from fear of you as because it was only in your absence that he could succeed as he did in getting all the guards out at once where he could handle them. He was a man with one accomplice or who worked alone, and who was almost exactly Seaton's size and build. He was undoubtedly an expert, as he blew the safe and searched the whole house without leaving a finger-print or any other clue, however slight, that I can find —a thing I have never before seen done in all my experience."

"His size should help in locating him," declared Crane. "While there are undoubtedly thousands of men of Dick's six-feet-one and two-fifths, they are fairly well scattered, are they not?"

"Yes, they are, but his very size only makes it worse. I have gone over all the records I could, in the short time I have had, and can't find an expert of that class with anywhere near that description."

"How about the third guard, the one who escaped?" asked Seaton.

"He wasn't here. It was his afternoon off, you know, and he said that he wouldn't come back into this job on a bet-that he wasn't afraid of anything ordinary, but he didn't like the looks of things out here. That sounded fishy to me, and I fired him. He may have been the leak, of course, though I have always found him reliable before. If he did leak, he must have got a whale of a slice for it. He is under constant watch, and if we can ever get anything on him, I will nail him to the cross. But that doesn't help get this affair straightened out. I haven't given up, of course, there are lots of things not tried yet, but I must admit that temporarily, at least, I am up a stump."

"Well," remarked Seaton, "that million-dollar reward will bring him in, sure. No honor that ever existed among thieves, or even among free-lances of diplomacy, could stand that strain."

"I'm not so sure of that, Dick," said Crane. "If either one of our ideas is the right one, very few men would know enough about the affair to give pertinent information, and they probably would not live long enough to enjoy the reward very thoroughly. Even a million dollars fails in that case."

"I rather agree with Mr. Crane, Seaton. If it were an ordinary affair-and I am as sure it is not as the police are that it is —a reward of that size would get us our man within two days. As it is, I doubt very much that the reward will do us any good. I'm afraid that it will never be claimed."

"Wonder if the Secret Service could help us out? They'd be interested if it should turn out to be some foreign power."

"I took it up with the Chief himself, just after it happened last night. He doesn't think that it can be a foreign country. He has their agents pretty well spotted, and the only one that could fill the bill-you know a man with that description and with the cold nerve to do the job would be apt to be known-was in San Francisco, the time this job was pulled off."

"The more you talk, the more I am convinced that it was DuQuesne himself," declared Seaton, positively. "He is almost exactly my size and build, is the only man I know of who could do anything with the solution after he got it, and he has nerve enough to do anything."

"I would like to think it was DuQuesne," replied the detective, thoughtfully, "but I'm afraid we'll have to count him out of it entirely. He has been under the constant surveillance of my best men ever since you mentioned him. We have detectaphones in his rooms, wires on his telephone, and are watching him night and day. He never goes out except to work, never has any except unimportant telephone calls, and the instruments register only the occasional scratching of a match, the rustle of papers, and other noises of a man studying. He's innocent."

"That may be true," assented Seaton doubtfully, "but you want to remember that he knows more about electricity than the guy that invented it, and I'm not sure that he can't talk to a detectaphone and make it say anything he wants it to. Anyway, we can soon settle it. Yesterday I made a special trip down to the Bureau, with some notes as an excuse, to set this object-compass on him," taking one of the small instruments from his pocket as he spoke. "I watched him a while last night, then fixed an alarm to wake me if the needle moved much, but it pointed steady all night. See! It's moving now. That means that he is going to work early, as usual. Now I'm morally certain that he's mixed up in this thing somewhere, and I'm not convinced that he isn't slipping one over on your men some way-he's a clever devil. I wonder if you wouldn't take this compass and watch him yourself tonight, just on general principles? Or let me do it. I'd be glad to. I say 'tonight' because if he did get the stuff here he didn't deliver it anywhere last night. It's just a chance, of course, but he may do it tonight."

After the compass had been explained to the detective he gladly consented to the plan, declaring that he would willingly spend the time just to watch such an unheard-of instrument work. After another hour of fruitless discussion Prescott took his leave, saying that he would mount an impregnable guard from that time on.

Late that evening Prescott joined the two men who were watching DuQuesne's house. They reported that all was perfectly quiet, as usual. The scientist was in his library, the instruments registering only the usual occasional faint sounds of a man absorbed in study. But after an hour of waiting, and while the microphones made a noise as of rustling papers, the needle of the compass moved. It dipped slowly toward the earth as though DuQuesne were descending into the cellar, but at the same time the shadow of his unmistakable profile was thrown upon the window shade as he apparently crossed the room.

"Can't you hear him walk?" demanded Prescott.

"No. He has heavy Turkish rugs all over the library, and he always walks very lightly, besides."

Prescott watched the needle in amazement as it dipped deeper and deeper, pointing down into the earth almost under his feet and then behind him, as though DuQuesne had walked beneath him. He did not, could not, believe it. He was certain that something had gone wrong with the strange instrument in his hand, nevertheless he followed the pointing needle. It led him beside Park Road, down the hill, straight toward the long bridge which forms one entrance to Rock Creek Park. Though skeptical, Prescott took no chances, and as he approached the bridge he left the road and concealed himself behind a clump of trees, from which point of vantage he could see the ground beneath the bridge as well as the roadway. Soon the bridge trembled under the weight of a heavy automobile going toward the city at a high rate of speed. He saw DuQuesne, with a roll of papers under his arm, emerge from under the bridge just in time to leap aboard the automobile, which slowed down only enough to enable him to board it in safety. The detective noticed that the car was a Pierce-Arrow limousine —a car not common, even in Washington-and rushed out to get its number, but the license plates were so smeared with oil and dust that the numbers could not be read by the light of the tail lamp. Glancing at the compass in his hand he saw that the delicate needle was now pointing steadily at the fleeing car, and all doubts as to the power of the instrument were dispelled. He rejoined his men, informed them that DuQuesne had eluded them, and took one of them up the hill to a nearby garage. There he engaged a fast car and set out in pursuit, choosing the path for the chauffeur by means of the compass. His search ended at the residence of Brookings, the General Manager of the great World Steel Corporation. Here he dismissed the car and watched the house while his assistant went to bring out the fast motorcycle used by Prescott when high speed was desirable.

After four hours a small car bearing the license number of a distant state-which was found, by subsequent telegraphing, to be unknown to the authorities of that state-drove under the porte-cochère, and the hidden watcher saw DuQuesne, without the papers, step into it. Knowing now what to expect, Prescott drove his racing motorcycle at full speed out to the Park Road Bridge and concealed himself beneath the structure, in a position commanding a view of the concrete abutment through which the scientist must have come. Soon he heard a car slow down overhead, heard a few rapid footfalls, and saw the dark form of a large man outlined against the gray face of the abutment. He saw the man lift his hand high above his head, and saw a black rectangle appear in the gray, engulf the man, and disappear. After a few minutes he approached the abutment and searched its face with the help of his flash-light. He finally succeeded in tracing the almost imperceptible crack which outlined the door, and the concealed button which DuQuesne had pressed to open it. He did not press the button, as it might be connected to an alarm. Deep in thought, he mounted his motorcycle and made his way to his home to get a few hours of sleep before reporting to Crane whom he was scheduled to see at breakfast next morning.

Both men were waiting for him when he appeared, and he noticed with pleasure that Shiro, with a heavily-bandaged head, was insisting that he was perfectly able to wait on the table instead of breakfasting in bed. He calmly proceeded to serve breakfast in spite of Crane's remonstrances, having ceremoniously ordered out of the kitchen the colored man who had been secured to take his place.

"Well, gentlemen," the detective began, "part of the mystery is straightened out. I was entirely wrong, and each of you were partly right. It was DuQuesne, in all probability. It is equally probable that a great company-in this case the World Steel Corporation-is backing him, though I don't believe there is a ghost of a show of ever being able to prove it in law. Your 'object-compass' did the trick."

He narrated all the events of the previous night.

"I'd like to send him to the chair for this job," said Seaton with rising anger. "We ought to shoot him anyway, damn him —I'm sorry duels have gone out of fashion, for I can't shoot him off-hand, the way things are now —I sure wish I could."

"No, you cannot shoot him," said Crane, thoughtfully, "and neither can I, worse luck. We are not in his class there. And you must not fight with him, either" —noting that Seaton's powerful hands had doubled into fists, the knuckles showing white through the tanned skin —"though that would be a fight worth watching and I would like to see you give him the beating of his life. A little thing like a beating is not a fraction of what he deserves and it would show him that we have found him out. No, we must do it legally or let him entirely alone. You think there is no hope of proving it, Prescott?"

"Frankly, I see very little chance of it. There is always hope, of course, and if that bunch of pirates ever makes a slip, we'll be right there waiting to catch 'em. While I don't believe in holding out false encouragement, they've never slipped yet. I'll take my men off DuQuesne, now that we've linked him up with Steel. It doesn't make any difference, does it, whether he goes to them every night or only once a week?"

"No."

"Then about all I can do is to get everything I can on that Steel crowd, and that is very much like trying to get blood out of a turnip. I intend to keep after them, of course, for I owe them something for killing two of my men here, as well as for other favors they have done me in the past, but don't expect too much. I have tackled them before, and so have police headquarters and even the Secret Service itself, under cover, and all that any of us has been able to get is an occasional small fish. We could never land the big fellows. In fact, we have never found the slightest material proof of what we are morally certain is the truth, that World Steel is back of a lot of deviltry all over the country. The little fellows who do the work either don't know anything or are afraid to tell. I'll see if I can find out what they are doing with the stuff they stole, but I'm not even sure of doing that. You can't plant instruments on that bunch-it would be like trying to stick a pin into a sleeping cat without waking him up. They undoubtedly have one of the best corps of detectives in the world. You haven't perfected an instrument which enables you to see into a closed room and hear what is going on there, have you?" And upon being assured that they had not, he took his leave.

"Optimistic cuss, ain't he?" remarked Seaton.

"He has cause to be, Dick. World Steel is a soulless corporation if there ever was one. They have the shrewdest lawyers in the country, and they get away legally with things that are flagrantly illegal, such as freezing out competitors, stealing patents, and the like. Report has it that they do not stop at arson, treason, or murder to attain their ends, but as Prescott said, they never leave any legal proof behind them."

"Well, *we* should fret, anyway. Of course, a monopoly is what they're after, but they can't form one because they can't possibly get the rest of our solution. Even if they should get it, we can get more. It won't be as easy as this last batch was, since the X was undoubtedly present in some particular lot of platinum in extraordinary quantities, but now that I know exactly what to look for, I can find more. So they can't get their monopoly unless they kill us off...."

"Exactly. Go on, I see you are getting the idea. If we should both conveniently die, they could get the solution from the company, and have the monopoly, since no one else can handle it."

"But they couldn't get away with it, Mart-never in a thousand years, even if they wanted to. Of course I am small fry, but you are too big a man for even Steel to do away with. It can't be done."

"I am not so sure of that. Airplane accidents are numerous, and I am an aviator. Also, has it ever occurred to you that the heavy forging for the Skylark, ordered a while ago, are of steel?"

Seaton paused, dumbfounded, in the act of lighting his pipe.

"But thanks to your object-compass, we are warned." Crane continued, evenly. "Those forgings are going through the most complete set of tests known to the industry, and if they go into the Skylark at all it will be after I am thoroughly convinced that they will not give way on our first trip into space. But we can do nothing until the steel arrives, and with the guard Prescott has here now we are safe enough. Luckily, the enemy knows nothing of the object-compass or the X-plosive, and we must keep them in ignorance. Hereinafter, not even the guards get a look at anything we do."

"They sure don't. Let's get busy!"

DuQuesne and Brookings met in conference in a private room of the Perkins Café.

"What's the good word, Doctor?"

"So-so," replied the scientist. "The stuff is all they said it was, but we haven't enough of it to build much of a power-plant. We can't go ahead with it, anyway, as long as Seaton and Crane have nearly all their original solution."

"No, we can't. We must find a way of getting it. I see now that we should have done as you suggested, and taken it before they had warning and put it out of our reach."

"There's no use holding post-mortems. We've got to get it, some way, and everybody that knows anything about that new metal, how to get it or how to handle it, must die. At first, it would have been enough to kill Seaton. Now, however, there is no doubt that Crane knows all about it, and he probably has left complete instructions in case he gets killed in an accident-he's the kind that would. We will have to keep our eyes open and wipe out those instructions and anyone who has seen them. You see that, don't you?"

"Yes, I am afraid that is the only way out. We must have the monopoly, and anyone who might be able to interfere with it must be removed. How has your search for more X prospered?"

"About as well as I expected. We bought up all the platinum wastes we could get, and reworked all the metallic platinum and allied metals we could buy in the open market, and got less than a gram of X out of the whole lot. It's scarcer than radium. Seaton's finding so much of it at once was an accident, pure and simple-it couldn't happen once in a million years."

"Well, have you any suggestions as to how we can get that solution?"

"No. I haven't thought of anything but that very thing ever since I found that they had hidden it, and I can't yet see any good way of getting it. My forte is direct action and that fails in this case, since no amount of force or torture could make Crane reveal the hiding-place of the solution. It's probably in the safest safe-deposit vault in the country. He wouldn't carry the key on him, probably wouldn't have it in the house. Killing Seaton or Crane, or both of them, is easy enough, but it probably wouldn't get us the solution, as I have no doubt that Crane has provided for everything."

"Probably he has. But if he should disappear the stuff would have to come to light, or the Seaton-Crane Company might start their power-plant. In that case, we probably could get it?"

"*Possibly*, you mean. That method is too slow to suit me, though. It would take months, perhaps years, and would be devilishly uncertain, to boot. They'll know something is in the wind, and the stuff will be surrounded by every safeguard they can think of. There must be some better way than that, but I haven't been able to think of it."

"Neither have I, but your phrase 'direct action' gives me an idea. You say that that method has failed. What do you think of trying indirect action in the shape of Perkins, who is indirection personified?"

"Bring him in. He may be able to figure out something."

Perkins was called in, and the main phases of the situation laid before him. The three men sat in silence for many minutes while the crafty strategist studied the problem. Finally he spoke.

"There's only one way, gentlemen. We must get a handle on either Seaton or Crane strong enough to make them give up their bottle of dope, their plans, and everything...."

"Handle!" interrupted DuQuesne. "You talk like a fool! You can't get anything on either of them."

"You misunderstand me, Doctor. You can get a handle of some kind on any living man. Not necessarily in his past, you understand —I know that anything like that is out of the question in this case-but in his future. With some men it is money, with others power, with others fame, with others women or some woman, and so on down the list. What can we use here? Money is out of the question, so are power and fame, as they already have both in plain sight. It seems to me that women would be our best chance."

"Hah!" snorted the chemist. "Crane has been chased by all the women of three continents so long that he's womanproof. Seaton is worse-he's engaged, and wouldn't realize that a woman was on his trail, even if you could find a better looking one to work on him than the girl he's engaged to-which would be a hard job. Cleopatra herself couldn't swing that order."

"Engaged? That makes it simple as A B C."

"Simple? In the devil's name, how?"

"Easy as falling off a log. You have enough of the dope to build a space-car from those plans, haven't you?"

"Yes. What has that to do with the case?"

"It has everything to do with it. I would suggest that we build such a car and use it to carry off the girl. After we have her safe we could tell Seaton that she is marooned on some distant planet, and that she will be returned to earth only after all the solution, all notes, plans, and everything pertaining to the new metal are surrendered. That will bring him, and Crane will consent. Then, afterward, Dr. Seaton may go away indefinitely, and if desirable, Mr. Crane may accompany him."

"But suppose they try to fight?" asked Brookings.

Perkins slid down into his chair in deep thought, his pale eyes under half-closed lids darting here and there, his stubby fingers worrying his watch-chain restlessly.

"Who is the girl?" he asked at last.

"Dorothy Vaneman, the daughter of the lawyer. She's that auburn-haired beauty that the papers were so full of when she came out last year."

"Vaneman is a director in the Seaton-Crane Company. That makes it still better. If they show fight and follow us, that beautiful car we are making for them will collapse and they will be out of the way. Vaneman, as Seaton's prospective father-in-law and a member of his company, probably knows something about the secret. Maybe all of it. With his daughter in a space-car, supposedly out in space, and Seaton and Crane out of the way, Vaneman would listen to reason and let go of the solution, particularly as nobody knows much about it except Seaton and Crane."

"That strikes me as a perfectly feasible plan," said Brookings. "But you wouldn't really take her to another planet, would you? Why not use an automobile or an airplane, and tell Seaton that it was a space-car?"

"I wouldn't advise that. He might not believe it, and they might make a lot of trouble. It must be a real space-car even if we don't take her out of the city. To make it more impressive, you should take her in plain sight of Seaton-no, that would be too dangerous, as I have found out from the police that Seaton has a permit to carry arms, and I know that he is one of the fastest men with a pistol in the whole country. Do it in plain sight of her folks, say, or a crowd of people; being masked, of course, or dressed in an aviator's suit, with the hood and goggles on. Take her straight up out of sight, then hide her somewhere until Seaton listens to reason. I know that he *will* listen, but if he doesn't, you might let him see you start out to visit her. He'll be sure to follow you in their rotten car. As soon as he does that, he's our meat. But that raises the question of who is going to drive the car?"

"I am," replied DuQuesne. "I will need some help, though, as at least one man must stay with the girl while I bring the car back."

"We don't want to let anybody else in on this if we can help it," cautioned Brookings. "You could go along, couldn't you, Perkins?"

"Is it safe?"

"Absolutely," answered DuQuesne. "They have everything worked out to the queen's taste."

"That's all right, then. I'll take the trip. Also," turning to Brookings, "it will help in another little thing we are doing-the Spencer affair."

"Haven't you got that stuff away from her yet, after having had her locked up in that hell-hole for two months?" asked Brookings.

"No. She's stubborn as a mule. We've given her the third degree time after time, but it's no use."

"What's this?" asked DuQuesne. "Deviltry in the main office?"

"Yes. This Margaret Spencer claims that we swindled her father out of an invention and indirectly caused his death. She secured a position with us in search of evidence. She is an expert stenographer, and showed such ability that she was promoted until she became my secretary. Our detectives must have been asleep, as she made away with some photographs and drawings before they caught her. She has no real evidence, of course, but she might cause trouble with a jury, especially as she is one of the best-looking women in Washington. Perkins is holding her until she returns the stolen articles."

"Why can't you kill her off?"

"She cannot be disposed of until after we know where the stuff is, because she says, and Perkins believes, that the evidence will show up in her effects. We must do something about her soon, as the search for her is dying down and she will be given up for dead."

"What's the idea about her and the space-car?"

"If the car proves reliable we might actually take her out into space and give her the choice between telling and walking back. She has nerve enough here on earth to die before giving up, but I don't believe any human being would be game to go it alone on a strange world. She'd wilt."

"I believe you're right, Perkins. Your suggestions are the best way out. Don't you think so, Doctor?"

"Yes, I don't see how we can fail-we're sure to win, either way. You are prepared for trouble afterward, of course?"

"Certainly, but I don't think there will be much trouble. They can't possibly link the three of us together. They aren't wise to you, are they, Doctor?"

"Not a chance!" sneered DuQuesne. "They ran themselves ragged trying to get something on me, but they couldn't do it. They have given me up as a bad job. I am still as careful as ever, though —I am merely a pure scientist in the Bureau of Chemistry!"

All three laughed, and Perkins left the room. The talk then turned to the construction of the space-car. It was decided to rush the work on it, so that DuQuesne could familiarize himself with its operation, but not to take any steps in the actual abduction until such time as Seaton and Crane were nearly ready to take their first flight, so that they could pursue the abductors in case Seaton was still obdurate after a few days of his fiancée's absence. DuQuesne insisted that the car should mount a couple of heavy guns, to destroy the pursuing car if the faulty members should happen to hold together long enough to carry it out into space.

After a long discussion, in which every detail of the plan was carefully considered, the two men left the restaurant, by different exits.

CHAPTER VII

The Trial Voyage

The great steel forgings which were to form the framework of the Skylark finally arrived and were hauled into the testing shed. There, behind closed doors, Crane inspected every square inch of the massive members with a lens, but could find nothing wrong. Still unsatisfied, he fitted up an electrical testing apparatus in order to search out flaws which might be hidden beneath the surface. This device revealed flaws in every piece, and after thoroughly testing each one and mapping out the imperfections he turned to Seaton with a grave face.

"Worse than useless, every one of them. They are barely strong enough to stand shipment. They figured that we would go slowly until we were well out of the atmosphere, then put on power-then something would give way and we would never come back."

"That's about the right dope, I guess. But now what'll we do? We can't cancel without letting them know we're onto them, and we certainly can't use this stuff."

"No, but we will go ahead and build this ship, anyway, so that they will think that we are going ahead with it. At the same time we will build another one, about four times this size, in absolute secrecy, and...."

"What d'you mean, absolute secrecy? How can you keep steel castings and forgings of that size secret from Steel?"

"I know a chap who owns and operates a small steel plant, so insignificant, relatively, that he has not yet been bought out or frozen out by Steel. I was able to do him a small favor once, and I am sure that he will be glad to return it. We will not be able to oversee the work, that is a drawback. We can get MacDougall to do it for us, however, and with him doing the work we can rest assured that there will be nothing off color. Even Steel couldn't buy *him*."

"MacDougall! The man who installed the Intercontinental plant? He wouldn't touch a little job like this with a pole!"

"I think he would. He and I are rather friendly, and after I tell him all about it he will be glad to take it. It means building the first interplanetary vessel, you know."

"Wouldn't Steel follow him up if he should go to work on a mysterious project? He's too big to hide."

"No. He will go camping-he often does. I have gone with him several times when we were completely out of touch with civilization for two months at a time. Now, about the ship we want. Have you any ideas?"

"It will cost more than our entire capital."

"That is easily arranged. We do not care how much it costs."

Seaton began to object to drawing so heavily upon the resources of his friend, but was promptly silenced.

"I told you when we started," Crane said flatly, "that your solution and your idea are worth far more than half a million. In fact, they are worth more than everything I have. No more talk of the money end of it, Dick."

"All right. We'll build a regular go-getter. Four times the size-she'll be a bear-cat, Mart. I'm glad this one is on the fritz. She'll carry a two-hundred-pound bar-Zowie! Watch our smoke! And say, why wouldn't it be a good idea to build an attractor —a thing like an object-compass, but mounting a ten-pound bar instead of a needle, so that if they chase us in space we can reach out and grab 'em? We might mount a machine-gun in each quadrant, shooting X-plosive bullets, through pressure gaskets in the walls. We should have something for defense —I don't like the possibility of having that gang of pirates after us, and nothing to fight back with except thought-waves."

"Right. We will do both those things. But we should make the power-plant big enough to avert any possible contingency-say four hundred pounds-and we should have everything in duplicate, from power-plant to push-buttons."

"I don't think that's necessary, Mart. Don't you think that's carrying caution to extremes?"

"Possibly-but I would rather be a live coward than a dead hero, wouldn't you?"

"You chirped it, old scout, I sure would. I never did like the looks of that old guy with the scythe, and I would hate to let DuQuesne feel that he had slipped something over on me at my own game. Besides, I've developed a lot of caution myself, lately. Double she is, with a skin of four-foot Norwegian armor. Let's get busy!"

They made the necessary alteration in the plans, and in a few days work was begun upon the huge steel shell in the little mountain steel-plant. The work was done under the constant supervision of the great MacDougall, by men who had been in his employ for years and who were all above suspicion. While it was being built Seaton and Crane employed a force of men and went ahead with the construction of the space-car in the testing shed. While they did not openly slight the work nearly all their time was spent in the house, perfecting the many essential things which were to go into the real Skylark. There was the attractor, for which they had to perfect a special sighting apparatus so that it could act in any direction, and yet would not focus upon the ship itself nor anything it contained. There were many other things.

It was in this work that the strikingly different temperaments and abilities of the two men were most clearly revealed. Seaton strode up and down the room, puffing great volumes of smoke from his hot and reeking briar, suggesting methods and ideas, his keen mind finding the way over, around, or through the apparently insuperable obstacles which beset their path. Crane, seated calmly at the drafting-table, occasionally inhaling a mouthful of smoke from one of his specially-made cigarettes, mercilessly tore Seaton's suggestions to shreds-pointing out their weaknesses, proving his points with his cold, incisive reasoning and his slide-rule calculations of factors, stresses, and strains. Seaton in turn would find a remedy for every defect, and finally, the idea complete and perfect, Crane would impale it upon the point of his drafting pencil and spread it in every detail upon the paper before him, while Seaton's active mind leaped to the next problem.

Not being vitally interested in the thing being built in the shed, they did not know that to the flawed members were being attached faulty plates, by imperfect welding. Even if they had been interested they could not have found the poor workmanship by any ordinary inspection, for it was being done by a picked crew of experts picked by Perkins. But to make things even, Perkins' crew did not know that the peculiar instruments installed by Seaton and Crane, of which their foreman took many photographs, were not real instruments, and were made only nearly enough like them to pass inspection. They were utterly useless, in design and function far different from the real instruments intended for the Skylark.

Finally, the last dummy instrument was installed in the worthless space-car, which the friends referred to between themselves as "The Cripple," a name which Seaton soon changed to "Old Crip." The construction crew was dismissed after Crane had let the foreman overhear a talk between Seaton and himself in which they decided not to start for a few days as they had some final experiments to make. Prescott reported that Steel had relaxed its vigilance and was apparently waiting for the first flight. About the same time word was received from MacDougall that the real Skylark was ready for the finishing touches. A huge triplane descended upon Crane Field and was loaded to its capacity with strange looking equipment. When it left Seaton and Crane went with it, "to make the final tests before the first flight," leaving a heavy guard over the house and the testing shed.

A few nights later, in inky blackness, a huge shape descended rapidly in front of the shed, whose ponderous doors opened to receive it and closed quickly after it. The Skylark moved lightly and easily as a wafted feather, betraying its thousands of tons of weight only by the hole it made in the hard-beaten earth of the floor as it settled to rest. Opening one of the heavy doors, Seaton and Crane sprang out into the darkness.

Dorothy and her father, who had been informed that the Skylark was to be brought home that night, were waiting. Seaton caught up his sweetheart in one mighty arm and extended his hand past her to Vaneman, who seized it in both his own. Upon the young man's face was the look of a victorious king returning from conquest. For a few minutes disconnected exclamations were all that any of the party could utter. Then Seaton, loosening slightly his bear's hold upon Dorothy, spoke.

"She flies!" he cried exultantly. "She flies, dearest, like a ray of light for speed and like a bit of thistledown for lightness. We've been around the moon!"

"Around the moon!" cried the two amazed visitors. "So soon?" asked Vaneman. "When did you start?"

"Almost an hour ago," replied Crane readily; he had already taken out his watch. His voice was calm, his face quiet, but to those who knew him best a deeper resonance in his voice and a deeper blue sparkle in his eyes betrayed his emotion. Both inventors were moved more than they could have told by their achievement, by the complete success of the great space-cruiser upon which they had labored for months with all the power of their marvelous intellects. Seaton stood now at the summit of his pride. No recognition by the masses, no applause by the multitudes, no praise even from the upper ten of his own profession could equal for him the silent adulation of the two before him. Dorothy's exquisite face was glorified as she looked at her lover. Her eyes wonderful as they told him how high he stood above all others in her world, how much she loved him. Seeing that look; that sweet face, more beautiful than ever in this, his hour of triumph; that perfect, adorable body, Seaton forgot the others and a more profound exaltation than that brought by his flight filled his being-humble thankfulness that he was the man to receive the untold treasure of her great giving.

"Every bit of mechanism we had occasion to use worked perfectly," Crane stated proudly. "We did not find it necessary to change any of our apparatus and we hope to make a longer flight soon. The hour we took on this trip might easily have been only a few minutes, for the Lark did not even begin to pick up speed."

Shiro looked at Crane with an air of utter devotion and bowed until his head approached the floor.

"Sir," he said in his stilted English. "Honorable Skylark shall be marvelous wonder. If permitting, I shall luxuriate in preparing suitable refreshment."

The permission granted, he trotted away into the house, and the travelers invited their visitors to inspect the new craft. Crane and the older man climbed through the circular doorway, which was at an elevation of several feet above the ground. Seaton and Dorothy exchanged a brief but enthusiastic caress before he lifted her lightly up to the opening and followed her up a short flight of stairs. Although she knew what to expect, from her lover's descriptions and from her own knowledge of "Old Crip," which she had seen many times, she caught her breath in amazement as she stood up and looked about the brilliantly-lighted interior of the great sky-rover. It was a sight such as had never before been seen upon earth.

She saw a spherical shell of hardened steel armor-plate, fully forty feet in diameter; though its true shape was not readily apparent from the inside, as it was divided into several compartments by horizontal floors or decks. In the exact center of the huge shell was a spherical network of enormous steel beams. Inside this structure could be seen a similar network which, mounted upon universal bearings, was free to revolve in any direction. This inner network was filled with machinery, surrounding a shining copper cylinder. From the outer network radiated six mighty supporting columns. These, branching as they neared the hull of the vessel, supported the power-plant and steering apparatus in the center and so strengthened the shell that the whole structure was nearly as strong as a solid steel ball. She noticed that the floor, perhaps eight feet below the center, was heavily upholstered in leather and did not seem solid; and that the same was true of the dozen or more seats-she could not call them chairs-which were built in various places. She gazed with interest at the two instrument boards, upon which flashed tiny lights and the highly-polished plate glass, condensite, and metal of many instruments, the use of which she could not guess.

After a few minutes of silence both visitors began to ask questions, and Seaton showed them the principal features of the novel craft. Crane accompanied them in silence, enjoying their pleasure, glorying in the mighty vessel. Seaton called attention to the great size and strength of the lateral supporting columns, one of which was immediately above their heads, and then led them over to the vertical column which pierced the middle of the floor. Enormous as the lateral had seemed, it appeared puny in comparison with this monster of fabricated steel. Seaton explained that the two verticals were many times stronger than the four laterals, as the center of gravity of the ship had been made lower than its geometrical center, so that the apparent motion of the vessel and therefore the power of the bar, would usually be merely vertical. Resting one hand caressingly upon the huge column, he exultantly explained that these members were "the last word in strength, made up of many separate I-beams and angles of the strongest known special steel, latticed and braced until no conceivable force could make them yield a millimeter."

"But why such strength?" asked the lawyer doubtfully. "This column alone would hold up Brooklyn Bridge."

"To hold down the power-plant, so that the bar won't tear through the ship when we cut her loose," replied Seaton. "Have you any idea how fast this bird can fly?"

"Well, I have heard you speak of traveling with the velocity of light, but that is overdrawn, isn't it?"

"Not very much. Our figures show that with this four-hundred-pound bar"—pointing to the copper cylinder in the exact center of the inner sphere—"we could develop not only the velocity of light, but an acceleration equal to that velocity, were it not for the increase in mass at high velocities, as shown by Einstein and others. We can't go very fast near the earth, of course, as the friction of the air would melt the whole works in a few minutes. Until we get out of the atmosphere our speed will be limited by the ability of steel to withstand melting by the friction of the air to somewhere in the neighborhood of four or five thousand miles per hour, but out in space we can develop any speed we wish, up to that of light as a limit."

"I studied physics a little in my youth. Wouldn't the mere force of such an acceleration as you mention flatten you on the floor and hold you there? And any sudden jar would certainly kill you."

"There can't be any sudden jar. This is a special floor, you notice. It is mounted on long, extremely heavy springs, to take up any possible jar. Also, whenever we are putting on power we won't try to stand up, our legs would crimple up like strings. We will ride securely strapped into those special seats, which are mounted the same as the floor, only a whole lot more so. As to the acceleration...."

"That word means picking up speed, doesn't it?" interrupted Dorothy.

"The rate of picking up speed," corrected Seaton. "That is, if you were going forty miles per hour one minute, and fifty the next minute, your acceleration would be ten miles per hour per minute. See? It's acceleration that makes you feel funny when you start up or down in an elevator."

"Then riding in this thing will be like starting up in an elevator so that your heart sinks into your boots and you can't breathe?"

"Yes, only worse. We will pick up speed faster and keep on doing it...."

"Seriously," interrupted the lawyer, "do you think that the human body can stand any such acceleration as that?"

"I don't know. We are going to find out, by starting out slowly and increasing our acceleration to as much as we can stand."

"I see," Vaneman replied. "But how are you going to steer her? How do you keep permanent reference points, since there are no directions in space?"

"That was our hardest problem," explained Seaton, "but Martin solved it perfectly. See the power-plant up there? Notice those big supporting rings and bearings? Well, the power-plant

51

is entirely separate from the ship, as it is inside that inner sphere, about which the outer sphere and the ship itself are free to revolve in any direction. No matter how much the ship rolls and pitches, as she is bound to do every time we come near enough to any star or planet to be influenced by its gravitation, the bar stays where it is pointed. Those six big jackets in the outer sphere, on the six sides of the bar, cover six pairs of gyroscope wheels, weighing several tons each, turning at a terrific speed in a vacuum. The gyroscopes keep the whole outer sphere in exactly the same position as long as they are kept turning, and afford us not only permanent planes of reference, but also a solid foundation in those planes which can be used in pointing the bar. The bar can be turned instantly to any direction whatever by special electrical instruments on the boards. You see, the outer sphere stays immovably fixed in that position, with the bar at liberty to turn in any direction inside it, and the ship at liberty to do the same thing outside it.

"Now we will show you where we sleep," Seaton continued. "We have eight rooms, four below and four above," leading the way to a narrow, steep steel stairway and down into a very narrow hall, from either side of which two doors opened. "This is my room, the adjoining one is Mart's. Shiro sleeps across the hall. The rest of the rooms are for our guests on future trips."

Sliding back the door, he switched on the light and revealed a small but fully-appointed bedroom, completely furnished with everything necessary, yet everything condensed into the least possible space. The floor, like the one above, was of cushioned leather supported by springs. The bed was a modification of the special seats already referred to. Opening another sliding door, he showed them an equally complete and equally compact bathroom.

"You see, we have all the comforts of home. This bathroom, however, is practical only when we have some force downward, either gravitation or our own acceleration. The same reasoning accounts for the hand-rails you see everywhere on board. Drifting in space, you know, there is no weight, and you can't walk; you must pull yourself around. If you tried to take a step you would bounce up and hit the ceiling, and stay there. That is why the ceilings are so well padded. And if you tried to wash your face you would throw water all over the place, and it would float around in the air instead of falling to the floor. As long as we can walk we can use the bathroom-if I should want to wash my face while we are drifting, I just press this button here, and the pilot will put on enough acceleration to make the correct use of water possible. There are a lot of surprising things about a trip into space."

"I don't doubt it a bit, and I'm simply wild to go for a ride with you. When will you take me, Dicky?" asked Dorothy eagerly.

"Very soon, Dottie. As soon as we get her in perfect running condition. You shall be the first to ride with us, I promise you."

"Where do you cook and eat? How do you see out? How about the air and water supply? How do you keep warm, or cool, as the case may be?" asked the girl's father, as though he were cross-examining a witness.

"Shiro has a galley on the main floor, and tables fold up into the wall of the main compartment. The passengers see out by sliding back steel panels, which normally cover the windows. The pilot can see in any direction from his seat at the instrument-board, by means of special instruments, something like periscopes. The windows are made of optical glass similar to that used in the largest telescopes. They are nearly as thick as the hull and have a compressive resistance almost equal to that of armor steel. Although so thick, they are crystal clear, and a speck of dust on the outer surface is easily seen. We have water enough in tanks to last us three months, or indefinitely if we should have to be careful, as we can automatically distill and purify all our waste water, recovering absolutely pure H_2O. We have compressed air, also in tanks, but we need very little, as the air is constantly being purified. Also, we have oxygen-generating apparatus aboard, in case we should run short. As to keeping warm, we have electric heating coils, run by the practically inexhaustible power of a small metal bar. If we get too near the sun and get too warm, we have a refrigerating machine to cool us off. Anything else?"

"You'd better give up, Dad," laughingly advised his daughter. "You've thought of everything, haven't you, Dick?"

"Mart has, I think. This is all his doing, you know. I wouldn't have thought of a tenth of it, myself."

"I must remind you young folks," said the older man, glancing at his watch, "that it is very late and high time for Dottie and me to be going home. We would like to stay and see the rest of it, but you know we must be away from here before daylight."

As they went into the house Vaneman asked:

"What does the other side of the moon look like? I have always been curious about it."

"We were not able to see much," replied Crane "It was too dark and we did not take the time to explore it, but from what we could see by means of our searchlights it is very much like this side-the most barren and desolate place imaginable. After we go to Mars, we intend to explore the moon thoroughly."

"Mars, then, is your first goal? When do you intend to start?"

"We haven't decided definitely. Probably in a day or two. Everything is ready now."

As the Vanemans had come out in the street car, in order to attract as little attention as possible, Seaton volunteered to take them home in one of Crane's cars. As they bade Crane goodnight after enjoying Shiro's "suitable refreshment" the lawyer took the chauffeur's seat, motioning his daughter and Seaton into the closed body of the car. As soon as they had started Dorothy turned in the embrace of her lover's arm.

"Dick," she said fiercely. "I would have been worried sick if I had known that you were way off there."

"I knew it, sweetheart. That's why I didn't tell you we were going. We both knew the Skylark was perfectly safe, but I knew that you would worry about our first trip. Now that we have been to the moon you won't be uneasy when we go to Mars, will you, dear?"

"I can't help it, boy. I will be afraid that something terrible has happened, every minute. Won't you take me with you? Then, if anything happens, it will happen to both of us, and that is as it should be. You know that I wouldn't want to keep on living if anything *should* happen to you."

He put both arms around her as his reply, and pressed his cheek to hers.

"Dorothy sweetheart, I know exactly how you feel. I feel the same way myself. I'm awfully sorry, dear, but I can't do it. I know the machine is safe, but I've got to prove it to everybody else before I take you on a long trip with me. Your father will agree with me that you ought not to go, on the first trip or two, anyway. And besides, what would Madam Grundy say?"

"Well, there *is* a way...." she began, and he felt her face turn hot.

His arms tightened around her and his breath came fast.

"I know it, sweetheart, and I would like nothing better in the world than to be married today and take our honeymoon in the Skylark, but I can't do it. After we come back from the first long trip we will be married just as soon as you say ready, and after that we will always be together wherever I go. But I can't take even the millionth part of a chance with anything as valuable as you are-you see that, don't you, Dottie?"

"I suppose so," she returned disconsolately, "but you'll make it a short trip, for my sake? I know I won't rest a minute until you get back."

"I promise you that we won't be gone more than four days. Then for the greatest honeymoon that ever was," and they clung together in the dark body of the car, each busy with solemn and beautiful thoughts of the happiness to come.

They soon reached their destination. As they entered the house Dorothy made one more attempt.

"Dad, Dick is just too perfectly mean. He says he won't take me on the first trip. If you were going out there wouldn't mother want to go along too?"

After listening to Seaton he gave his decision.

"Dick is right, Kitten. He must make the long trip first. Then, after the machine is proved reliable, you may go with him. I can think of no better way of spending a honeymoon-it will be a new one, at least. And you needn't worry about the boys getting back safely. I might not trust either of them alone, but together they are invincible. Good-night, children. I wish you success, Dick," as he turned away.

Seaton took a lover's leave of Dorothy, and went into the lawyer's study, taking an envelope from his pocket.

"Mr. Vaneman," he said in a low voice, "we think the Steel crowd is still camping on our trail. We are ready for them, with a lot of stuff that they never heard of, but in case anything goes wrong, Martin has written between the lines of this legal form, in invisible ink A-36, exactly how to get possession of all our notes and plans, so that the company can go ahead with everything. With those directions any chemist can find and use the stuff safely. Please put this envelope in the safest place you can think of, and then forget it unless they get both Crane and me. There's about one chance in a million of their doing that, but Mart doesn't gamble on even that chance."

"He is right, Dick. I believe that you can outwit them in any situation, but I will keep this paper where no one except myself can ever see it, nevertheless. Good-night, son, and good luck."

"The same to you, sir, and thank you. Good-night."

CHAPTER VIII

Indirect Action

The afternoon following the homecoming of the Skylark, Seaton and Dorothy returned from a long horseback ride in the park. After Seaton had mounted his motorcycle Dorothy turned toward a bench in the shade of an old elm to watch a game of tennis on the court next door. Scarcely had she seated herself when a great copper-plated ball alighted upon the lawn in front of her. A heavy steel door snapped open and a powerful figure clad in aviator's leather, the face completely covered by the hood, leaped out. She jumped to her feet with a cry of joyful surprise, thinking it was Seaton—a cry which died suddenly as she realized that Seaton had just left her and that this vessel was far too small to be the Skylark. She turned in flight, but the stranger caught her in three strides. She found herself helpless in a pair of arms equal in strength to Seaton's own. Picking her up lightly as a baby, DuQuesne carried her over to the space-car. Shriek after shriek rang out as she found that her utmost struggles were of no avail against the giant strength of her captor, that her fiercely-driven nails glanced harmlessly off the heavy glass and leather of his hood, and that her teeth were equally ineffective against his suit.

With the girl in his arms DuQuesne stepped into the vessel, and as the door clanged shut behind them Dorothy caught a glimpse of another woman, tied hand and foot in one of the side seats of the car.

"Tie her feet, Perkins," DuQuesne ordered brusquely, holding her around the body so that her feet extended straight out in front of him. "She's a wildcat."

As Perkins threw one end of a small rope around her ankles Dorothy doubled up her knees, drawing her feet as far away from him as possible. As he incautiously approached, she kicked out viciously, with all the force of her muscular young body behind her heavy riding-boots.

The sharp heel of one small boot struck Perkins squarely in the pit of the stomach—a true "solar-plexus" blow-and completely knocked out, he staggered back against the instrument-board. His out-flung arm pushed the speed lever clear out to its last notch, throwing the entire current of the batteries through the bar, which was pointed straight up, as it had been when they made their landing, and closing the switch which threw on the power of the repelling outer coating. There was a creak of the mighty steel fabric, stressed almost to its limit as the vessel darted upward with its stupendous velocity, and only the carefully-planned spring-and-cushion floor saved their lives as they were thrown flat and held there by the awful force of their acceleration as the space-car tore through the thin layer of the earth's atmosphere. So terrific was their speed, that the friction of the air did not have time to set them afire-they were through it and into the perfect vacuum of interstellar space before the thick steel hull was even warmed through. Dorothy lay flat upon her back, just as she had fallen, unable even to move her arms, gaining each breath only by a terrible effort. Perkins was a huddled heap under the instrument-board. The other captive, Brookings' ex-secretary, was in somewhat better case, as her bonds had snapped like string and she was lying at full length in one of the side-seats—forced into that position and held there, as the design of the seats was adapted for the most comfortable position possible under such conditions. She, like Dorothy, was gasping for breath, her straining muscles barely able to force air into her lungs because of the paralyzing weight of her chest.

DuQuesne alone was able to move, and it required all of his Herculean strength to creep and crawl, snake-like, toward the instrument-board. Finally attaining his goal, he summoned all his strength to grasp, not the controlling lever, which he knew was beyond his reach, but a cut-out switch only a couple of feet above his head. With a series of convulsive movements he fought his way up, first until he was crouching on his elbows and knees, and then into a squatting position. Placing his left hand under his right, he made a last supreme effort. Perspiration streamed from him, his mighty muscles stood out in ridges visible even under the heavy leather of his coat, his lips parted in a snarl over his locked teeth as he threw every ounce of his wonderful body into an effort to force his right hand up to the switch. His hand approached it slowly-closed over it and pulled it out.

The result was startling. With the mighty power instantly cut off, and with not even the ordinary force of gravitation to counteract the force DuQuesne was exerting, his own muscular effort hurled him up toward the center of the car and against the instrument-board. The switch, still in his grasp, was again closed. His shoulder crashed against the levers which controlled the direction of the bar, swinging it through a wide arc. As the ship darted off in the new direction with all its old acceleration, he was hurled against the instrument board, tearing one end loose from its supports and falling unconscious to the floor on the other side. After a time, which seemed like an eternity, Dorothy and the other girl felt their senses slowly leave them.

With four unconscious passengers, the space-car hurtled through empty space, its already inconceivable velocity being augmented every second by a quantity bringing its velocity near to that of light, driven onward by the incredible power of the disintegrating copper bar.

Seaton had gone only a short distance from his sweetheart's home when over the purring of his engine he thought he heard Dorothy's voice raised in a scream. He did not wait to make sure, but whirled his machine about and the purring changed instantly to a staccato roar as he threw open the throttle and advanced the spark. Gravel flew from beneath his skidding wheels as he negotiated the turn into the Vaneman grounds at suicidal speed. But with all his haste he arrived upon the scene just in time to see the door of the space-car close. Before he could reach it the vessel disappeared, with nothing to mark its departure save a violent whirl of grass and sod, uprooted and carried far into the air by the vacuum of its wake. To the excited tennis-players and the screaming mother of the abducted girl it seemed as though the great metal ball had vanished utterly-only Seaton, knowing what to expect, saw the line it made in the air and saw for an instant a minute dot in the sky before it disappeared.

Interrupting the clamor of the young people, each of whom was trying to tell him what had happened, he spoke to Mrs. Vaneman.

"Mother, Dottie's all right," he said rapidly but gently. "Steel's got her, but they won't keep her long. Don't worry, we'll get her. It may take a week or it may take a year, but we'll bring her back," and leaping upon his motorcycle, he shattered all the speed laws on his way to Crane's house.

"Mart!" he yelled, rushing into the shop, "they've got Dottie, in a bus made from our plans. Let's go!" as he started on a run for the testing shed.

"Wait a minute!" crisply shouted Crane. "Don't go off half-cocked. What is your plan?"

"Plan, hell!" barked the enraged chemist. "Chase 'em!"

"Which way did they go, and when?"

"Straight up, full power, twenty minutes ago."

"Too long ago. Straight up has changed its direction several degrees since then. They may have covered a million miles, or they may have come back and landed next door. Sit down and think-we need all your brains now."

Regaining his self-possession as the wisdom of his friend's advice came home to him, Seaton sat down and pulled out his pipe. There was a tense silence for an instant. Then he leaped to his feet and darted into his room, returning with an object-compass whose needle pointed upward.

"DuQuesne did it," he cried exultantly. "This baby is still looking right at him. Now let's go-make it snappy!"

"Not yet. We should find out how far away they are; that may give us an idea."

Suiting action to word, he took up his stopwatch and set the needle swinging. They watched it with strained faces as second after second went by and it still continued to swing. When it had come to rest Crane read his watch and made a rapid calculation.

"About three hundred and fifty million miles," he stated. "Clear out of our solar system already, and from the distance covered he must have had a constant acceleration so as to approximate the velocity of light, and he is still going with full...."

"But nothing can possibly go that fast, Mart, it's impossible. How about Einstein's theory?"

"That is a theory, this measurement of distance is a fact, as you know from our tests."

"That's right. Another good theory gone to pot. But how do you account for his distance? D'you suppose he's lost control?"

"He must have. I do not believe that he would willingly stand that acceleration, nor that he would have gone that far of his own accord. Do you?"

"I sure don't. We don't know how big a bar they are carrying, so we can't estimate how long it is going to take us to catch them. But let's not waste any more time, Mart. For Cat's sake, let's get busy!"

"We have only those four bars, Dick-two for each unit. Do you think that will be enough? Think of how far we may have to go, what we may possibly get into, and what it will mean to Dottie if we fail for lack of power."

Seaton, though furiously eager to be off, paused at this new idea, and half-regretfully he replied:

"We are so far behind them already that I guess a few hours more won't make much difference. It sure would be disastrous to get out near one of the fixed stars and have our power quit. I guess you're right, we'd better get a couple more-make it four, then we'll have enough to chase them half our lives. We'd better load up on grub and X-plosive ammunition, too."

While Crane and Shiro carried additional provisions and boxes of cartridges into the "Skylark," Seaton once more mounted his motorcycle and sped across the city to the brass foundry. The manager of the plant took his order, but blandly informed him that there was not that much copper in the city, that it would be a week or ten days before the order could be filled. Seaton suggested that they melt up some copper cable and other goods already manufactured, offering ten times their value, but the manager was obdurate, saying that he could not violate the rule of priority of orders. Seaton then went to other places, endeavoring to buy scrap copper, trolley wire, electric cable, anything made of the ruddy metal, but found none for sale in quantities large enough to be of any use. After several hours of fruitless search, he returned home in a towering rage and explained to Crane, in lurid language, his failure to secure the copper. The latter was unmoved.

"After you left, it occurred to me that you might not get any. You see, Steel is still watching us."

Fire shot from Seaton's eyes.

"I'm going to clean up that bunch," he gritted through his teeth as he started straight for the door.

"Not yet, Dick," Crane remonstrated. "We can go down to Wilson's in a few minutes, and I know we can get it there if he has it. The "Skylark" is all ready to travel."

No more words were needed. They hurried into the space-car and soon were standing in the office of the plant in which the vessel had been built. When they had made their wants known, the iron-master shook his head.

"I'm sorry, Crane, but I have only a few pounds of copper in the shop, and we have no suitable furnace."

Seaton broke out violently at this, but Crane interrupted him, explaining their inability to get the metal anywhere else and the urgency of their need. When he had finished, Wilson brought his fist down upon his desk.

"I'll get it if I have to melt up our dynamos," he roared. "We'll have to rig a crucible, but we'll have your bars out just as soon as the whole force of this damned scrap-heap can make 'em!"

Calling in his foreman, he bellowed orders, and while automobiles scoured the nearby towns for scrap copper, the crucible and molds were made ready.

Nearly two days passed before the gleaming copper cylinders were finished. During this time Crane added to their already complete equipment every article he could conceive of their having any use for, while Seaton raged up and down the plant in a black fury of impatience. Just before the bars were ready, they made another reading on the object-compass. Their faces grew tense and drawn and their hearts turned sick as second followed second and minute followed minute and the needle still oscillated. Finally, however, it came to rest, and Seaton's voice almost failed him as he read his figures.

"Two hundred and thirty-five light-years, Mart. They're lost, and still going. Good-bye, old scout," holding out his hand, "Tell Vaneman that I'll bring her back or else stay out there myself."

"You must be crazy, Dick. You know I am going."

"Why? No use in both of us taking such a chance. If Dottie's gone, of course I want to go too, but you don't."

"Nonsense, Dick. Of course this is somewhat farther than we had planned on going for our maiden voyage, but where is the difference? It is just as safe to go a thousand light-years as only one, and we have power and food for any contingency. There is no more danger in this trip than there is in one to Mars. At all events, I am going whether you want me to or not, so save your breath."

"You lie like a thief, Mart-you know what we are up against as well as I do. But if you insist on coming along, I'm sure glad to have you."

As their hands met in a crushing grip, the bars were brought up and loaded into the carriers. Waving good-bye to Wilson, they closed the massive door and took their positions. Seaton adjusted the bar parallel with the needle of the object-compass, turned on the coil, and advanced the speed-lever until Crane, reading the pyro-meters, warned him to slow down, as the shell was heating. Free of the earth's atmosphere, he slowly advanced the lever, one notch at a time, until he could no longer support the increasing weight of his hand, but had to draw out the rolling support designed for that emergency. He pushed the lever a few notches farther, and felt himself forced down violently into the seat. He was now lying at full length, the seat having automatically moved upward so that his hand still controlled the lever. Still he kept putting on more power, until the indicator showed that more than three-quarters of the power was in operation and he felt that he could stand but little more.

"How are you making it, Mart?" he asked, talking with difficulty because of the great weight of his tongue and jaws.

"All right so far," came the response, in a hesitating, almost stammering voice, "but I do not know how much more I can take. If you can stand it, go ahead."

"This is enough for awhile, until we get used to it. Any time you want to rest, tell me and I'll cut her down."

"Keep her at this for four or five hours. Then cut down until we can walk, so that we can eat and take another reading on distance. Remember that it will take as long to stop as it does to get up speed, and that we must be careful not to ram them. There would be nothing left of either car."

"All right. Talking's too darn much work, I'll talk to you again when we ease down. I sure am glad we're on our way at last."

CHAPTER IX

Lost In Space

For forty-eight hours the uncontrolled atomic motor dragged the masterless vessel with its four unconscious passengers through the illimitable reaches of empty space, with an awful and constantly increasing velocity. When only a few traces of copper remained in the power-plant, the acceleration began to decrease and the powerful springs began to restore the floor and the seats to their normal positions. The last particle of copper having been transformed into energy, the speed of the vessel became constant. Apparently motionless to those inside it, it was in reality traversing space with a velocity thousands of times greater than that of light. As the force which had been holding them down was relaxed, the lungs, which had been able to secure only air enough to maintain faint sparks of life, began to function more normally and soon all four recovered consciousness, drinking in the life-giving oxygen in a rapid succession of breaths so deep that it seemed as though their lungs must burst with each inhalation.

DuQuesne was the first to gain control of himself. His first effort to rise to his feet lifted him from the floor, and he floated lightly to the ceiling, striking it with a gentle bump and remaining suspended in the air. The others, who had not yet attempted to move, stared at him in wide-eyed amazement. Reaching out and clutching one of the supporting columns, he drew himself back to the floor and cautiously removed his leather suit, transferring two heavy automatic pistols as he did so. By gingerly feeling of his injured body, he discovered that no bones were broken, although he was terribly bruised. He then glanced around to learn how his companions were faring. He saw that they were all sitting up, the girls resting, Perkins removing his aviator's costume.

"Good morning, Doctor DuQuesne. What happened when I kicked your friend?"

DuQuesne smiled.

"Good morning, Miss Vaneman. Several things happened. He fell into the controls, turning on all the juice. We left shortly afterward. I tried to shut the power off, and in doing so I balled things up worse than ever. Then I went to sleep, and just woke up."

"Have you any idea where we are?"

"No, but I can make a fair estimate, I think," and glancing at the empty chamber in which the bar had been, he took out his notebook and pen and figured for a few minutes. As he finished, he drew himself along by a handrail to one of the windows, then to another. He returned with a puzzled expression on his face and made a long calculation.

"I don't know exactly what to make of this," he said thoughtfully. "We are so far away from the earth that even the fixed stars are unrecognizable. The power was on exactly forty-eight hours, since that is the life of that particular bar under full current. We should still be close to our own solar system, since it is theoretically impossible to develop any velocity greater than that of light. But in fact, we have. I know enough about astronomy to recognize the fixed stars from any point within a light-year or so of the sun, and I can't see a single familiar star. I never could see how mass could be a function of velocity, and now I am convinced that it is not. We have been accelerating for forty-eight hours!"

He turned to Dorothy.

"While we were unconscious, Miss Vaneman, we had probably attained a velocity of something like seven billion four hundred thirteen million miles per second, and that is the approximate speed at which we are now traveling. We must be nearly six quadrillion miles, and that is a space of several hundred light-years —away from our solar system, or, more plainly, about six times as far away from our earth as the North Star is. We couldn't see our sun with a telescope, even if we knew which way to look for it."

At this paralyzing news, Dorothy's face turned white and Margaret Spencer quietly fainted in her seat.

"Then we can never get back?" asked Dorothy slowly.

At this question, Perkins' self-control gave way and his thin veneer of decency disappeared completely.

"You got us into this whole thing!" he screamed as he leaped at Dorothy with murderous fury gleaming in his pale eyes and his fingers curved into talons. Instead of reaching her, however, he merely sprawled grotesquely in midair, and DuQuesne knocked him clear across the vessel with one powerful blow of his fist.

"Get back there, you cowardly cur," he said evenly. "Even though we are a long way from home, try to remember you're a man, at least. One more break like that and I'll throw you out of the boat. It isn't her fault that we are out here, but our own. The blame for it is a very small matter, anyway; the thing of importance is to get back as soon as possible."

"But how can we get back?" asked Perkins sullenly from the corner where he was crouching, fear in every feature. "The power is gone, the controls are wrecked, and we are hopelessly lost in space."

"Oh, I wouldn't say 'hopelessly,'" returned the other, "I have never been in any situation yet that I couldn't get out of, and I won't be convinced until I am dead that I can't get out of this one. We have two extra power bars, we can fix the board, and if I can't navigate us back close enough to our solar system to find it, I am more of a dub than I think I am. How about a little bite to eat?"

"Show us where it is!" exclaimed Dorothy. "Now that you mention it, I find that I am starved to death."

DuQuesne looked at her keenly.

"I admire your nerve, Miss Vaneman. I didn't suppose that that animal over there would show such a wide streak of yellow, but I was rather afraid that you girls might go to pieces."

"I'm scared blue, of course," Dorothy admitted frankly, "but hysterics won't do any good, and we simply *must* get back."

"Certainly, we must and we will," stated DuQuesne calmly. "If you like, you might find something for us to eat in the galley there, while I see what I can do with this board that I wrecked with my head. By the way, that cubby-hole there is the apartment reserved for you two ladies. We are in rather cramped quarters, but I think you will find everything you need."

As Dorothy drew herself along the handrail toward the room designated, accompanied by the other girl who, though conscious, had paid little attention to anything around her, she could not help feeling a thrill of admiration for the splendid villain who had abducted her. Calm and cool, always master of himself, apparently paying no attention to the terrible bruises which disfigured half his face and doubtless half his body as well, she admitted to herself that it was only his example, which had enabled her to maintain her self-control in their present plight. As she crawled over Perkins' discarded suit, she remembered that he had not taken any weapons from it. After a rapid glance around to assure herself that she was not being watched, she quickly searched the coat, bringing to light not one, but two pistols, which she thrust into her pocket. She saw with relief that they were regulation army automatics, with whose use she was familiar from much target practise with Seaton.

In the room, which was a miniature of the one she had seen on the Skylark, the girls found clothing, toilet articles, and everything necessary for a long trip. As they were setting themselves to rights, Dorothy electing to stay in her riding suit, they surveyed each other frankly and each was reassured by what she saw. Dorothy saw a girl of twenty-two, of her own stature, with a mass of heavy, wavy black hair. Her eyes, a singularly rich and deep brown, contrasted strangely with the beautiful ivory of her skin. She was normally a beautiful girl, thought Dorothy, but her beauty was marred by suffering and privation. Her naturally slender form was thin, her face was haggard and worn. The stranger broke the silence.

"I'm Margaret Spencer," she began abruptly, "former secretary to His Royal Highness, Brookings of Steel. They swindled my father out of an invention worth millions and he died, broken-hearted. I got the job to see if I couldn't get enough evidence to convict them, and I had quite a lot when they caught me. I had some things that they were afraid to lose, and I had them so well hidden that they couldn't find them, so they kidnapped me to make me give them back. They haven't dared kill me so far for fear the evidence will show up after my death-which it will. However, I will be legally dead before long, and then they know the whole thing will come out, so they have brought me out here to make me talk or kill me. Talking won't do me any good now, though, and I don't believe it ever would have. They would have killed me after they got the stuff back, anyway. So you see I, at least, will never get back to the earth alive."

"Cheer up-we'll all get back safely."

"No, we won't. You don't know that man Perkins-if that is his name. I never heard him called any real name before. He is simply unspeakable-vile-hideous-everything that is base. He was my jailer, and I utterly loathe and despise him. He is mean and underhanded and tricky-he reminds me of a slimy, poisonous snake. He will kill me: I know it."

"But how about Doctor DuQuesne? Surely he isn't that kind of man? He wouldn't let him."

"I've never met him before, but from what I heard of him in the office, he's even worse than Perkins, but in an entirely different way. There's nothing small or mean about him, and I don't believe he would go out of his way to hurt anyone, as Perkins would. But he is absolutely cold and hard, a perfect fiend. Where his interests are concerned, there's nothing under the sun, good or bad, that he won't do. But I'm glad that Perkins had me instead of 'The Doctor,' as they call him. Perkins raises such a bitter personal feeling, that anybody would rather die than give up to him in anything. DuQuesne, however, would have tortured me impersonally and scientifically-cold and self-contained all the while and using the most efficient methods, and I am sure he would have got it out of me some way. He always gets what he goes after."

"Oh, come, Miss Spencer!" Dorothy interrupted the half-hysterical girl. "You're too hard on him. Didn't you see him knock Perkins down when he came after me?"

"Well, maybe he has a few gentlemanly instincts, which he uses when he doesn't lose anything by it. More likely he merely intended to rebuke him for a useless action. He is a firm Pragmatist-anything that is useful is all right, anything that is useless is a crime. More probably yet, he wants you left alive. Of course that is his real reason. He went to the trouble of kidnapping you, so naturally he won't let Perkins or anybody else kill you until he is through with you. Otherwise he would have let Perkins do anything he wanted to with you, without lifting a finger."

"I can't quite believe that," Dorothy replied, though a cold chill struck at her heart as she remembered the inhuman crime attributed to this man, and she quailed at the thought of being in his charge, countless millions of miles from earth, a thought only partly counteracted by the fact that she was now armed. "He has treated us with every consideration so far, let's hope for the best. Anyway, I'm sure that we'll get back safely."

"Why so sure? Have you something up your sleeve?"

"No-or yes, in a way I have, though nothing very definite. I'm Dorothy Vaneman, and I am engaged to the man who discovered the thing that makes this space-car go...."

"That's why they kidnapped you, then-to make him give up all his rights to it. It's like them."

"Yes, I think that's why they did it. But they won't keep me long. Dick Seaton will find me, I know. I feel it."

"But that's exactly what they want!" cried Margaret excitedly. "In my spying around I heard a little about this very thing-the name Seaton brings it to my mind. His car is broken in some way, so that it will kill him the first time he tries to run it."

"That's where they underestimated Dick and his partner. You have heard of Martin Crane, of course?"

"I think I heard his name mentioned in the office, together with Seaton's, but that's all."

"Well, besides other things, Martin is quite a wonderful mechanic, and he found out that our Skylark was spoiled. So they built another one, a lot bigger, and I am sure that they are following us, right now."

"But how can they possibly follow us, when we are going so fast and are so far away?" queried the other girl, once more despondent.

"I don't quite know, but I do know that Dick will find a way. He's simply wonderful. He knows more now than that Doctor DuQuesne will ever learn in all his life, and he will find us in a few days. I feel it in my bones. Besides, I picked Perkins' pockets of these two pistols. Can you shoot an automatic?"

"Yes," replied the other girl, as she seized one of the guns, assured herself that its magazine was full, and slipped it into her pocket. "I used to practise a lot with my father's. This makes me feel a whole lot better. And call me Peggy, won't you? It will seem good to hear my name again. After what I've been through lately, even this trip will be a vacation for me."

"Well, then, cheer up, Peggy dear, we're going to be great friends. Let's go get us all something to eat. I'm simply starved, and I know you are, too."

The presence of the pistol in her pocket and Dorothy's unwavering faith in her lover, lifted the stranger out of the mood of despair into which the long imprisonment, the brutal treatment, and the present situation had plunged her, and she was almost cheerful as they drew themselves along the hand-rail leading to the tiny galley.

"I simply can't get used to the idea of nothing having any weight-look here!" laughed Dorothy, as she took a boiled ham out of the refrigerator and hung it upon an imaginary hook in the air, where it remained motionless. "Doesn't it make you feel funny?"

"It is a queer sensation. I feel light, like a toy balloon, and I feel awfully weird inside. If we have no weight, why does it hurt so when we bump into anything? And when you throw anything, like the Doctor did Perkins, why does it hit as hard as ever?"

"It's mass or inertia or something like that. A thing has it everywhere, whether it weighs anything or not. Dick explained it all to me. I understood it when he told me about it, but I'm afraid it didn't sink in very deep. Did you ever study physics?"

"I had a year of it in college, but it was more or less of a joke. I went to a girls' school, and all we had to do in physics was to get the credit; we didn't have to learn it."

"Me too. Next time I go to school I'm going to Yale or Harvard or some such place, and I'll learn so much mathematics and science that I'll have to wear a bandeau to keep my massive intellect in place."

During this conversation they had prepared a substantial luncheon and had arranged it daintily upon two large trays, in spite of the difficulty caused by the fact that nothing would remain in place by its own weight. The feast prepared, Dorothy took her tray from the table as carefully as she could, and saw the sandwiches and bottles start to float toward the ceiling. Hastily inverting the tray above the escaping viands, she pushed them back down upon the table. In doing so she lifted herself clear from the floor, as she had forgotten to hold herself down.

"What'll we do, anyway?" she wailed when she had recovered her position. "Everything wants to fly all over the place!"

"Put another tray on top of it and hold them together," suggested Margaret. "I wish we had a birdcage. Then we could open the door and grab a sandwich as it flies out."

By covering the trays the girls finally carried the luncheon out into the main compartment, where they gave DuQuesne and Perkins one of the trays and all fell to eating hungrily. DuQuesne paused with a glint of amusement in his one sound eye as he saw Dorothy trying to pour ginger ale out of a bottle.

"It can't be done, Miss Vaneman. You'll have to drink it through a straw. That will work, since our air pressure is normal. Be careful not to choke on it, though; your swallowing will have to be all muscular out here. Gravity won't help you. Or wait a bit—I have the control board fixed and it will be a matter of only a few minutes to put in another bar and get enough acceleration to take the place of gravity."

He placed one of the extra power bars in the chamber and pushed the speed lever into the first notch, and there was a lurch of the whole vessel as it swung around the bar so that the floor was once more perpendicular to it. He took a couple of steps, returned, and advanced the lever another notch.

"There that's about the same as gravity. Now we can act like human beings and eat in comfort."

"That's a wonderful relief, Doctor!" cried Dorothy. "Are we going back toward the earth?"

"Not yet. I reversed the bar, but we will have to use up all of this one before we can even start back. Until this bar is gone we will merely be slowing down."

As the meal progressed, Dorothy noticed that DuQuesne's left arm seemed almost helpless, and that he ate with great difficulty because of his terribly bruised face. As soon as they had removed the trays she went into her room, where she had seen a small medicine chest, and brought out a couple of bottles.

"Lie down here, Doctor DuQuesne," she commanded. "I'm going to apply a little first-aid to the injured. Arnica and iodine are all I can find, but they'll help a little."

"I'm all right," began the scientist, but at her imperious gesture he submitted, and she bathed his battered features with the healing lotion and painted the worst bruises with iodine.

"I see your arm is lame. Where does it hurt?"

"Shoulder's the worst. I rammed it through the board when we started out."

He opened his shirt at the throat and bared his shoulder, and Dorothy gasped-as much at the size and power of the muscles displayed, as at the extent and severity of the man's injuries. Stepping into the gallery, she brought out hot water and towels and gently bathed away the clotted blood that had been forced through the skin.

"Massage it a little with the arnica as I move the arm," he directed coolly, and she did so, pityingly. He did not wince and made no sign of pain, but she saw beads of perspiration appear upon his face, and wondered at his fortitude.

"That's fine," he said gratefully as she finished, and a peculiar expression came over his face. "It feels one hundred per cent better already. But why do you do it? I should think you would feel like crowning me with that basin instead of playing nurse."

"Efficiency," she replied with a smile. "I'm taking a leaf out of your own book. You are our chief engineer, you know, and it won't do to have you laid up."

"That's a logical explanation, but it doesn't go far enough," he rejoined, still studying her intently. She did not reply, but turned to Perkins.

"How are you, Mr. Perkins? Do you require medical attention?"

"No," growled Perkins from the seat in which he had crouched immediately after eating. "Keep away from me, or I'll cut your heart out!"

"Shut up!" snapped DuQuesne. "Remember what I said?"

"I haven't done anything," snarled the other.

"I said I would throw you out if you made another break," DuQuesne informed him evenly, "and I meant it. If you can't talk decently, keep still. Understand that you are to keep off Miss Vaneman, words and actions. I am in charge of her, and I will put up with no interference whatever. This is your last warning."

"How about Spencer, then?"

"I have nothing to say about her, she's not mine," responded DuQuesne with a shrug.

An evil light appeared in Perkins' eyes and he took out a wicked-looking knife and began to strop it carefully upon the leather of the seat, glaring at his victim the while.

"Well, *I* have something to say...." blazed Dorothy, but she was silenced by a gesture from Margaret, who calmly took the pistol from her pocket, jerked the slide back, throwing a cartridge into the chamber, and held the weapon up on one finger, admiring it from all sides.

"Don't worry about his knife. He has been sharpening it for my benefit for the last month. He doesn't mean anything by it."

At this unexpected show of resistance, Perkins stared at her for an instant, then glanced at his coat.

"Yes, this was yours, once. You needn't bother about picking up your coat, they're both gone. You might be tempted to throw that knife, so drop it on the floor and kick it over to me before I count three."

"One." The heavy pistol steadied into line with his chest and her finger tightened on the trigger.

"Two." He obeyed and she picked up the knife. He turned to DuQuesne, who had watched the scene unmoved, a faint smile upon his saturnine face.

"Doctor!" he cried, shaking with fear. "Why don't you shoot her or take that gun away from her? Surely you don't want to see me murdered?"

"Why not?" replied DuQuesne calmly. "It is nothing to me whether she kills you or you kill her. You brought it on yourself by your own carelessness. Any man with brains doesn't leave guns lying around within reach of prisoners, and a blind man could have seen Miss Vaneman getting your hardware."

"You saw her take them and didn't warn me?" croaked Perkins.

"Why should I warn you? If you can't take care of your own prisoner she earns her liberty, as far as I am concerned. I never did like your style, Perkins, especially your methods of handling-or rather mishandling-women. You could have made her give up the stuff she recovered from that ass Brookings inside of an hour, and wouldn't have had to kill her afterward, either."

"How?" sneered the other. "If you are so good at that kind of thing, why didn't you try it on Seaton and Crane?"

"There are seven different methods to use on a woman like Miss Spencer, each of which will produce the desired result. The reason I did not try them on either Seaton or Crane is that they would have failed. Your method of indirect action is probably the only one that will succeed. That is why I adopted it."

"Well, what are you going to do about it?" shrieked Perkins. "Are you going to sit there and lecture all day?"

"I am going to do nothing whatever," answered the scientist coldly. "If you had any brains you would see that you are in no danger. Miss Spencer will undoubtedly kill you if you attack her-not otherwise. That is an Anglo-Saxon weakness."

"Did you see me take the pistols?" queried Dorothy.

"Certainly. I'm not blind. You have one of them in your right coat pocket now."

"Then why didn't you, or don't you, try to take it away from me?" she asked in wonder.

"If I had objected to your having them, you would never have got them. If I didn't want you to have a gun now, I would take it away from you. You know that, don't you?" and his black eyes stared into her violet ones with such calm certainty of his ability that she felt her heart sink.

"Yes," she admitted finally, "I believe you could-that is, unless I were angry enough to shoot you."

"That wouldn't help you. I can shoot faster and straighter than you can, and would shoot it out of your hand. However, I have no objection to your having the gun, since it is no part of my plan to offer you any further indignity of any kind. Even if you had the necessary coldness of nerve or cruelty of disposition-of which I have one, Perkins the other, and you neither-you wouldn't shoot me now, because you can't get back to the earth without me. After we get back I will take the guns away from both of you if I think it desirable. In the meantime, play with them all you please."

"Has Perkins any more knives or guns or things in his room?" demanded Dorothy.

"How should I know?" indifferently; then, as both girls started for Perkins' room he ordered brusquely:

"Sit down, Miss Vaneman. Let them fight it out. Perkins has his orders to lay off you-you lay off him. I'm not taking any chances of getting you hurt, that's one reason I wanted you armed. If he gets gay, shoot him; otherwise, hands off completely."

Dorothy threw up her head in defiance, but meeting his cold stare she paused irresolutely and finally sat down, biting her lips in anger, while the other girl went on.

"That's better. She doesn't need any help to whip that yellow dog. He's whipped already. He never would think of fighting unless the odds were three to one in his favor."

When Margaret had returned from a fruitless search of Perkins' room and had assured herself that he had no more weapons concealed about his person, she thrust the pistol back into her pocket and sat down.

"That ends that," she declared. "I guess you will be good now, won't you, Mr. Perkins?"

"Yes," that worthy muttered. "I have to be, now that you've got the drop on me and DuQuesne's gone back on me. But wait until we get back! I'll get you then, you...."

"Stop right there!" sharply. "There's nothing I would rather do than shoot you right now, if you give me the slightest excuse, such as that name you were about to call me. Now go ahead!"

DuQuesne broke the silence that followed.

"Well, now that the battle is over, and since we are fed and rested, I suggest that we slow down a bit and get ready to start back. Pick out comfortable seats, everybody, and I'll shoot a little more juice through that bar."

Seating himself before the instrument board, he advanced the speed lever slowly until nearly three-quarters of the full power was on, as much as he thought the others could stand.

For sixty hours he drove the car, reducing the acceleration only at intervals during which they ate and walked about their narrow quarters in order to restore the blood to circulation in their suffering bodies. The power was not reduced for sleep; everyone slept as best he could.

Dorothy and Margaret talked together at every opportunity, and a real intimacy grew up between them. Perkins was for the most part sullenly quiet, knowing himself despised by all the others and having no outlet here for his particular brand of cleverness. DuQuesne was always occupied with his work and only occasionally addressed a remark to one or another of the party, except during meals. At those periods of general recuperation, he talked easily and well upon many topics. There was no animosity in his bearing nor did he seem to perceive any directed toward himself, but when any of the others ventured to infringe upon his ideas of how discipline should be maintained, DuQuesne's reproof was merciless. Dorothy almost liked him, but Margaret insisted that she considered him worse than ever.

When the bar was exhausted, DuQuesne lifted the sole remaining cylinder into place.

"We should be nearly stationary with respect to the earth," he remarked. "Now we will start back."

"Why, it felt as though we were picking up speed for the last three days!" exclaimed Margaret.

"Yes, it feels that way because we have nothing to judge by. Slowing down in one direction feels exactly like starting up in the opposite one. There is no means of knowing whether we are standing still, going away from the earth, or going toward it, since we have nothing stationary upon which to make observations. However, since the two bars were of exactly the same size and were exerted in opposite directions except for a few minutes after we left the earth, we are nearly stationary now. I will put on power until this bar is something less than half gone, then coast for three or four days. By the end of that time we should be able to recognize our solar system from the appearance of the fixed stars."

He again advanced the lever, and for many hours silence filled the car as it hurtled through space. DuQuesne, waking up from a long nap, saw that the bar no longer pointed directly toward the top of the ship, perpendicular to the floor, but was inclined at a sharp angle. He reduced the current, and felt the lurch of the car as it swung around the bar, increasing the angle many degrees. He measured the angle carefully and peered out of all the windows on one side of the car. Returning to the bar after a time, he again measured the angle, and found that it had increased greatly.

"What's the matter, Doctor DuQuesne?" asked Dorothy, who had also been asleep.

"We are being deflected from our course. You see the bar doesn't point straight up any more? Of course the direction of the bar hasn't changed, the car has swung around it."

"What does that mean?"

"We have come close enough to some star so that its attraction swings the bottom of the car around. Normally, you know, the bottom of the car follows directly behind the bar. It doesn't mean much yet except that we are being drawn away from our straight line, but if the attraction gets much stronger it may make us miss our solar system completely. I have been looking for the star in question, but can't see it yet. We'll probably pull away from it very shortly."

He threw on the power, and for some time watched the bar anxiously, expecting to see it swing back into the vertical, but the angle continually increased. He again reduced the current and searched the heavens for the troublesome body.

"Do you see it yet?" asked Dorothy with concern.

"No, there's apparently nothing near enough to account for all this deflection."

He took out a pair of large night-glasses and peered through them for several minutes.

"Good God! It's a dead sun, and we're nearly onto it! It looks as large as our moon!"

Springing to the board, he whirled the bar into the vertical. He took down a strange instrument, went to the bottom window, and measured the apparent size of the dark star. Then, after cautioning the rest of the party to sit tight, he advanced the lever farther than it had been before. After half an hour he again slackened the pace and made another observation, finding to his astonishment that the dark mass had almost doubled its apparent size! Dorothy, noting his expression, was about to speak, but he forestalled her.

"We lost ground, instead of gaining, that spurt," he remarked, as he hastened to his post. "It must be inconceivably large, to exert such an enormous attractive force at this distance. We'll have to put on full power. Hang onto yourselves as best you can."

He then pushed the lever out to its last notch and left it there until the bar was nearly gone, only to find that the faint disk of the monster globe was even larger than before, being now visible to the unaided eye. Revived, the three others saw it plainly—a great dim circle, visible as is the dark portion of the new moon-and, the power shut off, they felt themselves falling toward it with sickening speed. Perkins screamed with mad fear and flung himself grovelling upon the floor. Margaret, her nerves still unstrung, clutched at her heart with both hands. Dorothy, though her eyes looked like great black holes in her white face, looked DuQuesne in the eye steadily.

"This is the end, then?"

"Not yet," he replied in a calm and level voice. "The end will not come for a good many hours, as I have calculated that it will take at least two days, probably more, to fall the distance we have to go. We have all that time in which to think out a way of escape."

"Won't the outer repulsive shell keep us from striking it, or at least break the force of our fall?"

"No. It was designed only as protection from meteorites and other small bodies. It is heavy enough to swing us away from a small planet, but it will be used up long before we strike."

He lighted a cigarette and sat at ease, as though in his own study, his brow wrinkled in thought as he made calculations in his notebook. Finally he rose to his feet.

"There's only one chance that I can see. That is to gather up every scrap of copper we have and try to pull ourselves far enough out of line so that we will take an hyperbolic orbit around that body instead of falling into it."

"What good will that do us?" asked Margaret, striving for self-control. "We will starve to death finally, won't we?"

"Not necessarily. That will give us time to figure out something else."

"You won't have to figure out anything else, Doctor," stated Dorothy positively. "If we miss that moon, Dick and Martin will find us before very long."

"Not in this life. If they tried to follow us, they're both dead before now."

"That's where even you are wrong!" she flashed at him. "They knew you were wrecking our machine, so they built another one, a good one. And they know a lot of things about this new metal that you have never dreamed of, since they were not in the plans you stole."

DuQuesne went directly to the heart of the matter, paying no attention to her barbed shafts.

"Can they follow us through space without seeing us?" he demanded.

"Yes-or at least, I think they can."

"How do they do it?"

"I don't know—I wouldn't tell you if I did."

"You'll tell if you know," he declared, his voice cutting like a knife. "But that can wait until after we get out of this. The thing to do now is to dodge that world."

He searched the vessel for copper, ruthlessly tearing out almost everything that contained the metal, hammering it flat and throwing it into the power-plant. He set the bar at right angles to the line of their fall and turned on the current. When the metal was exhausted, he made another series of observations upon the body toward which they were falling, and reported quietly:

"We made a lot of distance, but not enough. Everything goes in, this time."

He tore out the single remaining light-wire, leaving the car in darkness save for the diffused light of his electric torch, and broke up the only remaining motor. He then took his almost priceless Swiss watch, his heavy signet ring, his scarf pin, and the cartridges from his pistol, and added them to the collection. Flashing his lamp upon Perkins, he relieved him of everything he had which contained copper.

"I think I have a few pennies in my pocketbook," suggested Dorothy.

"Get 'em," he directed briefly, and while she was gone he searched Margaret, without result save for the cartridges in her pistol, as she had no jewelry remaining after her imprisonment. Dorothy returned and handed him everything she had found.

"I would like to keep this ring," she said slowly, pointing to a slender circlet of gold set with a solitaire diamond, "if you think there is any chance of us getting clear."

"Everything goes that has any copper in it," he said coldly, "and I am glad to see that Seaton is too good a chemist to buy any platinum jewelry. You may keep the diamond, though," as he wrenched the jewel out of its setting and returned it to her.

He threw all the metal into the central chamber and the vessel gave a tremendous lurch as the power was again applied. It was soon spent, however, and after the final observation, the others waiting in breathless suspense for him to finish his calculations, he made his curt announcement.

"Not enough."

Perkins, his mind weakened by the strain of the last few days, went completely insane at the words. With a wild howl he threw himself at the unmoved scientist, who struck him with the butt of his pistol as he leaped, the mighty force of DuQuesne's blow crushing his skull like an eggshell and throwing him backward to the opposite side of the vessel. Margaret lay in her seat in a dead faint. Dorothy and DuQuesne looked at each other in the feeble light of the torch. To the girl's amazement, the man was as calm as though he were safe in his own house, and she made a determined effort to hold herself together.

"What next, Doctor DuQuesne?"

"I don't know. We have a couple of days yet, at least. I'll have to study awhile."

"In that time Dick will find us, I know."

"Even if they do find us in time, which I doubt, what good will it do? It simply means that they will go with us instead of saving us, for of course they can't pull away, since we couldn't. I hope they don't find us, but locate this star in time to keep away from it."

"Why?" she gasped. "You have been planning to kill both of them! I should think you would be delighted to take them with us?"

"Far from it. Please try to be logical. I intended to remove them because they stood in the way of my developing this new metal. If I am to be out of the way-and frankly, I see very little chance of getting out of this—I hope that Seaton goes ahead with it. It is the greatest discovery the world has ever known, and if both Seaton and I, the only two men in the world who know how to handle it, drop out, it will be lost for perhaps hundreds of years."

"If Dick's finding us means that he must go, too, of course I hope that he won't find us, but I don't believe that. I simply know that he could get us away from here."

She continued more slowly, almost speaking to herself, her heart sinking with her voice:

"He is following us, and he won't stop even if he does see this dead star and knows that he can't get away. We will die together."

"There's no denying the fact that our situation is critical, but you know a man isn't dead until after his heart stops beating. We have two whole days yet, and in that time, I can probably dope out some way of getting away from here."

"I hope so," she replied, keeping her voice from breaking only by a great effort. "But go ahead with your doping. I'm worn out." She drew herself down upon one of the seats and stared at the ceiling, fighting to restrain an almost overpowering impulse to scream.

Thus the hours wore by-Perkins dead; Margaret still unconscious; Dorothy lying in her seat, her thoughts a formless prayer, buoyed up only by her faith in God and in her lover; DuQuesne self-possessed, smoking innumerable cigarettes, his keen mind grappling with its most desperate problem, grimly fighting until the very last instant of life-while the powerless space-car fell with an appalling velocity, faster and faster; falling toward that cold and desolate monster of the heaven.

CHAPTER X

The Rescue

Seaton and Crane drove the Skylark in the direction indicated by the unwavering object-compass with the greatest acceleration they could stand, each man taking a twelve-hour watch at the instrument board.

Now, indeed, did the Skylark justify the faith of her builders, and the two inventors, with an exultant certainty of their success, flew out beyond man's wildest imaginings. Had it not been for the haunting fear for Dorothy's safety, the journey would have been one of pure triumph, and even that anxiety did not prevent a profound joy in the enterprise.

"If that misguided mutt thinks he can pull off a stunt like that and get away with it, he's got another think coming," asserted Seaton, after making a reading on the other car after several days of the flight. "He went off half-cocked this time, for sure, and we've got him foul. We'd better put on some negative pretty soon hadn't we, Mart? Only a little over a hundred light-years now."

Crane nodded agreement and Seaton continued:

"It'll take as long to stop, of course, as it has taken to get out here, and if we ram them-GOOD NIGHT! Let's figure it out as nearly as we can."

They calculated their own speed, and that of the other vessel, as shown by the various readings taken, and applied just enough negative acceleration to slow the Skylark down to the speed of the other space-car when they should come up with it. They smiled at each other in recognition of the perfect working of the mechanism when the huge vessel had spun, with a sickening lurch, through a complete half-circle, the instant the power was reversed. Each knew that they were actually traveling in a direction that to them seemed "down," but with a constantly diminishing velocity, even though they seemed to be still going "up" with an increasing speed.

Until nearly the end of the calculated time the two took turns as before, but as the time of meeting drew near both men were on the alert, taking readings on the object-compass every few minutes. Finally Crane announced:

"We are almost on them, Dick. They are so close that it is almost impossible to time the needle-less than ten thousand miles."

Seaton gradually increased the retarding force until the needle showed that they were very close to the other vessel and maintaining a constant distance from it. He then shut off the power, and both men hurried to the bottom window to search for the fleeing ship with their powerful night-glasses. They looked at each other in amazement as they felt themselves falling almost directly downward, with an astounding acceleration.

"What do you make of it, Dick?" asked Crane calmly, as he brought his glasses to his eyes and stared out into the black heavens, studded with multitudes of brilliant and unfamiliar stars.

"I don't make it at all, Mart. By the feel, I should say we were falling toward something that would make our earth look like a pin-head. I remember now that I noticed that the bus was getting a little out of plumb with the bar all this last watch. I didn't pay much attention to it, as I couldn't see anything out of the way. Nothing but a sun could be big enough to raise all this disturbance, and I can't see any close enough to be afraid of, can you?"

"No, and I cannot see the Steel space-car, either. Look sharp."

"Of course," Seaton continued to argue as he peered out into the night, "it is theoretically possible that a heavenly body can exist large enough so that it could exert even this much force and still appear no larger than an ordinary star, but I don't believe it is probable. Give me three or four minutes of visual angle and I'll believe anything, but none of these stars are big enough to have any visual angle at all. Furthermore...."

"There is at least half a degree of visual angle!" broke in his friend intensely. "Just to the left of that constellation that looks so much like a question mark. It is not bright, but dark, like a very dark moon-barely perceptible."

Seaton pointed his glass eagerly in the direction indicated.

"Great Cat!" he ejaculated. "I'll say that's some moon! Wouldn't that rattle your slats? And there's DuQuesne's bus, too, on the right edge. Get it?"

As they stood up, Seaton's mood turned to one of deadly earnestness, and a grave look came over Crane's face as the seriousness of their situation dawned upon them. Trained mathematicians both, they knew instantly that that unknown world was of inconceivable mass, and that their chance of escape was none too good, even should they abandon the other craft to its fate. Seaton stared at Crane, his fists clenched and drops of perspiration standing on his forehead. Suddenly, with agony in his eyes and in his voice, he spoke.

"Mighty slim chance of getting away if we go through with it, old man....Hate like the devil.... Have no right to ask you to throw yourself away, too."

"Enough of that, Dick. You had nothing to do with my coming: you could not have kept me away. We will see it through."

Their hands met in a fierce clasp, broken by Seaton, as he jumped to the levers with an intense:

"Well, let's get busy!"

In a few minutes they had reduced the distance until they could plainly see the other vessel, a small black circle against the faintly luminous disk. As it leaped into clear relief in the beam of his powerful searchlight, Seaton focused the great attractor upon the fugitive car and threw in the lever which released the full force of that mighty magnet, while Crane attracted the attention of the vessel's occupants by means of a momentary burst of solid machine-gun bullets, which he knew would glance harmlessly off the steel hull.

After an interminable silence, DuQuesne drew himself out of his seat. He took a long inhalation, deposited the butt of his cigarette carefully in his ash tray, and made his way to his room. He returned with three heavy fur suits provided with air helmets, two of which he handed to the girls, who were huddled in a seat with their arms around each other. These suits were the armor designed by Crane for use in exploring the vacuum and the intense cold of dead worlds. Air-tight, braced with fine steel netting, and supplied with air at normal pressure from small tanks by automatic valves, they made their wearers independent of surrounding conditions of pressure and temperature.

"The next thing to do," DuQuesne stated calmly, "is to get the copper off the outside of the ship. That is the last resort, as it robs us of our only safeguard against meteorites, but this is the time for last-resort measures. I'm going after that copper. Put these suits on, as our air will leave as soon as I open the door, and practically an absolute vacuum and equally absolute zero will come in."

As he spoke, the ship was enveloped in a blinding glare and they were thrown flat as the vessel slowed down in its terrific fall. The thought flashed across DuQuesne's mind that they had already entered the atmosphere of that monster globe and were being slowed down and set afire by its friction, but he dismissed it as quickly as it had come-the light in that case would be the green of copper, not this bluish-white. His next thought was that there had been a collision of meteors in the neighborhood, and that their retardation was due to the outer coating. While these thoughts were flickering through his mind, they heard an insistent metallic tapping, which DuQuesne recognized instantly.

"A machine-gun!" he blurted in amazement. "How in...."

"It's Dick!" screamed Dorothy, with flashing eyes. "He's found us, just as I knew he would. You couldn't beat Dick and Martin in a thousand years!"

The tension under which they had been laboring so long suddenly released, the two girls locked their arms around each other in a half-hysterical outburst of relief. Margaret's meaningless words and Dorothy's incoherent praises of her lover and Crane mingled with their racking sobs as each fought to recover self-possession.

DuQuesne had instantly mounted to the upper window. Throwing back the cover, he flashed his torch rapidly. The glare of the searchlight was snuffed out and he saw a flashing light spell out in dots and dashes:

"Can you read Morse?"

"Yes," he signalled back. "Power gone, drifting into...."

"We know it. Will you resist?"

"No."

"Have you fur pressure-suits?"

"Yes."

"Put them on. Shut off your outer coating. Will touch so your upper door against our lower. Open, transfer quick."

"O. K."

Hastily returning to the main compartment, he briefly informed the girls as to what had happened. All three donned the suits and stationed themselves at the upper opening. Rapidly, but with unerring precision, the two ships were brought into place and held together by the attractor. As the doors were opened, there was a screaming hiss as the air of the vessels escaped through the narrow crack between them. The passengers saw the moisture in the air turn into snow, and saw the air itself first liquefy and then freeze into a solid coating upon the metal around the orifices at the touch of the frightful cold outside-the absolute zero of interstellar space, about four hundred sixty degrees below zero in the every-day scale of temperature. The moisture of their breath condensed upon the inside of the double glasses of their helmets, rendering sight useless.

Dorothy pushed the other girl ahead of her. DuQuesne seized her and tossed her lightly through the doorway in such a manner that she would not touch the metal, which would have frozen instantly anything coming into contact with it. Seaton was waiting. Feeling a woman's slender form in his arms, he crushed her to him in a mighty embrace, and was astonished to feel movements of resistance, and to hear a strange, girlish voice cry out:

"Don't! It's me! Dorothy's next!"

Releasing her abruptly, he passed her on to Martin and turned just in time to catch his sweetheart, who, knowing that he would be there and recognizing his powerful arms at the first touch, returned his embrace with a fierce intensity which even he had never suspected that she could exert. They stood motionless, locked in each other's arms, while DuQuesne dove through the opening and snapped the door shut behind him.

The air-pressure and temperature back to normal, the cumbersome suits were hastily removed, and Seaton's lips met Dorothy's in a long, clinging caress. DuQuesne's cold, incisive voice broke the silence.

"Every second counts. I would suggest that we go somewhere."

"Just a minute!" snapped Crane. "Dick, what shall we do with this murderer?"

Seaton had forgotten DuQuesne utterly in the joy of holding his sweetheart in his arms, but at his friend's words, he faced about and his face grew stern.

"By rights, we ought to chuck him back into his own tub and let him go to the devil," he said savagely, doubling his fists and turning swiftly.

"No, no, Dick," remonstrated Dorothy, seizing his arm. "He treated us very well, and saved my life once. Anyway, you mustn't kill him."

"No, I suppose not," grudgingly assented her lover, "and I won't, either, unless he gives me at least half an excuse."

"We might iron him to a post?" suggested Crane, doubtfully.

"I think there's a better way," replied Seaton. "He may be able to work his way. His brain hits on all twelve, and he's strong as a bull. Our chance of getting back isn't a certainty, as you know." He turned to DuQuesne.

"I've heard that your word is good."

"It has never been broken."

"Will you give your word to act as one of the party, for the good of us all, if we don't iron you?"

"Yes-until we get back to the earth. Provided, of course, that I reserve the right to escape at any time between now and then if I wish to and can do so without injuring the vessel or any member of the party in any way."

"Agreed. Let's get busy-we're altogether too close to that dud there to suit me. Sit tight, everybody, we're on our way!" he cried, as he turned to the board, applied one notch of power, and shut off the attractor. The Skylark slowed down a trifle in its mad fall, the other vessel continued on its way—a helpless hulk, manned by a corpse, falling to destruction upon the bleak wastes of a desert world.

"Hold on!" said DuQuesne sharply. "Your power is the same as mine was, in proportion to your mass, isn't it?"

"Yes."

"Then our goose is cooked. I couldn't pull away from it with everything I had, couldn't even swing out enough to make an orbit, either hyperbolic or elliptical around it. With a reserve bar you will be able to make an orbit, but you can't get away from it."

"Thanks for the dope. That saves our wasting some effort. Our power-plant can be doubled up in emergencies, thanks to Martin's cautious old bean. We'll simply double her up and go away from here."

"There is one thing we didn't consider quite enough," said Crane, thoughtfully. "I started to faint back there before the full power of even one motor was in use. With the motor doubled, each of us will be held down by a force of many tons-we would all be helpless."

"Yes," added Dorothy, with foreboding in her eyes, "we were all unconscious on the way out, except Dr. DuQuesne."

"Well, then, Blackie and I, as the huskiest members of the party, will give her the juice until only one of us is left with his eyes open. If that isn't enough to pull us clear, we'll have to give her the whole works and let her ramble by herself after we all go out. How about it, Blackie?" unconsciously falling into the old Bureau nickname. "Do you think we can make it stop at unconsciousness with double power on?"

DuQuesne studied the two girls carefully.

"With oxygen in the helmets instead of air, we all may be able to stand it. These special cushions keep the body from flattening out, as it normally would under such a pressure. The unconsciousness is simply a suffocation caused by the lateral muscles being unable to lift the ribs-in other words, the air-pumps aren't strong enough for the added work put upon them. At least we stand a chance this way. We may live through the pressure while we are pulling away, and we certainly shall die if we don't pull away."

After a brief consultation, the men set to work with furious haste. While Crane placed extra bars in each of the motors and DuQuesne made careful observations upon the apparent size of the now plainly visible world toward which they were being drawn so irresistibly, Seaton connected the helmets with the air-and oxygen-tanks through a valve upon the board, by means of which he could change at will the oxygen content of the air they breathed. He then placed the strange girl, who seemed dazed by the frightful sensation of their never-ending fall, upon one of the seats, fitted the cumbersome helmet upon her head, strapped her carefully into place, and turned to Dorothy. In an instant they were in each other's arms. He felt her labored breathing and the wild beating of her heart, pressed so closely to his, and saw the fear of the unknown in the violet depths of her eyes, but she looked at him unflinchingly.

"Dick, sweetheart, if this is good-bye...."

He interrupted her with a kiss.

"It isn't good-bye yet, Dottie mine. This is merely a trial effort, to see what we will have to do to get away. Next time will be the time to worry."

"I'm not worried, really ... but in case ...you see ... I ... we ..."

The gray eyes softened and misted over as he pressed his cheek to hers.

"I understand, sweetheart," he whispered. "This is not good-bye, but if we don't pull through we'll go together, and that is what we both want."

As Crane and DuQuesne finished their tasks, Seaton fitted his sweetheart's helmet, placed her tenderly upon the seat, buckled the heavy restraining straps about her slender body, and donned his own helmet. He took his place at the main instrument board, DuQuesne stationing himself at the other.

"What did you read on it, Blackie?" asked Seaton.

"Two degrees, one minute, twelve seconds diameter," replied DuQuesne. "Altogether too close for comfort. How shall we apply the power? One of us must stay awake, or we'll go on as long as the bars last."

"You put on one notch, then I'll put on one. We can feel the bus jump with each notch. We'll keep it up until one of us is so far gone that he can't raise the bar-the one that raises last will have to let the ship run for thirty minutes or an hour, then cut down his power. Then the other fellow will revive and cut his off, for an observation. How's that?"

"All right."

They took their places, and Seaton felt the vessel slow down in its horrible fall as DuQuesne threw his lever into the first notch. He responded instantly by advancing his own, and notch after notch the power applied to the ship by the now doubled motor was rapidly increased. The passengers felt their suits envelope them and began to labor for breath. Seaton slowly turned the mixing valve, a little with each advance of his lever, until pure oxygen flowed through the pipes. The power levers had moved scarcely half of their range, yet minutes now intervened between each advance instead of seconds, as at the start.

As each of the two men was determined that he would make the last advance, the duel continued longer than either would have thought possible. Seaton made what he thought his final effort and waited-only to feel, after a few minutes, the upward surge telling him that DuQuesne was still able to move his lever. His brain reeled. His arm seemed paralyzed by its own enormous weight, and felt as though it, the rolling table upon which it rested, and the supporting framework were so immovably welded together that it was impossible to move it even the quarter-inch necessary to operate the ratchet-lever. He could not move his body, which was oppressed by a sickening weight. His utmost efforts to breathe forced only a little of the life-giving oxygen into his lungs, which smarted painfully at the touch of the undiluted gas, and he felt that he could not long retain consciousness under such conditions. Nevertheless, he summoned all his strength and advanced the lever one more notch. He stared at the clock-face above his head, knowing that if DuQuesne could advance his lever again he would lose consciousness and be beaten. Minute after minute went by, however, and the acceleration of the ship remained constant. Seaton, knowing that he was in sole control of the power-plant, fought to retain possession of his faculties, while the hands of the clock told off the interminable minutes.

After an eternity of time an hour had passed, and Seaton attempted to cut down his power, only to find with horror that the long strain had so weakened him that he could not reverse the ratchet. He was still able, however, to give the lever the backward jerk which disconnected the wires completely-and the safety straps creaked with the sudden stress as, half the power instantly shut off, the suddenly released springs tried to hurl five bodies against the ceiling. After a few minutes DuQuesne revived and slowly cut off his power. To the dismay of both men they were again falling!

DuQuesne hurried to the lower window to make the observation, remarking:

"You're a better man than I am, Gunga Din."

"Only because you're so badly bunged up. One more notch would've got my goat," replied Seaton frankly as he made his way to Dorothy's side. He noticed as he reached her, that Crane had removed his helmet and was approaching the other girl. By the time DuQuesne had finished the observation, the other passengers had completely recovered, apparently none the worse for their experience.

"Did we gain anything?" asked Seaton eagerly.

"I make it two, four, thirteen. We've lost about two minutes of arc. How much power did we have on?"

"A little over half-thirty-two points out of sixty possible."

"We were still falling pretty fast. We'll have to put on everything we've got. Since neither of us can put it on we'll have to rig up an automatic feed. It'll take time, but it's the only way."

"The automatic control is already there," put in Crane, forestalling Seaton's explanation. "The only question is whether we will live through it-and that is not really a question, since certain death is the only alternative. We must do it."

"We sure must," answered Seaton soberly.

Dorothy gravely nodded assent.

"What do you fellows think of a little plus pressure on the oxygen?" asked Seaton. "I think it would help a lot."

"I think it's a good idea," said DuQuesne, and Crane added:

"Four or five inches of water will be about all the pressure we can stand. Any more might burn our lungs too badly."

The pressure apparatus was quickly arranged and the motors filled to capacity with reserve bars-enough to last seventy-two hours-the scientists having decided that they must risk everything on one trial and put in enough, if possible, to pull them clear out of the influence of this center of attraction, as the time lost in slowing up to change bars might well mean the difference between success and failure. Where they might lie at the end of the wild dash for safety, how they were to retrace their way with their depleted supply of copper, what other dangers of dead star, planet, or sun lay in their path-all these were terrifying questions that had to be ignored.

DuQuesne was the only member of the party who actually felt any calmness, the quiet of the others expressing their courage in facing fear. Life seemed very sweet and desirable to them, the distant earth a very Paradise! Through Dorothy's mind flashed the visions she had built up during long sweet hours, visions of a long life with Seaton. As she breathed an inaudible prayer, she glanced up and saw Seaton standing beside her, gazing down upon her with his very soul in his eyes. Never would she forget the expression upon his face. Even in that crucial hour, his great love for her overshadowed every other feeling, and no thought of self was in his mind-his care was all for her. There was a long farewell caress. Both knew that it might be goodbye, but both were silent as the violet eyes and the gray looked into each other's depths and conveyed messages far beyond the power of words. Once more he adjusted her helmet and strapped her into place.

As Crane had in the meantime cared for the other girl, the men again took their places and Seaton started the motor which would automatically advance the speed levers, one notch every five seconds, until the full power of both motors was exerted. As the power was increased, he turned the valve as before, until the helmets were filled with pure oxygen under a pressure of five inches of water.

Margaret Spencer, weakened by her imprisonment, was the first to lose consciousness, and soon afterward Dorothy felt her senses leave her. A half-minute, in the course of which six mighty surges were felt, as more of the power of the doubled motor was released, and Crane had gone, calmly analyzing his sensations to the last. After a time DuQuesne also lapsed into unconsciousness, making no particular effort to avoid it, as he knew that the involuntary muscles would function quite as well without the direction of the will. Seaton, although he knew it was useless, fought to keep his senses as long as possible, counting the impulses he felt as the levers were advanced.

"Thirty-two." He felt exactly as he had before, when he had advanced the lever for the last time.

"Thirty-three." A giant hand shut off his breath completely, though he was fighting to his utmost for air. An intolerable weight rested upon his eyeballs, forcing them backward into his head. The universe whirled about him in dizzy circles-orange and black and green stars flashed before his bursting eyes.

"Thirty-four." The stars became more brilliant and of more variegated colors, and a giant pen dipped in fire was writing equations and mathematico-chemical symbols upon his quivering brain. He joined the circling universe, which he had hitherto kept away from him by main strength, and whirled about his own body, tracing a logarithmic spiral with infinite velocity-leaving his body an infinite distance behind.

"Thirty-five." The stars and the fiery pen exploded in a wild coruscation of searing, blinding light and he plunged from his spiral into a black abyss.

In spite of the terrific stress put upon the machine, every part functioned perfectly, and soon after Seaton had lost consciousness the vessel began to draw away from the sinister globe; slowly at first, faster and faster as more and more of the almost unlimited power of the mighty motor was released. Soon the levers were out to the last notch and the machine was exerting its maximum effort. One hour and an observer upon the Skylark would have seen that the apparent size of the massive unknown world was rapidly decreasing; twenty hours and it was so far away as to be invisible, though its effect was still great; forty hours and the effect was slight; sixty hours and the Skylark was out of range of the slightest measurable force of the monster it had left.

Hurtled onward by the inconceivable power of the unleashed copper demon in its center, the Skylark flew through the infinite reaches of interstellar space with an unthinkable, almost incalculable velocity-beside which the velocity of light was as that of a snail to that of a rifle bullet; a velocity augmented every second by a quantity almost double that of light itself.

CHAPTER XI

Through Space Into the Carboniferous

Seaton opened his eyes and gazed about him wonderingly. Only half conscious, bruised and sore in every part of his body, he could not at first realize what had happened. Instinctively drawing a deep breath, he coughed and choked as the undiluted oxygen filled his lungs, bringing with it a complete understanding of the situation. Knowing from the lack of any apparent motion that the power had been sufficient to pull the car away from that fatal globe, his first thought was for Dorothy, and he tore off his helmet and turned toward her. The force of even that slight movement, wafted him gently into the air where he hung suspended several minutes before his struggles enabled him to clutch a post and draw himself down to the floor. A quick glance around informed him that Dorothy, as well as the others, was still unconscious. Making his way rapidly to her, he placed her face downward upon the floor and began artificial respiration. Very soon he was rewarded by the coughing he had longed to hear. He tore off her helmet and clasped her to his breast in an agony of relief, while she sobbed convulsively upon his shoulder. The first ecstasy of their greeting over, Dorothy started guiltily.

"Oh, Dick!" she exclaimed. "How about Peggy? You must see how she is!"

"Never mind," answered Crane's voice cheerily. "She is coming to nicely."

Glancing around quickly, they saw that Crane had already revived the stranger, and that DuQuesne was not in sight. Dorothy blushed, the vivid wave of color rising to her glorious hair, and hastily disengaged her arms from around her lover's neck, drawing away from him. Seaton, also blushing, dropped his arms, and Dorothy floated away from him, frantically clutching at a brace just beyond reach.

"Pull me down, Dick!" she called, laughing gaily.

Seaton, seizing her instinctively, neglected his own anchorage and they hung in the air together, while Crane and Margaret, each holding a strap, laughed with unrestrained merriment.

"Tweet, tweet—I'm a canary!" chuckled Seaton. "Throw us a rope!"

"A Dicky-bird, you mean," interposed Dorothy.

"I knew that you were a sleight-of-hand expert, Dick, but I did not know that levitation was one of your specialties," remarked Crane with mock gravity. "That is a peculiar pose you are holding now. What are you doing-sitting on an imaginary pedestal?"

"I'll be sitting on your neck if you don't get a wiggle on with that rope!" retorted Seaton, but before Crane had time to obey the command the floating couple had approached close enough to the ceiling so that Seaton, with a slight pressure of his hand against the leather, sent them floating back to the floor, within reach of one of the handrails.

Seaton made his way to the power-plant, lifted in one of the remaining bars, and applied a little power. The Skylark seemed to jump under them, then it seemed as though they were back on Earth-everything had its normal weight once more, as the amount of power applied was just enough to equal the acceleration of gravity. After this fact had been explained, Dorothy turned to Margaret.

"Now that we are able to act intelligently, the party should be introduced to each other. Peggy, this is Dr. Dick Seaton, and this is Mr. Martin Crane. Boys, this is Miss Margaret Spencer, a dear friend of mine. These are the boys I have told you so much about, Peggy. Dick knows all about atoms and things; he found out how to make the Skylark go. Martin, who is quite a wonderful inventor, made the engines and things for it."

"I may have heard of Mr. Crane," replied Margaret eagerly. "My father was an inventor, and I have heard him speak of a man named Crane who invented a lot of instruments for airplanes. He used to say that the Crane instruments revolutionized flying. I wonder if you are that Mr. Crane?"

"That is rather unjustifiably high praise, Miss Spencer," replied Crane, "but as I have been guilty of one or two things along that line, I may be the man he meant."

"Pardon me if I seem to change the subject," put in Seaton, "but where's DuQuesne?"

"We came to at the same time, and he went into the galley to fix up something to eat."

"Good for him!" exclaimed Dorothy. "I'm simply starved to death. I would have been demanding food long ago, but I have so many aches and pains that I didn't realize how hungry I was until you mentioned it. Come on, Peggy, I know where our room is. Let's go powder our noses while these bewhiskered gentlemen reap their beards. Did you bring along any of my clothes, Dick, or did you forget them in the excitement?"

"I didn't think anything about clothes, but Martin did. You'll find your whole wardrobe in your room. I'm with you, Dot, on that eating proposition—I'm hungry enough to eat the jamb off the door!"

After the girls had gone, Seaton and Crane went to their rooms, where they exercised vigorously to restore the circulation to their numbed bodies, shaved, bathed, and returned to the saloon feeling like new men. They found the girls already there, seated at one of the windows.

"Hail and greeting!" cried Dorothy at sight of them. "I hardly recognized you without your whiskers. Do hurry over here and look out this perfectly wonderful window. Did you ever in your born days see anything like this sight? Now that I'm not scared pea-green, I can enjoy it thoroughly!"

The two men joined the girls and peered out into space through the window, which was completely invisible, so clear was the glass. As the four heads bent, so close together, an awed silence fell upon the little group. For the blackness of the interstellar void was not the dark of an earthly night, but the absolute black of the absence of all light, beside which the black of platinum dust is pale and gray; and laid upon this velvet were the jewel stars. They were not the twinkling, scintillating beauties of the earthly sky, but minute points, so small as to seem dimensionless, yet of dazzling brilliance. Without the interference of the air, their rays met the eye steadily and much of the effect of comparative distance was lost. All seemed nearer and there was no hint of familiarity in their arrangement. Like gems thrown upon darkness they shone in multi-colored beauty upon the daring wanderers, who stood in their car as easily as though they were upon their parent Earth, and gazed upon a sight never before seen by eye of man nor pictured in his imaginings.

Through the daze of their wonder, a thought smote Seaton like a blow from a fist. His eyes leaped to the instrument board and he exclaimed:

"Look there, Mart! We're heading almost directly away from the Earth, and we must be making billions of miles per second. After we lost consciousness, the attraction of that big dud back there would swing us around, of course, but the bar should have stayed pointed somewhere near the Earth, as I left it. Do you suppose it could have shifted the gyroscopes?"

"It not only could have, it did," replied Crane, turning the bar until it again pointed parallel with the object-compass which bore upon the Earth. "Look at the board. The angle has been changed through nearly half a circumference. We couldn't carry gyroscopes heavy enough to counteract that force."

"But they were heavier there-Oh, sure, you're right. It's mass, not weight, that counts. But we sure are in one fine, large jam now. Instead of being half-way back to the Earth we're-where are we, anyway?"

They made a reading on an object-compass focused upon the Earth. Seaton's face lengthened as seconds passed. When it had come to rest, both men calculated the distance.

"What d'you make it, Mart? I'm afraid to tell you my result."

"Forty-six point twenty-seven light-centuries," replied Crane, calmly. "Right?"

"Right, and the time was 11:32 P. M. of Thursday, by the chronometer there. We'll time it again after a while and see how fast we're traveling. It's a good thing you built the ship's chronometers to stand any kind of stress. My watch is a total loss. Yours is, too?"

"All of our watches must be broken. We will have to repair them as soon as we get time."

"Well, let's eat next! No human being can stand my aching void much longer. How about you, Dot?"

"Yes, for Cat's sake, let's get busy!" she mimicked him gaily. "Doctor DuQuesne's had dinner ready for ages, and we're all dying by inches of hunger."

The wanderers, battered, bruised, and sore, seated themselves at a folding table, Seaton keeping a watchful eye upon the bar and upon the course, while enjoying Dorothy's presence to the full. Crane and Margaret talked easily, but at intervals. Save when directly addressed. DuQuesne maintained silence-not the silence of one who knows himself to be an intruder, but the silence of perfect self-sufficiency. The meal over, the girls washed the dishes and busied themselves in the galley. Seaton and Crane made another observation upon the Earth, requesting DuQuesne to stay out of the "engine room" as they called the partially-enclosed space surrounding the main instrument board, where were located the object-compasses and the mechanism controlling the attractor, about which DuQuesne knew nothing. As they rejoined DuQuesne in the main compartment, Seaton said:

"DuQuesne, we're nearly five thousand light-years away from the Earth, and are getting farther at the rate of about one light-year per minute."

"I suppose that it would be poor technique to ask how you know?"

"It would-very poor. Our figures are right. The difficulty is that we have only four bars left-enough to stop us and a little to spare, but not nearly enough to get back with, even if we could take a chance on drifting straight that far without being swung off-which, of course, is impossible."

"That means that we must land somewhere and dig some copper, then."

"Exactly.

"The first thing to do is to find a place to land."

Seaton picked out a distant star in their course and observed it through the spectroscope. Since it was found to contain copper in notable amounts, all agreed that its planets probably also contained copper.

"Don't know whether we can stop that soon or not," remarked Seaton as he set the levers, "but we may as well have something to shoot at. We'd better take our regular twelve-hour tricks, hadn't we, Mart? It's a wonder we got as far as this without striking another snag. I'll take the first trick at the board-beat it to bed."

"Not so fast, Dick," argued Crane, as Seaton turned toward the engine-room: "It's my turn."

"Flip a nickel," suggested Seaton. "Heads I get it."

Crane flipped a coin. Heads it was, and the worn-out party went to their rooms, all save Dorothy, who lingered after the others to bid her lover a more intimate good-night.

Seated beside him, his arm around her and her head upon his shoulder, Dorothy exclaimed:

"Oh, Dicky, Dicky, it is wonderful to be with you again! I've lived as many years in the last week as we have covered miles!"

Seaton kissed her with ardor, then turned her fair face up to his and gazed hungrily at every feature.

"It sure was awful until we found you, sweetheart girl. Those two days at Wilson's were the worst and longest I ever put in. I could have wrung Martin's cautious old neck!"

"But isn't he a wiz at preparing for trouble? We sure owe him a lot, little dimpled lady."

Dorothy was silent for a moment, then a smile quirked at one corner of her mouth and a dimple appeared. Seaton promptly kissed it, whereupon it deepened audaciously.

"What are you thinking about-mischief?" he asked.

"Only of how Martin is going to be paid what we owe him," she answered teasingly. "Don't let the debt worry you any."

"Spill the news, Reddy," he commanded, as his arm tightened about her.

She stuck out a tiny tip of red tongue at him.

"Don't let Peggy find out he's a millionaire."

"Why not?" he asked wonderingly, then he saw her point and laughed:

"You little matchmaker!"

"I don't care, laugh if you want to. Martin's as nice a man as I know, and Peggy's a real darling. Don't you let slip a word about Martin's money, that's all!"

"She wouldn't think any less of him, would she?"

"Dick, sometimes you are absolutely dumb. It would spoil everything. If she knew he was a millionaire she would be scared to death-not of him, of course, but because she would think that he would think that she was chasing him, and then of course he would think that she was, see? As it is, she acts perfectly natural, and so does he. Didn't you notice that while we were eating they talked together for at least fifteen minutes about her father's invention and the way they stole the plans and one thing and another? I don't believe he has talked that much to any girl except me the last five years-and he wouldn't talk to me until he knew that I couldn't see any man except you. Much as we like Martin, we've got to admit that about him. He's been chased so much that he's wild. If any other girl he knows had talked to him that long, he would have been off to the North Pole or somewhere the next morning, and the best part of it is that he didn't think anything of it."

"You think she is domesticating the wild man?"

"Now, Dick, don't be foolish. You know what I mean. Martin is a perfect dear, but if she knew that he is *the* M. Reynolds Crane, everything would be ruined. You know yourself how horribly hard it is to get through his shell to the real Martin underneath. He is lonely and miserable inside, I know, and the right kind of girl, one that would treat him right, would make life Heaven for him, and herself too."

"Yes, and the wrong kind would make it...."

"She would," interrupted Dorothy hastily, "but Peggy's the right kind. Wouldn't it be fine to have Martin and Peggy as happy, almost, as you and I are?"

"All right, girlie, I'm with you," he answered, embracing her as though he intended never to let her go, "but you'd better go get some sleep-you're all in."

Considerably later, when Dorothy had finally gone, Seaton settled himself for the long vigil. Promptly at the end of the twelve hours Crane appeared, alert of eye and of bearing.

"You look fresh as a daisy, Mart. Feeling fit?"

"Fit as the proverbial fiddle. I could not have slept any better or longer if I had had a week off. Seven hours and a half is a luxury, you know."

"All wrong, old top. I need eight every night, and I'm going to take about ten this time."

"Go to it, twelve if you like. You have earned it."

Seaton stumbled to his room and slept as though in a trance for ten hours. Rising, he took his regular morning exercises and went into the saloon. All save Martin were there, but he had eyes only for his sweetheart, who was radiantly beautiful in a dress of deep bronze-brown.

"Good morning, Dick," she hailed him joyously. "You woke up just in time-we are all starving again, and were just going to eat without you!"

"Good morning, everybody. I would like to eat with you, Dottie, but I've got to relieve Martin. How'd it be for you to bring breakfast into the engine room and cheer my solitude, and let Crane eat with the others?"

"Fine-that's once you had a good idea, if you never have another!"

After the meal DuQuesne, who abhorred idleness with all his vigorous nature, took the watches of the party and went upstairs to the "shop," which was a completely-equipped mechanical laboratory, to repair them. Seaton stayed at the board, where Dorothy joined him as a matter of course. Crane and Margaret sat down at one of the windows.

She told him her story, frankly and fully, shuddering with horror as she recalled the awful, helpless fall, during which Perkins had met his end.

"Dick and I have a heavy score to settle with that Steel crowd and with DuQuesne," Crane said slowly. "We have no evidence that will hold in law, but some day DuQuesne will over-reach himself. We could convict him of abduction now, but the penalty for that is too mild for what he has done. Perkins' death was not murder, then?"

79

"Oh, no, it was purely self-defense. Perkins would have killed him if he could. And he really deserved it-Perkins was a perfect fiend. The Doctor, as they call him, is no better, although entirely different. He is so utterly heartless and ruthless, so cold and scientific. Do you know him very well?"

"We know all that about him, and more. And yet Dorothy said he saved her life?"

"He did, from Perkins, but I still think it was because he didn't want Perkins meddling in his affairs. He seems to me to be the very incarnation of a fixed purpose-to advance himself in the world."

"That expresses my thoughts exactly. But he slips occasionally, as in this instance, and he will again. He will have to walk very carefully while he is with us. Nothing would please Dick better than an excuse for killing him, and I must admit that I feel very much the same way."

"Yes, all of us do, and the way he acts proves what a machine he is. He knows just exactly how far to go, and never goes beyond it."

They felt the Skylark lurch slightly.

"Oh, Mart!" called Seaton. "Going to pass that star we were headed for-too fast to stop. I'm giving it a wide berth and picking out another one. There's a big planet a few million miles off in line with the main door, and another one almost dead ahead-that is, straight down. We sure are traveling. Look at that sun flit by!"

They saw the two planets, one like a small moon, the other like a large star, and saw the strange sun increase rapidly in size as the Skylark flew on at such a pace that any earthly distance would have been covered as soon as it was begun. So appalling was their velocity that their ship was bathed in the light of that sun for only a short time, then was again surrounded by the indescribable darkness. Their seventy-two-hour flight without a pilot had seemed a miracle, now it seemed entirely possible that they might fly in a straight line for weeks without encountering any obstacle, so vast was the emptiness in comparison with the points of light that punctuated it. Now and then they passed so close to a star that it apparently moved rapidly, but for the most part the silent sentinels stood, like distant mountain peaks to the travelers in an express train, in the same position for many minutes.

Awed by the immensity of the universe, the two at the window were silent, not with the silence of embarrassment, but with that of two friends in the presence of something beyond the reach of words. As they stared out into the infinity each felt as never before the pitiful smallness of even our whole solar system and the utter insignificance of human beings and their works. Silently their minds reached out to each other in mutual understanding.

Unconsciously Margaret half shuddered and moved closer to her companion, the movement attracting his attention but not her own. A tender expression came into Crane's steady blue eyes as he looked down at the beautiful young woman by his side. For beautiful she undoubtedly was. Untroubled rest and plentiful food had erased the marks of her imprisonment; Dorothy's deep, manifestly unassumed faith in the ability of Seaton and Crane to bring them safely back to Earth had quieted her fears; and a complete costume of Dorothy's simple but well-cut clothes, which fitted her perfectly, and in which she looked her best and knew it, had completely restored her self-possession. He quickly glanced away and again gazed at the stars, but now, in addition to the wonders of space, he saw masses of wavy black hair, high-piled upon a queenly head; deep down brown eyes half veiled by long, black lashes; sweet, sensitive lips; a firmly rounded but dimpled chin; and a perfectly-formed young body.

After a time she drew a deep, tremulous breath. As he turned, her eyes met his. In their shadowy depths, still troubled by the mystery of the unknowable, he read her very soul-the soul of a real woman.

"I had hoped," said Margaret slowly, "to take a long flight above the clouds, but anything like this never entered my mind. How unbelievably great it is! So much vaster than any perception we could get upon earth! It seems strange that we were ever awed by the sea or the mountains ... and yet...."

She paused, with her lip caught under two white teeth, then went on hesitatingly:

"Doesn't it seem to you, Mr. Crane, that there is something in man as great as all this? Otherwise, Dorothy and I could not be sailing here in a wonder like the Lark, which you and Dick Seaton have made."

Since from the first, Dorothy had timed her waking hours with those of Seaton-waiting upon him, preparing his meals, and lightening the long hours of his vigils at the board-Margaret took it upon herself to do the same thing for Crane. But often they assembled in the engine-room, and there was much fun and laughter, as well as serious talk, among the four. Margaret was quickly accepted as a friend, and proved a delightful companion. Her wavy, jet-black hair, the only color in the world that could hold its own with Dorothy's auburn glory, framed features self-reliant and strong, yet of womanly softness; and in this genial atmosphere her quick tongue had a delicate wit and a facility of expression that delighted all three. Dorothy, after the manner of Southern women, became the hostess of this odd "party," as she styled it, and unconsciously adopted the attitude of a lady in her own home.

Early in their flight, Crane suggested that they should take notes upon the systems of stars through which were passing.

"I know very little of astronomy," he said to Seaton, "but with our telescope, spectroscope, and other instruments, we should be able to take some data that will be of interest to astronomers. Possibly Miss Spencer would be willing to help us?"

"Sure," Seaton returned readily. "We'd be idiots to let a chance like this slide. Go to it!"

Margaret was delighted at the opportunity to help.

"Taking notes is the best thing I do!" she cried, and called for a pad and pencil.

Stationed at the window, they fell to work in earnest. For several hours Crane took observations, calculated distances, and dictated notes to Margaret.

"The stars are wonderfully different!" she exclaimed to him once. "That planet, I'm sure, has strange and lovely life upon it. See how its color differs from most of the others we have seen so near? It is rosy and soft like a home fire. I'm sure its people are happy."

They fell into a long discussion, laughing a little at their fancies. Were these multitudes of worlds peopled as the Earth? Could it be that only upon Earth had occurred the right combination for the generation of life, so that the rest of the Universe was unpeopled?

"It is unthinkable that they are all uninhabited," mused Crane. "There must be life. The beings may not exist in any form with which we are familiar-they may well be fulfilling some purpose in ways so different from ours that we should be unable to understand them at all."

Margaret's eyes widened in startled apprehension, but in a moment she shook herself and laughed.

"But there's no reason to suppose they would be awful," she remarked, and turned with renewed interest to the window.

Thus days went by and the Skylark passed one solar system after another, with a velocity so great that it was impossible to land upon any planet. Margaret's association with Crane, begun as a duty, soon became an intense pleasure for them both. Taking notes or seated at the board in companionable conversation or sympathetic silence, they compressed into a few days more real companionship than is ordinarily enjoyed in months. Oftener and oftener, as time went on, Crane found the vision of his dream home floating in his mind as he steered the Skylark in her meteoric flight or as he strapped himself into his narrow bed. Now, however, the central figure of the vision, instead of being an indistinct blur, was clear and sharply defined. And for her part, more and more was Margaret drawn to the quiet and unassuming, but utterly dependable and steadfast young inventor, with his wide knowledge and his keen, incisive mind.

* * * * *

Sometimes, when far from any star, the pilot would desert his post and join the others at meals. Upon one such occasion Seaton asked:

"How's the book on astronomy, oh, learned ones?"

"It will be as interesting as Egyptian hieroglyphics," Margaret replied, as she opened her notebook and showed him pages of figures and symbols.

"May I see it, Miss Spencer?" asked DuQuesne from across the small table, extending his hand.

She looked at him, hot hostility in her brown eyes, and he dropped his hand.

"I beg your pardon," he said, with amused irony.

After the meal Seaton and Crane held a short consultation, and the former called to the girls, asking them to join in the "council of war." There was a moment's silence before Crane said diffidently:

"We have been talking about DuQuesne, Miss Spencer, trying to decide a very important problem."

Seaton smiled in spite of himself as the color again deepened in Margaret's face, and Dorothy laughed outright.

"Talk about a red-headed temper! Your hair must be dyed, Peggy!"

"I know I acted like a naughty child," Margaret said ruefully, "but he makes me perfectly furious and scares me at the same time. A few more remarks like that 'I beg your pardon' of his and I wouldn't have a thought left in my head!"

Seaton, who had opened his mouth, shut it again ludicrously, without saying a word, and Margaret gave him a startled glance.

"Now I *have* said it!" she exclaimed. "I'm not afraid of him, boys, really. What do you want me to do?"

Seaton plunged in.

"What we were trying to get up nerve enough to say is that he'd be a good man on the astronomy job," and Crane added quickly:

"He undoubtedly knows more about it than I do, and it would be a pity to lose the chance of using him. Besides, Dick and I think it rather dangerous to leave him so much time to himself, in which to work up a plan against us."

"He's cooking one right now, I'll bet a hat," Seaton put in, and Crane added:

"If you are sure that you have no objections, Miss Spencer, we might go below, where we can have it dark, and all three of us see what we can make of the stargazing. We are really losing an unusual opportunity."

Margaret hid gallantly any reluctance she might have felt.

"I wouldn't deserve to be here if I can't work with the Doctor and hate him at the same time."

"Good for you, Peg, you're a regular fellow!" Seaton exclaimed. "You're a trump!"

Finally, the enormous velocity of the cruiser was sufficiently reduced to effect a landing, a copper-bearing sun was located, and a course was laid toward its nearest planet.

As the vessel approached its goal a deep undercurrent of excitement kept all the passengers feverishly occupied. They watched the distant globe grow larger, glowing through its atmosphere more and more clearly as a great disk of white light, its outline softened by the air about it. Two satellites were close beside it. Its sun, a great, blazing orb, a little nearer than the planet, looked so great and so hot that Margaret became uneasy.

"Isn't it dangerous to get so close, Dick? We might burn up, mightn't we?"

"Not without an atmosphere," he laughed.

"Oh," murmured the girl apologetically, "I might have known that."

Dropping rapidly into the atmosphere of the planet, they measured its density and analyzed it in apparatus installed for that purpose, finding that its composition was very similar to the Earth's air and that its pressure was not enough greater to be uncomfortable. When within one thousand feet of the surface, Seaton weighed a five-pound weight upon a spring-balance, finding that it weighed five and a half pounds, thus ascertaining that the planet was either somewhat larger than the Earth or more dense. The ground was almost hidden by a rank growth of vegetation, but here and there appeared glade-like openings.

Seaton glanced at the faces about him. Tense interest marked them all. Dorothy's cheeks were flushed, her eyes shone. She looked at him with awe and pride.

"A strange world, Dorothy," he said gravely. "You are not afraid?"

"Not with you," she answered. "I am only thrilled with wonder."

"Columbus at San Salvador," said Margaret, her dark eyes paying their tribute of admiration.

A dark flush mounted swiftly into Seaton's brown face and he sought to throw most of the burden upon Crane, but catching upon his face also a look of praise, almost of tenderness, he quickly turned to the controls.

"Man the boats!" he ordered an imaginary crew, and the Skylark descended rapidly.

Landing upon one of the open spaces, they found the ground solid and stepped out. What had appeared to be a glade was in reality a rock, or rather, a ledge of apparently solid metal, with scarcely a loose fragment to be seen. At one end of the ledge rose a giant tree wonderfully symmetrical, but of a peculiar form. Its branches were longer at the top than at the bottom, and it possessed broad, dark-green leaves, long thorns, and odd, flexible, shoot-like tendrils. It stood as an outpost of the dense vegetation beyond. Totally unlike the forests of Earth were those fern-like trees, towering two hundred feet into the air. They were of an intensely vivid green and stood motionless in the still, hot air of noonday. Not a sign of animal life was to be seen; the whole landscape seemed asleep.

The five strangers stood near their vessel, conversing in low tones and enjoying the sensation of solid ground beneath their feet. After a few minutes DuQuesne remarked:

"This is undoubtedly a newer planet than ours. I should say that it was in the Carboniferous age. Aren't those trees like those in the coal-measures, Seaton?"

"True as time, Blackie-there probably won't be a human race here for ages, unless we bring out some colonists."

Seaton kicked at one of the loose lumps of metal questioningly with his heavy shoe, finding that it was as immovable as though it were part of the ledge. Bending over, he found that it required all his great strength to lift it and he stared at it with an expression of surprise, which turned to amazement as he peered closer.

"DuQuesne! Look at this!"

DuQuesne studied the metal, and was shaken out of his habitual taciturnity.

"Platinum, by all the little gods!"

"We'll grab some of this while the grabbing's good," announced Seaton, and the few visible lumps were rolled into the car. "If we had a pickaxe we could chop some more off one of those sharp ledges down there."

"There's an axe in the shop," replied DuQuesne. "I'll go get it. Go ahead, I'll soon be with you."

"Keep close together," warned Crane as the four moved slowly down the slope. "This is none too safe, Dick."

"No, it isn't, Mart. But we've got to see whether we can't find some copper, and I would like to get some more of this stuff, too. I don't think it's platinum, I believe that it's X."

As they reached the broken projections, Margaret glanced back over her shoulder and screamed. The others saw that her face was white and her eyes wide with horror, and Seaton instinctively drew his pistol as he whirled about, only to check his finger on the trigger and lower his hand.

"Nothing but X-plosive bullets," he growled in disgust, and in helpless silence the four watched an unspeakably hideous monster slowly appear from behind the Skylark. Its four huge, squat legs supported a body at least a hundred feet long, pursy and ungainly; at the extremity of a long and sinuous neck a comparatively small head seemed composed entirely of a cavernous mouth armed with row upon row of carnivorous teeth. Dorothy gasped with terror and both girls shrank closer to the two men, who maintained a baffled silence as the huge beast passed his revolting head along the hull of the vessel.

"I dare not shoot, Martin," Seaton whispered, "it would wreck the bus. Have you got any solid bullets?"

"No. We must hide behind these small ledges until it goes away," answered Crane, his eyes upon Margaret's colorless face. "You two hide behind that one, we will take this one."

"Oh, well, it's nothing to worry about, anyway. We can kill him as soon as he gets far enough away from the boat," said Seaton as, with Dorothy clinging to him, he dropped behind one of the ledges. Margaret, her staring eyes fixed upon the monster, remained standing until Crane touched her gently and drew her down beside him.

"He will go away soon," his even voice assured her. "We are in no danger."

In spite of their predicament, a feeling of happiness flowed through Crane's whole being as he crouched beside the wall of metal with one arm protectingly around Margaret, and he longed to protect her through life as he was protecting her then. Accustomed as he was to dangerous situations, he felt no fear. He felt only a great tenderness for the girl by his side, who had ceased trembling but was still staring wide-eyed at the monster through a crevice.

"Scared, Peggy?" he whispered.

"Not now, Martin, but if you weren't here I would die of fright."

At this reply his arm tightened involuntarily, but he forced it to relax.

"It will not be long," he promised himself silently, "until she is back at home among her friends, and then...."

There came the crack of a rifle from the Skylark. There was an awful roar from the dinosaur, which was quickly silenced by a stream of machine-gun bullets.

"Blackie's on the job—let's go!" cried Seaton, and they raced up the slope. Making a detour to avoid the writhing and mutilated mass they plunged through the opening door. DuQuesne shut it behind them and in overwhelming relief, the adventurers huddled together as from the wilderness without there arose an appalling tumult.

The scene, so quiet a few moments before, was instantly changed. The trees, the swamp, and the air seemed filled with monsters so hideous as to stagger the imagination. Winged lizards of prodigious size hurtled through the air, plunging to death against the armored hull. Indescribable flying monsters, with feathers like birds, but with the fangs of tigers, attacked viciously. Dorothy screamed and started back as a scorpion-like thing with a body ten feet in length leaped at the window in front of her, its terrible sting spraying the glass with venom. As it fell to the ground, a huge spider—if an eight-legged creature with spines instead of hair, many-faceted eyes, and a bloated, globular body weighing hundreds of pounds, may be called a spider—leaped upon it and, mighty mandibles against poisonous sting, the furious battle raged. Several twelve-foot cockroaches climbed nimbly across the fallen timber of the morass and began feeding voraciously upon the body of the dead dinosaur, only to be driven away by another animal, which all three men recognized instantly as that king of all prehistoric creatures, the saber-toothed tiger. This newcomer, a tawny beast towering fifteen feet high at the shoulder, had a mouth disproportionate even to his great size —a mouth armed with four great tiger-teeth more than three feet in length. He had barely begun his meal, however, when he was challenged by another nightmare, a something apparently half-way between a dinosaur and a crocodile. At the first note the tiger charged. Clawing, striking, rending each other with their terrible teeth, a veritable avalanche of bloodthirsty rage, the combatants stormed up and down the little island. But the fighters were rudely interrupted, and the earthly visitors discovered that in this primitive world it was not only animal life that was dangerous.

The great tree standing on the farther edge of the island suddenly bent over, lashing out like a snake and grasping both. It transfixed them with the terrible thorns, which were now seen to be armed with needlepoints and to possess barbs like fish-hooks. It ripped at them with the long branches, which were veritable spears. The broad leaves, armed with revolting sucking disks, closed about the two animals, while the long, slender twigs, each of which was now seen to have an eye at its extremity, waved about, watching each movement of the captives from a safe distance.

If the struggle between the two animals had been awful, this was Titanic. The air was torn by the roars of the reptile, the screams of the great cat, and the shrieks of the tree. The very ground rocked with the ferocity of the conflict. There could be but one result-soon the tree, having absorbed the two gladiators, resumed its upright position in all its beauty.

The members of the little group stared at each other, sick at heart.

"This is NO place to start a copper-mine. I think we'd better beat it," remarked Seaton presently, wiping drops of perspiration from his forehead.

"I think so," acquiesced Crane. "We found air and Earth-like conditions here; we probably will elsewhere."

"Are you all right, Dottie?" asked Seaton.

"All right, Dicky," she replied, the color flowing back into her cheeks. "It scared me stiff, and I think I have a lot of white hairs right now, but I wouldn't have missed it for anything."

She paused an instant, and continued:

"Dick, there must be a queer streak of brutality in me, but would you mind blowing up that frightful tree? I wouldn't mind its nature if it were ugly-but look at it! It's so deceptively beautiful! You wouldn't think it had the disposition of a fiend, would you?"

A general laugh relieved the nervous tension, and Seaton stepped impulsively toward DuQuesne with his hand outstretched.

"You've squared your account, Blackie. Say the word and the war's all off."

DuQuesne ignored the hand and glanced coldly at the group of eager, friendly faces.

"Don't be sentimental," he remarked evenly as he turned away to his room. "Emotional scenes pain me. I gave my word to act as one of the party."

"Well, may I be kicked to death by little red spiders!" exclaimed Seaton, dumbfounded, as the other disappeared. "He ain't a man, he's a fish!"

"He's a machine. I always thought so, and now I know it," stated Margaret, and the others nodded agreement.

"Well, we'll sure pull his cork as soon as we get back!" snapped Seaton. "He asked for it, and we'll give him both barrels!"

"I know I acted the fool out there," Margaret apologized, flushing hotly and looking at Crane. "I don't know what made me act so stupid. I used to have a little nerve."

"You were a regular little brick, Peg," Seaton returned instantly. "Both you girls are all to the good-the right kind to have along in ticklish places."

Crane held out his steady hand and took Margaret's in a warm clasp.

"For a girl in your weakened condition you were wonderful. You have no reason to reproach yourself."

Tears filled the dark eyes, but were held back bravely as she held her head erect and returned the pressure of his hand.

"Just so you don't leave me behind next time," she returned lightly, and the last word concerning the incident had been said.

Seaton applied the power and soon they were approaching another planet, which was surrounded by a dense fog. Descending slowly, they found it to be a mass of boiling-hot steam and rank vapors, under enormous pressure.

The next planet they found to have a clear atmosphere, but the ground had a peculiar, barren look; and analysis of the gaseous envelope proved it to be composed almost entirely of chlorin. No life of an earthly type could be possible upon such a world, and a search for copper, even with the suits and helmets, would probably be fruitless if not impossible.

"Well," remarked Seaton as they were again in space, "we've got enough copper to visit several more worlds-several more solar systems, if necessary. But there's a nice, hopeful-looking planet right in front of us. It may be the one we're looking for."

Arrived in the belt of atmosphere, they tested it as before, and found it satisfactory.

CHAPTER XII

The Mastery of Mind Over Matter

They descended rapidly, directly over a large and imposing city in the middle of a vast, level, beautifully-planted plain. While they were watching it, the city vanished and the plain was transformed into a heavily-timbered mountain summit, the valleys falling away upon all sides as far as the eye could reach.

"Well, I'll say that's SOME mirage!" exclaimed Seaton, rubbing his eyes in astonishment. "I've seen mirages before, but never anything like that. Wonder what this air's made of? But we'll land, anyway, if we finally have to swim!"

The ship landed gently upon the summit, the occupants half expecting to see the ground disappear before their eyes. Nothing happened, however, and they disembarked, finding walking somewhat difficult because of the great mass of the planet. Looking around, they could see no sign of life, but they *felt* a presence near them—a vast, invisible something.

Suddenly, out of the air in front of Seaton, a man materialized: a man identical with him in every feature and detail, even to the smudge of grease under one eye, the small wrinkles in his heavy blue serge suit, and the emblem of the American Chemical Society upon his watch-fob.

"Hello, folks," the stranger began in Seaton's characteristic careless speech. "I see you're surprised at my knowing your language. You're a very inferior race of animals-don't even understand telepathy, don't understand the luminiferous ether, or the relation between time and space. Your greatest things, such as the Skylark and your object-compass, are merely toys."

Changing instantly from Seaton's form to that of Dorothy, likewise a perfect imitation, the stranger continued without a break:

"Atoms and electrons and things, spinning and whirling in their dizzy little orbits...." It broke off abruptly, continuing in the form of DuQuesne:

"Couldn't make myself clear as Miss Vaneman-not a scientific convolution in her foolish little brain. You are a freer type, DuQuesne, unhampered by foolish, soft fancies. But you are very clumsy, although working fairly well with your poor tools-Brookings and his organization, the Perkins Café and its clumsy wireless telephones. All of you are extremely low in the scale. Such animals have not been known in our universe for ten million years, which is as far back as I can remember. You have millions of years to go before you will amount to anything; before you will even rise above death and its attendant necessity, sex."

The strange being then assumed form after form with bewildering rapidity, while the spectators stared in dumb astonishment. In rapid succession it took on the likeness of each member of the party, of the vessel itself, of the watch in Seaton's pocket-reappearing as Seaton.

"Well, bunch," it said in a matter-of-fact voice, "there's no mental exercise in you and you're such a low form of life that you're of no use on this planet; so I'll dematerialize you."

A peculiar light came into its eyes as they stared intently into Seaton's, and he felt his senses reel under the impact of an awful mental force, but he fought back with all his power and remained standing.

"What's this?" the stranger demanded in surprise, "This is the first time in history that mere matter-which is only a manifestation of mind-has ever refused to obey mind. There's a screw loose somewhere."

"I must reason this out," it continued analytically, changing instantaneously into Crane's likeness. "Ah! I am not a perfect reproduction. This is the first matter I have ever encountered that I could not reproduce perfectly. There is some subtle difference. The external form is the same, the organic structure likewise. The molecules of substance are arranged as they should be, as are also the atoms in the molecule. The electrons in the atom-ah! There is the difficulty. The arrangement and number of electrons, as well as positive charges, are entirely different from what I had supposed. I must derive the formula."

"Let's go, folks!" said Seaton hastily, drawing Dorothy back toward the Skylark. "This dematerialization stunt may be play for him, but I don't want any of it in my family."

"No, you really *must* stay," remonstrated the stranger. "Much as it is against my principles to employ brute force, you must stay and be properly dematerialized, alive or dead. Science demands it."

As he spoke, he started to draw his automatic pistol. Being in Crane's form, he drew slowly, as Crane did; and Seaton, with the dexterity of much sleight-of-hand work and of years of familiarity with his weapon, drew and fired in one incredibly rapid movement, before the other had withdrawn the pistol from his pocket. The X-plosive shell completely volatilized the stranger and hurled the party backward toward the Skylark, into which they fled hastily. As Crane, the last one to enter the vessel, fired his pistol and closed the massive door, Seaton leaped to the levers. As he did so, he saw a creature materialize in the air of the vessel and fall to the floor with a crash as he threw on the power. It was a frightful thing, like nothing ever before seen upon any world; with great teeth, long, sharp claws, and an automatic pistol clutched firmly in a human hand. Forced flat by the terrific acceleration of the vessel, it was unable to lift either itself or the weapon, and lay helpless.

"We take one trick, anyway!" blazed Seaton, as he threw on the power of the attractor and diffused its force into a screen over the party, so that the enemy could not materialize in the air above them and crush them by mere weight. "As pure mental force, you're entirely out of my class, but when you come down to matter, which I can understand, I'll give you a run for your money until my angles catch fire."

"That is a childish defiance. It speaks well for your courage, but ill for your intelligence," the animal said, and vanished.

A moment later Seaton's hair almost stood on end as he saw an automatic pistol appear upon the board directly in front of him, clamped to it by bands of steel. Paralyzed by this unlooked-for demonstration of the mastery of mind over matter, unable to move a muscle, he lay helpless, staring at the engine of death in front of him. Although the whole proceeding occupied only a fraction of a second, it seemed to Seaton as though he watched the weapon for hours. As the sleeve drew back, cocking the pistol and throwing a cartridge into the chamber, the trigger moved, and the hammer descended to speed on its way the bullet which was to blot out his life. There was a sharp click as the hammer fell-Seaton was surprised to find himself still alive until a voice spoke, apparently from the muzzle of the pistol, with the harsh sound of a metallic diaphragm.

"I was almost certain that it wouldn't explode," the stranger said, chattily. "You see, I haven't derived that formula yet, so I couldn't make a real explosive. I could of course, materialize beside you, under your protective screen, and crush you in a vise. I could materialize as a man of metal, able to stand up under this acceleration, and do you to death. I could even, by a sufficient expenditure of mental energy, materialize a planet around your ship and crush it. However, these crude methods are distasteful in the extreme, especially since you have already given me some slight and unexpected mental exercise. In return, I shall give you one chance for your lives. I cannot dematerialize either you or your vessel until I work out the formula for your peculiar atomic structure. If I can derive the formula before you reach the boundaries of my home-space, beyond which I cannot go, I shall let you go free. Deriving the formula will be a neat little problem. It should be fairly easy, as it involves only a simple integration in ninety-seven dimensions."

Silence ensued, and Seaton advanced his lever to the limit of his ability to retain consciousness. Almost overcome by the horror of their position, in an agony of suspense, expecting every instant to be hurled into nothingness, he battled on, with no thought of yielding, even in the face of those overwhelming mental odds.

"You can't do it, old top," he thought savagely, concentrating all the power of his highly-trained mind against the intellectual monster. "You can't dematerialize us, and you can't integrate above ninety-five dimensions to save your neck. You can't do it-you're slipping-you're all balled up right now!"

For more than an hour the silent battle raged, during which time the Skylark flew millions upon millions of miles toward Earth. Finally the stranger spoke again.

"You three win," it said abruptly. In answer to the unspoken surprise of all three men it went on: "Yes, all three of you got the same idea and Crane even forced his body to retain consciousness to fight me. Your efforts were very feeble, of course, but were enough to interrupt my calculations at a delicate stage, every time. You are a low form of life, undoubtedly, but with more mentality than I supposed at first. I could get that formula, of course, in spite of you, if I had time, but we are rapidly approaching the limits of my territory, outside of which even I could not think my way back. That is one thing in which your mechanical devices are superior to anything my own race developed before we became pure intellectuals. They point the way back to your Earth, which is so far away that even my mentality cannot grasp the meaning of the distance. I can understand the Earth, can visualize it from your minds, but I cannot project myself any nearer to it than we are at present. Before I leave you, I will say that you have conferred a real favor upon me-you have given me something to think about for thousands of cycles to come. Good-bye."

Assured that their visitor had really gone, Seaton reduced the power to that of gravity and Dorothy soon sat up, Margaret reviving more slowly.

"Dick," said Dorothy solemnly, "did that happen or have I been unconscious and just had a nightmare?"

"It happened, all right," returned her lover, wiping his brow in relief. "See that pistol clamped upon the top of the board? That's a token in remembrance of him."

Dorothy, though she had been only half conscious, had heard the words of the stranger. As she looked at the faces of the men, white and drawn with the mental struggle, she realized what they had gone through, and she drew Seaton down into one of the seats, stroking his hair tenderly.

Margaret went to her room immediately, and as she did not return, Dorothy followed. She came back presently with a look of concern upon her face.

"This life is a little hard on Peggy. I didn't realize how much harder for her it would be than it is for me until I went in there and found her crying. It is much harder for her, of course, since I am with you, Dick, and with you, Martin, whom I know so well. She must feel terribly alone."

"Why should she?" demanded Seaton. "We think she's some game little guy. Why, she's one of the bunch! She must know that!"

"Well, it isn't the same," insisted Dorothy. "You be extra nice to her, Dick. But don't you dare let her know I told you about the tears, or she'd eat me alive!"

Crane said nothing—a not unusual occurrence-but his face grew thoughtful and his manner, when Margaret appeared at mealtime, was more solicitous than usual and more than brotherly in its tenderness.

"I shall be an interstellar diplomat," Dorothy whispered to Seaton as soon as they were alone. "Wasn't that a beautiful bee I put upon Martin?"

Seaton stared at her a moment, then shook her gently before he took her into his arms.

The information, however, did not prevent him from calling to Crane a few minutes later, even though he was still deep in conversation with Margaret. Dorothy gave him an exasperated glance and walked away.

"I sure pulled a boner that time," Seaton muttered as he plucked at his hair ruefully. "It nearly did us.

"Let's test this stuff out and see if it's X, Mart, while DuQuesne's out of the way. If it is X, it's SOME find!"

Seaton cut off a bit of metal with his knife, hammered it into a small piece of copper, and threw the copper into the power-chamber, out of contact with the plating. As the metal received the current the vessel started slightly.

"It *is* X! Mart, we've got enough of this stuff to supply three worlds!"

"Better put it away somewhere," suggested Crane, and after the metal had been removed to Seaton's cabin, the two men again sought a landing-place. Almost in their line of flight they saw a close cluster of stars, each emitting a peculiar greenish light which, in the spectroscope, revealed a blaze of copper lines.

"That's our meat, Martin. We ought to be able to grab some copper in that system, where there's so much of it that it colors their sunlight."

"The copper is undoubtedly there, but it might be too dangerous to get so close to so many suns. We may have trouble getting away."

"Well, our copper's getting horribly low. We've got to find some pretty quick, somewhere, or else walk back home, and there's our best chance. We'll feel our way along. If it gets too strong, we'll beat it."

When they had approached so close that the suns were great stars widely spaced in the heavens, Crane relinquished the controls to Seaton.

"If you will take the lever awhile, Dick, Margaret and I will go downstairs and see if we can locate a planet."

After a glance through the telescope, Crane knew that they were still too far from the group of suns to place any planet with certainty, and began taking notes. His mind was not upon his work, however, but was completely filled with thoughts of the girl at his side. The intervals between his comments became longer and longer until they were standing in silence, both staring with unseeing eyes out into the trackless void. But it was in no sense their usual companionable silence. Crane was fighting back the words he longed to say. This lovely girl was not here of her own accord-she had been torn forcibly from her home and from her friends, and he would not, could not, make her already difficult position even more unpleasant by forcing his attentions upon her. Margaret sensed something unusual and significant in his attitude and held herself tense, her heart beating wildly.

At that moment an asteroid came within range of the Skylark's watchful repeller, and at the lurch of the vessel, as it swung around the obstruction, Margaret would have fallen had not Crane instinctively caught her with one arm. Ordinarily this bit of courtesy would have gone unnoticed by both, as it had happened many times before, but in that heavily-charged atmosphere it took on a new significance. Both blushed hotly, and as their eyes met each saw that which held them spellbound. Slowly, almost as if without volition, Crane put his other arm around her. A wave of deeper crimson swept over her face and she bent her handsome head as her slender body yielded to his arms with no effort to free itself. Finally Crane spoke, his usually even voice faltering.

"Margaret, I hope you will not think this unfair of me...but we have been through so much together that I feel as though we had known each other forever. Until we went through this last experience I had intended to wait-but why should we wait? Life is not lived in years alone, and you know how much I love you, my dearest!" he finished, passionately.

Her arms crept up around his neck, her bowed head lifted, and her eyes looked deep into his as she whispered her answer:

"I think I do...Oh, Martin!"

Presently they made their way back to the engine-room, keeping the singing joy in their hearts inaudible and the kisses fresh upon their lips invisible. They might have kept their secret for a time, had not Seaton promptly asked:

"Well, what did you find, Mart?"

A panicky look appeared upon Crane's self-possessed countenance and Margaret's fair face glowed like a peony.

"*Yes*, what *did* you find?" demanded Dorothy, as she noticed their confusion.

"My future wife," Crane answered steadily.

The two girls rushed into each other's arms and the two men silently gripped hands in a clasp of steel; for each of the four knew that these two unions were not passing fancies, lightly entered into and as lightly cast aside, but were true partnerships which would endure throughout the entire span of life.

A planet was located and the Skylark flew toward it. Discovering that it was apparently situated in the center of the cluster of suns, they hesitated; but finding that there was no dangerous force present, they kept on. As they drew nearer, so that the planet appeared as a very small moon, they saw that the Skylark was in a blaze of green light, and looking out of the windows, Crane counted seventeen great suns, scattered in all directions in the sky! Slowing down abruptly as the planet was approached, Seaton dropped the vessel slowly through the atmosphere, while Crane and DuQuesne tested and analyzed it.

"Pressure, thirty pounds per square inch. Surface gravity as compared to that of the Earth, two-fifths. Air-pressure about double that of the Earth, while a five-pound weight weighs only two pounds. A peculiar combination," reported Crane, and DuQuesne added:

"Analysis about the same as our air except for two and three-tenths per cent of a gas that isn't poisonous and which has a peculiar, fragrant odor. I can't analyze it and think it probably an element unknown upon Earth, or at least very rare."

"It would have to be rare if you don't know what it is," acknowledged Seaton, locking the Skylark in place and going over to smell the strange gas.

Deciding that the air was satisfactory, the pressure inside the vessel was slowly raised to the value of that outside and two doors were opened, to allow the new atmosphere free circulation.

Seaton shut off the power actuating the repeller and let the vessel settle slowly toward the ocean which was directly beneath them—an ocean of a deep, intense, wondrously beautiful blue, which the scientists studied with interest. Arrived at the surface, Seaton moistened a rod in a wave, and tasted it cautiously, then uttered a yell of joy—a yell broken off abruptly as he heard the sound of his own voice. Both girls started as the vibrations set up in the dense air smote upon their eardrums. Seaton moderated his voice and continued:

"I forgot about the air-pressure. But hurrah for this ocean-it's ammoniacal copper sulphate solution! We can sure get all the copper we want, right here, but it would take weeks to evaporate the water and recover the metal. We can probably get it easier ashore. Let's go!"

They started off just above the surface of the ocean toward the nearest continent, which they had observed from the air.

CHAPTER XIII

Nalboon of Mardonale

As the Skylark approached the shore, its occupants heard a rapid succession of heavy detonations, apparently coming from the direction in which they were traveling.

"Wonder what that racket is?" asked Seaton.

"It sounds like big guns," said Crane, and DuQuesne nodded agreement.

"Big guns is right. They're shooting high explosive shells, too, or I never heard any. Even allowing for the density of the air, that kind of noise isn't made by pop-guns."

"Let's go see what's doing," and Seaton started to walk toward one of the windows with his free, swinging stride. Instantly he was a-sprawl, the effort necessary to carry his weight upon the Earth's surface lifting him into the air in a succession of ludicrous hops, but he soon recovered himself and walked normally.

"I forgot this two-fifths gravity stuff," he laughed. "Walk as though we had only a notch of power on and it goes all right. It sure is funny to feel so light when we're so close to the ground."

He closed the doors to keep out a part of the noise and advanced the speed lever a little, so that the vessel tilted sharply under the pull of the almost horizontal bar.

"Go easy," cautioned Crane. "We do not want to get in the way of one of their shells. They may be of a different kind than those we are familiar with."

"Right-easy it is. We'll stay forty miles above them, if necessary."

As the great speed of the ship rapidly lessened the distance, the sound grew heavier and clearer-like one continuous explosion. So closely did one deafening concussion follow another that the ear could not distinguish the separate reports.

"I see them," simultaneously announced Crane, who was seated at one of the forward windows searching the country with his binoculars, and Seaton, who, from the pilot's seat, could see in any direction.

The others hurried to the windows with their glasses and saw an astonishing sight.

"Aerial battleships, eight of 'em!" exclaimed Seaton, "as big as the Idaho. Four of 'em are about the same shape as our battleships. No wings-they act like helicopters."

"Four of them are battleships, right enough, but what about the other four?" asked DuQuesne. "They are not ships or planes or anything else that I ever heard of."

"They are animals," asserted Crane. "Machines never were and never will be built like that."

As the Skylark cautiously approached, it was evident to the watchers that four of the contestants were undoubtedly animals. Here indeed was a new kind of animal, an animal able to fight on even terms with a first-class battleship! Frightful aerial monsters they were. Each had an enormous, torpedo-shaped body, with scores of prodigiously long tentacles like those of a devil-fish and a dozen or more great, soaring wings. Even at that distance they could see the row of protruding eyes along the side of each monstrous body and the terrible, prow-like beaks tearing through the metal of the warships opposing them. They could see, by the reflection of the light from the many suns, that each monster was apparently covered by scales and joints of some transparent armor. That it was real and highly effective armor there could be no doubt, for each battleship bristled with guns of heavy caliber and each gun was vomiting forth a continuous stream of fire. Shells bursting against each of the creatures made one continuous blaze, and the uproar was indescribable-an uninterrupted cataclysm of sound appalling in its intensity.

The battle was brief. Soon all four of the battleships had crumpled to the ground, their crews absorbed by the terrible sucking arms or devoured by the frightful beaks. They did not die in vain-three of the monsters had been blown to atoms by shells which had apparently penetrated their armor. The fourth was pursuing something, which Seaton now saw was a fleet of small airships, which had flown away from the scene of conflict. Swift as they were, the monster covered three feet to their one.

91

"We can't stand for anything like that," cried Seaton, as he threw on the power and the Skylark leaped ahead. "Get ready to bump him off, Mart, when I jerk him away. He acts hard-boiled, so give him a real one-fifty milligrams!"

Sweeping on with awful speed the monster seized the largest and most gaily decorated plane in his hundred-foot tentacles just as the Skylark came within sighting distance. In four practically simultaneous movements Seaton sighted the attractor at the ugly beak, released all its power, pointed the main bar of the Skylark directly upward, and advanced his speed lever. There was a crash of rending metal as the thing was torn loose from the plane and jerked a hundred miles into the air, struggling so savagely in that invisible and incomprehensible grip that the three-thousand-ton mass of the Skylark tossed and pitched like a child's plaything. Those inside her heard the sharp, spiteful crack of the machine-gun, and an instant later they heard a report that paralyzed their senses, even inside the vessel and in the thin air of their enormous elevation, as the largest X-plosive bullet prepared by the inventors struck full upon the side of the hideous body. There was no smoke, no gas or vapor of any kind-only a huge volume of intolerable flame as the energy stored within the atoms of copper, instantaneously liberated, heated to incandescence and beyond all the atmosphere within a radius of hundreds of feet. The monster disappeared utterly, and Seaton, with unerring hand, reversed the bar and darted back down toward the fleet of airships. He reached them in time to focus the attractor upon the wrecked and helpless plane in the middle of its five-thousand-foot fall and lowered it gently to the ground, surrounded by the fleet.

The Skylark landed easily beside the wrecked machine, and the wanderers saw that their vessel was completely surrounded by a crowd of people-men and women identical in form and feature with themselves. They were a superbly molded race, the men fully as large as Seaton and DuQuesne; the women, while smaller than the men, were noticeably taller than the two women in the car. The men wore broad collars of metal, numerous metallic ornaments, and heavily-jeweled leather belts and shoulder-straps which were hung with weapons of peculiar patterns. The women carried no weapons, but were even more highly decorated than were the men—each slender, perfectly-formed body scintillated with the brilliance of hundreds of strange gems, flashing points of fire. Jeweled bands of metal and leather restrained their carefully-groomed hair; jeweled collars encircled their throats; jeweled belts, jeweled bracelets, jeweled anklets, each added its quota of brilliance to the glittering whole. The strangers wore no clothing, and their smooth skins shone a dark, livid, utterly indescribable color in the peculiar, unearthly, yellowish-bluish-green glare of the light. Green their skins undoubtedly were, but not any shade of green visible in the Earthly spectrum. The "whites" of their eyes were a light yellowish-green. The heavy hair of the women and the close-cropped locks of the men were green as well—a green so dark as to be almost black, as were also their eyes.

"Well, what d'you know about that?" pondered Seaton, dazedly. "They're human, right enough, but ye gods, what a color!"

"It is hard to tell how much of that color is real, and how much of it is due to this light," answered Crane. "Wait until you get outside, away from our daylight lamps, and you will probably look like a Chinese puzzle. As to the form, it is logical to suppose that wherever conditions are similar to those upon the Earth, and the age is anywhere nearly the same, development would be along the same lines as with us."

"That's right, too. Dottie, your hair will sure look gorgeous in this light. Let's go out and give the natives a treat!"

"I wouldn't look like that for a million dollars!" retorted Dorothy, "and if I'm going to look like that I won't get out of the ship, so there!"

"Cheer up, Dottie, you won't look like that. Your hair will be black in this light."

"Then what color will mine be?" asked Margaret.

Seaton glanced at her black hair.

"Probably a very dark and beautiful green," he grinned, his gray eyes sparkling, "but we'll have to wait and see. Friends and fellow-countrymen, I've got a hunch that this is going to be SOME visit. How about it, shall we go ahead with it?"

Dorothy went up to him, her face bright with eagerness.

"Oh, what a lark! Let's go!"

Even in DuQuesne's cold presence, Margaret's eyes sought those of her lover, and his sleeve, barely touching her arm, was enough to send a dancing thrill along it.

"Onward, men of Earth!" she cried, and Seaton, stepping up to the window, rapped sharply upon the glass with the butt of his pistol and raised both hands high above his head in the universal sign of peace. In response, a man of Herculean mold, so splendidly decorated that his harness was one blazing mass of jewels, waved his arm and shouted a command. The crowd promptly fell back, leaving a clear space of several hundred yards. The man, evidently one in high command, unbuckled his harness, dropping every weapon, and advanced toward the Skylark, both arms upraised in Seaton's gesture.

Seaton went to the door and started to open it.

"Better talk to him from inside," cautioned Crane.

"I don't think so, Mart. He's peaceable, and I've got my gun in my pocket. Since he doesn't know what clothes are he'll think I'm unarmed, which is as it should be; and if he shows fight, it won't take more than a week for me to get into action."

"All right, go on. DuQuesne and I will come along."

"Absolutely not. He's alone, so I've got to be. I notice that some of his men are covering us, though. You might do the same for them, with a couple of the machine guns."

Seaton stepped out of the car and went to meet the stranger. When they had approached to within a few feet of each other the stranger stopped. He flexed his left arm smartly, so that the finger-tips touched his left ear, and smiled broadly, exposing a row of splendid, shining, green teeth. Then he spoke, a meaningless jumble of sounds. His voice, though light and thin, nevertheless seemed to be of powerful timbre.

Seaton smiled in return and saluted.

"Hello, Chief. I get your idea all right, and we're glad you're peaceable, but your language doesn't mean a thing in my young life."

The Chief tapped himself upon the chest, saying distinctly and impressively:

"Nalboon."

"Nalboon," repeated Seaton, and added, pointing to himself:

"Seaton."

"See Tin," answered the stranger, and again indicating himself, "Domak gok Mardonale."

"That must be his title," thought Seaton rapidly. "Have to give myself one, I guess."

"Boss of the Road," he replied, drawing himself up with pride.

The introduction made, Nalboon pointed to the wrecked plane, inclined his head in thanks, and turned to his people with one arm upraised, shouting an order in which Seaton could distinguish something that sounded like "See Tin, Bass uvvy Rood." Instantly every right arm in the assemblage was aloft, that of each man bearing a weapon, while the left arms snapped into the peculiar salute and a mighty cry arose as all repeated the name and title of the distinguished visitor.

Seaton turned to the Skylark, motioning to Crane to open the door.

"Bring out one of those big four-color signal rockets, Mart!" he called. "They're giving us a royal reception-let's acknowledge it right."

The party appeared, Crane carrying the huge rocket with an air of deference. As they approached, Seaton shrugged one shoulder and his cigarette-case appeared in his hand. Nalboon started, and in spite of his utmost efforts at self-control, he glanced at it in surprise. The case flew open and Seaton, taking a cigarette, extended the case.

"Smoke?" he asked affably. The other took one, but showed plainly that he had no idea of the use to which it was to be put. This astonishment of the stranger at a simple sleight-of-hand

93

feat and his apparent ignorance of tobacco emboldened Seaton. Reaching into his mouth, he pulled out a flaming match, at which Nalboon started violently. While all the natives watched in amazement, Seaton lighted the cigarette, and after half consuming it in two long inhalations, he apparently swallowed the remainder, only to bring it to light again. Having smoked it, he apparently swallowed the butt, with evident relish.

"They don't know anything about matches or smoking," he said, turning to Crane. "This rocket will tie them up in a knot. Step back, everybody."

He bowed deeply to Nalboon, pulling a lighted match from his ear as he did so, and lighted the fuse. There was a roar, a shower of sparks, a blaze of colored fire as the great rocket flew upward; but to Seaton's surprise, Nalboon took it quite as a matter of course, saluting as an acknowledgment of the courtesy.

Seaton motioned to his party to approach, and turned to Crane.

"Better not, Dick. Let him think that you are the king of everything in sight."

"Not on your life. If he is one king, we are two," and he introduced Crane, with great ceremony, to the Domak as the "Boss of the Skylark," at which the salute by his people was repeated.

Nalboon then shouted an order and a company of soldiers led by an officer came toward them, surrounding a small group of people, apparently prisoners. These captives, seven men and seven women, were much lighter in color than the rest of the gathering, having skins of a ghastly, pale shade, practically the same color as the whites of their eyes. In other bodily aspects they were the same as their captors in appearance, save that they were entirely naked except for the jeweled metal collars worn by all and a massive metal belt worn by one man. They walked with a proud and lofty carriage, scorn for their captors in every step.

Nalboon barked an order to the prisoners. They stared in defiance, motionless, until the man wearing the belt who had studied Seaton closely, spoke a few words in a low tone, when they all prostrated themselves. Nalboon then waved his hand, giving the whole group to Seaton as slaves. Seaton, with no sign of his surprise, thanked the giver and motioned his slaves to rise. They obeyed and placed themselves behind the party-two men and two women behind Seaton and the same number behind Crane; one man and one woman behind each of the others.

Seaton then tried to make Nalboon understand that they wanted copper, pointing to his anklet, the only copper in sight. The chief instantly removed the trinket and handed it to Seaton; who, knowing by the gasp of surprise of the guard that it was some powerful symbol, returned it with profuse apologies. After trying in vain to make the other understand what he wanted, he led him into the Skylark and showed him the remnant of the power-bar. He showed him its original size and indicated the desired number by counting to sixteen upon his fingers. Nalboon nodded his comprehension and going outside, pointed upward toward the largest of the eleven suns visible, motioning its rising and setting, four times.

He then invited the visitors, in unmistakable sign language, to accompany him as guests of honor, but Seaton refused.

"Lead on, MacDuff, we follow," he replied, explaining his meaning by signs as they turned to enter the vessel. The slaves followed closely until Crane remonstrated.

"We don't want them aboard, do we, Dick? There are too many of them."

"All right," Seaton replied, and waved them away. As they stepped back the guard seized the nearest, a woman, and forced her to her knees; while a man, adorned with a necklace of green human teeth and carrying a shining broadsword, prepared to decapitate her.

"We must take them with us, I see," said Crane, as he brushed the guards aside. Followed by the slaves, the party entered the Skylark, and the dark green people embarked in their airplanes and helicopters.

Nalboon rode in a large and gaily-decorated plane, which led the fleet at its full speed of six hundred miles an hour, the Skylark taking a placing a few hundred yards above the flagship.

"I don't get these folks at all, Mart," said Seaton, after a moment's silence. "They have machines far ahead of anything we have on Earth and big guns that shoot as fast as machine-guns, and yet are scared to death at a little simple sleight-of-hand. They don't seem to understand matches at all, and yet treat fire-works as an every-day occurrence."

"We will have to wait until we know them better," replied Crane, and DuQuesne added:

"From what I have seen, their power seems to be all electrical. Perhaps they aren't up with us in chemistry, even though they are ahead of us in mechanics?"

Flying above a broad, but rapid and turbulent stream, the fleet soon neared a large city, and the visitors from Earth gazed with interest at this metropolis of the unknown world. The buildings were all the same height, flat-roofed, and arranged in squares very much as our cities are arranged. There were no streets, the spaces between the buildings being park-like areas, evidently laid out for recreation, amusement, and sport. There was no need for streets; all traffic was in the air. The air seemed full of flying vehicles, darting in all directions, but it was soon evident that there was exact order in the apparent confusion, each class of vessel and each direction of traffic having its own level. Eagerly the three men studied the craft, which ranged in size from one-man helicopters, little more than single chairs flying about in the air, up to tremendous multiplane freighters, capable of carrying thousands of tons.

Flying high over the city to avoid its congested air-lanes, the fleet descended toward an immense building just outside the city proper, and all landed upon its roof save the flagship, which led the Skylark to a landing-dock nearby—a massive pile of metal and stone, upon which Nalboon and his retinue stood to welcome the guests. After Seaton had anchored the vessel immovably by means of the attractor, the party disembarked, Seaton remarking with a grin:

"Don't be surprised at anything I do, folks. I'm a walking storehouse of junk of all kinds, so that if occasion arises I can put on a real exhibition."

As they turned toward their host, a soldier, in his eagerness to see the strangers, jostled another. Without a word two keen swords flew from their scabbards and a duel to the death ensued. The visitors stared in amazement, but no one else paid any attention to the combat, which was soon over; the victor turning away from the body of his opponent and resuming his place without creating a ripple of interest.

Nalboon led the way into an elevator, which dropped rapidly to the ground-floor level. Massive gates were thrown open, and through ranks of people prostrate upon their faces the party went out into the palace grounds of the Domak, or Emperor, of the great nation of Mardonale.

Never before had Earthly eyes rested upon such scenes of splendor. Every color and gradation of their peculiar spectrum was present, in solid, liquid, and gas. The carefully-tended trees were all colors of the rainbow, as were the grasses and flowers along the walks. The fountains played streams of many and constantly-changing hues, and even the air was tinted and perfumed, swirling through metal arches in billows of ever-varying colors and scents. Colors and combinations of colors impossible to describe were upon every hand, fantastically beautiful in that peculiar, livid light. Diamonds and rubies, their colors so distorted by the green radiance as to be almost unrecognizable; emeralds glowing with an intense green impossible in earthly light, together with strange gems peculiar to this strange world, sparkled and flashed from railings, statues, and pedestals throughout the ground.

"Isn't this gorgeous, Dick?" whispered Dorothy. "But what do I look like? I wish I had a mirror-you look simply awful. Do I look like you do?"

"Not being able to see myself, I can't say, but I imagine you do. You look as you would under a county-fair photographer's mercury-vapor arc lamps, only worse. The colors can't be described. You might as well try to describe cerise to a man born blind as to try to express these colors in English, but as near as I can come to it, your eyes are a dark sort of purplish green, with the whites of your eyes and your teeth a kind of plush green. Your skin is a pale yellowish green, except for the pink of your cheeks, which is a kind of black, with orange and green mixed up in it. Your lips are black, and your hair is a funny kind of color, halfway between black and old rose, with a little green and...."

"Heavens, Dick, stop! That's enough!" choked Dorothy. "We all look like hobgoblins. We're even worse than the natives."

"Sure we are. They were born here and are acclimated to it-we are strangers and aren't. I would like to see what one of these people would look like in Washington."

Nalboon led them into the palace proper and into a great dining hall, where a table was already prepared for the entire party. This room was splendidly decorated with jewels, its many windows being simply masses of gems. The walls were hung with a cloth resembling silk, which fell to the floor in shimmering waves of color.

Woodwork there was none. Doors, panels, tables, and chairs were cunningly wrought of various metals. Seaton and DuQuesne could recognize a few of them, but for the most part they were unknown upon the Earth; and were, like the jewels and vegetation of this strange world, of many and various peculiar colors. A closer inspection of one of the marvelous tapestries showed that it also was of metal, its threads numbering thousands to the inch. Woven of many different metals, of vivid but harmonious colors in a strange and intricate design, it seemed to writhe as its colors changed with every variation in the color of the light; which, pouring from concealed sources, was reflected by the highly-polished metal and innumerable jewels of the lofty, domed ceiling.

"Oh ... isn't this too perfectly gorgeous?" breathed Dorothy. "I'd give anything for a dress made out of that stuff, Dick. Cloth-of-gold is common by comparison!"

"Would you dare wear it, Dottie?" asked Margaret.

"*Would* I? I'd wear it in a minute if I could only get it. It would take Washington by storm!"

"I'll try to get a piece of it, then," smiled Seaton. "I'll see about it while we are getting the copper."

"We'd better be careful in choosing what we eat here, Seaton," suggested DuQuesne, as the Domak himself led them to the table.

"We sure had. With a copper ocean and green teeth, I shouldn't be surprised if copper, arsenic, and other such trifles formed a regular part of their diet."

"The girls and I will wait for you two chemists to approve every dish before we try it, then," said Crane.

Nalboon placed his guests, the light-skinned slaves standing at attention behind them, and numerous servants, carrying great trays, appeared. The servants were intermediate in color between the light and the dark races, with dull, unintelligent faces, but quick and deft in their movements.

The first course —a thin, light wine, served in metal goblets-was approved by the chemists, and the dinner was brought on. There were mighty joints of various kinds of meat; birds and fish, both raw and cooked in many ways; green, pink, purple, and white vegetables and fruits. The majordomo held each dish up to Seaton for inspection, the latter waving away the fish and the darkest green foods, but approving the others. Heaping plates, or rather metal trays, of food were placed before the diners, and the attendants behind their chairs handed them peculiar implements-knives with razor edges, needle-pointed stilettoes instead of forks, and wide, flexible spatulas, which evidently were to serve the purposes of both forks and spoons.

"I simply can't eat with these things!" exclaimed Dorothy in dismay, "and I don't like to drink soup out of a can, so there!"

"That's where my lumberjack training comes in handy," grinned Seaton. "With this spatula I can eat faster than I could with two forks. What do you want, girls, forks or spoons, or both?"

"Both, please."

Seaton reached out over the table, seizing forks and spoons from the air and passing them to the others, while the natives stared in surprise. The Domak took a bowl filled with brilliant blue crystals from the major-domo, sprinkled his food liberally with the substance, and passed it to Seaton, who looked at the crystals attentively.

"Copper sulphate," he said to Crane. "It's a good thing they add it at the table instead of cooking with it, or we'd be out of luck."

Waving the copper sulphate away, he again reached out, this time producing a pair of small salt-and pepper-shakers, which he passed to the Domak after he had seasoned the dishes before him. Nalboon tasted the pepper cautiously and smiled in delight, half-emptying the shaker upon his plate. He then sprinkled a few grains of salt into his palm, stared at them with an expression of doubting amazement, and after a few rapid sentences poured them into a dish held by an officer who had sprung to his side. The officer studied them closely, then carefully washed his chief's hand. Nalboon turned to Seaton, plainly asking for the salt-cellar.

"Sure, old top. Keep 'em both, there's lots more where those came from," as he produced several more sets in the same mysterious way and handed them to Crane, who in turn passed them to the others.

The meal progressed merrily, with much conversation in the sign-language between the two parties. It was evident that Nalboon, usually stern and reticent, was in an unusually pleasant mood. The viands, though of peculiar flavor, were in the main pleasing to the palates of the Earthly visitors.

"This fruit salad, or whatever it is, is divine," remarked Dorothy, after an experimental bite. "May we eat as much as we like, or had we better just eat a little?"

"Go as far as you like," returned her lover. "I wouldn't recommend it, as a steady diet, as I imagine everything contains copper and other heavy metals in noticeable amounts, and probably considerable arsenic, but for a few days it can't very well hurt us much."

After the meal, Nalboon bade them a ceremonious farewell, and they were escorted to a series of five connecting rooms by the royal usher, escorted by an entire company of soldiers, who mounted guard outside the doors. Gathered in one room, they discussed sleeping arrangements. The girls insisted that they would sleep together, and that the men should occupy the rooms at either side. As the girls turned away, the four slaves followed.

"We don't want these people, and I can't make them go away!" cried Dorothy.

"I don't want them, either," replied Seaton, "but if we chase them out they'll get their heads chopped off. You girls take the women and we'll take the men."

Seaton waved all the women into the girls' room, but they paused irresolutely. One of them went up to the man wearing the metal belt, evidently their leader, and spoke to him rapidly as she threw her arms around his neck. He shook his head, motioning toward Seaton several times as he spoke to her reassuringly. With his arm about her tenderly, he led her to the door, the other women following. Crane and DuQuesne having gone to their rooms with their attendants, the man wearing the belt drew the blinds and turned to assist Seaton in taking off his clothes.

"I never had a valet before, but go as far as you like if it pleases you," remarked Seaton, as he began to throw off his clothes. A multitude of small articles fell from their hiding-places in his garments as he removed them. Almost stripped, Seaton stretched vigorously, the muscles writhing and rippling in great ridges under the satin skin of his broad back and mighty arms and shoulders as he filled his capacious lungs and twisted about, working off the stiffness caused by the days of comparative confinement.

The four slaves stared in open-mouthed astonishment at this display of muscular development and conversed among themselves as they gathered up Seaton's discarded clothing. Their leader picked up a salt-shaker, a couple of silver knives and forks, and some other articles, and turned to Seaton, apparently asking permission to do something with them. Seaton nodded assent carelessly and turned to his bed. As he did so, he heard a slight clank of arms in the hall as the guard was changed, and lifting the blind a trifle he saw that guards were stationed outside as well. As he went to bed, he wondered whether the guards were guards of honor or jailers; whether he and his party were honored guests or prisoners.

Three of the slaves, at a word from their chief, threw themselves upon the floor and slept, but he himself did not rest. Opening the apparently solid metal belt, he took out a great number of small tools, many tiny instruments, and several spools of insulated wire. He then took the articles Seaton had given him, taking great pains not to spill a single grain of salt, and set to work. Hour after hour he labored, a strange, exceedingly complex instrument taking form under his clever fingers.

CHAPTER XIV

Nalboon Unmasked

After a long, sound sleep, Seaton awoke and sprang out of bed. No sooner had he started to shave, however, than one of the slaves touched his arm, motioning him into a reclining chair and showing him a keen blade, long and slightly curved. Seaton lay down and the slave shaved him with a rapidity and smoothness he had never before experienced, so wonderfully sharp was the peculiar razor. After Seaton had dressed, the barber started to shave the chief slave, without any preliminary treatment save rubbing his face with a perfumed oil.

"Hold on a minute," interjected Seaton, who was watching the process with interest, "here's something that helps a lot." He lathered the face with his brush and the man looked up in surprised pleasure as his stiff beard was swept away without a sound.

Seaton called to the others and soon the party was assembled in his room, all dressed very lightly, because of the unrelieved and unvarying heat, which was constant at one hundred degrees. A gong sounded, and one of the slaves opened the door, ushering in a party of servants bearing a table, ready set. During the meal, Seaton was greatly surprised at hearing Dorothy carrying on a halting conversation, with one of the women standing behind her.

"I knew that you were a language shark, Dottie, with five or six different ones to your credit, but I didn't suppose you could learn to talk this stuff in one day."

"I can't," she replied, "but I've picked up a few words of it. I can understand very little of what they are trying to tell me."

The woman spoke rapidly to the man standing behind Seaton, and as soon as the table had been carried away, he asked permission to speak to Dorothy. Fairly running across to her, he made a slight obeisance and in eager tones poured forth such a stream of language that she held up her hand to silence him.

"Go slower, please," she said, and added a couple of words in his own tongue.

There ensued a strange dialogue, with many repetitions and much use of signs. She turned to Seaton, with a puzzled look.

"I can't make out all he says, Dick, but he wants you to take him into another room of the palace here, to get back something or other that they took from him when they captured him. He can't go alone—I think he says he will be killed if he goes anywhere without you. And he says that when you get there, you must be sure not to let the guards come inside."

"All right, let's go!" and Seaton motioned the man to precede him. As Seaton started for the door, Dorothy fell into step beside him.

"Better stay back, Dottie, I'll be back in a minute," he said at the door.

"I will not stay back. Wherever you go, I go," she replied in a voice inaudible to the others. "I simply will not stay away from you a single minute that I don't have to."

"All right, little girl," he replied in the same tone. "I don't want to be away from you, either, and I don't think that we're in any danger here."

Preceded by the chief slave and followed by half a dozen others, they went out into the hall. No opposition was made to their progress, but a full half-company of armed guards fell in around them as an escort, regarding Seaton with looks composed of equal parts of reverence and fear. The slave led the way rapidly to a room in a distant wing of the palace and opened the door. As Seaton stepped in, he saw that it was evidently an audience-chamber or court-room, and that it was now entirely empty. As the guard approached the door, Seaton waved them back. All retreated across the hall except the officer in charge, who refused to move. Seaton, the personification of offended dignity, first stared at the offender, who returned the stare, and stepped up to him insolently, then pushed him back roughly, forgetting that his strength, great upon Earth, would be gigantic upon this smaller world. The officer spun across the corridor, knocking down three of his men in his flight. Picking himself up, he drew his sword and rushed, while his men fled in panic to the extreme end of the corridor. Seaton did not wait for him, but in one bound leaped half-way across the intervening space to meet him. With the vastly superior agility of his earthly muscles he dodged the falling broadsword and drove his left fist full against the fellow's chin, with all the force of his mighty arm and all the momentum of his rapidly moving body behind the blow. The crack of breaking bones was distinctly audible as the officer's head snapped back. The force of the blow lifted him high into the air, and after turning a complete somersault, he brought up with a crash against the opposite wall, dropping to the floor stone dead. As several of his men, braver than the others, lifted their peculiar rifles, Seaton drew and fired in one incredibly swift motion, the X-plosive bullet obliterating the entire group of men and demolishing that end of the palace.

In the meantime the slave had taken several pieces of apparatus from a cabinet in the room and had placed them in his belt. Stopping only to observe for a few moments a small instrument which he clamped upon the head of the dead man, he rapidly led the way back to the room they had left and set to work upon the instrument he had constructed while the others had been asleep. He connected it, in an intricate system of wiring, with the pieces of apparatus he had just recovered.

"That's a complex job of wiring," said DuQuesne admiringly. "I've seen several intricate pieces of apparatus myself, but he has so many circuits there that I'm lost. It would take an hour to figure out the lines and connections alone."

Straightening abruptly, the slave clamped several electrodes upon his temples and motioned to Seaton and the others, speaking to Dorothy as he did so.

"He wants us to let him put those things on our heads," she translated. "Shall we let him, Dick?"

"Yes," he replied without hesitation. "I've got a real hunch that he's our friend, and I'm not sure of Nalboon. He doesn't act right."

"I think so, too," agreed the girl, and Crane added:

"I can't say that I relish the idea, but since I know that you are a good poker player, Dick, I am willing to follow your hunch. How about you, DuQuesne?"

"Not I," declared that worthy, emphatically. "Nobody wires me up to anything I can't understand, and that machine is too deep for me."

Margaret elected to follow Crane's example, and, impressed by the need for haste evident in the slave's bearing, the four walked up to the machine without further talk. The electrodes were clamped into place quickly and the slave pressed a lever. Instantly the four visitors felt that they had a complete understanding of the languages and customs of both Mardonale, the nation in which they now were, and of Kondal, to which nation the slaves belonged, the only two civilized nations upon Osnome. While the look of amazement at this method of receiving instruction was still upon their faces, the slave-or rather, as they now knew him, Dunark, the Kofedix or Crown Prince of the great nation of Kondal-began to disconnect the wires. He cut out the wires leading to the two girls and to Crane, and was reaching for Seaton's, when there was a blinding flash, a crackling sound, the heavy smoke of burning metal and insulation, and both Dunark and Seaton fell to the floor.

Before Crane could reach them, however, they were upon their feet and the stranger said in his own tongue, now understood by every one but DuQuesne:

"This machine is a mechanical educator, a thing entirely new, in our world at least. Although I have been working on it for a long time, it is still in a very crude form. I did not like to use it in its present state of development, but it was necessary in order to warn you of what Nalboon is going to do to you, and to convince you that the best way of saving your lives would save our lives as well. The machine worked perfectly until something, I don't know what, went wrong. Instead of stopping, as it should have done, at teaching your party to speak our languages, it short-circuited us two completely, so that every convolution in each of our brains has been imprinted upon the brain of the other. It was the sudden formation of all the new convolutions that rendered us unconscious. I can only apologize for the break-down, and assure you that my intentions were of the best."

"You needn't apologize," returned Seaton. "That was a wonderful performance, and we're both gainers, anyway, aren't we? It has taken us all our lives to learn what little we know, and now we each have the benefit of two lifetimes, spent upon different worlds! I must admit, though, that I have a whole lot of knowledge that I don't know how to use."

"I am glad you take it that way," returned the other warmly, "for I am infinitely the better off for the exchange. The knowledge I imparted was nothing, compared to that which I received. But time presses—I must tell you our situation. I am, as you now know, the Kofedix of Kondal. The other thirteen are fedo and fediro, or, as you would say, princes and princesses of the same nation. We were captured by one of Nalboon's raiding parties while upon a hunting trip, being overcome by some new, stupefying gas, so that we could not kill ourselves. As you know, Kondal and Mardonale have been at war for over ten thousand karkamo-something more than six thousand years of your time. The war between us is one of utter extermination. Captives are never exchanged and only once during an ordinary lifetime does one ever escape. Our attendants were killed immediately. We were being taken to furnish sport for Nalboon's party by being fed to one of his captive kolono-animals something like your earthly devilfish-when the escort of battleships was overcome by those four karlono, the animals you saw, and one of them seized Nalboon's plane, in which we were prisoners. You killed the karlon, saving our lives as well as those of Nalboon and his party.

"Having saved his life, you and your party should be honored guests of the most honored kind, and I venture to say that you would be so regarded in any other nation of the universe. But Nalboon, the Domak—a title equivalent to your word 'Emperor' and our word 'Karfedix'—of Mardonale, is utterly without either honor or conscience, as are all Mardonalians. At first he was afraid of you, as were we all. We thought you visitors from a planet of our fifteenth sun, which is now at its nearest possible approach to us. After your display of superhuman power and ability, we expected instant annihilation. However, after seeing the Skylark as a machine, discovering that you are short of power, and finding that you are gentle instead of bloodthirsty by nature, Nalboon lost his fear of you and resolved to rob you of your vessel, with its wonderful secrets of power. Though we are so ignorant of chemistry that I cannot understand the thousandth part of what I just learned from you, we are a race of mechanics and have developed machines of many kinds to a high state of efficiency, including electrical machines of all kinds. In fact, electricity, generated by our great waterfalls, is our only power. No scientist upon Osnome has ever had an inkling that intra-atomic energy exists. Nalboon cannot understand the power, but he solved the means of liberating it at a glance-and that glance sealed your death-warrants. With the Skylark, he could conquer Kondal, and to assure the downfall of my nation he would do anything.

"Also, he or any other Osnomian scientist would go to any lengths whatever-would challenge the great First Cause itself-to secure even one of those little bottles of the chemical you call 'salt.' It is far and away the scarcest and most precious substance in the world. It is so rare that those bottles you produced at the table held more than the total amount previously known to exist upon Osnome. We have great abundance of all the heavy metals, but the lighter metals are rare. Sodium and chlorin are the rarest of all known elements. Its immense value is due, not to its rarity, but to the fact that it is an indispensable component of the controlling instruments of our wireless power stations and that it is used as a catalyst in the manufacture of our hardest metals.

"For these reasons, you understand why Nalboon does not intend to let you escape and why he intends that this kokam (our equivalent of a day) shall be your last. About the second or third kam (hour) of the sleeping period he intends to break into the Skylark, learn its control, and secure the salt you undoubtedly have in the vessel. Then my party and myself will be thrown to the kolon. You and your party will be killed and your bodies smelted to recover the salt that is in them. This is the warning I had to give you. Its urgency explains the use of my untried mechanical educator; the hope that my party could escape with yours, in your vessel, explains why you saw me, the Kofedix of Kondal, prostrate myself before that arch-fiend Nalboon."

"How do you, a captive prince of another nation, know these things?" asked Crane, doubtfully.

"I read Nalboon's ideas from the brain of that officer whom the Karfedix Seaton killed. He was a ladex of the guards-an officer of about the same rank as one of your colonels. He was high in Nalboon's favor, and he was to have been in charge of the work of breaking into the Skylark and killing us all. Let me caution you now; do not let any Mardonalian touch our hands with a wire, for if you do, your thoughts will be recorded and the secrets of the Skylark and your many other mysterious things, such as smoking, matches, and magic feats, will be secrets no longer."

"Thanks for the information," responded Seaton, "but I want to correct your title for me. I'm no Karfedix-merely a plain citizen."

"In one way I see that that is true," replied the Kofedix with a puzzled look. "I cannot understand your government at all-but the inventor of the Skylark must certainly rank as a Karfedix."

As he spoke, a smile of understanding passed over his face and he continued:

"I see. Your title is Doctor of Philosophy, which must mean that you are the Karfedix of Knowledge of the Earth."

"No, no. You're way off. I'm...."

"Certainly Seaton is the Karfedix of Knowledge," broke in DuQuesne. "Let it go at that, anyway, whatever it means. The thing to do now is to figure a way out of this."

"You chirped it then, Blackie. Dunark, you know this country better than we do; what do you suggest?"

"I suggest that you take my party into the Skylark and escape from Mardonale as soon as possible. I can pilot you to Kondalek, the capital city of our nation. There, I can assure you, you will be welcomed as you deserve. My father, the Karfedix, will treat you as a Karfedix should be treated. As far as I am concerned, nothing I can ever do will lighten the burden of my indebtedness to you, but I promise you all the copper you want, and anything else you may desire that is within the power of man to give you."

Seaton thought deeply a moment, then shook Dunark's hand vigorously.

"That suits me, Kofedix," he said warmly. "I thought from the first that you were our friend. Shall we make for the Skylark right now, or wait a while?"

"We had better wait until after the second meal," the prince replied. "We have no armor, and no way of making any. We would be helpless against the bullets of any except a group small enough so that you could kill them all before they could fire. The kam after the second meal is devoted to strolling about the grounds, so that our visiting the Skylark would look perfectly natural. As the guard is very lax at that time, it is the best time for the attempt."

"But how about my killing his company of guards and blowing up one wing of his palace? Won't he have something to say about that?"

"I don't know," replied the Kofedix doubtfully. "It depends upon whether his fear of you or his anger is the greater. He should pay his call of state here in your apartment in a short time, as it is the inviolable rule of Osnome, that any visitor shall receive a call of state from one of his own rank before leaving his apartment for the first time. His actions may give you some idea as to his feelings, though he is an accomplished diplomat and may conceal his real feelings entirely. But let me caution you not to be modest or soft-spoken. He will mistake softness for fear."

"All right," grinned Seaton. "In that case I won't wait to try to find out what he thinks. If he shows any signs of hostility at all, I'll open up on him."

"Well," remarked Crane, calmly, "if we have some time to spare, we may as well wait comfortably instead of standing in the middle of the room. I, for one, have a lot of questions to ask about this new world."

Acting upon this suggestion, the party seated themselves upon comfortable divans, and Dunark rapidly dismantled the machine he had constructed. The captives remained standing, always behind the visitors until Seaton remonstrated.

"Please sit down, everybody. There's no need of keeping up this farce of your being slaves as long as we're alone, is there, Dunark?"

"No, but at the first sound of the gong announcing a visitor we must be in our places. Now that we are all comfortable and waiting, I will introduce my party to yours.

"Fellow Kondalians, greet the Karfedo Seaton and Crane," he began, his tongue fumbling over the strange names, "of a distant world, the Earth, and the two noble ladies, Miss Vaneman and Miss Spencer, soon to be their Karfediro.

"Guests from Earth, allow me to present to you the Kofedir Sitar, the only one of my wives who accompanied me upon our ill-fated hunting expedition."

Then, still ignoring DuQuesne as a captive, he introduced the other Kondolians in turn as his brothers, sisters, cousins, nieces, and nephews-all members of the great ruling house of Kondal.

"Now," he concluded, "after I have a word with you in private, Doctor Seaton, I will be glad to give the others all the information in my power."

He led Seaton out of earshot of the others and said in a low voice:

"It is no part of Nalboon's plan to kill the two women. They are so beautiful, so different from our Osnomian women, that he intends to keep them-alive. Understand?"

"Yes," returned Seaton grimly, his eyes turning hard, "I get you all right-but what he'll do and what he thinks he'll do are two entirely different breeds of cats."

Returning to the others, they found Dorothy and Sitar deep in conversation.

"So a man has half a dozen or so wives?" Dorothy was asking in surprise. "How do you get along together? I'd fight like a wildcat if my husband tried to have other wives!"

"We get along splendidly, of course," returned the Osnomian princess in equal surprise. "I would not think of being a man's only wife. I wouldn't consider marrying a man who could win only one wife-think what a disgrace it would be! And think how lonely one would be while her husband is away at war-we would go insane if we did not have the company of the other wives. There are six of us, and we could not get along at all without each other."

"I've got a compliment for you and Peggy, Dottie," said Seaton. "Dunark here thinks that you two girls look good enough to eat-or words to that effect." Both girls flushed slightly, the purplish-black color suffusing their faces. They glanced at each other and Dorothy voiced the thought of both as she said:

"How can you, Kofedix Dunark? In this horrible light we both look perfectly dreadful. These other girls would be beautiful, if we were used to the colors, but we two look simply hideous."

"Oh, no," interrupted Sitar. "You have a wonderfully rich coloring. It is a shame to hide so much of yourselves with robes."

"Their eyes interpret colors differently than ours do," explained Seaton. "What to us are harsh and discordant colors are light and pleasing to their eyes. What looks like a kind of sloppy greenish black to us may-in fact, does-look a pale pink to them."

"Are Kondal and Mardonale the only two nations upon Osnome?" asked Crane.

"The only civilized nations, yes. Osnome is divided into two great and almost equal continents, separated by a wide ocean which encircles the globe. One is Kondal, the other Mardonale. Each nation has several nations or tribes of savages, which inhabit various waste places."

"You are the light race, Mardonale the dark," continued Crane. "What are the servants, who seem half-way between?"

"They are slaves...."

"Captured savages?" interrupted Dorothy.

"No. They are a separate race. They are a race so low in intelligence that they cannot exist except as slaves, but they can be trained to understand language and to do certain kinds of work. They are harmless and mild, making excellent servants, otherwise they would have perished ages ago. All menial work and most of the manual labor is done by the slave race. Formerly criminals were sterilized and reduced to unwilling slavery, but there have been no unwilling slaves in Kondal for hundreds of karkamo."

"Why? Are there no criminals any more?"

"No. With the invention of the thought recorder an absolutely fair trial was assured and the guilty were all convicted. They could not reproduce themselves, and as a natural result crime died out."

"That is," he added hastily, "what we regard as crime. Duelling, for instance, is a crime upon Earth; here it is a regular custom. In Kondal duels are rather rare and are held only when honor is involved, but here in Mardonale they are an every-day affair, as you saw when you landed."

"What makes the difference?" asked Dorothy curiously.

"As you know, with us every man is a soldier. In Kondal we train our youth in courage, valor, and high honor-in Mardonale they train them in savage blood-thirstiness alone. Each nation fixed its policy in bygone ages to produce the type of soldier it thought most efficient."

"I notice that everyone here wears those heavy collars," said Margaret. "What are they for?"

"They are identification marks. When a child is nearly grown, a collar bearing his name and the device of his house is cast about his neck. This collar is made of 'arenak,' a synthetic metal which, once formed, cannot be altered by any usual means. It cannot be scratched, cut, bent, broken, or worked in any way except at such a high temperature that death would result, if such heat were applied to the collar. Once the arenak collar is cast about a person's neck he is identified for life, and any adult Osnomian not wearing a collar is put to death."

"That must be an interesting metal," remarked Crane. "Is your belt a similar mark?"

"This belt is an idea of my own," and Dunark smiled broadly. "It looks like opaque arenak, but isn't. It is merely a pouch in which I carry anything I am particularly interested in. Even Nalboon thought it was arenak, so he didn't trouble to try to open it. If he had opened it and taken my tools and instruments, I couldn't have built the educator."

"Is that transparent armor arenak?"

"Yes, the only difference being that nothing is added to the matrix to color or make opaque the finished metal. It is in the preparation of this metal that salt is indispensable. It acts only as a catalyst, being recovered afterward, but neither nation has ever had enough salt to make all the armor they want."

"Aren't those monsters-karlono, I think you called them-covered by the same thing? And what are those animals, anyway?" Dorothy asked.

"Yes, they are armored with arenak, and it is thought that the beasts grow it, the same as fishes grow scales. The karlono are the most frightful scourge of Osnome. Very little is known of them, though every scientist has theorized upon them since time immemorial. It is very seldom that one is ever killed, as they easily outfly our swiftest battleships, and only fight when they can be victorious. To kill one requires a succession of the heaviest high-explosive shells in the same spot, a joint in the armor; and after the armor is once penetrated, the animal is blown into such small fragments that reconstruction is impossible. From such remains it has been variously described as a bird, a beast, a fish, and a vegetable; sexual, asexual, and hermaphroditic. Its habitat is unknown, it being variously supposed to live high in the air, deep in the ocean, and buried in the swamps. Another theory is that they live upon one of our satellites, which encounters our belt of atmosphere every karkam. Nothing is certainly known about the monsters except their terrible destructiveness and their insatiable appetites. One of them will devour five or six airships at one time, absorbing the crews and devouring the cargo and all of the vessels except the very hardest of the metal parts."

"Do they usually go in groups?" asked Crane. "If they do, I should think that a fleet of warships would be necessary for every party."

"No, they are almost always found alone. Only very rarely are two found together. This is the first time in history that more than two have ever been seen together. Two battleships can always defeat one karlon, so they are never attacked. With four battleships Nalboon considered his expedition perfectly safe, especially as they are now rare. The navies hunted down and killed what was supposed to be the last one upon Osnome more than a karkam ago, and none have been seen since, until we were attacked...."

The gong over the door sounded and the Kondalians leaped to their positions back of the Earthly visitors. The Kofedix went to the door. Nalboon brushed him aside and entered, escorted by a full company of heavily-armed soldiery. A scowl of anger was upon his face and he was plainly in an ugly mood.

"Stop, Nalboon of Mardonale!" thundered Seaton in the Mardonalian tongue and with the full power of his mighty voice. "Dare you invade my privacy unannounced and without invitation?"

The escort shrank back, but the Domak stood his ground, although he was plainly taken aback. With an apparent effort he smoothed his face into lines of cordiality.

"I merely came to inquire why my guards are slain and my palace destroyed by my honored guest?"

"As for slaying your guards, they sought to invade my privacy. I warned them away, but one of them was foolish enough to try to kill me. Then the others attempted to raise their childish rifles against me, and I was obliged to destroy them. As for the wall, it happened to be in the way of the thought-waves I hurled against your guards-consequently it was demolished. An honored guest! Bah! Are honored guests put to the indignity of being touched by the filthy hands of a mere ladex?"

"You do not object to the touch of slaves!" with a wave of his hand toward the Kondalians.

"That is what slaves are for," coldly. "Is a Domak to wait upon himself in the court of Mardonale? But to return to the issue. Were I an honored guest this would never have happened. Know, Nalboon, that when you attempt to treat a visiting Domak of MY race as a low-born captive, you must be prepared to suffer the consequences of your rashness!"

"May I ask how you, so recently ignorant, know our language?"

"You question me? That is bold! Know that I, the Boss of the Road, show ignorance or knowledge, when and where I please. You may go."

CHAPTER XV

The Escape from Mardonale

"That was a wonderful bluff, Dick!" exclaimed the Kofedix in English as soon as Nalboon and his guards had disappeared. "That was exactly the tone to take with him, too-you've sure got him guessing!"

"It seemed to get him, all right, but I'm wondering how long it'll hold him. I think we'd better make a dash for the Skylark right now, before he has time to think it over, don't you?"

"That is undoubtedly the best way," Dunark replied, lapsing into his own tongue. "Nalboon is plainly in awe of you now, but if I understand him at all, he is more than ever determined to seize your vessel, and every darkam's delay is dangerous."

The Earth-people quickly secured the few personal belongings they had brought with them. Stepping out into the hall and waving away the guards, Seaton motioned Dunark to lead the way. The other captives fell in behind, as they had done before, and the party walked boldly toward the door of the palace. The guards offered no opposition, but stood at attention and saluted as they passed. As they approached the entrance, however, Seaton saw the major-domo hurrying away and surmised that he was carrying the news to Nalboon. Outside the door, walking directly toward the landing dock, Dunark spoke in a low voice to Seaton, without turning.

"Nalboon knows by this time that we are making our escape, and it will be war to the death from here to the Skylark. I do not think there will be any pursuit from the palace, but he has warned the officers in charge of the dock and they will try to kill us as soon as we step out of the elevator, perhaps sooner. Nalboon intended to wait, but we have forced his hand and the dock is undoubtedly swarming with soldiers now. Shoot first and oftenest. Shoot first and think afterward. Show no mercy, as you will receive none-remember that the quality you call 'mercy' does not exist upon Osnome."

Rounding a great metal statue about fifty feet from the base of the towering dock, they saw that the door leading into one of the elevators was wide open and that two guards stood just inside it. As they caught sight of the approaching party, the guards raised their rifles; but, quick as they were, Seaton was quicker. At the first sight of the open door he had made two quick steps and had hurled himself across the intervening forty feet in a long football plunge. Before the two guards could straighten, he crashed into them, his great momentum hurling them across the elevator cage and crushing them into unconsciousness against its metal wall.

"Good work!" said Dunark, as he preceded the others into the elevator, and, after receiving Seaton's permission, distributed the weapons of the two guards among the men of his party. "Now we can surprise those upon the roof. That was why you didn't shoot?"

"Yes, I was afraid to risk a shot-it would give the whole thing away," Seaton replied, as he threw the unconscious guards out into the grounds and closed the massive door.

"Aren't you going to kill them?" asked Sitar, amazement in every feature and a puzzled expression in her splendid eyes. A murmur arose from the other Kondalians, which was quickly silenced by the Kofedix.

"It is dishonorable for a soldier of Earth to kill a helpless prisoner," he said briefly. "We cannot understand it, but we must not attempt to sway him in any point of honor."

Dunark stepped to the controls and the elevator shot upward, stopping at a landing several stories below the top of the dock. He took a peculiar device from his belt and fitted it over the muzzle of his strange pistol.

"We will get out here," he instructed the others, "and go up the rest of the way by a little-used flight of stairs. We will probably encounter some few guards, but I can dispose of them without raising an alarm. You will all stay behind me, please."

Seaton remonstrated, and Dunark went on:

"No, Seaton, you have done your share, and more. I am upon familiar ground now, and can do the work alone better than if you were to help me. I will call upon you, however, before we reach the dock."

The Kofedix led the way, his pistol resting lightly against his hip, and at the first turn of the corridor they came full upon four guards. The pistol did not move from its place at the side of the leader, but there were four subdued clicks and the four guards dropped dead, with bullets through their brains.

"Seaton, that is *some* silencer," whispered DuQuesne. "I didn't suppose a silencer could work that fast."

"They don't use powder," Seaton replied absently, all his faculties directed toward the next corner. "The bullets are propelled by an electrical charge."

In the same manner Dunark disposed of several more guards before the last stairway was reached.

"Seaton," he whispered in English, "now is the time we need your rapid pistol-work and your high-explosive shells. There must be hundreds of soldiers on the other side of that door, armed with machine-cannon shooting high-explosive shells at the rate of a thousand per minute. Our chance is this-their guns are probably trained upon the elevators and main stairways, since this passage is unused and none of us would be expected to know of it. Most of them don't know of it themselves. It will take them a second or two to bring their guns to bear upon us. We must do all the damage we can-kill them all, if possible-in that second or two. If Crane will lend me a pistol, we'll make the rush together."

"I've a better scheme than that," interrupted DuQuesne. "Next to you, Seaton, I'm the fastest man with a gun here. Also, like you, I can use both hands at once. Give me a couple of clips of those special cartridges and you and I will blow that bunch into the air before they know we're here."

It was decided that the two pistol experts should take the lead, closely followed by Crane and Dunark. The weapons were loaded to capacity and put in readiness for instant use.

"Let's go, bunch!" said Seaton. "The quicker we start the quicker we'll get back. Get ready to run out there, all the rest of you, as soon as the battle's over. Ready? On your marks-get set-go!"

He kicked the door open and there was a stuttering crash as the four automatic pistols simultaneously burst into practically continuous flame —a crash obliterated by an overwhelming concussion of sound as the X-plosive shells, sweeping the entire roof with a rapidly-opening fan of death, struck their marks and exploded. Well it was for the little group of wanderers that the two men in the door were past masters in the art of handling their weapons; well it was that they had in their tiny pistol-bullets the explosive force of hundreds of giant shells! For rank upon rank of soldiery were massed upon the roof; rapid-fire cannon, terrible engines of destruction, were pointing toward the elevators and toward the main stairways and approaches. But so rapid and fierce was the attack, that even those trained gunners had no time to point their guns. The battle lasted little more than a second, being over before either Crane or Dunark could fire a shot, and silence again reigned even while broken and shattered remnants of the guns and fragments of the metal and stone of the dock were still falling to the ground through a fine mist of what had once been men.

Assured by a rapid glance that not a single Mardonalian remained upon the dock, Seaton turned back to the others.

"Make it snappy, bunch! This is going to be a mighty unhealthy spot for us in a few minutes."

Dorothy threw her arms around his neck in relief. With one arm about her, he hastily led the way across the dock toward the Skylark, choosing the path with care because of the yawning holes blown into the structure by the terrific force of the explosions. The Skylark was still in place, held immovable by the attractor, but what a sight she was! Her crystal windows were shattered; her mighty plates of four-foot Norwegian armor were bent and cracked and twisted; two of her doors, warped and battered, hung awry from their broken hinges. Not a shell had struck her: all this damage had been done by flying fragments of the guns and of the dock itself; and Seaton and Crane, who had developed the new explosive, stood aghast at its awful power.

They hastily climbed into the vessel, and Seaton assured himself that the controls were uninjured.

"I hear battleships," Dunark said. "Is it permitted that I operate one of your machine guns?"

"Go as far as you like," responded Seaton, as he placed the women beneath the copper bar-the safest place in the vessel-and leaped to the instrument board. Before he reached it, and while DuQuesne, Crane, and Dunark were hastening to the guns, the whine of giant helicopter-screws was plainly heard. A ranging shell from the first warship, sighted a little low, exploded against the side of the dock beneath them. He reached the levers just as the second shell screamed through the air a bare four feet above them. As he shot the Skylark into the air under five notches of power, a steady stream of the huge bombs poured through the spot where, an instant before, the vessel had been. Crane and DuQuesne aimed several shots at the battleships, which were approaching from all sides, but the range was so extreme that no damage was done.

They heard the continuous chattering of the machine gun operated by the Kofedix, however, and turned toward him. He was shooting, not at the warships, but at the city rapidly growing smaller beneath them; moving the barrel of the rifle in a tiny spiral; spraying the entire city with death and destruction! As they looked, the first of the shells reached the ground, just as Dunark ceased firing for lack of ammunition. They saw the palace disappear as if by magic, being instantly blotted out in a cloud of dust —a cloud which, with a spiral motion of dizzying rapidity, increased in size until it obscured the entire city.

Having attained sufficient altitude to be safe from any possible pursuit and out of range of even the heaviest guns, Seaton stopped the vessel and went out into the main compartment to consult with the other members of the group, about their next move.

"It sure does feel good to get a breath of cool air, folks," he said, as he drew with relief a deep breath of the air, which, at that great elevation, was of an icy temperature and very thin. He glanced at the little group of Kondalians as he spoke, then leaped back to the instrument board with an apology on his lips-they were gasping for breath and shivering with the cold. He switched on the heating coils and dropped the Skylark rapidly in a long descent toward the ocean.

"If that is the temperature you enjoy, I understand at last why you wear clothes," said the Kofedix, as soon as he could talk.

"Do not your planes fly up into the regions of low temperature?" asked Crane.

"Only occasionally, and all high-flying vessels are enclosed and heated to our normal temperature. We have heavy wraps, but we dislike to wear them so intensely that we never subject ourselves to any cold."

"Well, there's no accounting for tastes," returned Seaton, "but I can't hand your climate a thing. It's hotter even than Washington in August; 'and that,' as the poet feelingly remarked, 'is going some!'

"But there's no reason for sitting here in the dark," he continued, as he switched on the powerful daylight lamps which lighted the vessel with the nearest approach to sunlight possible to produce. As soon as the lights were on, Dorothy looked intently at the strange women.

"Now we can see what color they really are," she explained to her lover in a low voice. "Why, they aren't so very different from what they were before, except that the colors are much softer and more pleasing. They really are beautiful, in spite of being green. Don't you think so, Dick?"

"They're a handsome bunch, all right," he agreed, and they were. Their skins were a light, soft green, tanned to an olive shade by their many fervent suns. Their teeth were a brilliant and shining grass-green. Their eyes and their long, thick hair were a glossy black.

The Kondalians looked at the Earthly visitors and at each other, and the women uttered exclamations of horror.

"What a frightful light?" exclaimed Sitar. "Please shut it off. I would rather be in total darkness than look like this!"

"What's the matter, Sitar?" asked the puzzled Dorothy as Seaton turned off the lights. "You look perfectly stunning in this light."

"They see things differently than we do," explained Seaton. "Their optic nerves react differently than ours do. While we look all right to them, and they look all right to us, in both kinds of light, they look just as different to themselves under our daylight lamps as we do to ourselves in their green light. Is that explanation clear?"

"It's clear enough as far as it goes, but what do they look like to themselves?"

"That's too deep for me—I can't explain it, any better than you can. Take the Osnomian color 'mlap,' for instance. Can you describe it?"

"It's a kind of greenish orange-but it seems as though it ought not to look like that color either."

"That's it, exactly. From the knowledge you received from the educator, it should be a brilliant purple. That is due to the difference in the optic nerves, which explains why we see things so differently from the way the Osnomians do. Perhaps they can describe the way they look to each other in our white light."

"Can you, Sitar?" asked Dorothy.

"One word describes it—'horrible.'" replied the Kondalian princess, and her husband added:

"The colors are distorted and unrecognizable, just as your colors are to your eyes in our light."

"Well, now that the color question is answered, let's get going. I pretty nearly asked you the way, Dunark-forgot that I know it as well as you do."

The Skylark set off at as high an altitude as the Osnomians could stand. As they neared the ocean several great Mardonalian battleships, warned of the escape, sought to intercept them; but the Skylark hopped over them easily, out of range of their heaviest guns, and flew onward at such speed that pursuit was not even attempted. The ocean was quickly crossed. Soon the space-car came to rest over a great city, and Seaton pointed out the palace; which, with its landing dock nearby, was very similar to that of Nalboon, in the capital city of Mardonale.

Crane drew Seaton to one side.

"Do you think it is safe to trust these Kondalians, any more than it was the others? How would it be to stay in the Lark instead of going into the palace?"

"Yes, Mart, this bunch can be trusted. Dunark has a lot of darn queer ideas, but he's square as a die. He's our friend, and will get us the copper. We have no choice now, anyway, look at the bar. We haven't an ounce of copper left-we're down to the plating in spots. Besides, we couldn't go anywhere if we had a ton of copper, because the old bus is a wreck. She won't hold air-you could throw a cat out through the shell in any direction. She'll have to have a lot of work done on her before we can think of leaving. As to staying in her, that wouldn't help us a bit. Steel is as soft as wood to these folks-their shells would go through her as though she were made of mush. They are made of metal that is harder than diamond and tougher than rubber, and when they strike they bore in like drill-bits. If they are out to get us they'll do it anyway, whether we're here or there, so we may as well be guests. But there's no danger, Mart. You know I swapped brains with him, and I know him as well as I know myself. He's a good, square man-one of our kind of folks."

Convinced, Crane nodded his head and the Skylark dropped toward the dock. While they were still high in air, Dunark took an instrument from his belt and rapidly manipulated a small lever. The others felt the air vibrate—a peculiar, pulsating wave, which, to the surprise of the Earthly visitors, they could read without difficulty. It was a message from the Kofedix to the entire city, telling of the escape of his party and giving the news that he was accompanied by two great Karfedo from another world. Then the pulsations became unintelligible, and all knew that he had tuned his instrument away from the "general" key into the individual key of some one person.

"I just let my father, the Karfedix, know that we are coming," he explained, as the vibrations ceased.

From the city beneath them hundreds of great guns roared forth a welcome, banners and streamers hung from every possible point, and the air became tinted and perfumed with a bewildering variety of colors and scents and quivered with the rush of messages of welcome. The Skylark was soon surrounded by a majestic fleet of giant warships, who escorted her with impressive ceremony to the landing dock, while around them flitted great numbers of other aircraft. The tiny one-man helicopters darted hither and thither, apparently always in imminent danger of colliding with some of their larger neighbors, but always escaping as though by a miracle. Beautiful pleasure-planes soared and dipped and wheeled like giant gulls; and, cleaving their stately way through the numberless lesser craft; immense multiplane passenger liners partially supported by helicopter screws turned aside from their scheduled courses to pay homage to the Kofedix of Kondal.

As the Skylark approached the top of the dock, all the escorting vessels dropped away and Crane saw that instead of the brilliant assemblage he had expected to see upon the landing-place there was only a small group of persons, as completely unadorned as were those in the car. In answer to his look of surprise, the Kofedix said, with deep feeling:

"My father, mother, and the rest of the family. They know that we, as escaped captives, would be without harness or trappings, and are meeting us in the same state."

Seaton brought the vessel to the dock near the little group, and the Earthly visitors remained inside their vessel while the rulers of Kondal welcomed the sons and daughters they had given up for dead.

After the affecting reunion, which was very similar to an earthly one under similar circumstances, the Kofedix led his father up to the Skylark and his guests stepped down upon the dock.

"Friends," Dunark began, "I have told you of my father, Roban, the Karfedix of Kondal. Father, it is a great honor to present to you those who rescued us from Mardonale-Seaton, Karfedix of Knowledge; Crane, Karfedix of Wealth; Miss Vaneman; and Miss Spencer. Karfedix DuQuesne," waving his hand toward him, "is a lesser Karfedix of Knowledge, captive to the others."

"The Kofedix Dunark exaggerates our services," deprecated Seaton, "and doesn't mention the fact that he saved all our lives. But for him we all should have been killed."

The Karfedix, disregarding Seaton's remark, acknowledged the indebtedness of Kondal in heartfelt accents before he led them back to the other party and made the introductions. As all walked toward the elevators, the emperor turned to his son with a puzzled expression.

"I know from your message, Dunark, that our guests are from a distant solar system, and I can understand your accident with the educator, but I cannot understand the titles of these men. Knowledge and wealth are not ruled over. Are you sure that you have translated their titles correctly?"

"As correctly as I can-we have no words in our language to express the meaning. Their government is a most peculiar one, the rulers all being chosen by the people of the whole nation...."

"Extraordinary!" interjected the older man. "How, then, can anything be accomplished?"

"I do not understand the thing myself, it is so utterly unheard-of. But they have no royalty, as we understand the term. In America, their country, every man is equal.

"That is," he hastened to correct himself, "they are not all equal, either, as they have two classes which would rank with royalty-those who have attained to great heights of knowledge and those who have amassed great wealth. This explanation is entirely inadequate and does not give the right idea of their positions, but it is as close as I can come to the truth in our language."

"I am surprised that you should be carrying a prisoner with you, Karfedo," said Roban, addressing Seaton and Crane. "You will, of course, be at perfect liberty to put him to death in any way that pleases you, just as though you were in your own kingdoms. But perchance you are saving him so that his death will crown your home-coming?"

The Kofedix spoke in answer while Seaton, usually so quick to speak, was groping for words.

"No, father, he is not to be put to death. That is another peculiar custom of the Earth-men; they consider it dishonorable to harm a captive, or even an unarmed enemy. For that reason we must treat the Karfedix DuQuesne with every courtesy due his rank, but at the same time he is to be allowed to do only such things as may be permitted by Seaton and Crane."

"Yet they do not seem to be a weak race," mused the older man.

"They are a mighty race, far advanced in evolution," replied his son. "It is not weakness, but a peculiar moral code. We have many things to learn from them, and but few to give them in return. Their visit will mean much to Kondal."

During this conversation they had descended to the ground and had reached the palace, after traversing grounds even more sumptuous and splendid than those surrounding the palace of Nalboon. Inside the palace walls the Kofedix himself led the guests to their rooms, accompanied by the major-domo and an escort of guards. He explained to them that the rooms were all inter-communicating, each having a completely equipped bathroom.

"Complete except for cold water, you mean," said Seaton with a smile.

"There is cold water," rejoined the other, leading him into the bathroom and releasing a ten-inch stream of lukewarm water into the small swimming pool, built of polished metal, which forms part of every Kondalian bathroom. "But I am forgetting that you like extreme cold. We will install refrigerating machines at once."

"Don't do it-thanks just the same. We won't be here long enough to make it worth while."

Dunark smilingly replied that he would make his guests as comfortable as he could, and after informing them that in one kam he would return and escort them in to koprat, took his leave. Scarcely had the guests freshened themselves when he was back, but he was no longer the Dunark they had known. He now wore a metal-and-leather harness which was one blaze of precious gems, and a leather belt hung with jeweled weapons replaced the familiar hollow girdle of metal. His right arm, between the wrist and the elbow, was almost covered by six bracelets of a transparent metal, deep cobalt-blue in color, each set with an incredibly brilliant stone of the same shade. On his left wrist he wore an Osnomian chronometer. This was an instrument resembling the odometer of an automobile, whose numerous revolving segments revealed a large and constantly increasing number-the date and time of the Osnomian day, expressed in a decimal number of the karkamo of Kondalian history.

"Greetings, oh guests from Earth! I feel more like myself, now that I am again in my trappings and have my weapons at my side. Will you accompany me to koprat, or are you not hungry?" as he attached the peculiar timepieces to the wrists of the guests, with bracelets of the deep-blue metal.

"We accept with thanks," replied Dorothy promptly. "We're starving to death, as usual."

As they walked toward the dining hall, Dunark noticed that Dorothy's eyes strayed toward his bracelets, and he answered her unasked question:

"These are our wedding rings. Man and wife exchange bracelets as part of the ceremony."

"Then you can tell whether a man is married or not, and how many wives he has, simply by looking at his arm? We should have something like that on Earth, Dick-then married men wouldn't find it so easy to pose as bachelors!"

Roban met them at the door of the great dining hall. He also was in full panoply, and Dorothy counted ten of the heavy bracelets upon his right arm as he led them to places near his own. The room was a replica of the other Osnomian dining hall they had seen and the women were decorated with the same barbaric splendor of scintillating gems.

After the meal, which was a happy one, taking the nature of a celebration in honor of the return of the captives, DuQuesne went directly to his room while the others spent the time until the zero hour in strolling about the splendid grounds, always escorted by many guards. Returning to the room occupied by the two girls, the couples separated, each girl accompanying her lover to the door of his room.

Margaret was ill at ease, though trying hard to appear completely self-possessed.

"What is the matter, sweetheart Peggy?" asked Crane, solicitously.

"I didn't know that you...." she broke off and continued with a rush: "What did the Kofedix mean just now, when he called you the Karfedix of Wealth?"

"Well, you see, I happen to have some money...." he began.

"Then you are the great M. Reynolds Crane?" she interrupted, in consternation.

"Leave off 'the great,'" he said, then, noting her expression, he took her in his arms and laughed slightly.

"Is that all that was bothering you? What does a little money amount to between you and me?"

"Nothing-but I'm awfully glad that I didn't know it before," she replied, as she returned his caress with fervor. "That is, it means nothing if you are perfectly sure I'm not...."

Crane, the imperturbable, broke a life-long rule and interrupted her.

"Do not say that, dear. You know as well as I do that between you and me there never have been, are not now, and never shall be, any doubts or any questions."

"If I could have a real cold bath now, I'd feel fine," remarked Seaton, standing in his own door with Dorothy by his side. "I'm no blooming Englishman but in weather as hot as this I sure would like to dive into a good cold tank. How do you feel after all this excitement, Dottie? Up to standard?"

"I'm scared purple," she replied, nestling against him, "or, at least, if not exactly scared, I'm apprehensive and nervous. I always thought I had good nerves, but everything here is so horrible and unreal, that I can't help but feel it. When I'm with you I really enjoy the experience, but when I'm alone or with Peggy, especially in the sleeping-period, which is so awfully long and when it seems that something terrible is going to happen every minute, my mind goes off in spite of me into thoughts of what may happen. Why, last night, Peggy and I just huddled up to each other in a ghastly yellow funk-dreading we knew not what-the two of us slept hardly at all."

"I'm sorry, little girl," replied Seaton, embracing her tenderly, "sorrier than I can say. I know that your nerves are all right, but you haven't roughed it enough, or lived in strange environments enough, to be able to feel at home. The reason you feel safer with me is that I feel perfectly at home here myself, not that your nerves are going to pieces or anything like that. It won't be for long, though, sweetheart-as soon as we get the chariot fixed up we'll beat it back to the Earth so fast it'll make your head spin."

"Yes, I think that's the reason, lover. I hope you won't think I'm a clinging vine, but I can't help being afraid of something here every time I'm away from you. You're so self-reliant, so perfectly at ease here, that it makes me feel the same way."

"I am perfectly at ease. There's nothing to be afraid of. I've been in hundreds of worse places, right on Earth. I sure wish I could be with you all the time, sweetheart girl-only you can understand just how much I wish it-but, as I said before, it won't be long until we can be together all the time."

Dorothy pushed him into his room, followed him within it, closed the door, and put both hands on his arm.

"Dick, sweetheart," she whispered, while a hot blush suffused her face, "you're not as dumb as I thought you were-you're dumber! But if you simply won't say it, I will. Don't you know that a marriage that is legal where it is performed is legal anywhere, and that no law says that the marriage must be performed upon the Earth?"

He pressed her to his heart in a mighty embrace, and his low voice showed in every vibration the depth of the feeling he held for the beautiful woman in his arms as he replied:

"I never thought of that, sweetheart, and I wouldn't have dared mention it if I had. You're so far away from your family and your friends that it would seem...."

"It wouldn't seem anything of the kind," she broke in earnestly. "Don't you see, you big, dense, wonderful man, that it is the only thing to do? We need each other, or at least, I need you, so much now...."

"Say 'each other'; it's right," declared her lover with fervor.

"It's foolish to wait. Mother would like to have seen me married, of course; but there will be great advantages, even on that side. A grand wedding, of the kind we would simply have to have in Washington, doesn't appeal to me any more than it does to you-and it would bore you to extinction. Dad would hate it, too-it's better all around to be married here."

Seaton, who had been trying to speak, silenced her.

"I'm convinced, Dottie, have been ever since the first word. If you can see it that way I'm so glad that I can't express it. I've been scared stiff every time I thought of our wedding. I'll speak to the Karfedix the first thing in the morning, and we'll be married tomorrow-or rather today, since it is past the zero kam," as he glanced at the chronometer upon his wrist, which, driven by wireless impulses from the master-clock in the national observatory, was clicking off the darkamo with an almost inaudible purr of its smoothly-revolving segments.

"How would it be to wake him up and have it done now?"

"Oh, Dick, be reasonable! That would never do. Tomorrow will be most awfully sudden, as it is! And Dick, please speak to Martin, will you? Peggy's even more scared than I am, and Martin, the dear old stupid, is even less likely to suggest such a thing as this kind of a wedding than you are. Peggy's afraid to suggest it to him."

"Woman!" he said in mock sternness, "Is this a put-up job?"

"It certainly is. Did you think I had nerve enough to do it without help?"

Seaton turned and opened the door.

"Mart! Bring Peggy over here!" he called, as he led Dorothy back into the girls' room.

"Heavens, Dick, be careful! You'll spoil the whole thing!"

"No, I won't. Leave it to me —I bashfully admit that I'm a regular bear-cat at this diplomatic stuff. Watch my smoke!"

"Folks," he said, when the four were together, "Dottie and I have been talking things over, and we've decided that today's the best possible date for a wedding. Dottie's afraid of these long, daylight nights, and I admit that I'd sleep a lot sounder if I knew where she was all the time instead of only part of it. She says she's willing, provided you folks see it the same way and make it double. How about it?"

Margaret blushed furiously and Crane's lean, handsome face assumed a darker color as he replied:

"A marriage here would, of course, be legal anywhere, provided we have a certificate, and we could be married again upon our return if we think it desirable. It might look as though we were taking an unfair advantage of the girls, Dick, but considering all the circumstances, I think it would be the best thing for everyone concerned."

He saw the supreme joy in Margaret's eyes, and his own assumed a new light as he drew her into the hollow of his arm.

"Peggy has known me only a short time, but nothing else in the world is as certain as our love. It is the bride's privilege to set the date, so I will only say that it cannot be too soon for me."

"The sooner the better," said Margaret, with a blush that would have been divine in any earthly light, "did you say 'today,' Dick?"

"I'll see the Karfedix as soon as he gets up," he answered, and walked with Dorothy to his door.

"I'm just too supremely happy for words," Dorothy whispered in Seaton's ear as he bade her good-night. "I won't be able to sleep or anything!"

CHAPTER XVI

An Osnomian Marriage

Seaton awoke, hot and uncomfortable, but with a great surge of joy in his heart-this was his wedding day! Springing from the bed, he released the full stream of the "cold" water, filling the tank in a few moments. Poising lightly upon the edge, he made a clean, sharp dive, and yelled in surprise as he came snorting to the surface. For Dunark had made good his promise-the water was only a few degrees above the freezing point! After a few minutes of vigorous splashing in the icy water, he rubbed himself down with a coarse towel, shaved, threw on his clothes, and lifted his powerful, but musical, bass voice in the wedding chorus from "The Rose Maiden."

"Rise, sweet maid, arise, arise,
Rise, sweet maid, arise, arise,
'Tis the last fair morning for thy maiden eyes,"

he sang lustily, out of his sheer joy in being alive, and was surprised to hear Dorothy's clear soprano, Margaret's pleasing contralto, and Crane's mellow tenor chime in from the adjoining room. Crane threw open the door and Seaton joined the others.

"Good morning. Dick, you sound happy," said Crane.

"Who wouldn't be? Look what's doing today," as he ardently embraced his bride-to-be. "Besides, I found some cold water this morning."

"Everyone in the palace heard you discovering it," dryly returned Crane, and the girls laughed merrily.

"It surprised me at first," admitted Seaton, "but it's great after a fellow once gets wet."

"We warmed ours a trifle," said Dorothy. "I like a cold bath myself, but not in ice-water."

All four became silent, thinking of the coming event of the day, until Crane said:

"They have ministers here, I know, and I know something of their religion, but my knowledge is rather vague. You know more about it than we do, Dick, suppose you tell us about it while we wait."

Seaton paused a moment, with an odd look on his face. As one turning the pages of an unfamiliar book of reference, he was seeking the answer to Crane's question in the vast store of Osnomian information received from Dunark. His usually ready speech came a little slowly.

"Well, as nearly as I can explain it, it's a funny kind of a mixture-partly theology, partly Darwinism, or at least, making a fetish of evolution, and partly pure economic determinism. They believe in a Supreme Being, whom they call the First Cause-that is the nearest English equivalent-and they recognize the existence of an immortal and unknowable life-principle, or soul. They believe that the First Cause has decreed the survival of the fittest as the fundamental law, which belief accounts for their perfect physiques...."

"Perfect physiques? Why, they're as weak as children," interrupted Dorothy.

"Yes, but that is because of the smallness of the planet," returned Seaton. "You see, a man of my size weighs only eighty-six pounds here, on a spring balance, so he would need only the muscular development of a boy of twelve or so. In a contest of strength, either of you girls could easily handle two of the strongest men upon Osnome. In fact, the average Osnomian could stand up on our Earth only with the greatest difficulty. But that isn't the fault of the people; they are magnificently developed for their surroundings. They have attained this condition by centuries of weeding out the unfit. They have no hospitals for the feeble-minded or feeble-bodied —abnormal persons are not allowed to live. The same reasoning accounts for their perfect cleanliness, moral and physical. Vice is practically unknown. They believe that clean living and clean thinking are rewarded by the production of a better physical and mental type...."

"Yes, especially as they correct wrong living by those terrible punishments the Kofedix told us about," interrupted Margaret.

"That probably helps some. They also believe that the higher the type is, the faster will evolution proceed, and the sooner will mankind reach what they call the Ultimate Goal, and know all things. Believing as they do that the fittest must survive, and thinking themselves, of course, the superior type, it is ordained that Mardonale must be destroyed utterly, root and branch. They believe that the slaves are so low in the scale, millions of years behind in evolution, that they do not count. Slaves are simply intelligent and docile animals, little more than horses or oxen. Mardonalians and savages are unfit to survive and must be exterminated.

"Their ministers are chosen from the very fittest. They are the strongest, cleanest-living, and most vigorous men of this clean and vigorous nation, and are usually high army officers as well as ministers."

An attendant announced the coming of the Karfedix and his son, to pay the call of state. After the ceremonious greetings had been exchanged, all went into the dining hall for darprat. As soon as the meal was over, Seaton brought up the question of the double wedding that kokam, and the Karfedix was overjoyed.

"Karfedix Seaton," he said earnestly, "nothing could please us more than to have such a ceremony performed in our palace. Marriage between such highly-evolved persons as are you four is wished by the First Cause, whose servants we are. Aside from that, it is an unheard-of honor for any ruler to have even one karfedix married beneath his roof, and you are granting me the privilege of two! I thank you, and assure you that we will do our poor best to make the occasion memorable."

"Don't do anything fancy," said Seaton hastily. "A simple, plain wedding will do."

Unheeding Seaton's remark, the Karfedix took his wireless from its hook at his belt and sent a brief message.

"I have summoned Karbix Tarnan to perform the ceremony. Our usual time for ceremonies is just before koprat-is that time satisfactory to you?"

Assured that it was, he turned to his son.

"Dunark, you are more familiar than I with the customs of our illustrious visitors. May I ask you to take charge of the details?"

While Dunark sent a rapid succession of messages, Dorothy whispered to Seaton:

"They must be going to make a real function of our double wedding, Dick. The Karbix is the highest dignitary of the church, isn't he?"

"Yes, in addition to being the Commander-in-Chief of all the Kondalian armies. Next to the Karfedix he is the most powerful man in the empire. Something tells me, Dottie, that this is going to be SOME ceremony!"

As Dunark finished telegraphing, Seaton turned to him.

"Dorothy said, a while ago, that she would like to have enough of that tapestry-fabric for a dress. Do you suppose it could be managed?"

"Certainly. In all state ceremonials we always wear robes made out of the same fabric as the tapestries, but much finer and more delicate. I would have suggested it, but thought perhaps the ladies would prefer their usual clothing. I know that you two men do not care to wear our robes?"

"We will wear white ducks, the dressiest and coolest things we have along," replied Seaton. "Thank you for your offer, but you know how it is. We should feel out of place in such gorgeous dress."

"I understand. I will call in a few of our most expert robe-makers, who will weave the gowns. Before they come, let us decide upon the ceremony. I think you are familiar with our marriage customs, but I will explain them to make sure. Each couple is married twice. The first marriage is symbolized by the exchange of plain bracelets and lasts four karkamo, during which period divorce may be obtained at will. The children of such divorced couples formerly became wards of the state, but in my lifetime I have not heard of there being any such children-all divorces are now between couples who discover their incompatibility before children are conceived."

"That surprises me greatly," said Crane. "Some system of trial-marriage is advocated among us on Earth every few years, but they all so surely degenerate into free love that no such system has found a foothold."

"We are not troubled in that way at all. You see, before the first marriage, each couple, from the humblest peasantry to the highest royalty, must submit to a mental examination. If they are marrying for any reason at all other than love, such as any thought of trifling in the mind of the man, or if the woman is marrying him for his wealth or position, he or she is summarily executed, regardless of station."

No other questions being asked, Dunark continued:

"At the end of four karkamo the second marriage is performed, which is indissoluble. In this ceremony jeweled bracelets are substituted for the plain ones. In the case of highly-evolved persons it is permitted that the two ceremonies be combined into one. Then there is a third ceremony, used only in the marriage of persons of the very highest evolution, in which the 'eternal' vows are taken and the faidon, the eternal jewel, is exchanged. As you are all in the permitted class, you may use the eternal ceremony if you wish."

"I think we all know our minds well enough to know that we want to be married for good-the longer the better," said Seaton, positively. "We'll make it the eternal, won't we, folks?"

"I should like to ask one question," said Crane, thoughtfully. "Does that ceremony imply that my wife would be breaking her vows if she married again upon my death?"

"Far from it. Numbers of our men are killed every karkam. Their wives, if of marriageable age, are expected to marry again. Then, too, you know that most Kondalian men have several wives. No matter how many wives or husbands may be linked together in that way, it merely means that after death their spirits will be grouped into one. Just as in your chemistry," smiling in comradely fashion at Seaton, "a varying number of elements may unite to form a stable compound."

After a short pause, the speaker went on:

"Since you are from the Earth and unaccustomed to bracelets, rings will be substituted for them. The plain rings will take the place of your Earthly wedding rings, the jeweled ones that of your engagement rings. The only difference is that while we discard the plain bracelets, you will continue to wear them. Have you men any objections to wearing the rings during the ceremony? You may discard them later if you wish and still keep the marriage valid."

"Not I! I'll wear mine all my life," responded Seaton earnestly, and Crane expressed the same thought.

"There is only one more thing," added the Kofedix. "That is, about the mental examination. Since it is not your custom, it is probable that the justices would waive the ruling, especially since everyone must be examined by a jury of his own or a superior rank, so that only one man, my father alone, could examine you."

"Not in a thousand years!" replied Seaton emphatically. "I want to be examined, and have Dorothy see the record. I don't care about having her put through it, but I want her to know exactly the kind of a guy she is getting."

Dorothy protested at this, but as all four were eager that they themselves should be tested, the Karfedix was notified and Dunark clamped sets of multiple electrodes, connected to a set of instruments, upon the temples of his father, Dorothy, and Seaton. He pressed a lever, and instantly Dorothy and Seaton read each other's minds to the minutest detail, and each knew that the Karfedix was reading the minds of both.

After Margaret and Crane had been examined, the Karfedix expressed himself as more than satisfied.

"You are all of the highest evolution and your minds are all untainted by any base thoughts in your marriage. The First Cause will smile upon your unions," he said solemnly.

"Let the robe-makers appear," the Karfedix ordered, and four women, hung with spools of brilliantly-colored wire of incredible fineness and with peculiar looms under their arms, entered the room and accompanied the two girls to their apartment.

As soon as the room was empty save for the four men, Dunark said:

"While I was in Mardonale, I heard bits of conversation regarding an immense military discovery possessed by Nalboon, besides the gas whose deadly effects we felt. I could get no inkling of its nature, but feel sure that it is something to be dreaded. I also heard that both of these secrets had been stolen from Kondal, and that we were to be destroyed by our own superior inventions."

The Karfedix nodded his head gloomily.

"That is true, my son-partly true, at least. We shall not be destroyed, however. Kondal shall triumph. The discoveries were made by a Kondalian, but I am as ignorant as are you concerning their nature. An obscure inventor, living close to the bordering ocean, was the discoverer. He was rash enough to wireless me concerning them. He would not reveal their nature, but requested a guard. The Mardonalian patrol intercepted the message and captured both him and his discoveries before our guard could arrive."

"That's easily fixed," suggested Seaton. "Let's get the Skylark fixed up, and we'll go jerk Nalboon out of his palace-if he's still alive-bring him over here, and read his mind."

"That might prove feasible," answered the Kofedix, "and in any event we must repair the Skylark and replenish her supply of copper immediately. That must be our first consideration, so that you, our guests, will have a protection in any emergency."

The Karfedix went to his duties and the other three made their way to the wrecked space-car. They found that besides the damage done to the hull, many of the instruments were broken, including one of the object-compasses focused upon the Earth.

"It's a good thing you had three of them, Mart. I sure hand it to you for preparedness," said Seaton, as he tossed the broken instruments out upon the dock. Dunark protested at this treatment, and placed the discarded instruments in a strong metal safe, remarking:

"These things may prove useful at some future time."

"Well, I suppose the first thing to do is to get some powerful jacks and straighten these plates," said Seaton.

"Why not throw away this soft metal, steel, and build it of arenak, as it should be built? You have plenty of salt," suggested Dunark.

"Fine! We have lots of salt in the galley, haven't we, Mart?"

"Yes, nearly a hundred pounds. We are stocked for emergencies, with two years' supply of food, you know."

Dunark's eyes opened in astonishment at the amount mentioned, in spite of his knowledge of earthly conditions. He started to say something, then stopped in confusion, but Seaton divined his thought.

"We can spare him fifty pounds as well as not, can't we, Mart?"

"Certainly. Fifty pounds of salt is a ridiculously cheap price for what he is doing for us, even though it is very rare here."

Dunark acknowledged the gift with shining eyes and heartfelt, but not profuse, thanks, and bore the precious bag to the palace under a heavy escort. He returned with a small army of workmen, and after making tests to assure himself that the power-bar would work as well through arenak as through steel, he instructed the officers concerning the work to be done. As the wonderfully skilled mechanics set to work without a single useless motion, the prince stood silent, with a look of care upon his handsome face.

"Worrying about Mardonale, Dunark?"

"Yes. I cannot help wondering what that terrible new engine of destruction is, which Nalboon now has at his command."

"Say, why don't you build a bus like the Skylark, and blow Mardonale off the map?"

"Building the vessel would be easy enough, but X is as yet unknown upon Osnome."

"We've got a lot of it...."

"I could not accept it. The salt was different, since you have plenty. X, however, is as scarce upon Earth as salt is upon Osnome."

"Sure you can accept it. We stopped at a planet that has lots of it, and we've got an object-compass pointing at it so that we can go back and get more of it any time we want it. We've got more of it on hand now than we're apt to need for a long time, so have a hunk and get busy," and he easily carried one of the lumps out of his cabin and tossed it upon the dock, from whence it required two of Kondal's strongest men to lift it.

The look of care vanished from the face of the prince and he summoned another corps of mechanics.

"How thick shall the walls be? Our battleships are armed with arenak the thickness of a hand, but with your vast supply of salt you may have it any thickness you wish, since the materials of the matrix are cheap and abundant."

"One inch would be enough, but everything in the bus is designed for a four-foot shell, and if we change it from four feet we'll have to redesign our guns and all our instruments. Let's make it four feet."

Seaton turned to the crippled Skylark, upon which the first crew of Kondalian mechanics were working with skill and with tools undreamed-of upon Earth. The whole interior of the vessel was supported by a complex falsework of latticed metal, then the four-foot steel plates and the mighty embers, the pride of the great MacDougall, were cut away as though they were made of paper by revolving saws and enormous power shears. The sphere, grooved for the repellers and with the members, braces, and central machinery complete, of the exact dimensions of the originals, was rapidly moulded of a stiff, plastic substance resembling clay. This matrix soon hardened into a rock-like mass into which the doors, machine-gun emplacements, and other openings were carefully cut. All surfaces were then washed with a dilute solution of salt, which the workmen handled as though it were radium. Two great plates of platinum were clamped into place upon either side of the vessel, each plate connected by means of silver cables as large as a man's leg to the receiving terminal of an enormous wireless power station. The current was applied and the great spherical mass apparently disappeared, being transformed instantly into the transparent metal arenak. Then indeed had the Earth-men a vehicle such as had never been seen before! A four-foot shell of metal five hundred times as strong and hard as the strongest and hardest steel, cast in one piece with the sustaining framework designed by the world's foremost engineer —a structure that no conceivable force could deform or injure, housing an inconceivable propulsive force!

The falsework was rapidly removed and the sustaining framework was painted with opaque varnish to render it plainly visible. At Seaton's suggestion the walls of the cabins were also painted, leaving transparent several small areas to serve as windows.

The second work-period was drawing to a close, and as Seaton and Crane were to be married before koprat, they stopped work. They marveled at the amount that had been accomplished, and the Kofedix told them:

"Both vessels will be finished tomorrow, except for the controlling instruments, which we will have to make ourselves. Another crew will work during the sleeping-period, installing the guns and other fittings. Do you wish to have your own guns installed, or guns of our pattern? You are familiar with them now."

"Our own, please. They are slower and less efficient than yours, but we are used to them and have a lot of X-plosive ammunition for them," replied Seaton, after a short conference with Crane.

After instructing the officers in charge of the work, the three returned to the palace, the hearts of two of them beating high in anticipation. Seaton went into Crane's room, accompanied by two attendants bearing his suitcase and other luggage.

"We should have brought along dress clothes, Mart. Why didn't you think of that, too?"

"Nothing like this ever entered my mind. It is a good thing we brought along ducks and white soft shirts. I must say that this is extremely informal garb for a state wedding, but since the natives are ignorant of our customs, it will not make any difference."

"That's right, too-we'll make 'em think it's the most formal kind of dress. Dunark knows what's what, but he knows that full dress would be unbearable here. We'd melt down in a minute. It's plenty hot enough as it is, with only duck trousers and sport-shirts on. They'll look green instead of white, but that's a small matter."

Dunark, as best man, entered the room some time later.

"Give us a look, Dunark," begged Seaton, "and see if we'll pass inspection. I was never so rattled in my life."

They were clad in spotless white, from their duck oxfords to the white ties encircling the open collars of their tennis shirts. The two tall figures-Crane's slender, wiry, at perfect ease; Seaton's broad-shouldered, powerful, prowling about with unconscious, feline suppleness and grace-and the two handsome, high-bred, intellectual faces, each wearing a look of eager happiness, fully justified Dunark's answer.

"You sure will do!" he pronounced enthusiastically, and with Seaton's own impulsive good will he shook hands and wished them an eternity of happiness.

"When you have spoken with your brides," he continued, "I shall be waiting to escort you into the chapel. Sitar told me to say that the ladies are ready."

Dorothy and Margaret had been dressed in their bridal gowns by Sitar and several other princesses, under the watchful eyes of the Karfedir herself. Sitar placed the two girls side by side and drew off to survey her work.

"You are the loveliest creatures in the whole world!" she cried.

They looked at each other's glittering gowns, then Margaret glanced at Dorothy's face and a look of dismay overspread her own.

"Oh, Dottie!" she gasped. "Your lovely complexion! Isn't it terrible for the boys to see us in this light?"

There was a peal of delighted laughter from Sitar and she spoke to one of the servants, who drew dark curtains across the windows and pressed a switch, flooding the room with brilliant white light.

"Dunark installed lamps like those of your ship for you," she explained with intense satisfaction. "I knew in advance just how you would feel about your color."

Before the girls had time to thank their thoughtful hostess she disappeared and their bridegrooms stood before them. For a moment no word was spoken. Seaton stared at Dorothy hungrily, almost doubting the evidence of his senses. For white was white, pink was pink, and her hair shone in all its natural splendor of burnished bronze.

In their wondrous Osnomian bridal robes the beautiful Earth-maidens stood before their lovers. Upon their feet were jeweled slippers. Their lovely bodies were clothed in softly shimmering garments that left their rounded arms and throats bare-garments infinitely more supple than the finest silk, thick-woven of metallic threads of such fineness that the individual wires were visible only under a lens; garments that floated and clung about their perfect forms in lines of exquisite grace. For black-haired Margaret, with her ivory skin, the Kondalian princess had chosen a background of a rare white metal, upon which, in complicated figures, glistened numberless jewels of pale colors, more brilliant than diamonds. Dorothy's dress was of a peculiar, dark-green shade, half-hidden by an intricate design of blazing green gems-the strange, luminous jewels of this strange world. Both girls wore their long, heavy hair unbound, after the Kondalian bridal fashion, brushed until it fell like mist about them and confined at the temples by metallic bands entirely covered with jewels.

Seaton looked from Dorothy to Margaret and back again; looked down into her violet eyes, deep with wonder and with love, more beautiful than any jewel in all her gorgeous costume. Unheeding the presence of the others, she put her dainty hands upon his mighty shoulders and stood on tiptoe.

"I love you, Dick. Now and always, here or at home or anywhere in the Universe. We'll never be parted again," she whispered, and her own beloved violin had no sweeter tones than had her voice.

A few minutes later, her eyes wet and shining, she drew herself away from him and glanced at Margaret.

"Isn't she the most beautiful thing you ever laid eyes on?"

"No," Seaton answered promptly, "she is not-but poor old Mart thinks she is!"

Accompanied by the Karfedix and his son, Seaton and Crane went into the chapel, which, already brilliant, had been decorated anew with even greater splendor. Glancing through the wide arches they saw, for the first time, Osnomians clothed. The great room was filled with the highest nobility of Kondal, wearing their heavily-jeweled, resplendent robes of state. Every color of the rainbow and numberless fantastic patterns were there, embodied in the soft, lustrous, metallic fabric.

As the men entered one door Dorothy and Margaret, with the Karfedir and Sitar, entered the other, and the entire assemblage rose to its feet and snapped into the grand salute. Moving to the accompaniment of strange martial music from concealed instruments, the two parties approached each other, meeting at the raised platform or pulpit where Karbix Tarnan, a handsome, stately, middle-aged man who carried easily his hundred and fifty karkamo of age, awaited them. As he raised his arms, the music ceased.

It was a solemn and wonderfully impressive spectacle. The room, of burnished metal, with its bizarre decorations wrought in scintillating gems; the constantly changing harmony of colors as the invisible lamps were shifted from one shade to another; the group of mighty nobles standing rigidly at attention in a silence so profound that it was an utter absence of everything audible as the Karbix lifted both arms in a silent invocation of the great First Cause-all these things deepened the solemnity of that solemn moment.

When Tarnan spoke, his voice, deep with some great feeling, inexplicable even to those who knew him best, carried clearly to every part of the great chamber.

"Friends, it is our privilege to assist today in a most notable event, the marriage of four personages from another world. For the first time in the history of Osnome, one karfedix has the privilege of entertaining the bridal party of another. It is not for this fact alone, however, that this occasion is to be memorable. A far deeper reason is that we are witnessing, possibly for the first time in the history of the Universe, the meeting upon terms of mutual fellowship and understanding of the inhabitants of two worlds separated by unthinkable distances of trackless space and by equally great differences in evolution, conditions of life, and environment. Yet these strangers are actuated by the spirit of good faith and honor which is instilled into every worthy being by the great First Cause, in the working out of whose vast projects all things are humble instruments.

"In honor of the friendship of the two worlds, we will proceed with the ceremony.

"Richard Seaton and Martin Crane, exchange the plain rings with Dorothy Vaneman and Margaret Spencer."

They did so, and repeated, after the Karbix, simple vows of love and loyalty.

"May the First Cause smile upon this temporary marriage and render it worthy of being made permanent. As a lowly servant of the all-powerful First Cause I pronounce you two, and you two, husband and wife. But we must remember that the dull vision of mortal man cannot pierce the veil of futurity, which is as crystal to the all-beholding eye of the First Cause. Though you love each other truly, unforeseen things may come between you to mar the perfection of your happiness. Therefore a time is granted you during which you may discover whether or not your unions are perfect."

A pause ensued, then Tarnan went on:

"Martin Crane, Margaret Spencer, Richard Seaton, and Dorothy Vaneman, you are before us to take the final vows which shall bind your bodies together for life and your spirits together for eternity. Have you considered the gravity of this step sufficiently to enter into this marriage without reservation?"

"I have," solemnly replied the four, in unison.

"Exchange the jeweled rings. Do you, Richard Seaton and Dorothy Vaneman; and you, Martin Crane and Margaret Spencer; individually swear, here in the presence of the First Cause and that of the Supreme Justices of Kondal, that you will be true and loyal, each helping his chosen one in all things, great and small; that never throughout eternity, in thought or in action, will either your body or your mind or your conscious spirit stray from the path of fairness and truth and honor?"

"I do."

"I pronounce you married with the eternal marriage. Just as the faidon which you each now wear-the eternal jewel which no force of man, however applied, has yet been able to change or deform in any particular; and which continues to give off its inward light without change throughout eternity-shall endure through endless cycles of time after the metal of the ring which holds it shall have crumbled in decay: even so shall your spirits, formerly two, now one and indissoluble, progress in ever-ascending evolution throughout eternity after the base material which is your bodies shall have returned to the senseless dust from whence it arose."

The Karbix lowered his arms and the bridal party walked to the door through a double rank of uplifted weapons. From the chapel they were led to another room, where the contracting parties signed their names in a register. The Kofedix then brought forward two marriage certificates-heavy square plates of a brilliant purple metal, beautifully engraved in parallel columns of English and Kondalian script, and heavily bordered with precious stones. The principals and witnesses signed below each column, the signatures being deeply engraved by the royal engraver. Leaving the registry, they were escorted to the dining hall, where a truly royal repast was served. Between courses the highest nobles of the nation welcomed the visitors and wished them happiness in short but earnest addresses. After the last course had been disposed of, the Karbix rose at a sign from the Karfedix and spoke, his voice again agitated by the emotion which had puzzled his hearers during the marriage service.

"All Kondal is with us here in spirit, trying to aid us in our poor attempts to convey our welcome to these our guests, of whose friendship no greater warrant could be given than their willingness to grant us the privilege of their marriage. Not only have they given us a boon that will make their names revered throughout the nation as long as Kondal shall exist, but they have also been the means of showing us plainly that the First Cause is upon our side, that our age-old institution of honor is in truth the only foundation upon which can be built a race fitted to survive. At the same time they have been the means of showing us that our hated foe, entirely without honor, building his race upon a foundation of bloodthirsty savagery alone, is building wrongly and must perish utterly from the face of Osnome."

His hearers listened, impressed by his earnestness, but plainly not understanding his meaning.

"You do not understand?" he went on, with a deep light shining in his eyes. "It is inevitable that two peoples inhabiting worlds so widely separated as are our two should be possessed of widely-varying knowledge and abilities, and these strangers have already made it possible for us to construct engines of destruction which shall obliterate Mardonale completely...." A fierce shout of joy interrupted the speaker and the nobles sprang to their feet, saluting the visitors with upraised weapons. As soon as they had reseated themselves, the Karbix continued:

"That is the boon. The vindication of our system of evolution is easily explained. The strangers landed first upon Mardonale. Had Nalboon met them in honor, he would have gained the boon. But he, with the savagery characteristic of his evolution, attempted to kill his guests and steal their treasures, with what results you already know. We, on our part, in exchange for the few and trifling services we have been able to render them, have received even more than Nalboon would have obtained, had his plans not been nullified by their vastly superior state of evolution."

The orator seated himself and there was a deafening clamor of cheering as the nobles formed themselves into an escort of honor and conducted the two couples to their apartments.

Alone in their room, Dorothy turned to her husband with tears shining in her beautiful eyes.

"Dick, sweetheart, wasn't that the most wonderful thing that anybody ever heard of? Using the word in all its real meaning, it was indescribably grand, and that old man is simply superb. It makes me ashamed of myself to think that I was ever afraid or nervous here."

"It sure was all of that, Dottie mine, little bride of an hour. The whole thing gets right down to where a fellow lives —I've got a lump in my throat right now so big that it hurts me to think. Earthly marriages are piffling in comparison with that ceremony. It's no wonder they're happy, after taking those vows-especially as they don't have to take them until after they are sure of themselves.

"But we're sure already, sweetheart," as he embraced her with all the feeling of his nature. "Those vows are not a bit stronger than the ones we have already exchanged-bodily and mentally and spiritually we are one, now and forever."

CHAPTER XVII

Bird, Beast, or Fish?

"These jewels rather puzzle me, Dick. What are they?" asked Martin, as the four assembled, waiting for the first meal. As he spoke he held up his third finger, upon which gleamed the royal jewel of Osnome in its splendid Belcher mounting of arenak as transparent as the jewel itself and having the same intense blue color. "I know the name, 'faidon,' but that's all I seem to know."

"That's about all that anybody knows about them. It is a naturally-occurring, hundred-faceted crystal, just as you see it there-deep blue, perfectly transparent, intensely refractive, and constantly emitting that strong, blue light. It is so hard that it cannot be worked, cut, or ground. No amount of the hardest known abrasive will even roughen its surface. No blow, however great, will break it-it merely forces its way into the material of the hammer, however hard the hammer may be. No extremity of either heat or cold affects it in any degree, it is the same when in the most powerful electric arc as it is when immersed in liquid helium."

"How about acids?"

"That is what I am asking myself. Osnomians aren't much force at chemistry. I'm going to try to get hold of another one, and see if I can't analyze it, just for fun. I can't seem to convince myself that a real atomic structure could be that large."

"No, it is rather large for an atom," and turning to the two girls, "How do you like your solitaires?"

"They're perfectly beautiful, and the Tiffany mounting is exquisite," replied Dorothy, enthusiastically, "but they're so awfully big! They're as big as ten-carat diamonds, I do believe."

"Just about," replied Seaton, "but at that, they're the smallest Dunark could find. They have been kicking around for years, he says-so small that nobody wanted them. They wear big ones on their bracelets, you know. You sure will make a hit in Washington, Dottie. People will think you're wearing a bottle-stopper until they see it shining in the dark, then they'll think it's an automobile headlight. But after a few jewelers have seen these stones, one of them will be offering us five million dollars apiece for them, trying to buy them for some dizzy old dame who wants to put out the eyes of some of her social rivals. Yes? No?"

"That's about right, Dick," replied Crane, and his face wore a thoughtful look. "We can't keep it secret that we have a new jewel, since all four of us will be wearing them continuously, and anyone who knows jewels at all will recognize these as infinitely superior to any known Earthly jewel. In fact, they may get some of us into trouble, as fabulously valuable jewels usually do."

"That's true, too. So we'll let it out casually that they're as common as mud up here-that we're just wearing them for sentiment, which is true, and that we're thinking of bringing back a shipload to sell for parking lights."

"That would probably keep anyone from trying to murder our wives for their rings, at least."

"Have you read your marriage certificate, Dick?" asked Margaret.

"Not yet. Let's look at it, Dottie."

She produced the massive, heavily-jeweled document, and the auburn head and the brown one were very close to each other as they read together the English side of the certificate. Their vows were there, word for word, with their own signatures beneath them, all deeply engraved into the metal. Seaton smiled as he saw the legal form engraved below their signatures, and read aloud:

> "I, the Head of the Church and the Commander-in-Chief of the armed forces of Kondal, upon the planet Osnome, certify that I have this day, in the city of Kondalek, of said nation and planet, joined in indissoluble bonds of matrimony, Richard Ballinger Seaton, Doctor of Philosophy, and Dorothy Lee Vaneman; Doctor of Music; both of the city of Washington, District of Columbia, United States

of America, upon the planet Earth, in strict compliance with the marriage laws, both of Kondal and of the United States of America.

TARNAN."

Witnesses:
ROBAN, Emperor of Kondal.
TURAL, Empress of Kondal.
DUNARK, Crown Prince of Kondal.
SITAR, Crown Princess of Kondal.
MARC C. DuQUESNE, Ph. D., Washington, D. C.

"That is SOME document," remarked Seaton. "Probably a lawyer could find fault with his phraseology, but I'll bet that this thing would hold in any court in the world. Think you'll get married again when we get back, Mart?"

Both girls protested, and Crane answered:

"No, I think not. Our ceremony would be rather an anticlimax after this one, and this one will undoubtedly prove legal. I intend to register this just as it is, and get a ruling from the courts. But it is time for breakfast. Pardon me —I should have said 'darprat,' for it certainly is not breakfast-time by Washington clocks. My watch says that it is eleven-thirty P. M."

"This system of time is funny," remarked Dorothy. "I just can't get used to having no night, and...."

"And it's such a long time between eats, as the famous governor said about the drinks," broke in Seaton.

"How did you know what I was going to say, Dick?"

"Husbandly intuition," he grinned, "aided and abetted by a normal appetite that rebels at seventeen hours between supper and breakfast, and nine hours between the other meals. Well, it's time to eat-let's go!"

After eating, the men hurried to the Skylark. During the sleeping-period the vessel had been banded with the copper repellers: the machine guns and instruments, including the wonderful Osnomian wireless system, had been installed; and, except for the power-bars, she was ready for a voyage. The Kondalian vessel was complete, even to the cushions, but was without instruments.

After a brief conversation with the officer in charge, Dunark turned to Seaton.

"Didn't you find that your springs couldn't stand up under the acceleration?"

"Yes, they flattened out dead."

"The Kolanix Felan, in charge of the work, thought so, and substituted our compound-compensated type, made of real spring metal, for them. They'll hold you through any acceleration you can live through."

"Thanks, that's fine. What's next, instruments?"

"Yes. I have sent a crew of men to gather up what copper they can find-you know that we use practically no metallic copper, as platinum, gold, and silver are so much better for ordinary purposes-and another to erect a copper-smelter near one of the mines which supply the city with the copper sulphate used upon our tables. While they are at work I think I will work on the instruments, if you two will be kind enough to help me."

Seaton and Crane offered to supply him with instruments from their reserve stock, but the Kofedix refused to accept them, saying that he would rather have their help in making them, so that he would thoroughly understand their functions. The electric furnaces were rapidly made ready and they set to work; Crane taking great delight in working that hitherto rare and very refractory metal, iridium, of which all the Kondalian instruments were to be made.

"They have a lot of our rare metals here, Dick."

"They sure have. I'd like to set up a laboratory and live here a few years —I'd learn something about my specialty or burst. They use gold and silver where we use copper, and platinum and its alloys where we use iron and soft steel. All their weapons are made of iridium, and all their most highly-tempered tools, such as their knives, razors, and so on, are made of opaque arenak. I suppose you've noticed the edge on your razor?"

"How could I help it? It is hard to realize that a metal can be so hard that it requires forty years on a diamond-dust abrasive machine to hone a razor-or that once honed, it shaves generation after generation of men without losing in any degree its keenness."

"I can't understand it, either—I only know that it's so. They have all our heavy metals in great abundance, and a lot more that we don't know anything about on Earth, but they apparently haven't any light metals at all. It must be that Osnome was thrown off the parent sun late, so that the light metals were all gone?"

"Something like that, possibly."

The extraordinary skill of the Kofedix made the manufacture of the instruments a short task, and after Crane had replaced the few broken instruments of the Skylark from their reserve stock, they turned their attention to the supply of copper that had been gathered. They found it enough for only two bars.

"Is this all we have?" asked Dunark, sharply.

"It is, your Highness," replied the Kolanix. "That is every scrap of metallic copper in the city."

"Oh, well, that'll be enough to last until we can smelt the rest," said Seaton. "With one bar apiece we're ready for anything Mardonale can start. Let 'em come!"

The bars were placed in the containers and both vessels were tried out, each making a perfect performance. Upon the following kokam, immediately after the first meal, the full party from the Earth boarded the Skylark and accompanied the Kofedix to the copper smelter. Dunark himself directed the work of preparing the charges and the molds, though he was continually being interrupted by wireless messages in code and by messengers bearing tidings too important to trust into the air.

"I hope you will excuse all of these delays," said Dunark, after the twentieth interruption, "but...."

"That's all right, Dunark. We know that you're a busy man."

"I can tell you about it, but I wouldn't want to tell many people. With the salt you gave us, I am preparing a power-plant that will enable us to blow Mardonale into...."

He broke off as a wireless call for help sounded. All listened intently, learning that a freight-plane was being pursued by a karlon a few hundred miles away.

"Now's the time for you to study one, Dunark!" Seaton exclaimed. "Get your gang of scientists out here while we go get him and drag him in!"

As Dunark sent the message, the Skylark's people hurried aboard, and Seaton drove the vessel toward the calls for help. With its great speed it reached the monster before the plane was overtaken. Focusing the attractor upon the enormous metallic beak of the karlon, Seaton threw on the power and the beast halted in midair as it was jerked backward and upward. As it saw the puny size of the attacking Skylark, it opened its cavernous mouth in a horrible roar and rushed at full speed. Seaton, unwilling to have the repellers stripped from the vessel, turned on the current actuating them. The karlon was hurled backward to the point of equilibrium of the two forces, where it struggled demoniacally.

Seaton carried his captive back to the smelter, where finally, by judicious pushing and pulling, he succeeded in turning the monster flat upon its back and pinning it to the ground in spite of its struggles to escape.

Soon the scientists arrived and studied the animal thoroughly, at as close a range as its flailing arms permitted.

"I wish we could kill him without blowing him to bits," wirelessed Dunark. "Do you know any way of doing it?"

"We could if we had a few barrels of ether, or some of our own poison gases, but they are all unknown here and it would take a long time to build the apparatus to make them. I'll see if I can't tire him out and get him that way as soon as you've studied him enough. We may be able to find out where he lives, too."

The scientists having finished their observations, Seaton jerked the animal a few miles into the air and shut off the forces acting upon it. There was a sudden crash, and the karlon, knowing that this apparently insignificant vessel was its master, turned in headlong flight.

"Have you any idea what caused the noise just then, Dick?" asked Crane; who, with characteristic imperturbability, had taken out his notebook and was making exact notes of all that transpired.

"I imagine we cracked a few of his plates," replied Seaton with a laugh, as he held the Skylark in place a few hundred feet above the fleeing animal.

Pitted for the first time in its life against an antagonist, who could both outfly and outfight it, the karlon redoubled its efforts and fled in a panic of fear. It flew back over the city of Kondalek, over the outlying country, and out over the ocean, still followed easily by the Skylark. As they neared the Mardonalian border, a fleet of warships rose to contest the entry of the monster. Seaton, not wishing to let the foe see the rejuvenated Skylark, jerked his captive high into the thin air. As soon as it was released, it headed for the ocean in an almost perpendicular dive, while Seaton focused an object-compass upon it.

"Go to it, old top," he addressed the plunging monster. "We'll follow you clear to the bottom of the ocean if you go that far!"

There was a mighty double splash as the karlon struck the water, closely followed by the Skylark. The girls gasped as the vessel plunged below the surface at such terrific speed, and seemed surprised that it had suffered no injury and that they had felt no jar. Seaton turned on the powerful searchlights and kept close enough so that he could see the monster through the transparent walls. Deeper and deeper the quarry dove, until it was plainly evident to the pursuers that it was just as much at home in the water as it was in the air. The beams of the lights revealed strange forms of life, among which were huge, staring-eyed fishes, which floundered about blindly in the unaccustomed glare. As the karlon bored still deeper, the living things became scarcer, but still occasional fleeting glimpses were obtained of the living nightmares which inhabited the oppressive depths of these strange seas. Continuing downward, the karlon plumbed the nethermost pit of the ocean and came to rest upon the bottom, stirring up a murk of ooze.

"How deep are we, Mart?"

"About four miles. I have read the pressure, but will have to calculate later exactly what depth it represents, from the gravity and density readings."

As the animal showed no sign of leaving its retreat, Seaton pulled it out with the attractor and it broke for the surface. Rising through the water at full speed, it burst into the air and soared upward to such an incredible height that Seaton was amazed.

"I wouldn't have believed that anything could fly in air this thin!" he exclaimed.

"It is thin up here," assented Crane. "Less than three pounds to the square inch. I wonder how he does it?"

"It doesn't look as though we are ever going to find out-he's sure a bear-cat!" replied Seaton, as the karlon, unable to ascend further, dropped in a slanting dive toward the lowlands of Kondal-the terrible, swampy region covered with poisonous vegetation and inhabited by frightful animals and even more frightful savages. The monster neared the ground with ever-increasing speed. Seaton, keeping close behind it, remarked to Crane:

"He'll have to flatten out pretty quick, or he'll burst something, sure."

But it did not flatten out. It struck the soft ground head foremost and disappeared, its tentacles apparently boring a way ahead of it.

Astonished at such an unlooked-for development, Seaton brought the Skylark to a stop and stabbed into the ground with the attractor. The first attempt brought up nothing but a pillar of muck, the second brought to light a couple of wings and one writhing arm, the third brought the whole animal, still struggling as strongly as it had in the first contest. Seaton again lifted the animal high into the air.

"If he does that again, we'll follow him."

"Will the ship stand it?" asked DuQuesne, with interest.

"Yes. The old bus wouldn't have, but this one can stand anything. We can go anywhere that thing can, that's a cinch. If we have enough power on, we probably won't even feel a jolt when we strike ground."

Seaton reduced the force acting upon the animal until just enough was left to keep the attractor upon it, and it again dived into the swamp. The Skylark followed, feeling its way in the total darkness, until the animal stopped, refusing to move in any direction, at a depth estimated by Crane to be about three-quarters of a mile. After waiting some time Seaton increased the power of the attractor and tore the karlon back to the surface and into the air, where it turned on the Skylark with redoubled fury.

"We've dug him out of his last refuge and he's fighting like a cornered rat," said Seaton as he repelled the monster to a safe distance. "He's apparently as fresh as when he started, in spite of all this playing. Talk about a game fish! He doesn't intend to run any more, though, so I guess we'll have to put him away. It's a shame to bump him off, but it's got to be done."

Crane aimed one of the heavy X-plosive bullets at the savagely-struggling monster, and the earth rocked with the concussion as the shell struck its mark. They hurried back to the smelter, where Dunark asked eagerly:

"What did you find out about it?"

"Nothing much," replied Seaton, and in a few words described the actions of the karlon. "What did your savants think of it?"

"Very little that any of us can understand in terms of any other known organism. It seems to combine all the characteristics of bird, beast, and fish, and to have within itself the possibilities of both bisexual and asexual reproduction."

"I wouldn't doubt it-it's a queer one, all right."

The copper bars were cool enough to handle, and the Skylark was loaded with five times its original supply of copper, the other vessel taking on a much smaller amount. After the Kofedix had directed the officer in charge to place the remaining bars in easily-accessible places throughout the nation, the two vessels were piloted back to the palace, arriving just in time for the last meal of the kokam.

"Well, Dunark," said Seaton after the meal was over, "I'm afraid that we must go back as soon as we can. Dorothy's parents and Martin's bankers will think they are dead by this time. We should start right now, but...."

"Oh, no, you must not do that. That would rob our people of the chance of bidding you goodbye."

"There's another reason, too. I have a mighty big favor to ask of you."

"It is granted. If man can do it, consider it done."

"Well, you know platinum is a very scarce and highly useful metal with us. I wonder if you could let us have a few tons of it? And I would like to have another faidon, too—I want to see if I can't analyze it."

"You have given us a thousand times the value of all the platinum and all the jewels your vessel can carry. As soon as the foundries are open tomorrow we will go and load up your store-rooms—or, if you wish, we will do it now."

"That isn't necessary. We may as well enjoy your hospitality for one more sleeping-period, get the platinum during the first work-period, and bid you goodbye just before the second meal. How would that be?"

"Perfectly satisfactory."

The following kokam, Dunark piloted the Skylark, with Seaton, Crane, and DuQuesne as crew, to one of the great platinum foundries. The girls remained behind to get ready for their departure, and for the great ceremony which was to precede it. The trip to the foundry was a short one, and the three scientists of Earth stared at what they saw-thousands of tons of platinum, cast into bars and piled up like pig-iron, waiting to be made into numerous articles of every-day use throughout the nation. Dunark wrote out an order, which his chief attendant handed to the officer in charge of the foundry, saying:

"Please have it loaded at once."

Seaton indicated the storage compartment into which the metal was to be carried, and a procession of slaves, two men staggering under one ingot, was soon formed between the pile and the storage room.

"How much are you loading on, Dunark?" asked Seaton, when the large compartment was more than half full.

"My order called for about twenty tons, in your weight, but I changed it later-we may as well fill that room full, so that the metal will not rattle around in flight. It doesn't make any difference to us, we have so much of it. It is like your gift of the salt, only vastly smaller."

"What are you going to do with it all, Dick?" asked Crane. "That is enough to break the platinum market completely."

"That's exactly what I'm going to do," returned Seaton, with a gleam in his gray eyes. "I'm going to burst this unjustifiable fad for platinum jewelry so wide open that it'll never recover, and make platinum again available for its proper uses, in laboratories and in the industries.

"You know yourself," he rushed on hotly, "that the only reason platinum is used at all for jewelry is that it is expensive. It isn't nearly so handsome as either gold or silver, and if it wasn't the most costly common metal we have, the jewelry-wearing crowd wouldn't touch it with a ten-foot pole. Useless as an ornament, it is the one absolutely indispensable laboratory metal, and literally hundreds of laboratories that need it can't have it because over half the world's supply is tied up in jeweler's windows and in useless baubles. Then, too, it is the best thing known for contact points in electrical machinery. When the Government and all the scientific societies were abjectly begging the jewelers to let loose a little of it they refused-they were selling it to profiteering spendthrifts at a hundred and fifty dollars an ounce. The condition isn't much better right now; it's a vicious circle. As long as the price stays high it will be used for jewelry, and as long as it is used for jewelry the price will stay high, and scientists will have to fight the jewelers for what little they get."

"While somewhat exaggerated, that is about the way matters stand. I will admit that I, too, am rather bitter on the subject," said Crane.

"Bitter? Of course you're bitter. Everybody is who knows anything about science and who has a brain in his head. Anybody who claims to be a scientist and yet stands for any of his folks buying platinum jewelry ought to be shot. But they'll get theirs as soon as we get back. They wouldn't let go of it before, they had too good a thing, but they'll let go now, and get their fingers burned besides. I'm going to dump this whole shipment at fifty cents a pound, and we'll take mighty good care that jewelers don't corner the supply."

"I'm with you, Dick, as usual."

Soon the storage room was filled to the ceiling with closely-stacked ingots of the precious metal, and the Skylark was driven back to the landing dock. She alighted beside Dunark's vessel, the *Kondal*, whose gorgeously-decorated crew of high officers sprang to attention as the four men stepped out. All were dressed for the ceremonial leave-taking, the three Americans wearing their spotless white, the Kondalians wearing their most resplendent trappings.

"This formal stuff sure does pull my cork!" exclaimed Seaton to Dunark. "I want to get this straight. The arrangement was that we were to be here at this time, all dressed up, and wait for the ladies, who are coming under the escort of your people?"

"Yes. Our family is to escort the ladies from the palace here. As they leave the elevator the surrounding war-vessels will salute, and after a brief ceremony you two will escort your wives into the Skylark, Doctor DuQuesne standing a little apart and following you in. The war-vessels will escort you as high as they can go, and the Kondal will accompany you as far as our most distant sun before turning back."

For a few moments Seaton nervously paced a short beat in front of the door of the space-car.

"I'm getting more fussed every second," he said abruptly, taking out his wireless instrument. "I'm going to see if they aren't about ready."

"What seems to be the trouble, Dick? Have you another hunch, or are you just rattled?" asked Crane.

"Rattled, I guess, but I sure do want to get going," he replied, as he worked the lever rapidly.

"Dottie," he sent out, and, the call being answered, "How long will you be? We're all ready and waiting, chewing our finger-nails with impatience."

"We'll soon be ready. The Karfedix is coming for us now."

Scarcely had the tiny sounder become silent when the air was shaken by an urgently-vibrated message, and every wireless sounder gave warning.

CHAPTER XVIII

The Invasion

The pulsating air and the chattering sounders were giving the same dire warning, the alarm extraordinary of invasion, of imminent and catastrophic danger from the air.

"Don't try to reach the palace. Everyone on the ground will have time enough to hide in the deep, arenak-protected pits beneath the buildings, and you would be killed by the invaders long before you could reach the palace. If we can repel the enemy and keep them from landing, the women will be perfectly safe, even though the whole city is destroyed. If they effect a landing we are lost."

"They'll not land, then," Seaton answered grimly, as he sprang into the Skylark and took his place at the board. As Crane took out his wireless, Seaton cautioned him.

"Send in English, and tell the girls not to answer, as these devils can locate the calls within a foot and will be able to attack the right spot. Just tell them we're safe in the Skylark. Tell them to sit tight while we wipe out this gang that is coming, and that we'll call them, once in a while, when we have time, during the battle."

Before Crane had finished sending the message the crescendo whine of enormous propellers was heard. Simultaneously there was a deafening concussion and one entire wing of the palace disappeared in a cloud of dust, in the midst of which could be discerned a few flying fragments. The air was filled with Mardonalian warships. They were huge vessels, each mounting hundreds of guns, and the rain of high-explosive shells was rapidly reducing the great city to a wide-spread heap of debris.

Seaton's hand was upon the lever which would hurl the Skylark upward into the fray. Crane and DuQuesne, each hard of eye and grim of jaw, were stationed at their machine-guns.

"Something's up!" exclaimed Seaton. "Look at the Kondal!"

Something had happened indeed. Dunark sat at the board, his hand upon the power lever, and each of his crew was in place, grasping his weapon, but every man was writhing in agony, unable to control his movements. As they stared, momentarily spellbound, the entire crew ceased their agonized struggles and hung, apparently lifeless, from their supports.

"They've got to 'em some way–let's go!" yelled Seaton.

As his hand tightened upon the lever, a succession of shells burst upon the dock, wrecking it completely, all three men fancied that the world had come to an end as the stream of high explosive was directed against their vessel. But the four-foot shell of arenak was impregnable, and Seaton shot the Skylark upward into the midst of the enemy fleet. The two gunners fired as fast as they could sight their weapons, and with each shot one of the great warships was blown into fragments. The Mardonalians then concentrated the fire of their entire fleet upon their tiny opponent.

From every point of the compass, from above and below, the enemy gunners directed streams of shells against the dodging vessel. The noise was more than deafening, it was one continuous, shattering explosion, and the Earth-men were surrounded by such a blaze of fire from the exploding shells that they could not see the enemy vessels. Seaton sought to dodge the shells by a long dive toward one side, only to find that dozens of new opponents had been launched against them–the deadly airplane-torpedoes of Osnome. Steered by wireless and carrying no crews, they were simply winged bombs carrying thousands of pounds of terrific electrical explosive–enough to kill the men inside the vessel by the concussion of the explosion, even should the arenak armor be strong enough to withstand the blow. Though much faster than the Osnomian vessels, they were slow beside the Skylark, and Seaton could have dodged a few of them with ease. As he dodged, however, they followed relentlessly, and in spite of those which were blown up by the gunners, their number constantly increased until Seaton thought of the repellers.

"'Nobody Holme' is right!" he exclaimed, as he threw on the power actuating the copper bands which encircled the hull in all directions. Instantly the torpedoes were hurled backward, exploding as the force struck them, and even the shells were ineffective, exploding harmlessly, as they encountered the zone of force. The noise of the awful detonations lessened markedly.

"Why the silence, I wonder?" asked Seaton, while the futile shells of the enemy continued to waste their force some hundreds of feet distant from their goal, and while Crane and DuQuesne were methodically destroying the huge vessels as fast as they could aim and fire. At every report one of the monster warships disappeared-its shattered fragments and the bodies of its crew hurtling to the ground. His voice could not be heard in even the lessened tumult, but he continued:

"It must be that our repellers have set up a partial vacuum by repelling even the air!"

Suddenly the shelling ceased and the Skylark was enveloped by a blinding glare from hundreds of great reflectors; an intense, searching, bluish-violet light that burned the flesh and seared through eyelids and eyeballs into the very brain.

"Ultra-violet!" yelled Seaton at the first glimpse of the light, as he threw on the power. "Shut your eyes! Turn your heads down!"

Out in space, far beyond reach of the deadly rays, the men held a short conference, then donned heavy leather-and-canvas suits, which they smeared liberally with thick red paint, and replaced the plain glasses of their helmets with heavy lenses of deep ruby glass.

"This'll stop any ultra-violet ray ever produced," exulted Seaton, as he again threw the vessel into the Mardonalian fleet. A score of the great vessels met their fate before the Skylark was located, and, although the terrible rays were again focused upon the intruder in all their intensity, the carnage continued.

In a few minutes, however, the men heard, or rather felt, a low, intense vibration, like a silent wave of sound —a vibration which smote upon the eardrums as no possible sound could smite, a vibration which racked the joints and tortured the nerves as though the whole body were disintegrating. So sudden and terrible was the effect that Seaton uttered an involuntary yelp of surprise and pain as he once more fled into the safety of space.

"What the devil was that?" demanded DuQuesne. "Was it infra-sound? I didn't suppose such waves could be produced."

"Infra-sound is right. They produce most anything here," replied Seaton, and Crane added:

"Well, about three fur suits apiece, with cotton in our ears, ought to kill any wave propagated through air."

The fur suits were donned forthwith, Seaton whispering in Crane's ear:

"I've found out something else, too. The repellers repel even the air. I'm going to shoot enough juice through them to set up a perfect vacuum outside. That'll kill those air-waves."

Scarcely were they back within range of the fleet when DuQuesne, reaching for his gun to fire the first shot, leaped backward with a yell.

"Beat it!"

Once more at a safe distance, DuQuesne explained.

"It's lucky I'm so used to handling hot stuff that from force of habit I never make close contact with anything at the first touch. That gun carried thousands of volts, with lots of amperage behind them, and if I had had a good hold on it I couldn't have let go. We'll block that game quick enough, though. Thick, dry gloves covered with rubber are all that is necessary. It's a good thing for all of us that you have those fancy condensite handles on your levers, Seaton."

"That was how they got Dunark, undoubtedly," said Crane, as he sent a brief message to the girls, assuring them that all was well, as he had been doing at every respite. "But why were we not overcome at the same time?"

"They must have had the current tuned to iridium, and had to experiment until they found the right wave for steel," Seaton explained.

"I should think our bar would have exploded, with all that current. They must have hit the copper range, too?"

Seaton frowned in thought before he answered.

"Maybe because it's induced current, and not a steady battery impulse. Anyway, it didn't. Let's go!"

"Just a minute," put in Crane. "What are they going to do next, Dick?"

"Search me. I'm not used to my new Osnomian mind yet. I recognize things all right after they happen, but I can't seem to figure ahead-it's like a dimly-remembered something that flashes up as soon as mentioned. I get too many and too new ideas at once. I know, though, that the Osnomians have defenses against all these things except this last stunt of the charged guns. That must be the new one that Mardonale stole from Kondal. The defenses are, however, purely Osnomian in character and material. As we haven't got the stuff to set them up as the Osnomians do, we'll have to do it our own way. We may be able to dope out the next one, though. Let's see, what have they given us so far?"

"We've got to hand it to them," responded DuQuesne, admiringly. "They're giving us the whole range of wave-lengths, one at a time. They've given us light, both ultra-violet and visible, sound, infra-sound, and electricity—I don't know what's left unless they give us a new kind of X-rays, or Hertzian, or infra-red heat waves, or...."

"That's it, heat!" exclaimed Seaton. "They produce heat by means of powerful wave-generators and by setting up heavy induced currents in the armor. They can melt arenak that way."

"Do you suppose we can handle the heat with our refrigerators?" asked Crane.

"Probably. We have a lot of power, and the new arenak cylinders of our compressors will stand anything. The only trouble will be in cooling the condensers. We'll run as long as we have any water in our tanks, then go dive into the ocean to cool off. We'll try it a whirl, anyway."

Soon the Skylark was again dealing out death and destruction in the thick of the enemy vessels, who again turned from the devastation of the helpless city to destroy this troublesome antagonist. But in spite of the utmost efforts of light-waves, sound-waves, and high-tension electricity, the space-car continued to take its terrible toll. As Seaton had foretold, the armor of the Skylark began to grow hot, and he turned on the full power of the refrigerating system. In spite of the cooling apparatus, however, the outer walls finally began to glow redly, and, although the interior was comfortably cool, the ends of the rifle-barrels, which were set flush with the surface of the revolving arenak globes which held them, softened, rendering the guns useless. The copper repellers melted and dripped off in flaming balls of molten metal, so that shells once more began to crash against the armor. DuQuesne, with no thought of quitting apparent in voice or manner, said calmly:

"Well, it looks as though they had us stopped for a few minutes. Let's go back into space and dope out something else."

Seaton, thinking intensely, saw a vast fleet of enemy reinforcements approaching, and at the same time received a wireless call directed to Dunark. It was from the grand fleet of Kondal, hastening from the bordering ocean to the defense of the city. Using Dunark's private code, Seaton told the Karbix, who was in charge of the fleet, that the enemy had a new invention which would wipe them out utterly without a chance to fight, and that he and his vessel were in control of the situation; and ordered him to see that no Kondalian ship came within battle range of a Mardonalian. He then turned to Crane and DuQuesne, his face grim and his fighting jaw set.

"I've got it doped right now. Give the Lark speed enough and she's some bullet herself. We've got four feet of arenak, they've got only an inch, and arenak doesn't even begin to soften until far above a blinding white temperature. Strap yourselves in solid, for it's going to be a rough party from now on."

They buckled their belts firmly, and Seaton, holding the bar toward their nearest antagonist, applied twenty notches of power. The Skylark darted forward and crashed completely through the great airship. Torn wide open by the forty-foot projectile, its engines wrecked and its helicopter-screws and propellers completely disabled, the helpless hulk plunged through two miles of empty air, a mass of wreckage.

Darting hither and thither, the space-car tore through vessel after vessel of the Mardonalian fleet. She was an embodied thunderbolt; a huge, irresistible, indestructible projectile, directed by a keen brain inside it-the brain of Richard Seaton, roused to his highest fighting pitch and fighting for everything that man holds dear. Tortured by the terrible silent waves, which, now that the protecting vacuum had been destroyed, were only partially stopped by the fur suits; shaken and battered by the terrific impacts and the even greater shocks occurring every second as the direction of the vessel was changed; made sick and dizzy by the nauseating swings and lurches as the Skylark spun about the central chamber; Seaton's wonderful physique and his nerves of steel stood him in good stead in this, the supreme battle of his life, as with teeth tight-locked and eyes gray and hard as the fracture of high-carbon steel, he urged the Skylark on to greater and greater efforts.

Though it was impossible for the eye to follow the flight of the space-car, the mechanical sighting devices of the Mardonalian vessels kept her in as perfect focus as though she were stationary, and the great generators continued to hurl into her the full power of their death-dealing waves. The enemy guns were still spitting forth their streams of high-explosive shells, but unlike the waves, the shells moved so slowly compared to their target that only a few found their mark, and many of the vessels fell to the ground, riddled by the shells of their sister-ships.

With anxious eyes Seaton watched the hull of his animated cannon-ball change in color. From dull red it became cherry, and as the cherry red gave place to bright red heat, Seaton threw even more power into the bar as he muttered through his set teeth:

"Well, Seaton, old top, you've got to cut out this loafing on the job and get busy!"

In spite of his utmost exertions and in spite of the powerful ammonia plant, now exerting its full capacity, but sadly handicapped by the fact that its cooling-water was now boiling, Seaton saw the arenak shell continue to heat. The bright red was succeeded by orange, which slowly changed, first to yellow, then to light yellow, and finally to a dazzling white; through which, with the aid of his heavy red lenses, he could still see the enemy ships. After a time he noted that the color had gone down to yellow and he thrilled with exultation, knowing that he had so reduced the numbers of the enemy fleet that their wave-generators could no longer overcome his refrigerators. After a few minutes more of the awful carnage there remained only a small fraction of the proud fleet which, thousands strong, had invaded Kondal —a remnant that sought safety in flight. But even in flight, they still fought with all their weapons, and the streams of bombs dropped from their keel-batteries upon the country beneath marked the path of their retreat with a wide swath of destruction. Half inclined to let the few remaining vessels escape, Seaton's mind changed instantly as he saw the bombs spreading devastation upon the countryside, and not until the last of the Mardonalian vessels had been destroyed did he drop the Skylark into the area of ruins which had once been the palace grounds, beside the Kondal, which was still lying as it had fallen.

After several attempts to steady their whirling senses, the three men finally were able to walk, and, opening a door, they leaped out through the opening in the still glowing wall. Seaton's first act was to wireless the news to Dorothy, who replied that they were coming as fast as they could. The men then removed their helmets, revealing faces pale and drawn, and turned to the helpless space-car.

"There's no way of getting into this thing from the outside...." Seaton began, when he saw that the Kofedix and his party were beginning to revive. Soon Dunark opened the door and stumbled out.

"I have to thank you for more than my life this time," he said, his voice shaken by uncontrollable emotion as he grasped the hands of all three men. "Though unable to move, I was conscious and saw all that happened-you kept them so busy that they didn't have a chance to give us enough to kill us outright. You have saved the lives of millions of our nation and have saved Kondal itself from annihilation."

"Oh, it's not that bad," answered Seaton, uncomfortably. "Both nations have been invaded before."

"Yes-once when we developed the ultra-violet ray, once when Mardonale perfected the machine for producing the silent sound-wave, and again when we harnessed the heat-wave. But this would have been the most complete disaster in history. The other inventions were not so deadly as was this one, and there were terrible battles, from which the victors emerged so crippled that they could not completely exterminate the vanquished, who were able to re-establish themselves in the course of time. If it had not been for you, this would have been the end, as not a Kondalian soldier could move-any person touching iridium was helpless and would have been killed."

He ceased speaking and saluted as the Karfedix and his party rounded a heap of boulders. Dorothy and Margaret screamed in unison as they saw the haggard faces of their husbands, and saw their suits, dripping with a thick substance which they knew to be red, in spite of its purplish-black color. Seaton dodged nimbly as Dorothy sought to take him in her arms, and tore off his suit.

"Nothing but red paint to stop their light-rays," he reassured her as he lifted her clear from the ground in a soul-satisfying embrace. Out of the corner of his eye he saw the Kondalians staring in open-mouthed amazement at the Skylark. Wheeling swiftly, he laughed as he saw a gigantic ball of frost and snow! Again donning his fur suit, he shut off the refrigerators and returned to his party, where the Karfedix gave him thanks in measured terms. As he fell silent, Dunark added:

"Thanks to you, the Mardonalian forces, instead of wiping us out, are themselves destroyed, while only a handful of our vessels have been lost, since the grand fleet could not arrive until the battle was over, and since the vessels that would have thrown themselves away were saved by your orders, which I heard. Thanks to you, we are not even crippled, though our capital is destroyed and the lives of some unfortunates, who could not reach the pits in time, have probably been lost.

"Thanks to you," he continued in a ringing voice, "and to the salt and the new source of power you have given us, Mardonale shall now be destroyed utterly!"

After sending out ships to relieve the suffering of the few wounded and the many homeless, Dunark summoned a corps of mechanics, who banded on new repellers and repaired the fused barrels of the machine-guns, all that was necessary to restore the Skylark to perfect condition.

Facing the party from Earth, the Karfedix stood in the ruins of his magnificent palace. Back of him were the nobles of Kondal, and still further back, in order of rank, stood a multitude of people.

"Is it permitted, oh noble Karfedo, that I reward your captive for his share in the victory?" he asked.

"It is," acquiesced Seaton and Crane, and Roban stepped up to DuQuesne and placed in his hand a weighty leather bag. He then fastened about his left wrist the Order of Kondal, the highest order of the nation.

He then clasped about Crane's wrist a heavily-jeweled, peculiarly-ornamented disk wrought of a deep ruby-red metal, supported by a heavy bracelet of the same material, the most precious metal of Osnome. At sight of the disk the nobles saluted and Seaton barely concealed a start of surprise, for it bore the royal emblem and delegated to its bearer power second only to that of the Karfedix himself.

"I bestow upon you this symbol, Karfedix Crane, in recognition of what you have this day done for Kondal. Wherever you may be upon Kondalian Osnome, which from this day henceforth shall be all Osnome, you have power as my personal representative, as my eldest son."

He drew forth a second bracelet, similar to the first except that it bore seven disks, each differently designed, which he snapped upon Seaton's wrist as the nobles knelt and the people back of them threw themselves upon their faces.

"No language spoken by man possesses words sufficiently weighty to express our indebtedness to you, Karfedix Seaton, our guest and our savior. The First Cause has willed that you should be the instrument through which Kondal is this day made supreme upon Osnome.

In small and partial recognition of that instrumentality, I bestow upon you these symbols, which proclaim you our overlord, the ultimate authority of Osnome.

While this is not the way in which I had thought to bid you farewell, the obligations which you have heaped upon us render all smaller things insignificant. When you return, as I hope and trust you soon will, the city shall be built anew and we can welcome you as befits your station."

Lifting both arms above his head he continued:

"May the great First Cause smile upon you in all your endeavors until you solve the Mystery: may your descendants soon reach the Ultimate Goal. Goodbye."

Seaton uttered a few heartfelt words in response and the party stepped backward toward the Skylark. As they reached the vessel the standing Karfedix and the ranks of kneeling nobles snapped into the double salute-truly a rare demonstration in Kondal.

"What'll we do now?" whispered Seaton.

"Bow, of course," answered Dorothy.

They bowed, deeply and slowly, and entered their vessel. As the Skylark shot into the air with the greatest acceleration that would permit its passengers to move about, the grand fleet of Kondalian warship fired a deafening salute.

It had been planned before the start that each person was to work sixteen hours out of the twenty-four. Seaton was to drive the vessel during the first two eight-hour periods of each day. Crane was to observe the stars during the second and to drive during the third. DuQuesne was to act as observer during the first and third periods. Margaret had volunteered to assist the observer in taking his notes during her waking hours, and Dorothy appointed herself cook and household manager.

As soon as the Skylark had left Osnome, Crane told DuQuesne that he and his wife would work in the observation room until four o'clock in the afternoon, at which time the prearranged system of relief would begin, and DuQuesne retired to his room.

Crane and Margaret made their way to the darkened room which housed the instruments and seated themselves, watching intently and making no effort to conceal their emotion as first the persons beneath them, then the giant war-vessels, and finally the ruined city itself, were lost to view. Osnome slowly assumed the proportions of a large moon, grew smaller, and as it disappeared Crane began to take notes. For a few hours the seventeen suns of this strange solar system shone upon the flying space-car, after which they assumed the aspect of a widely-separated cluster of enormous stars, slowly growing smaller and smaller and shrinking closer and closer together.

At four o'clock in the afternoon, Washington time, DuQuesne relieved Crane, who made his way to the engine room.

"It is time to change shifts, Dick. You have not had your sixteen hours, but everything will be regular from now on. You two had better get some rest."

"All right," replied Seaton, as he relinquished the controls to Crane, and after bidding the new helmsman goodnight he and Dorothy went below to their cabin.

Standing at a window with their arms around each other they stared down with misty eyes at the very faint green star, which was rapidly decreasing in brilliance as the Skylark increased its already inconceivable velocity. Finally, as it disappeared altogether, Seaton turned to his wife and tenderly, lovingly, took her in his arms.

"Littlest Girl....Sweetheart...." he whispered, and paused, overcome by the intensity of his feelings.

"I know, husband mine," she answered, while tears dimmed her glorious eyes. "It is too deep. With nothing but words, we can't say a single thing."

CHAPTER XIX

The Return to Earth

DuQuesne's first act upon gaining the privacy of his own cabin was to open the leather bag presented to him by the Karfedix. He expected to find it filled with rare metals, with perhaps some jewels, instead of which the only metal present was a heavily-insulated tube containing a full pound of metallic radium. The least valuable items in the bag were scores of diamonds, rubies, and emeralds of enormous size and of flawless perfection. Merely ornamental glass upon Osnome, Dunark knew that they were priceless upon Earth, and had acted accordingly. To this great wealth of known gems, he had added a rich and varied assortment of the rare and strange jewels peculiar to his own world, the faidon alone being omitted from the collection. DuQuesne's habitual calmness of mind almost deserted him as he classified the contents of the bag.

The radium alone was worth millions of dollars, and the scientist in him exulted that at last his brother scientists should have ample supplies of that priceless metal with which to work, even while he was rejoicing in the price he would exact for it. He took out the familiar jewels, estimating their value as he counted them—a staggering total. The bag was still half full of the strange gems, some of them glowing like miniature lamps in the dark depths, and he made no effort to appraise them. He knew that once any competent jeweler had compared their cold, hard, scintillating beauty with that of any Earthly gems, he could demand his own price.

"At last," he breathed to himself, "I will be what I have always longed to be—a money power. Now I can cut loose from that gang of crooks and go my own way."

He replaced the gems and the tube of radium in the bag, which he stowed away in one of his capacious pockets, and made his way to the galley.

The return voyage through space was uneventful, the Skylark constantly maintaining the same velocity with which she had started out. Several times, as the days wore on, she came within the zone of attraction of various gigantic suns, but the pilot had learned his lesson. He kept a vigilant eye upon the bar, and at the first sign of a deviation from the perpendicular he steered away, far from the source of the attraction. Not content with these precautions, the man at the board would, from time to time, shut off the power, to make sure that the space-car was not falling toward a body directly in its line of flight.

When half the distance had been covered, the bar was reversed, the travelers holding an impromptu ceremony as the great vessel spun around its center through an angle of one hundred and eighty degrees. A few days later the observers began to recognize some of the fixed stars in familiar constellations and knew that the yellowish-white star directly in their line of flight was the sun of their own solar system. After a time they saw that their course, instead of being directly toward that rapidly-brightening star, was bearing upon a barely visible star a little to one side of it. Pointing their most powerful telescope toward that point of light, Crane made out a planet, half of its disk shining brightly. The girls hastened to peer through the telescope, and they grew excited as they made out the familiar outlines of the continents and oceans upon the lighted portion of the disk.

It was not long until these outlines were plainly visible to the unaided vision. The Earth appeared as a great, softly shining, greenish half-moon, with parts of its surface obscured by fleecy wisps of cloud, and with its two gleaming ice-caps making of its poles two brilliant areas of white. The returning wanderers stared at their own world with their hearts in their throats as Crane, who was at the board, increased the retarding force sufficiently to assure himself that they would not be traveling too fast to land upon the Earth.

After Dorothy and Margaret had gone to prepare a meal, DuQuesne turned to Seaton.

"Have you gentlemen decided what you intend to do with me?"

"No. We haven't discussed it yet. I can't make up my own mind what I want to do to you, except that I sure would like to get you inside a square ring with four-ounce gloves on. You have been of too much real assistance on this trip for us to see you hanged, as you deserve. On the other hand, you are altogether too much of a thorough-going scoundrel for us to let you go free. You see the fix we are in. What would you suggest?"

"Nothing," replied DuQuesne calmly. "As I am in no danger whatever of hanging, nothing you can say on that score affects me in the least. As for freeing me, you may do as you please-it makes no difference to me, one way or the other, as no jail can hold me for a day. I can say, however, that while I have made a fortune on this trip, so that I do not have to associate further with Steel unless it is to my interest to do so, I may nevertheless find it desirable at some future time to establish a monopoly of X. That would, of course, necessitate the death of yourself and Crane. In that event, or in case any other difference should arise between us, this whole affair will be as though it had never existed. It will have no weight either way, whether or not you try to hang me."

"Go as far as you like," Seaton answered cheerfully. "If we're not a match for you and your gang, on foot or in the air, in body or in mind, we'll deserve whatever we get. We can outrun you, outjump you, throw you down, or lick you; we can run faster, hit harder, dive deeper, and come up dryer, than you can. We'll play any game you want to deal, whenever you want to deal it; for fun, money, chalk, or marbles."

His brow darkened in anger as a thought struck him, and the steady gray eyes bored into the unflinching black ones as he continued, with no trace of his former levity in his voice:

"But listen to this. Anything goes as far as Martin and I personally are concerned. But I want you to know that I could be arrested for what I think of you as a man; and if any of your little schemes touch Dottie or Peggy in any way, shape or form, I'll kill you as I would a snake-or rather, I'll take you apart as I would any other piece of scientific apparatus. This isn't a threat, it's a promise. Get me?"

"Perfectly. Good-night."

For many hours the Earth had been obscured by clouds, so that the pilot had only a general idea of what part of the world was beneath them, but as they dropped rapidly downward into the twilight zone, the clouds parted and they saw that they were directly over the Panama Canal. Seaton allowed the Skylark to fall to within ten miles of the ground, when he stopped so that Martin could get his bearings and calculate the course to Washington, which would be in total darkness before their arrival.

DuQuesne had retired, cold and reticent as usual. Glancing quickly about his cabin to make sure that he had overlooked nothing he could take with him, he opened a locker, exposing to view four suits which he had made in his spare time, each adapted to a particular method of escape from the Skylark. The one he selected was of heavy canvas, braced with steel netting, equipped with helmet and air-tanks, and attached to a strong, heavy parachute. He put it on, tested all its parts, and made his way unobserved to one of the doors in the lower part of the vessel. Thus, when the chance for escape came, he was ready for it. As the Skylark paused over the Isthmus, his lips parted in a sardonic smile. He opened the door and stepped out into the air, closing the door behind him as he fell. The neutral color of the parachute was lost in the gathering twilight a few seconds after he left the vessel.

The course laid, Seaton turned almost due north and the Skylark tore through the air. After a short time, when half the ground had been covered, Seaton spoke suddenly.

"Forgot about DuQuesne, Mart. We'd better iron him, hadn't we? Then we'll decide whether we want to keep him or turn him loose."

"I will go fetch him," replied Crane, and turned to the stairs.

He returned shortly, with the news of the flight of the captive.

"Hm...he must have made himself a parachute. I didn't think even he would tackle a sixty-thousand-foot drop. I'll tell the world that he sure has established a record. I can't say I'm sorry that he got away, though. We can get him again any time we want him, anyway, as that little object-compass in my drawer is still looking right at him," said Seaton.

"I think he earned his liberty," declared Dorothy, stoutly, and Margaret added:

"He deserves to be shot, but I'm glad he's gone. He gives me the shivers."

At the end of the calculated time they saw the lights of a large city beneath them, and Crane's fingers clenched upon Seaton's arm as he pointed downward. There were the landing-lights of Crane Field, seven peculiarly-arranged searchlights throwing their mighty beams upward into the night.

"Nine weeks, Dick," he said, unsteadily, "and Shiro would have kept them burning nine years if necessary."

The Skylark dropped easily to the ground in front of the testing shed and the wanderers leaped out, to be greeted by the half-hysterical Jap. Shiro's ready vocabulary of peculiar but sonorous words failed him completely, and he bent himself double in a bow, his yellow face wreathed in the widest possible smile. Crane, one arm around his wife, seized Shiro's hand and wrung it in silence. Seaton swept Dorothy off her feet, pressing her slender form against his powerful body. Her arms tightened about his neck as they kissed each other fervently and he whispered in her ear:

"Sweetheart wife, isn't it great to be back on our good old Earth again?"

THE END

Skylark Three

CHAPTER I

DuQuesne Goes Traveling

In the innermost private office of Steel, Brookings and DuQuesne stared at each other across the massive desk. DuQuesne's voice was cold, his black brows were drawn together.

"Get this, Brookings, and get it straight. I'm shoving off at twelve o'clock tonight. My advice to you is to lay off Richard Seaton, absolutely. Don't do a thing. *Nothing, hold everything.* Keep on holding it until I get back, no matter how long that may be," DuQuesne shot out in an icy tone.

"I am very much surprised at your change of front, Doctor. You are the last man I would have expected to be scared off after one engagement."

"Don't be any more of a fool than you have to, Brookings. There's a lot of difference between scared and knowing when you are simply wasting effort. As you remember, I tried to abduct Mrs. Seaton by picking her off with an attractor from a space-ship. I would have bet that nothing could have stopped me. Well, when they located me-probably with an automatic Osnomian ray-detector —and heated me red-hot while I was still better than two hundred miles up, I knew then and there that they had us stopped; that there was nothing we could do except go back to my plan, abandon the abduction idea, and eventually kill them all. Since my plan would take time, you objected to it, and sent an airplane to drop a five-hundred-pound bomb on them. Airplane, bomb, and all simply vanished. It didn't explode, you remember, just flashed into light and disappeared, with scarcely any noise. Then you pulled several more of your fool ideas, such as long-range bombardment, and so on. None of them worked. Still you've got the nerve to think that you can get them with ordinary gunmen! I've drawn you diagrams and shown you figures —I've told you in great detail and in one-syllable words exactly what we're up against. Now I tell you again that they've *got something*. If you had the brains of a pinhead, you would know that anything I can't do with a space-ship can't be done by a mob of ordinary gangsters. I'm telling you, Brookings, that you can't do it. My way is absolutely the only way that will work."

"But five years, Doctor!"

"I may be back in six months. But on a trip of this kind anything can happen, so I am planning on being gone five years. Even that may not be enough—I am carrying supplies for ten years, and that box of mine in the vault is not to be opened until ten years from today."

"But surely we shall be able to remove the obstructions ourselves in a few weeks. We always have."

"Oh, quit kidding yourself, Brookings! This is no time for idiocy! You stand just as much chance of killing Seaton———"

"Please, Doctor, please don't talk like that!"

"Still squeamish, eh? Your pussyfooting always did give me an acute pain. I'm for direct action, word and deed, first, last, and all the time. I repeat, you have exactly as much chance of killing Richard Seaton as a blind kitten has."

"How do you arrive at that conclusion, Doctor? You seem very fond of belittling our abilities. Personally, I think that we shall be able to attain our objectives within a few weeks-certainly long before you can possibly return from such an extended trip as you have in mind. And since you are so fond of frankness, I will say that I think that Seaton has you buffaloed, as you call it. Nine-tenths of these wonderful Osnomian things, I am assured by competent authorities, are scientifically impossible, and I think that the other one-tenth exists only in your own imagination. Seaton was lucky in that the airplane bomb was defective and exploded prematurely; and your space-ship got hot because of your injudicious speed through the atmosphere. We shall have everything settled by the time you get back."

"If you have, I'll make you a present of the controlling interest in Steel and buy myself a chair in some home for feeble-minded old women. Your ignorance and unwillingness to believe any new idea do not change the facts in any particular. Even before they went to Osnome, Seaton was hard to get, as you found out. On that trip he learned so much new stuff that it is now impossible to kill him by any ordinary means. You should realize that fact when he kills every gangster you send against him. At all events be very, *very* careful not to kill his wife in any of your attacks, even by accident, until after you have killed him."

"Such an event would be regrettable, certainly, in that it would remove all possibility of the abduction."

"It would remove more than that. Remember the explosion in our laboratory, that blew an entire mountain into impalpable dust? Draw in your mind a nice, vivid picture of one ten times the size in each of our plants and in this building. I know that you are fool enough to go ahead with your own ideas, in spite of everything I've said; and, since I do not yet actually control Steel, I can't forbid you to, officially. But you should know that I know what I'm talking about, and I say again that you're going to make an utter fool of yourself; just because you won't believe anything possible, that hasn't been done every day for a hundred years. I wish that I could make you understand that Seaton and Crane have got something that we haven't —but for the good of our plants, and incidentally for your own, please remember one thing, anyway; for if you forget it, we won't have a plant left and you personally will be blown into a fine red mist. Whatever you start, kill Seaton first, and be absolutely certain that he is definitely, completely, finally and totally dead before you touch one of Dorothy Seaton's red hairs. As long as you only attack him personally he won't do anything but kill every man you send against him. If you kill her while he's still alive, though-Blooie!" and the saturnine scientist waved both hands in an expressive pantomime of wholesale destruction.

"Probably you are right in that," Brookings paled slightly. "Yes, Seaton would do just that. We shall be very careful, until after we succeed in removing him."

"Don't worry-you won't succeed. I shall attend to that detail myself, as soon as I get back. Seaton and Crane and their families, the directors and employees of their plants, the banks that by any possibility may harbor their notes or solutions-in short, every person and everything standing between me and a monopoly of 'X' —all shall disappear."

"That is a terrible program, Doctor. Wouldn't the late Perkins' plan of an abduction, such as I have in mind, be better, safer and quicker?"

"Yes-except for the fact that it will not work. I've talked until I'm blue in the face —I've proved to you over and over that you can't abduct her now without first killing him, and that you can't even touch him. My plan is the only one that will work. Seaton isn't the only one who learned anything—I learned a lot myself. I learned one thing in particular. Only four other inhabitants of either Earth or Osnome ever had even an inkling of it, and they died, with their brains disintegrated beyond reading. That thing is my ace in the hole. I'm going after it. When I get it, and not until then, will I be ready to take the offensive."

"You intend starting open war upon your return?"

"The war started when I tried to pick off the women with my attractor. That is why I am leaving at midnight. He always goes to bed at eleven-thirty, and I will be out of range of his object-compass before he wakes up. Seaton and I understand each other perfectly. We both know that the next time we meet one of us is going to be resolved into his component atoms, perhaps into electrons. He doesn't know that he's going to be the one, but I do. My final word to you is to lay off-if you don't, you and your 'competent authorities' are going to learn a lot."

"You do not care to inform me more fully as to your destination or your plans?"

"I do not. Goodbye."

CHAPTER II

Dunark Visits Earth

Martin Crane reclined in a massive chair, the fingers of his right hand lightly touching those of his left, listening attentively. Richard Seaton strode up and down the room before his friend, his unruly brown hair on end, speaking savagely between teeth clenched upon the stem of his reeking, battered briar, brandishing a sheaf of papers.

"Mart, we're stuck-stopped dead. If my head wasn't made of solid blue mush I'd have had a way figured out of this thing before now, but I can't. With that zone of force the Skylark would have everything imaginable-without it, we're exactly where we were before. That zone is immense, man-terrific-its possibilities are unthinkable-and I'm so cussed dumb that I can't find out how to use it intelligently-can't use it at all, for that matter. By its very nature it is impenetrable to any form of matter, however applied; and this calc here," slapping viciously the sheaf of papers containing his calculations, "shows that it must also be opaque to any wave whatever, propagated through air or through ether, clear down to cosmic rays. Behind it, we would be blind and helpless, so we can't use it at all. It drives me frantic! Think of a barrier of pure force, impalpable, immaterial, and exerted along a geometrical surface of no thickness whatever-and yet actual enough to stop even a Millikan ray that travels a hundred thousand light-years and then goes through twenty-seven feet of solid lead just like it was so much vacuum! That's what we're up against! However, I'm going to try out that model, Mart, right now. Come on, guy, snap into it! Let's get busy!"

"You are getting idiotic again, Dick," Crane rejoined calmly, without moving. "You know, even better than I do, that you are playing with the most concentrated essence of energy that the world has ever seen. That zone of force probably can be generated — —"

"Probably, nothing!" barked Seaton. "It's just as evident a fact as that stool," kicking the unoffending bit of furniture half-way across the room as he spoke. "If you'd've let me, I'd've shown it to you yesterday!"

"Undoubtedly, then. Grant that it is impenetrable to all matter and to all known waves. Suppose that it should prove impenetrable also to gravitation and to magnetism? Those phenomena probably depend upon the ether, but we know nothing fundamental of their nature, nor of that of the ether. Therefore your calculations, comprehensive though they are, cannot predict the effect upon them of your zone of force. Suppose that that zone actually does set up a barrier in the ether, so that it nullifies gravitation, magnetism, and all allied phenomena; so that the power-bars, the attractors and repellers, cannot work through it? Then what? As well as showing me the zone of force, you might well have shown me yourself flying off into space, unable to use your power and helpless if you released the zone. No, we must know more of the fundamentals before you try even a small-scale experiment."

"Oh, bugs! You're carrying caution to extremes, Mart. What can happen? Even if gravitation should be nullified, I would rise only slowly, heading south the angle of our latitude-that's thirty-nine degrees-away from the perpendicular. I couldn't shoot off on a tangent, as some of these hot-heads have been claiming. Inertia would make me keep pace, approximately, with the earth in its rotation. I would rise slowly-only as fast as the tangent departs from the curvature of the earth's surface. I haven't figured out how fast that is, but it must be pretty slow."

"Pretty slow?" Crane smiled. "Figure it out."

"All right-but I'll bet it's slower than the rise of a toy balloon." Seaton threw down the papers and picked up his slide-rule, a twenty-inch trigonometrical duplex. "You'll concede that it is allowable to neglect the radial component of the orbital velocity of the earth for a first approximation, won't you-or shall I figure that in too?"

"You may ignore that factor."

"All right-let's see. Radius of rotation here in Washington would be cosine latitude times equatorial radius, approximately-call it thirty-two hundred miles. Angular velocity, fifteen degrees an hour. I want secant fifteen less one times thirty-two hundred. Right? Secant equals one over cosine-um-m-m-m —one point oh three five. Then point oh three five times thirty-two hundred. Hundred and twelve miles first hour. Velocity constant with respect to sun, accelerated respecting point of departure. Ouch! You win, Mart —I'd kinda step out! Well, how about this, then? I'll put on a vacuum suit and carry rations. Harness outside, with the same equipment I used in the test flights before we built *Skylark I*—*plus* the new stuff and a coil. Then throw on the zone, and see what happens. There can't be any jar in taking off, and with that outfit I can get back O. K. if I go clear to Jupiter!"

Crane sat in silence, his keen mind considering every aspect of the motions possible, of velocity, of acceleration, of inertia. He already knew well Seaton's resourcefulness in crises and his physical and mental strength.

"As far as I can see, that might be safe," he admitted finally, "and we really should know something about it besides the theory."

"Fine, Mart-let's get busy! I'll be ready in five minutes. Yell for the girls, will you? They'd break us off at the ankles if we pull anything new without letting them in on it."

A few minutes later the "girls" strolled out into Crane Field, arms around each other-Dorothy Seaton, her gorgeous auburn hair framing violet eyes and vivid coloring; black-haired, dark-eyed Margaret Crane.

"Br-r-r, it's cold!" Dorothy shivered, wrapping her coat more closely about her. "This must be the coldest day Washington has seen for years!"

"It is cold," Margaret agreed. "I wonder what they are going to do out here, this kind of weather?"

As she spoke, the two men stepped out of the "testing shed" —the huge structure that housed their Osnomian-built space-cruiser, "Skylark II." Seaton waddled clumsily, wearing as he did a Crane vacuum-suit which, built of fur, canvas, metal and transparent silica, braced by steel netting and equipped with air-tanks and heaters, rendered its wearer independent of outside conditions of temperature and pressure. Outside this suit he wore a heavy harness of leather, buckled about his body, shoulders, and legs, attached to which were numerous knobs, switches, dials, bakelite cases, and other pieces of apparatus. Carried by a strong aluminum framework in turn supported by the harness, the universal bearing of a small power-bar rose directly above his grotesque-looking helmet.

"What do you think you're going to do in that thing, Dickie?" Dorothy called. Then, knowing that he could not hear her voice, she turned to Crane. "What are you letting that precious husband of mine do now, Martin? He looks as though he were up to something."

While she was speaking, Seaton had snapped the release of his face plate.

"Nothing much, Dottie. Just going to show you-all the zone of force. Mart wouldn't let me turn it on, unless I got all cocked and primed for a year's journey into space."

"Dot, what is that zone of force, anyway?" asked Margaret.

"Oh, it's something Dick got into his head during that awful fight they had on Osnome. He hasn't thought of anything else since we got back. You know how the attractors and repellers work? Well, he found out something funny about the way everything acted while the Mardonalians were bombarding them with a certain kind of wave-length. He finally figured out the exact ray that did it, and found out that if it is made strongly enough, it acts as if a repeller and attractor were working together-only so much stronger that nothing can get through the boundary, either way-in fact, it's so strong that it cuts anything in two that's in the way. And the funny thing is that there's nothing there at all, really; but Dick says that the forces meeting there, or something, make it act as though something really important were there. See?"

"Uh-huh," assented Margaret, doubtfully, just as Crane finished the final adjustments and moved toward them. A safe distance away from Seaton, he turned and waved his hand.

Instantly Seaton disappeared from view, and around the place where he had stood there appeared a shimmering globe some twenty feet in diameter —a globe apparently a perfect spherical mirror, which darted upward and toward the south. After a moment the globe disappeared and Seaton was again seen. He was now standing upon a hemispherical mass of earth. He darted back toward the group upon the ground, while the mass of earth fell with a crash a quarter of a mile away. High above their heads the mirror again encompassed Seaton, and again shot upward and southward. Five times this maneuver was repeated before Seaton came down, landing easily in front of them and opening his helmet.

"It's just what we thought it was, only worse," he reported tersely. "Can't do a thing with it. Gravitation won't work through it-bars won't —nothing will. And dark? *Dark!* Folks, you ain't never seen no darkness, nor heard no silence. It scared me stiff!"

"Poor little boy-afraid of the dark!" exclaimed Dorothy. "We saw absolute blackness in space."

"Not like this, you didn't. I just saw absolute darkness and heard absolute silence for the first time in my life. I never imagined anything like it-come on up with me and I'll show it to you."

"No you won't!" his wife shrieked as she retreated toward Crane. "Some other time, perhaps."

Seaton removed the harness and glanced at the spot from which he had taken off, where now appeared a hemispherical hole in the ground.

"Let's see what kind of tracks I left, Mart," and the two men bent over the depression. They saw with astonishment that the cut surface was perfectly smooth, with not even the slightest roughness or irregularity visible. Even the smallest loose grains of sand had been sheared in two along a mathematically exact hemispherical surface by the inconceivable force of the disintegrating copper bar.

"Well, that sure wins the ——"

An alarm bell sounded. Without a glance around, Seaton seized Dorothy and leaped into the testing shed. Dropping her unceremoniously to the floor he stared through the telescope sight of an enormous ray-generator which had automatically aligned itself upon the distant point of liberation of intra-atomic energy which had caused the alarm to sound. One hand upon the switch, his face was hard and merciless as he waited to make sure of the identity of the approaching space-ship, before he released the frightful power of his generator upon it.

"I've been expecting DuQuesne to try it again," he gritted, striving to make out the visitor, yet more than two hundred miles distant. "He's out to get you, Dot-and this time I'm not just going to warm him up and scare him away, as I did last time. This time that misguided mutt's going to get frizzled right....I can't locate him with this small telescope, Mart. Line him up in the big one and give me the word, will you?"

"I see him, Dick, but it is not DuQuesne's ship. It is built of transparent arenak, like the 'Kondal.' Even though it seems impossible, I believe it is the 'Kondal'."

"Maybe so, and again maybe DuQuesne built it-or stole it. On second thought, though, I don't believe that DuQuesne would be fool enough to tackle us again in the same way-but I'm taking no chances....O. K., it is the 'Kondal,' I can see Dunark and Sitar myself, now."

The transparent vessel soon neared the field and the four Terrestrials walked out to greet their Osnomian friends. Through the arenak walls they recognized Dunark, Kofedix of Kondal, at the controls, and saw Sitar, his beautiful young queen, lying in one of the seats near the wall. She attempted a friendly greeting, but her face was strained as though she were laboring under a burden too great for her to bear.

As they watched, Dunark slipped a helmet over his head and one over Sitar's, pressed a button to open one of the doors, and supported her toward the opening.

"They mustn't come out, Dick!" exclaimed Dorothy in dismay. "They'll freeze to death in five minutes without any clothes on!"

"Yes, and Sitar can't stand up under our gravitation, either —I doubt if Dunark can, for long," and Seaton dashed toward the vessel, motioning the visitor back.

But misunderstanding the signal, Dunark came on. As he clambered heavily through the door he staggered as though under an enormous weight, and Sitar collapsed upon the frozen ground. Trying to help her, half-kneeling over her, Dunark struggled, his green skin paling to a yellowish tinge at the touch of the bitter and unexpected cold. Seaton leaped forward and gathered Sitar up in his mighty arms as though she were a child.

"Help Dunark back in, Mart," he directed crisply. "Hop in, girls-we've got to take these folks back up where they can live."

Seaton shut the door, and as everyone lay flat in the seats Crane, who had taken the controls, applied one notch of power and the huge vessel leaped upward. Miles of altitude were gained before Crane brought the cruiser to a stop and locked her in place with an anchoring attractor.

"There," he remarked calmly, "gravitation here is approximately the same as it is upon Osnome."

"Yes," put in Seaton, standing up and shedding clothing in all directions, "and I rise to remark that we'd better undress as far as the law allows-perhaps farther. I never did like Osnomian ideas of comfortable warmth, but we can endure it by peeling down to bedrock— —"

Sitar jumped up happily, completely restored, and the three women threw their arms around each other.

"What a horrible, terrible, frightful world!" exclaimed Sitar, her eyes widening as she thought of her first experience with our earth. "Much as I love you, I shall never dare try to visit you again. I have never been able to understand why you Terrestrials wear what you call 'clothes,' nor why you are so terribly, brutally strong. Now I really know—I will feel the utterly cold and savage embrace of that awful earth of yours as long as I live!"

"Oh, it's not so bad, Sitar." Seaton, who was shaking both of Dunark's hands vigorously, assured her over his shoulder. "All depends on where you were raised. We like it that way, and Osnome gives us the pip. But you poor fish," turning again to Dunark, "with all my brains inside your skull, you should have known what you were letting yourself in for."

"That's true, after a fashion," Dunark admitted, "but your brain told me that Washington was *hot*. If I'd have thought to recalculate your actual Fahrenheit degrees into our loro ... but that figures only forty-seven and, while very cold, we could have endured it-wait a minute, I'm getting it. You have what you call 'seasons.' This, then, must be your 'winter.' Right?"

"Right the first time. That's the way your brain works behind my pan, too. I could figure anything out all right after it happened, but hardly ever beforehand-so I guess I can't blame you much, at that. But what I want to know is, how'd you get here? It would take more than my brains-you can't see our sun from anywhere near Osnome, even if you knew exactly where to look for it."

"Easy. Remember those wrecked instruments you threw out of *Skylark I* when we built *Skylark II*?" Having every minute detail of the configuration of Seaton's brain engraved upon his own, Dunark spoke English in Seaton's own characteristic careless fashion. Only when thinking deeply or discussing abstruse matter did Seaton employ the carefully selected and precise phrasing, which he knew so well how to use. "Well, none of them was beyond repair and the juice was still on most of them. One was an object-compass bearing on the Earth. We simply fixed the bearings, put on some minor improvements, and here we are."

"Let us all sit down and be comfortable," he continued, changing into the Kondalian tongue without a break, "and I will explain why we have come. We are in most desperate need of two things which you alone can supply-salt, and that strange metal, 'X'. Salt I know you have in great abundance, but I know that you have very little of the metal. You have only the one compass upon that planet?"

"That's all-one is all we set on it. However, we've got close to half a ton of the metal on hand-you can have all you want."

"Even if I took it all, which I would not like to do, that would be less than half enough. We must have at least one of your tons, and two tons would be better."

"Two tons! Holy cat! Are you going to plate a fleet of battle cruisers?"

145

"More than that. We must plate an area of copper of some ten thousand square miles-in fact, the very life of our entire race depends upon it."

"It's this way," he continued, as the four earth-beings stared at him in wonder. "Shortly after you left Osnome we were invaded by the inhabitants of the third planet of our fourteenth sun. Luckily for us they landed upon Mardonale, and in less than two days there was not a single Osnomian left alive upon that half of the planet. They wiped out our grand fleet in one brief engagement, and it was only the *Kondal* and a few more like her that enabled us to keep them from crossing the ocean. Even with our full force of these vessels, we cannot defeat them. Our regular Kondalian weapons were useless. We shot explosive copper charges against them of such size as to cause earthquakes all over Osnome, without seriously crippling their defenses. Their offensive weapons are almost irresistible-they have generators that burn arenak as though it were so much paper, and a series of deadly frequencies against which only a copper-driven ray screen is effective, and even that does not stand up long."

"How come you lasted till now, then?" asked Seaton.

"They have nothing like the *Skylark*, and no knowledge of intra-atomic energy. Therefore their space-ships are of the rocket type, and for that reason they can cross only at the exact time of conjunction, or whatever you call it-no, not conjunction, exactly, either, since the two planets do not revolve around the same sun: but when they are closest together. Our solar system is so complex, you know, that unless the trips are timed exactly, to the hour, the vessels will not be able to land upon Osnome, but will be drawn aside and be lost, if not actually drawn into the vast central sun. Although it may not have occurred to you, a little reflection will show that the inhabitants of all the central planets, such as Osnome, must perforce be absolutely ignorant of astronomy, and of all the wonders of outer space. Before your coming we knew nothing beyond our own solar system, and very little of that. We knew of the existence of only such of the closest planets as were brilliant enough to be seen in our continuous sunlight, and they were few. Immediately after your coming I gave your knowledge of astronomy to a group of our foremost physicists and mathematicians, and they have been working ceaselessly from space-ships —close enough so that observations could be recalculated to Osnome, and yet far enough away to afford perfect 'seeing,' as you call it."

"But I don't know any more about astronomy than a pig does about Sunday," protested Seaton.

"Your knowledge of details is, of course, incomplete," conceded Dunark, "but the detailed knowledge of the best of your Earthly astronomers would not help us a great deal, since we are so far removed from you in space. You, however, have a very clear and solid knowledge of the fundamentals of the science, and that is what we need, above all things."

"Well, maybe you're right, at that. I do know the general theory of the motions, and I studied some Celestial Mechanics. I'm awfully weak on advanced theory, though, as you'll find out when you get that far."

"Perhaps-but since our enemies have no knowledge of astronomy whatever, it is not surprising that their rocket-ships can be launched only at one particularly favorable time; for there are many planets and satellites, of which they can know nothing, to throw their vessels off the course.

"Some material essential to the operation of their war machinery apparently must come from their own planet, for they have ceased attacking, have dug in, and are simply holding their ground. It may be that they had not anticipated as much resistance as we could offer with space-ships and intra-atomic energy. At any rate, they have apparently saved enough of that material to enable them to hold out until the next conjunction —I cannot think of a better word for it-shall occur. Our forces are attacking constantly, with all the armament at our command, but it is certain that if the next conjunction is allowed to occur, it means the end of the entire Kondalian nation.'"

"What d'you mean 'if the next conjunction is *allowed* to occur?'" interjected Seaton. "Nobody can stop it."

"I am stopping it," Dunark stated quietly, grim purpose in every lineament. "That conjunction shall never occur. That is why I must have the vast quantities of salt and 'X'. We are building abutments of arenak upon the first satellite of our seventh planet, and upon our sixth planet itself. We shall cover them with plated active copper, and install chronometers to throw the switches at precisely the right moment. We have calculated the exact times, places, and magnitudes of the forces to be used. We shall throw the sixth planet some distance out of its orbit, and force the first satellite of the seventh planet clear out of that planet's influence. The two bodies whose motions we have thus changed will collide in such a way that the resultant body will meet the planet of our enemies in head-on collision, long before the next conjunction. The two bodies will be of almost equal masses, and will have opposite and approximately equal velocities; hence the resultant fused or gaseous mass will be practically without velocity and will fall directly into the fourteenth sun."

"Wouldn't it be easier to destroy it with an explosive copper bomb?"

"Easier, yes, but much more dangerous to the rest of our solar system. We cannot calculate exactly the effect of the collisions we are planning-but it is almost certain that an explosion of sufficient violence to destroy all life upon the planet would disturb its motion sufficiently to endanger the entire system. The way we have in mind will simply allow the planet and one satellite to drop out quietly-the other planets of the same sun will soon adjust themselves to the new conditions, and the system at large will be practically unaffected-at least, so we believe."

Seaton's eyes narrowed as his thoughts turned to the quantities of copper and "X" required and to the engineering features of the project; Crane's first thought was of the mathematics involved in a computation of that magnitude and character; Dorothy's quick reaction was one of pure horror.

"He can't, Dick! He mustn't! It would be too ghastly! It's outrageous-it's unthinkable-it's — it's —it's simply too horrible!" Her violet eyes flamed, and Margaret joined in:

"That would be awful, Martin. Think of the destruction of a whole planet-of an entire world-with all its inhabitants! It makes me shudder, even to think of it."

Dunark leaped to his feet, ablaze. But before he could say a word, Seaton silenced him.

"Shut up, Dunark! Pipe down! Don't say anything you'll be sorry for-let *me* tell 'em! Close your mouth, I tell you!" as Dunark still tried to get a word in, "I tell you I'll tell 'em, and when I tell 'em they stay told! Now listen, you two girls-you're going off half-cocked and you're both full of little red ants. What do you think Dunark is up against? Sherman chirped it when he described war-and this is a real he-war; a brand totally unknown on our Earth. It isn't a question of whether or not to destroy a population-the only question is which population is to be destroyed. One of them's got to go. Remember those folks go into a war thoroughly, and there isn't a thought, even remotely resembling our conception of mercy in any of their minds on either side. If Dunark's plans go through the enemy nation will be wiped out. That is horrible, of course. But on the other hand, if we block him off from salt and 'X,' the entire Kondalian nation will be destroyed just as thoroughly and efficiently, and even more horribly-not one man, woman, or child would be spared. Which nation do you want saved? Play that over a couple of times on your adding machine, Dot, and let me know what you get."

Dorothy, taken aback, opened and closed her mouth twice before she found her voice.

"But, Dick, they couldn't possibly. Would they kill them all, Dick? Surely they wouldn't — they *couldn't*."

"Surely they would-and could. They do-it's good technique in those parts of the Galaxy. Dunark has just told us of how they killed every member of the entire race of Mardonalians, in forty hours. Kondal would go the same way. Don't kid yourself, Dimples-don't be a child. War up there is *no* species of pink tea, believe me-half of my brain has been through thirty years of Osnomian warfare, and I know precisely what I'm talking about. Let's take a vote. Personally, I'm in favor of Osnome. Mart?"

"Osnome."

"Dottie? Peggy?" Both remained silent for some time, then Dorothy turned to Margaret.

"You tell him, Peggy-we both feel the same way."

"Dick, you know that we wouldn't want the Kondalians destroyed-but the other is so-such a —well, such an utter *shrecklichkeit* —isn't there some other way out?"

"I'm afraid not-but if there is any other possible way out, I'll do my da-to help find it," he promised. "The ayes have it. Dunark, we'll skip over to that 'X' planet and load you up."

Dunark grasped Seaton's hand. "Thanks, Dick," he said, simply. "But before you help me farther, and lest I might be in some degree sailing under false colors, I must tell you that, wearer of the seven disks though you are, Overlord of Osnome though you are, my brain brother though you are; had you decided against me, nothing but my death could have kept me away from that salt and your 'X' compass."

"Why sure," assented Seaton, in surprise. "Why not? Fair enough! Anybody would do the same-don't let that bother you."

"How is your supply of platinum?" asked Dunark.

"Mighty low. We had about decided to hop over there after some. I want some of your textbooks on electricity and so on, too. I see you brought a load of platinum with you."

"Yes, a few hundred tons. We also brought along an assortment of books I knew you would be interested in, a box of radium, a few small bags of gems of various kinds, and some of our fabrics, Sitar thought your Karfediro would like to have. While we are here, I would like to get some books on chemistry and some other things."

"We'll get you the Congressional Library, if you want it, and anything else you think you'd like. Well, gang, let's go places and do things! What to do, Mart?"

"We had better drop back to Earth, have the laborers unload the platinum, and load on the salt, books, and other things. Then both ships will go to the 'X' planet, as we will each want compasses on it, for future use. While we are loading, I should like to begin remodeling our instruments; to make them something like these; with Dunark's permission. These instruments are wonders, Dick-vastly ahead of anything I have ever seen. Come and look at them, if you want to see something really beautiful."

"Coming up. But say, Mart, while I think of it, we mustn't forget to install a zone-of-force apparatus on this boat, too. Even though we can't use it intelligently, it certainly would be a winner as a defense. We couldn't hurt anybody through it, of course, but if we should happen to be getting licked anywhere, all we'd have to do would be to wrap ourselves up in it. They couldn't touch us. Nothing in the ether spectrum is corkscrewy enough to get through it."

"That's the second idea you've had since I've known you, Dicky," Dorothy smiled at Crane. "Do you think he should be allowed to run at large, Martin?"

"That is a real idea. We may need it-you never can tell. Even if we never find any other use for the zone of force, that one is amply sufficient to justify its installation."

"Yes, it would be, for you-and I'm getting to be a regular Safety-First Simon myself, since they opened up on us. What about those instruments?"

The three men gathered around the instrument-board and Dunark explained the changes he had made-and to such men as Seaton and Crane it was soon evident that they were examining an installation embodying sheer perfection of instrumental control—a system which only those wonder instrument-makers, the Osnomians, could have devised. The new object-compasses were housed in arenak cases after setting, and the housings were then exhausted to the highest attainable vacuum. Oscillation was set up by means of one carefully standardized electrical impulse, instead of by the clumsy finger-touch Seaton had used. The bearings, built of arenak and Osnomian jewels, were as strong as the axles of a truck and yet were almost perfectly frictionless.

"I like them myself," admitted Dunark. "Without a load the needles will rotate freely more than a thousand hours on the primary impulse, as against a few minutes in the old type; and under load they are many thousands of times as sensitive."

"You're a blinding flash and a deafening report, ace!" declared Seaton, enthusiastically. "That compass is as far ahead of my model as the *Skylark* is ahead of Wright's first glider."

The other instruments were no less noteworthy. Dunark had adopted the Perkins telephone system, but had improved it until it was scarcely recognized and had made it capable of almost unlimited range. Even the guns-heavy rapid-firers, mounted in spherical bearings in the walls-were aimed and fired by remote control, from the board. He had devised full automatic steering controls; and meters and recorders for acceleration, velocity, distance, and flight-angle. He had perfected a system of periscopic vision, which enabled the pilot to see the entire outside surfaces of the shell, and to look toward any point of the heavens without interference.

"This kind of takes my eye, too, prince," Seaton said, as he seated himself, swung a large, concave disk in front of him, and experimented with levers and dials. "You certainly can't call this thing a periscope-it's no more a periscope than I am a polyp. When you look through this plate, it's better than looking out of a window-it subtends more than the angle of vision, so that you can't see anything but out-of-doors —I thought for a second I was going to fall out. What do you call 'em, Dunark?"

"Kraloto. That would be in English ... Seeing-plate? Or rather, call it 'visiplate'."

"That's a good word. Mart, take a look if you want to see a set of perfect lenses and prisms."

Crane looked into the visiplate and gasped. The vessel had disappeared-he was looking directly down upon the Earth below him!

"No trace of chromatic, spherical, or astigmatic aberration," he reported in surprise. "The refracting system is invisible-it seems as though nothing intervenes between the eye and the object. You perfected all these things since we left Osnome, Dunark? You are in a class by yourself. I could not even copy them in less than a month, and I never could have invented them."

"I did not do it alone, by any means. The Society of Instrument-Makers, of which I am only one member, installed and tested more than a hundred systems. This one represents the best features of all the systems tried. It will not be necessary for you to copy them. I brought along two complete duplicate sets for the *Skylark*, as well as a dozen or so of the compasses. I thought that perhaps these particular improvements might not have occurred to you, since you Terrestrials are not as familiar as we are with complex instrumental work."

Crane and Seaton spoke together.

"That was thoughtful of you, Dunark, and we appreciated it fully."

"That puts four more palms on your *Croix de Guerre*, ace. Thanks a lot."

"Say, Dick," called Dorothy, from her seat near the wall. "If we're going down to the ground, how about Sitar?"

"By lying down and not doing anything, and by staying in the vessel, where it is warm, she will be all right for the short time we must stay here," Dunark answered for his wife. "I will help all I can, but I do not know how much that will be."

"It isn't so bad lying down." Sitar agreed. "I don't like your Earth a bit, but I can stand it a little while. Anyway, I *must* stand it, so why worry about it?"

"'At-a-girl!" cheered Seaton. "And as for you, Dunark, you'll pass the time just like Sitar does-lying down. If you do much chasing around down there where we live, you're apt to get your lights and liver twisted all out of shape-so you'll stay put, horizontal. We've got men enough around the shop to eat this cargo in three hours, let alone unload it. While they unload and load you up, we'll install the zone apparatus, put a compass on you, put one of yours on us, and then you can hop back up here where you're comfortable. Then as soon as we can get the 'Lark' ready for the trip, we'll jump up here and be on our way. Everything clear? Cut the rope, Mart-let the old bucket drop!"

CHAPTER III

Skylark Two Sets Out

"Say, Mart, I just got conscious! It never occurred to me until just now, as Dunark left, that I'm as good an instrument-maker as Dunark is-the same one, in fact-and I've got a hunch. You know that needle on DuQuesne hasn't been working for quite a while? Well, I don't believe it's out of commission at all. I think he's gone somewhere, so far away that it can't read on him. I'm going to house it in, re-jewel it, and find out where he is."

"An excellent idea. He has even you worrying, and as for myself——"

"Worrying! That bird is simply pulling my cork! I'm so scared he'll get Dottie, that I'm running around in circles and biting myself in the small of the back. He's got a hen on, you can bet your shirt on that-what gravels me is he's aiming at the girls, not at us or the job."

"I should say that someone had aimed at you fairly accurately, judging by the number of bullets stopped lately by that arenak armor of yours. I wish that I could take some of the strain, but they are centering all their attacks upon you."

"Yes—I can't stick my nose outside our yard without somebody throwing lead at it. It's funny, too. You're more important to the power-plant than I am."

"You should know why. They are not afraid of me. While my spirit is willing enough, it was your skill and rapidity with a pistol that frustrated four attempts at abduction in as many days. It is positively uncanny, the way you explode into action. With all my practice, I didn't even have my pistol out yesterday until it was all over. And besides Prescott's guards, we had four policemen with us-detailed to 'guard' us-because of the number of gunmen you had to kill before that!"

"It ain't practice so much, Mart-it's a gift. I've always been fast, and I react automatically. You think first, that's why you're slow. Those cops were funny. They didn't know what it was all about until it was all over-all but calling the wagon. That was the worst yet. One of their slugs struck directly in front of my left eye-it was kinda funny, at that, seeing it splash-and I thought I was inside a boiler in a riveting shop when those machine-guns cut loose. It was hectic, all right, while it lasted. But one thing I'll tell the attentive world-we're not doing all the worrying. Very few, if any, of the gangsters they send after us are getting back. Wonder what they think when they shoot at us and we don't drop?

"But I'm afraid I'm beginning to crack, Mart," Seaton went on, his voice becoming grimly earnest. "I don't like anything about this whole mess. I don't like all four of us wearing armor all the time. I don't like living constantly under guard. I don't like all this killing. And this constant menace of losing Dorothy, if I let her out of my sight for five seconds, is driving me mad. To tell you the real truth, I'm devilishly afraid that they'll figure out something that'll work. I could grab off two women, or kill two men, if they had armor and guns enough to stock a war. I believe that DuQuesne could, too-and the rest of that bunch aren't imbeciles, either, by any means. I won't feel safe until all four of us are in the *Skylark* and a long ways from here. I'm sure glad we're pulling out; and I don't intend to come back until I get a good line on DuQuesne. He's the bird I'm going to get, and get right-and when I get him I'll tell the cock-eyed world he'll stay got. There won't be any two atoms of his entire carcass left in the same township. I meant that promise when I gave it to him!"

"He realizes that fully. He knows that it is now definitely either his life or our own, and he is really dangerous. When he took Steel over and opened war upon us, he did it with his eyes wide open. With his ideas, he must have a monopoly of 'X' or nothing; and he knows the only possible way of getting it. However, you and I both know that he would not let either one of us live, even though we surrendered."

"You chirped it! But that guy's going to find he's started something, unless I get paralysis of the intentions. Well, how about turning up a few R. P. M.? We don't want to keep Dunark waiting too long."

"There is very little to do beyond installing the new instruments; and that is nearly done. We can finish pumping out the compass *en route*. You have already installed every weapon of offense and defense known to either Earthly or Osnomian warfare, including those ray-generators and screens you moaned so about not having during the battle over Kondal. I believe that we have on board every article for which either of us has been able to imagine even the slightest use."

"Yes, we've got her so full of plunder that there's hardly room left for quarters. You ain't figuring on taking anybody but Shiro along, are you?"

"No. I suppose there is no real necessity for taking even him, but he wants very much to go, and may prove himself useful."

"I'll say he'll be useful. None of us really enjoys polishing brass or washing dishes-and besides, he's one star cook and an A-1 housekeeper."

The installation of the new instruments was soon completed, and while Dorothy and Margaret made last-minute preparations for departure, the men called a meeting of the managing directors and department heads of the "Seaton-Crane Co., Engineers." The chiefs gave brief reports in turn. Units Number One and Number Two of the immense new central super-power plant were in continuous operation. Number Three was almost ready to cut in. Number Four was being rushed to completion. Number Five was well under way. The research laboratory was keeping well up on its problems. Troubles were less than had been anticipated. Financially, it was a gold mine. With no expense for boilers or fuel, and thus with a relatively small investment in plant and a very small operating cost, they were selling power at one-sixth of prevailing rates, and still profits were almost paying for all new construction. With the completion of Number Five, rates would be reduced still further.

"In short, Dad, everything's slick," remarked Seaton to Mr. Vaneman, after the others had gone.

"Yes; your plan of getting the best men possible, paying them well, and giving them complete authority and sole responsibility, has worked to perfection. I have never seen an undertaking of such size go forward so smoothly and with such fine co-operation."

"That's the way we wanted it. We hand-picked the directors, and put it up to you, strictly. You did the same to the managers. Everybody knows that his end is up to him, and him alone-so he digs in."

"However, Dick, while everything at the works is so fine, when is this other thing going to break?"

"We've won all the way so far, but I'm afraid something's about due. That's the big reason I want to get Dot away for a while. You know what they're up to?"

"Too well," the older man answered. "Dottie or Mrs. Crane, or both. Her mother-she is telling her goodbye now-and I agree that the danger here is greater than out there."

"Danger out there? With the old can fixed the way she is now, Dot's a lot safer there than you are in bed. Your house might fall down, you know."

"You're probably right, son —I know you, and I know Martin Crane. Together, and in the *Skylark*, I believe you invincible."

"All set, Dick?" asked Dorothy, appearing in the doorway.

"All set. You've got the dope for Prescott and everybody Dad. We may be back in six months, or we may see something to investigate, and be gone a year or so. Don't begin to lose any sleep until after we've been out-oh, say three years. We'll make it a point to be back by then."

Farewells were said; the party embarked, and *Skylark Two* shot upward. Seaton flipped a phone set over his head and spoke.

"Dunark!... Coming out, heading directly for 'X'.... No, better stay quite a ways off to one side when we get going good.... Yes, I'm accelerating twenty six point oh oh oh.... Yes. I'll call you now and then, until the radio waves get lost, to check the course with you. After that,

151

keep on the last course, reverse at the calculated distance, and by the time we're pretty well slowed down, we'll feel around for each other with the compasses and go in together....Right.... Uh-huh....Fine! So long!"

In order that the two vessels should keep reasonably close together, it had been agreed that each should be held at an acceleration of exactly twenty-six feet per second, positive and negative. This figure represented a compromise between the gravitational forces of the two worlds upon which the different parties lived. While considerably less than the acceleration of gravitation at the surface of the Earth, the Terrestrials could readily accustom themselves to it; and it was not enough greater than that of Osnome to hamper seriously the activities of the green people.

Well clear of the Earth's influence, Seaton assured himself that everything was functioning properly, then stretched to his full height, wreathed his arms over his head, and heaved a deep sigh of relief.

"Folks," he declared, "This is the first time I've felt right since we got out of this old bottle. Why, I feel so good a cat could walk up to me and scratch me right in the eye, and I wouldn't even scratch back. Yowp! I'm a wild Siberian catamount, and this is my night to howl. Whee-ee-yerow!"

Dorothy laughed, a gay, lilting carol.

"Haven't I always told you he had cat blood in him, Peggy? Just like all tomcats, every once in a while he has to stretch his claws and yowl. But go ahead, Dickie, I like it-this is the first uproar you've made in weeks. I believe I'll join you!"

"It most certainly is a relief to get this load off our minds: I could do a little ladylike yowling myself," Margaret said; and Crane, lying completely at ease, a thin spiral of smoke curling upward from his cigarette, nodded agreement.

"Dick's yowling is quite expressive at times. All of us feel the same way, but some of us are unable to express ourselves quite so vividly. However, it is past bedtime, and we should organize our crew. Shall we do it as we did before?"

"No, it isn't necessary. Everything is automatic. The bar is held parallel to the guiding compass, and signal bells ring whenever any of the instruments show a trace of abnormal behavior. Don't forget that there is at least one meter registering and recording every factor of our flight. With this control system we can't get into any such jam as we did last trip."

"Surely you are not suggesting that we run all night with no one at the controls?"

"Exactly that. A man camping at this board is painting the lily and gilding fine gold. Awake or asleep nobody need be closer to it than is necessary to hear a bell if one should ring, and you can hear them all over the ship. Furthermore, I'll bet a hat we won't hear a signal a week. Simply as added precaution, though, I've run lines so that any time one of these signals lets go, it sounds a buzzer on the head of our bed, so I'm automatically taking the night shift. Remember, Mart, these instruments are thousands of times as sensitive as the keenest human senses-they'll spot trouble long before we could, even if we were looking right at it."

"Of course, you understand these instruments much better than I do, as yet. If you trust them, I am perfectly willing to do the same. Goodnight."

Seaton sat down and Dorothy nestled beside him, her head snuggled into the curve of his shoulder.

"Sleepy, cuddle-pup?"

"Heavens, no! I couldn't sleep now, lover-could you?"

"Not any. What's the use?"

His arm tightened around her. Apparently motionless to its passengers, the cruiser bored serenely on into space, with ever-mounting velocity. There was not the faintest sound, not the slightest vibration-only the peculiar violet glow surrounding the shining copper cylinder in its massive universal bearing gave any indication of the thousands of kilowatts being generated in the mighty intra-atomic power-plant. Seaton studied it thoughtfully.

"You know, if that violet aura and copper bar were a little different in shade and tone of color, they'd be just like your eyes and hair," he remarked finally.

"You burn me up, Dick!" she retorted, her entrancing low chuckle bubbling through her words. "You do say the weirdest things at times! Possibly they would-and if the moon were made of different stuff than it is and had a different color, it might be green cheese, too! What say we go over and look at the stars?"

"As you were, Rufus!" he commanded sternly. "Don't move a millimeter-you're a drive fit, right where you are. I'll get you any stars you want, and bring them right in here to you. What constellation would you like? I'll get you the Southern Cross-we never see it in Washington."

"No, I want something familiar; the Pleiades or the Big Dipper-no, get me Canis Major — 'where Sirius, brightest jewel in the diadem of the firmament, holds sway'," she quoted. "There! Thought I'd forgotten all the astronomy you ever taught me, didn't you? Think you can find it?"

"Sure. Declination about minus twenty, as I remember it, and right ascension between six and seven hours. Let's see-where would that be from our course?"

He thought for a moment, manipulated several levers and dials, snapped off the lights, and swung number one exterior visiplate around, directly before their eyes.

"Oh....Oh...this is magnificent, Dick!" she exclaimed. "It's stupendous. It seems as though we were right out there in space itself, and not in here at all. It's...it's just too perfectly darn wonderful!"

Although neither of them was unacquainted with interstellar space, it presents a spectacle that never fails to awe even the most seasoned observer: and no human being had ever before viewed the wonders of space from such a coign of vantage. Thus the two fell silent and awed as they gazed out into the abysmal depths of the interstellar void. The darkness of Earthly night is ameliorated by light-rays scattered by the atmosphere: the stars twinkle and scintillate and their light is diffused, because of the same medium. But here, what a contrast! They saw the utter, absolute darkness of the complete absence of all light: and upon that indescribable blackness they beheld superimposed the almost unbearable brilliance of enormous suns concentrated into mathematical points, dimensionless. Sirius blazed in blue-white splendor, dominating the lesser members of his constellation, a minute but intensely brilliant diamond upon a field of black velvet-his refulgence unmarred by any trace of scintillation or distortion.

As Seaton slowly shifted the field of vision, angling toward and across the celestial equator and the ecliptic, they beheld in turn mighty Rigel; The Belt, headed by dazzlingly brilliant-white Delta-Orionis; red Betelguese; storied Aldebaran, the friend of mariners; and the astronomically constant Pleiades.

Seaton's arm contracted, swinging Dorothy into his embrace; their lips met and held.

"Isn't it wonderful, lover," she murmured, "to be out here in space this way, together, away from all our troubles and worries? I am so happy."

"It's all of that, sweetheart mine!"

"I almost died, every time they shot at you. Suppose your armor cracked or something? I wouldn't want to go on living—I'd just naturally die!"

"I'm glad it didn't —and I'm twice as glad that they didn't succeed in grabbing you away from me...." His jaw set rigidly, his gray eyes became hard as tempered drills. "Blackie DuQuesne has something coming to him. So far, I have always paid my debts....I shall settle with him ... IN FULL."

"That was an awfully quick change of subject," he continued, his voice changing instantly into a lighter vein, "but that's one penalty of being human. We can't live in high altitudes all our lives-if we could there would be no thrill in ascending them so often.

"Yes, we love each other just the same-more than anybody else I ever heard of." After a moment she eyed him shrewdly and continued:

"You've got something on your mind besides that tangled mop of hair, big boy. Tell it to Red-Top."

"Nothing much...."

"Come on, 'fess up-it's good for the soul. You can't fool your own wife, guy; I know your little winning ways too well."

"Let me finish, woman; I was about to bare my very soul. To resume-nothing much to go on but a hunch, but I think DuQuesne's somewhere out here in the great open spaces, where men are sometimes schemers as well as men; and if so, I'm after him-foot, horse, and marines."

"That object compass?"

"Yes. You see, I built that thing myself, and I know darn well it isn't out of order. It's still on him, but doesn't indicate. Ergo, he is too far away to reach-and with his weight, I could find him anywhere up to about one and a half light-years. If he wants to go that far away from home, where is his logical destination? It can't be anywhere but Osnome, since that is the only place we stopped at for any length of time-the only place where he could have learned anything. He's learned something, or found something useful to him there, just as we did. That is certain, since he is not the type of man to do anything without a purpose. Uncle Dudley is on his trail-and will be able to locate him pretty soon."

"When will you get that new compass-case exhausted to a skillionth of a whillimeter or something, whatever it is? I thought Dunark said it took five hundred hours of pumping to get it where he wanted it?"

"It did him-but while the Osnomians are wonders at some things, they're not so hot at others. You see, I've got three pumps on that job, in series. First, a Rodebush-Michalek superpump then, backing that, an ordinary mercury-vapor pump, and last, backing both the others, a Cenco-Hyvac motor-driven oil pump. In less than fifty hours that case will be as empty as a flapper's skull. Just to make sure of cleaning up the last infinitesimal traces, though, I'm going to flash a getter charge of tantalum in it. After that, the atmosphere in that case will be tenuous-take my word for it."

"I'll have to; most of that contribution to science being over my head like a circus tent. What say we let *Skylark Two* drift by herself for a while, and catch us some of Nature's sweet restorer?"

CHAPTER IV

The Zone of Force Is Tested

Seaton strode into the control room with a small oblong box in his hand. Crane was seated at the desk, poring over an abstruse mathematical treatise in *Science*. Margaret was working upon a bit of embroidery. Dorothy, seated upon a cushion on the floor with one foot tucked under her, was reading, her hand straying from time to time to a box of chocolates conveniently near.

"Well, this is a peaceful, home-like scene-too bad to bust it up. Just finished sealing off and flashing out this case, Mart. Going to see if she'll read. Want to take a look?"

He placed the compass upon the plane table, so that its final bearing could be read upon the master circles controlled by the gyroscopes; then simultaneously started his stop-watch and pressed the button which caused a minute couple to be applied to the needle. Instantly the needle began to revolve, and for many minutes there was no apparent change in its motion in either the primary or secondary bearings.

"Do you suppose it is out of order, after all?" asked Crane, regretfully.

"I don't think so," Seaton pondered. "You see, they weren't designed to indicate such distances on such small objects as men, so I threw a million ohms in series with the impulse. That cuts down the free rotation to less than half an hour, and increases the sensitivity to the limit. There, isn't she trying to quit it?"

"Yes, it is settling down. It must be on him still." Finally the ultra-sensitive needle came to rest. When it had done so, Seaton calculated the distance, read the direction, and made a reading upon Osnome.

"He's there, all right. Bearings agree, and distances check to within a light-year, which is as close as we can hope to check on as small a mass as a man. Well, that's that-nothing to do about it until after we get there. One sure thing, Mart-we're not coming straight back home from 'X'."

"No, an investigation is indicated."

"Well, that puts me out of a job. What to do? Don't want to study, like you. Can't crochet, like Peg. Darned if I'll sit cross-legged on a pillow and eat candy, like that Titian blonde over there on the floor. I know what —I'll build me a mechanical educator and teach Shiro to talk English instead of that mess of language he indulges in. How'd that be, Mart?"

"Don't do it," put in Dorothy, positively. "He's just too perfect the way he is. Especially don't do it if he'd talk the way you do-or could you teach him to talk the way you write?"

"Ouch! That's a dirty dig. However, Mrs. Seaton, I am able and willing to defend my customary mode of speech. You realize that the spoken word is ephemeral, whereas the thought, whose nuances have once been expressed in imperishable print is not subject to revision-its crudities can never be remodeled into more subtle, more gracious shading. It is my contention that, due to these inescapable conditions, the mental effort necessitated by the employment of nice distinctions in sense and meaning of words and a slavish adherence to the dictates of the more precise grammarians should be reserved for the print...."

He broke off as Dorothy, in one lithe motion, rose and hurled her pillow at his head.

"Choke him, somebody! Perhaps you had better build it, Dick, after all."

"I believe that he would like it, Dick. He is trying hard to learn, and the continuous use of a dictionary is undoubtedly a nuisance to him."

"I'll ask him. Shiro!"

"You have call, sir?" Shiro entered the room from his galley, with his unfailing bow.

"Yes. How'd you like to learn to talk English like Crane there does-without taking lessons?"

Shiro smiled doubtfully, unable to take such a thought seriously.

"Yes, it can be done," Crane assured him. "Doctor Seaton can build a machine which will teach you all at once, if you like."

"I like, sir, enormously, yes, sir. I years study and pore, but honorable English extraordinary difference from Nipponese-no can do. Dictionary useful but ..." he flipped pages dexterously, "extremely cumbrous. If honorable Seaton can do, shall be extreme ... gratification."

He bowed again, smiled, and went out.

"I'll do just that little thing. So long, folks, I'm going up to the shop."

Day after day the *Skylark* plunged through the vast emptiness of the interstellar reaches. At the end of each second she was traveling exactly twenty-six feet per second faster than she had been at its beginning; and as day after day passed, her velocity mounted into figures which became meaningless, even when expressed in thousands of miles per second. Still she seemed stationary to her occupants, and only different from a vessel motionless upon the surface of the Earth in that objects within her hull had lost three-sixteenths of their normal weight. Acceleration, too, had its effect. Only the rapidity with which the closer suns and their planets were passed gave any indication of the frightful speed at which they were being hurtled along by the inconceivable power of that disintegrating copper bar.

When the vessel was nearly half-way to "X," the bar was reversed in order to change the sign of their acceleration, and the hollow sphere spun through an angle of one hundred and eighty degrees around the motionless cage which housed the enormous gyroscopes. Still apparently motionless and exactly as she had been before, the *Skylark* was now actually traveling in a direction which seemed "down" and with a velocity which was being constantly decreased by the amount of their negative acceleration.

A few days after the bar had been reversed Seaton announced that the mechanical educator was complete, and brought it into the control room.

In appearance it was not unlike a large radio set, but it was infinitely more complex. It possessed numerous tubes, kino-lamps, and photo-electric cells, as well as many coils of peculiar design-there were dozens of dials and knobs, and a multiple set of head-harnesses.

"How can a thing like that possibly work as it does?" asked Crane. "I know that it does work, but I could scarcely believe it, even after it had educated me."

"That is nothing like the one Dunark used, Dick," objected Dorothy. "How come?"

"I'll answer you first, Dot. This is an improved model-it has quite a few gadgets of my own in it. Now, Mart, as to how it works-it isn't so funny after you understand it-it's a lot like radio in that respect. It operates on a band of frequencies lying between the longest light and heat waves and the shortest radio waves. This thing here is the generator of those waves and a very heavy power amplifier. The headsets are stereoscopic transmitters, taking or receiving a three-dimensional view. Nearly all matter is transparent to those waves; for instance bones, hair, and so on. However, cerebin, a cerebroside peculiar to the thinking structure of the brain, is opaque to them. Dunark, not knowing chemistry, didn't know why the educator worked or what it worked on-he found out by experiment that it did work; just as we found out about electricity. This three-dimensional model, or view, or whatever you want to call it, is converted into electricity in the headsets, and the resulting modulated wave goes back to the educator. There it is heterodyned with another wave-this second frequency was found after thousands of trials and is, I believe, the exact frequency existing in the optic nerves themselves-and sent to the receiving headset. Modulated as it is, and producing a three-dimensional picture, after rectification in the receiver, it reproduces exactly what has been 'viewed,' if due allowance has been made for the size and configuration of the different brains involved in the transfer. You remember a sort of flash —a sensation of seeing something-when the educator worked on you? Well, you did see it, just as though it had been transmitted to the brain by the optic nerve, but everything came at once, so the impression of sight was confused. The result in the brain, however, was clear and permanent. The only drawback is that you haven't the visual memory of what you have learned, and that sometimes makes it hard to use your knowledge. You don't know whether you know anything about a certain subject or not until after you go digging around in your brain looking for it."

"I see," said Crane, and Dorothy, the irrepressible, put in:

"Just as clear as so much mud. What are the improvements you added to the original design?"

"Well, you see, I had a big advantage in knowing that cerebrin was the substance involved, and with that knowledge I could carry matters considerably farther than Dunark could in his original model. I can transfer the thoughts of somebody else to a third party or to a record. Dunark's machine couldn't work against resistance-if the subject wasn't willing to give up his thoughts he couldn't get them. This one can take them away by force. In fact, by increasing plate and grid voltages in the amplifier, I can pretty nearly burn out a man's brain. Yesterday, I was playing with it, transferring a section of my own brain to a magnetized tape-for a permanent record, you know-and found out that above certain rather low voltages it becomes a form of torture that would make the best efforts of the old Inquisition seem like a petting party."

"Did you succeed in the transfer?" Crane was intensely interested.

"Sure. Push the button for Shiro, and we'll start something."

"Put your head against this screen," he directed when Shiro had come in, smiling and bowing as usual. "I've got to caliper your brains to do a good job."

The calipering done, he adjusted various dials and clamped the electrodes over his own head and over the heads of Crane and Shiro.

"Want to learn Japanese while we're at it, Mart? I'm going to."

"Yes, please. I tried to learn it while I was in Japan, but it was altogether too difficult to be worth while."

Seaton threw in a switch, opened it, depressed two more, opened them, and threw off the power.

"All set," he reported crisply, and barked a series of explosive syllables at Shiro, ending upon a rising note.

"Yes, sir," answered the Japanese. "You speak Nipponese as though you had never spoken any other tongue. I am very grateful to you, sir, that I may now discard my dictionary."

"How about you two girls-anything you want to learn in a hurry?"

"Not me!" declared Dorothy emphatically. "That machine is too darn weird to suit me. Besides, if I knew as much about science as you do, we'd probably fight about it."

"I do not believe I care to...." began Margaret.

She was interrupted by the penetrating sound of an alarm bell.

"That's a new note!" exclaimed Seaton, "I never heard that note before."

He stood in surprise at the board, where a brilliant purple light was flashing slowly. "Great Cat! That's a purely Osnomian war-gadget —kind of a battleship detector-shows that there's a boatload of bad news around here somewhere. Grab the visiplates quick, folks," as he rang Shiro's bell. "I'll take visiplate area one, dead ahead. Mart, take number two. Dot, three; Peg, four; Shiro, five. Look sharp!...Nothing in front. See anything, any of you?"

None of them could discover anything amiss, but the purple light continued to flash, and the bell to ring. Seaton cut off the bell.

"We're almost to 'X'," he thought aloud. "Can't be more than a million miles or so, and we're almost stopped. Wonder if somebody's there ahead of us? Maybe Dunark is doing this, though. I'll call him and see." He threw in a switch and said one word —"Dunark!"

"Here!" came the voice of the Kofedix from the speaker. "Are you generating?"

"No-just called to see if you were. What do you make of it?"

"Nothing as yet. Better close up?"

"Yes, edge over this way and I'll come over to meet you. Leave your negative as it is-we'll be stopped directly. Whatever it is, it's dead ahead. It's a long ways off yet, but we'd better get organized. Wouldn't talk much, either-they may intercept our wave, narrow as it is."

"Better yet, shut off your radio entirely. When we get close enough together, we'll use the hand-language. You may not know that you know it, but you do. Turn your heaviest searchlight toward me —I'll do the same."

There was a click as Dunark's power was shut off abruptly, and Seaton grinned as he cut his own.

"That's right, too, folks. In Osnomian battles we always used a sign-language when we couldn't hear anything-and that was most of the time. I know it as well as I know English, now that I am reminded of the fact."

He shifted his course to intercept that of the Osnomian vessel. After a time the watchers picked out a minute point of light, moving comparatively rapidly against the stars, and knew it to be the searchlight of the *Kondal*. Soon the two vessels were almost side by side, moving cautiously forward, and Seaton set up a sixty-inch parabolic reflector, focused upon a coil. As they went on, the purple light continued to flash more and more rapidly, but still nothing was to be seen.

"Take number six visiplate, will you, Mart? It's telescopic, equivalent to a twenty-inch refractor. I'll tell you where to look in a minute-this reflector increases the power of the regular indicator." He studied meters and adjusted dials. "Set on nineteen hours forty-three minutes, and two hundred seventy-one degrees. He's too far away yet to read exactly, but that'll put him in the field of vision."

"Is this radiation harmful?" asked Margaret.

"Not yet-it's too weak. Pretty soon we may be able to feel it; then I'll throw out a screen against it. When it's strong enough, it's pretty deadly stuff. See anything, Mart?"

"I see something, but it is very indistinct. It is moving in sharper now. Yes, it is a space-ship, shaped like a dirigible airship."

"See it yet, Dunark?" Seaton signaled.

"Just sighted it. Ready to attack?"

"I am not. I'm going to run. Let's go, and go fast!"

Dunark signaled violently, and Seaton shook his head time after time, stubbornly.

"A difficulty?" asked Crane.

"Yes. He wants to go jump on it, but I'm not looking for trouble with any such craft as that-it must be a thousand feet long and is certainly neither Terrestrial nor Osnomian. I say beat it while we're all in one piece. How about it?"

"Absolutely," concurred Crane and both women.

The bar was reversed and the *Skylark* leaped away. The *Kondal* followed, although the observers could see that Dunark was raging. Seaton swung number six visiplate around, looked once, and switched on the radio.

"Well, Dunark," he said grimly. "You get your wish. That bird is coming out, with at least twice the acceleration we could get with both motors full on. He saw us all the time, and was waiting for us."

"Go on-get away if you can. You can stand a higher acceleration than we can. We'll hold him as long as possible."

"I would, if it would do any good, but it won't. He's so much faster than we are that he could catch us anyway, if he wanted to, no matter how much of a start we had-and it looks now as though he wanted us. Two of us stand a lot better chance than one of licking him if he's looking for trouble. Spread out a mile or two, and pretend this is all the speed we've got. What'll we give him first?"

"Give him everything at once. Rays six, seven, eight, nine, and ten...." Crane, with Seaton, began making contacts, rapidly but with precision. "Heat wave two-seven. Induction, five-eight. Oscillation, everything under point oh six three. All the explosive copper we can get in. Right?"

"Right-and if worse comes to worst, remember the zone of force. Let him shoot first, because he may be peaceable-but it doesn't look like olive branches to me."

"Got both your screens out?"

"Yes. Mart, you might take number two visiplate and work the guns—I'll handle the rest of this stuff. Better strap yourselves in solid, folks-this may develop into a kind of rough party, by the looks of things right now."

As he spoke, a pyrotechnic display enveloped the entire ship as a radiation from the foreign vessel struck the other neutralizing screen and dissipated its force harmlessly in the ether. Instantly Seaton threw on the full power of his refrigerating system and shot in the master switch that actuated the complex offensive armament of his dreadnought of the skies. An intense, livid violet glow hid completely main and auxiliary power bars, and long flashes leaped between metallic objects in all parts of the vessel. The passengers felt each hair striving to stand on end as the very air became more and more highly charged-and this was but the slight corona-loss of the frightful stream of destruction being hurled at the other space-cruiser, now scarcely a mile away!

Seaton stared into number one visiplate, manipulating levers and dials as he drove the *Skylark* hither and yon, dodging frantically, the while the automatic focusing devices remained centered upon the enemy and the enormous generators continued to pour forth their deadly frequencies. The bars glowed more fiercely as they were advanced to full working load-the stranger was one blaze of incandescent ionization, but she still fought on; and Seaton noticed that the pyrometers recording the temperature of the shell were mounting rapidly, in spite of the refrigerators.

"Dunark, put everything you've got upon one spot-right on the end of his nose!"

As the first shell struck the mark, Seaton concentrated every force at his command upon the designated point. The air in the *Skylark* crackled and hissed and intense violet flames leaped from the bars as they were driven almost to the point of disruption. From the forward end of the strange craft there erupted prominence after prominence of searing, unbearable flame as the terrific charges of explosive copper struck the mark and exploded, liberating instantaneously their millions upon millions of kilowatt-hours of intra-atomic energy. Each prominence enveloped all three of the fighting vessels and extended for hundreds of miles out into space-but still the enemy warship continued to hurl forth solid and vibratory destruction.

A brilliant orange light flared upon the panel, and Seaton gasped as he swung his visiplate upon his defenses, which he had supposed impregnable. His outer screen was already down, although its mighty copper generator was exerting its utmost power. Black areas had already appeared and were spreading rapidly, where there should have been only incandescent radiance; and the inner screen was even now radiating far into the ultra-violet and was certainly doomed. Knowing as he did the stupendous power driving those screens, he knew that there were superhuman and inconceivable forces being directed against them, and his right hand flashed to the switch controlling the zone of force. Fast as he was, much happened in the mere moment that passed before his flying hand could close the switch. In the last infinitesimal instant of time before the zone closed in, a gaping black hole appeared in the incandescence of the inner screen, and a small portion of a ray of energy so stupendous as to be palpable, struck, like a tangible projectile, the exposed flank of the *Skylark*. Instantly the refractory arenak turned an intense, dazzling white and more than a foot of the forty-eight-inch skin of the vessel melted away, like snow before an oxy-acetylene flame: melting and flying away in molten globes and sparkling gases-the refrigerating coils lining the hull were of no avail against the concentrated energy of that titanic thrust. As Seaton shut off his power, intense darkness and utter silence closed in, and he snapped on the lights.

"They take one trick!" he blazed, his eyes almost emitting sparks, and leaped for the generators. He had forgotten the efforts of the zone of force, however, and only sprawled grotesquely in the air until he floated within reach of a line.

"Hold everything, Dick!" Crane snapped, as Seaton bent over one of the bars. "What are you going to do?"

"I'm going to put as heavy bars in these ray-generators as they'll stand and go out and get that bird. We can't lick him with Osnomian rays or with our explosive copper, but I can carve that sausage into slices with a zone of force, and I'm going to do it."

"Steady, old man-take it easy. I see your point, but remember that you must release the zone of force before you can use it as a weapon. Furthermore, you must discover his exact location, and must get close enough to him to use the zone as a weapon, all without its protection.

Can those ray-screens be made sufficiently powerful to withstand the beam they employed last, even for a second?"

"Hm ... m ... m. Never thought of that, Mart," Seaton replied, the fire dying out of his eyes. "Wonder how long the battle lasted?"

"Eight and two-tenths seconds, from first to last, but they had had that heavy ray in action only a fraction of one second when you cut in the zone of force. Either they underestimated our strength at first, or else it required about eight seconds to tune in their heavy generators-probably the former."

"But we've *got* to do something, man! We can't just sit here and twiddle our thumbs!"

"Why, and why not? That course seems eminently wise and proper. In fact, at the present time, thumb-twiddling is distinctly indicated."

"Oh, you're full of little red ants! We can't do a thing with that zone on-and you say just sit here. Suppose they know all about that zone of force? Suppose they can crack it? Suppose they ram us?"

"I shall take up your objections in order," Crane had lighted a cigarette and was smoking meditatively. "First, they may or may not know about it. At present, that point is immaterial. Second, whether or not they know about it, it is almost a certainty that they cannot crack it. It had been up for more than three minutes, and they have undoubtedly concentrated everything possible upon us during that time. It is still standing. I really expected it to go down in the first few seconds, but now that it has held this long it will, in all probability, continue to hold indefinitely. Third, they most certainly will not ram us, for several reasons. They probably have encountered few, if any, foreign vessels able to stand against them for a minute, and will act accordingly. Then, too, it is probably safe to assume that their vessel is damaged, to some slight extent at least; for I do not believe that any possible armament could withstand the forces you directed against them and escape entirely unscathed. Finally, if they did ram us, what would happen? Would we feel the shock? That barrier in the ether seems impervious, and if so, it could not transmit a blow. I do not see exactly how it would affect the ship dealing the blow. You are the one who works out the new problems in unexplored mathematics-some time you must take a few months off and work it out."

"Yes, it would take that long, too, I guess-but you're right, he can't hurt us. That's using the old bean, Mart! I was going off half-cocked again, darn it! I'll pipe down, and we'll go into a huddle."

Seaton noticed that Dorothy's face was white and that she was fighting for self-control. Drawing himself over to her, he picked her up in a tight embrace.

"Cheer up, Red-Top! This man's war ain't started yet!"

"Not started? What do you mean? Haven't you and Martin just been admitting to each other that you can't do anything? Doesn't that mean that we are beaten?"

"Beaten! Us? How do you get that way? Not on your sweet young life!" he ejaculated, and the surprise on his face was so manifest that she recovered instantly. "We've just dug a hole and pulled the hole in after us, that's all! When we get everything doped out to suit us, we'll snap out of it and that bird'll think he's been petting a wildcat!"

"Mart, you're the thinking end of this partnership," he continued, thoughtfully. "You've got the analytical mind and the judicial disposition, and can think circles around me. From what little you've seen of those folks, tell me who, what, and where they are. I'm getting the germ of an idea, and maybe we can make it work."

"I will try it." Crane paused. "They are, of course, neither from the Earth nor from Osnome. It is also evident that they have solved the secret of intra-atomic energy. Their vessels are not propelled as ours are-they have so perfected that force that it acts upon every particle of the structure and its contents...."

"How do you figure that?" blurted Seaton.

"Because of the acceleration they can stand. Nothing even semi-human, and probably nothing living, could endure it otherwise. Right?"

"Yes—I never thought of that."

"Furthermore, they are far from home, for if they were from anywhere nearby, the Osnomians would have known of them-particularly since it is evident from the size of the vessel that it is not a recent development with them, as it is with us. Since the green system is close to the center of the Galaxy, it seems reasonable, as a working hypothesis, to assume that they are from some system far from the center, perhaps close to the outer edge. They are very evidently of a high degree of intelligence. They are also highly treacherous and merciless...."

"Why?" asked Dorothy, who was listening eagerly.

"I deduce those characteristics from their unprovoked attack upon peaceful ships, vastly smaller and supposedly of inferior armament; and also from the nature of that attack. This vessel is probably a scout or an exploring ship, since it seems to be alone. It is not altogether beyond the bounds of reason to imagine it upon a voyage of discovery, in search of new planets to be subjugated and colonized...."

"That's a sweet picture of our future neighbors-but I guess you're hitting the old nail on the head, at that."

"If these deductions are anywhere nearly correct, they are terrible neighbors. For my next point, are we justified in assuming that they do or do not know about the zone of force?"

"That's a hard one. Knowing what they evidently do know, it's hard to see how they could have missed it. And yet, if they had known about it for a long time, wouldn't they be able to get through it? Of course it may be a real and total barrier in the ether-in that case they'd know that they couldn't do a thing as long as we keep it on. Take your choice, but I believe that they know about it, and know more than we do-that it is a total barrier set up in the ether."

"I agree with you, and we shall proceed upon that assumption. They know, then, that neither they nor we can do anything as long as we maintain the zone-that it is a stalemate. They also know that it takes an enormous amount of power to keep the zone in place. Now we have gone as far as we can go upon the meager data we have-considerably farther than we really are justified in going. We must now try to come to some conclusion concerning their present activities. If our ideas as to their natures are even approximately correct, they are waiting, probably fairly close at hand, until we shall be compelled to release the zone, no matter how long that period of waiting shall be. They know, of course, from our small size, that we cannot carry enough copper to maintain it indefinitely, as they could. Does that sound reasonable?"

"I check you to nineteen decimal places, Mart, and from your ideas I'm getting surer and surer that we can pull their corks. I can get into action in a hurry when I have to, and my idea now is to wait until they relax a trifle, and then slip a fast one over on them. One more bubble out of the old think-tank and I'll let you off for the day. At what time will their vigilance be at lowest ebb? That's a poser, I'll admit, but the answer to it may answer everything-the first shot will, of course, be the best chance we'll ever have."

"Yes, we should succeed in the first attempt. We have very little information to guide us in answering that question." He studied the problem for many minutes before he resumed, "I should say that for a time they would keep all their rays and other weapons in action against the zone of force, expecting us to release it immediately. Then, knowing that they were wasting power uselessly, they would cease attacking, but would be very watchful, with every eye fastened upon us and with every weapon ready for instant use. After this period of vigilance, regular ship's routine would be resumed. Half the force, probably, would go off duty-for, if they are even remotely like any organic beings with which we are familiar, they require sleep or its equivalent at intervals. The men on duty-the normal force, that is-would be doubly careful for a time. Then habit will assert itself, if we have done nothing to create suspicion, and their watchfulness will relax to the point of ordinary careful observation. Toward the end of their watch, because of the strain of the battle and because of the unusually long period of duty, they will become careless, and their vigilance will be considerably below normal. But the exact time of all these things depends entirely upon their conception of time, concerning which we have no information whatever. Though it is purely a speculation, based upon Earthly and Osnomian experience, I should say that after twelve or thirteen hours would come the time for us to make the attack."

"That's good enough for me. Fine, Mart, and thanks. You've probably saved the lives of the party. We will now sleep for eleven or twelve hours."

"Sleep, Dick! How could you?" Dorothy exclaimed.

CHAPTER V

First Blood

The next twelve hours dragged with terrible slowness. Sleep was impossible and eating was difficult, even though all knew that they would have need of the full measure of their strength. Seaton set up various combinations of switching devices connected to electrical timers, and spent hours trying, with all his marvelous quickness of muscular control, to cut shorter and ever shorter the time between the opening and the closing of the switch. At last he arranged a powerful electro-magnetic device so that one impulse would both open and close the switch, with an open period of one one-thousandth of a second. Only then was he satisfied.

"A thousandth is enough to give us a look around, due to persistence of vision; and it is short enough so that they won't see it unless they have a recording observer on us. Even if they still have rays on us, they can't possibly neutralize our screens in that short an exposure. All right, gang? We'll take five visiplates and cover the sphere. If any of you get a glimpse of him, mark the exact spot and outline on the glass. All set?"

He pressed the button. The stars flashed in the black void for an instant, then were again shut out.

"Here he is, Dick!" shrieked Margaret. "Right here-he covered almost half the visiplate!"

She outlined for him, as nearly as she could, the exact position of the object she had seen, and he calculated rapidly.

"Fine business!" he exulted. "He's within half a mile of us, three-quarters on-perfect! I thought he'd be so far away that I'd have to take photographs to locate him. He hasn't a single ray on us, either. That bird's goose is cooked right now, folks, unless every man on watch has his hand right on the controls of a generator and can get into action in less than a tenth of a second! Hang on, gang, I'm going to step on the gas!"

After making sure that everyone was fastened immovably in their seats he strapped himself in the pilot's seat, then set the bar toward the strange vessel and applied fully one-third of its full power. The *Skylark*, of course, did not move. Then, with bewildering rapidity, he went into action; face glued to the visiplate, hands moving faster than the eye could follow-the left closing and opening the switch controlling the zone of force, the right swinging the steering controls to all points of the sphere. The mighty vessel staggered this way and that, jerking and straining terribly as the zone was thrown on and off, lurching sickeningly about the central bearing as the gigantic power of the driving bar was exerted, now in one direction, now in another. After a second or two of this mad gyration, Seaton shut off the power. He then released the zone, after assuring himself that both inner and outer screens were operating at the highest possible rating.

"There, that'll hold 'em for a while, I guess. This battle was even shorter than the other one-and a lot more decisive. Let's turn on the flood-lights and see what the pieces look like."

The lights revealed that the zone of force had indeed sliced the enemy vessel into pieces. No fragment was large enough to be navigable or dangerous and each was sharply cut, as though sheared from its neighbor by some gigantic curved blade. Dorothy sobbed with relief in Seaton's arms as Crane, with one arm around his wife, grasped his hand.

"That was flawless, Dick. As an exhibition of perfect co-ordination and instantaneous timing under extreme physical difficulties, I have never seen its equal."

"You certainly saved all our lives," Margaret added.

"Only fifty-fifty, Peg," Seaton protested, and blushed vividly. "Mart did most of it, you know. I'd have gummed up everything back there if he had let me. Let's see what we can find out about them."

He touched the lever and the *Skylark* moved slowly toward the wreckage, the scattered fragments of which were beginning to move toward and around each other because of their mutual gravitational forces. Snapping on a searchlight, he swung its beam around, and as it settled upon one of the larger sections he saw a group of hooded figures; some of them upon the metal, others floating slowly toward it through space.

"Poor devils-they didn't have a chance," he remarked regretfully. "However, it was either they or we-look out! Sweet spirits of niter!"

He leaped back to the controls and the others were hurled bodily to the floor as he applied the power-for at a signal each of the hooded figures had leveled a tube and once more the outer screen had flamed into incandescence.

As the *Skylark* leaped away, Seaton focussed an attractor upon the one who had apparently signaled the attack. Rolling the vessel over in a short loop, so that the captive was hurled off into space upon the other side, he snatched the tube from the figure's grasp with one auxiliary attractor, and anchored head and limbs with others, so that the prisoner could scarcely move a muscle. Then, while Crane and the women scrambled up off the floor and hurried to the visiplates, Seaton cut in rays six, two-seven, and five-eight. Ray six, "the softener," was a band of frequencies extending from violet far up into the ultra-violet. When driven with sufficient power, this ray destroyed eyesight and nervous tissue, and its power increased still further, actually loosened the molecular structure of matter. Ray two-seven was operated in a range of frequencies far below the visible red. It was pure heat-under its action matter became hotter and hotter as long as it was applied, the upper limit being only the theoretical maximum of temperature. Ray five-eight was high-tension, high-frequency alternating current. Any conductor in its path behaved precisely as it would in the Ajax-Northrup induction furnace, which can boil platinum in ten seconds! These three rays composed the beam which Seaton directed upon the mass of metal from which the enemy had elected to continue the battle-and behind each ray, instead of the small energy at the command of its Osnomian inventor, were the untold millions of kilowatts developed by a one-hundred-pound bar of disintegrating copper!

There ensued a brief but appalling demonstration of the terrible effectiveness of those Osnomian weapons against anything not protected by ultra-powered ray screens. Metal and men-if men they were-literally vanished. One moment they were outlined starkly in the beam; there was a moment of searing, coruscating, blinding light-the next moment the beam bored on into the void, unimpeded. Nothing was visible save an occasional tiny flash, as some condensed or solidified droplet of the volatilized metal re-entered the path of that ravening beam.

"We'll see if there's any more of them loose," Seaton remarked, as he shut off the force and probed into the wreckage with a searchlight.

No sign of life or of activity was revealed, and the light was turned upon the captive. He was held motionless in the invisible grip of the attractors, at the point where the force of those peculiar magnets was exactly balanced by the outward thrust of the repellers. By manipulating the attractor holding it, Seaton brought the strange tubular weapon into the control-room through a small air-lock in the wall and examined it curiously, but did not touch it.

"I never heard of a hand-ray before, so I guess I won't play with it much until after I learn something about it."

"So you have taken a captive?" asked Margaret. "What are you going to do with him?"

"I'm going to drag him in here and read his mind. He's one of the officers of that ship, I believe, and I'm going to find out how to build one exactly like it. This old can is now as obsolete as a 1920 flivver, and I'm going to make us a later model. How about it, Mart, don't we want something really up-to-date if we're going to keep on space-hopping?"

"We certainty do. Those denizens seem to be particularly venomous, and we will not be safe unless we have the most powerful and most efficient space-ship possible. However, that fellow may be dangerous, even now-in fact, it is practically certain that he is."

"You chirped it, ace. I'd much rather touch a pound of dry nitrogen iodide. I've got him spread-eagled so that he can't destroy his brain until after we've read it, though, so there's no particular hurry about him. We'll leave him out there for a while, to waste his sweetness on the desert air. Let's all look around for the *Kondal*. I sure hope they didn't get her in that fracas."

They diffused the rays of eight giant searchlights into a vertical fan, and with it swept slowly through almost a semi-circle before anything was seen. Then there was revealed a cluster of cylindrical objects amid a mass of wreckage, which Crane recognized at once.

"The *Kondal* is gone, Dick. There is what is left of her, and most of her cargo of salt, in jute bags."

As he spoke, a series of green flashes played upon the bags, and Seaton yelled in relief.

"They got the ship all right, but Dunark and Sitar got away-they're still with their salt!"

The *Skylark* moved over to the wreck and Seaton, relinquishing the controls to Crane, donned a vacuum suit, entered the main air-lock and snapped on the motor which sealed off the lock, pumped the air into a pressure-tank, and opened the outside door. He threw a light line to the two figures and pushed himself lightly toward them. He then talked briefly to Dunark in the hand-language, and handed the end of the line to Sitar, who held it while the two men explored the fragments of the strange vessel, gathering up various things of interest as they came upon them.

Back in the control-room, Dunark and Sitar let their pressure decrease gradually to that of the terrestrial vessel and removed the face-plates from their helmets.

"Again, oh Karfedo of Earth, we thank you for our lives," Dunark began, gasping for breath, when Seaton leaped to the air-gauge with a quick apology.

"Never thought of the effect our atmospheric pressure would have on you two. We can stand yours all right, but you'd pretty nearly pass out on ours. There, that'll suit you better. Didn't you throw out your zone of force?"

"Yes, as soon as I saw that our screens were not going to hold." The Osnomians' labored breathing became normal as the air-pressure increased to a value only a little below that of the dense atmosphere of their native planet. "I then increased the power of the screens to the extreme limit and opened the zone for a moment to see how the screens would hold with the added power. That instant was enough. In that period a concentrated beam, such as I had no idea could ever be generated, went through the outer and inner screens as though they were not there, through the four-foot arenak of the hull, through the entire central installation, and through the hull on the other side. Sitar and I were wearing suits...."

"Say, Mart, that's one bet we overlooked. It's a good idea, too-those strangers wore them all the time as regular equipment, apparently. Next time we get into a jam, be sure we do it; they might come in handy. Excuse me, Dunark-go ahead."

"We had suits on, so as soon as the ray was shut off, which was almost instantly, I phoned the crew to jump, and we leaped out through the hole in the hull. The air rushing out gave us an impetus that carried us many miles out into space, and it required many hours for the slight attraction of the mass here to draw us back to it. We just got back a few minutes ago. That air-blast is probably what saved us, as they destroyed our vessel with atomic bombs and hunted down the four men of our crew, who stayed comparatively close to the scene. They rayed you for about an hour with the most stupendous beams imaginable-no such generators have ever been considered possible of construction-but couldn't make any impression upon you. Then they shut off their power and stood by, waiting. I wasn't looking at you when you released your zone. One moment it was there, and the next, the stranger had been cut in pieces. The rest you know."

"We're sure glad you two got away, Dunark. Well, Mart, what say we drag that guy in and give him the once-over?"

Seaton swung the attractors holding the prisoner until they were in line with the main air-lock, then reduced the power of the repellers. As he approached the lock various controls were actuated, and soon the stranger stood in the control room, held immovable against one wall, while Crane, with a 0.50-caliber elephant gun, stood against the other.

"Perhaps you girls should go somewhere else," suggested Crane.

"Not on your life!" protested Dorothy, who, eyes wide and flushed with excitement, stood near a door, with a heavy automatic pistol in her hand. "I wouldn't miss this for a farm!"

"Got him solid," declared Seaton, after a careful inspection of the various attractors and repellers he had bearing upon the prisoner, "Now let's get him out of that suit. No-better read his air first, temperature and pressure-might analyze it, too."

Nothing could be seen of the person of the stranger, since he was encased in vacuum armor, but it was plainly evident that he was very short and immensely broad and thick. By means of hollow needles forced through the leather-like material of the suit Seaton drew off a sample of the atmosphere within, into an Orsat apparatus, while Crane made pressure and temperature readings.

"Temperature, one hundred ten degrees. Pressure, twenty-eight pounds-about the same as ours is, now that we have stepped it up to keep the Osnomians from suffering."

Seaton soon reported that the atmosphere was quite similar to that of the *Skylark*, except that it was much higher in carbon dioxide and carried an extremely high percentage of water vapor. He took up a pair of heavy shears and laid the suit open full length, on both sides, knowing that the powerful attractors would hold the stranger immovable. He then wrenched off the helmet and cast the whole suit aside, revealing the enemy officer, clad in a tunic of scarlet silk.

He was less than five feet tall. His legs were merely blocks, fully as great in diameter as they were in length, supporting a torso of Herculean dimensions. His arms were as large as a strong man's thigh and hung almost to the floor. His astounding shoulders, fully a yard across, merged into and supported an enormous head. The being possessed recognizable nose, ears, and mouth; and the great domed forehead and huge cranium bespoke an immense and a highly developed brain.

But it was the eyes of this strange creature that fixed and held the attention. Large they were, and black-the dull, opaque, lusterless black of platinum sponge. The pupils were a brighter black, and in them flamed ruby lights: pitiless, mocking, cold. Plainly to be read in those sinister depths were the untold wisdom of unthinkable age, sheer ruthlessness, mighty power, and ferocity unrelieved. His baleful gaze swept from one member of the party to another, and to meet the glare of those eyes was to receive a tangible physical blow-it was actually ponderable force; that of embodied hardness and of ruthlessness incarnate, generated in that merciless brain and hurled forth through those flame-shot, Stygian orbs.

"If you don't need us for anything, Dick, I think Peggy and I will go upstairs," Dorothy broke the long silence.

"Good idea, Dot. This isn't going to be pretty to watch-or to do, either, for that matter."

"If I stay here another minute I'll see that thing as long as I live; and I might be very ill. Goodbye," and heartless and bloodthirsty Osnomian though she was, Sitar had gone to join the two Terrestrial women.

"I didn't want to say much before the girls, but I want to check a couple of ideas with you two. Don't you think it's a safe bet that this bird reported back to his headquarters?"

"I have been thinking that very thing," Crane spoke gravely, and Dunark nodded agreement. "Any race capable of developing such a vessel as this would almost certainly have developed systems of communication in proportion."

"That's the way I doped it out-and that's why I'm going to read his mind, if I have to burn out his brain to do it. We've got to know how far away from home he is, whether he has turned in any report about us, and all about it. Also, I'm going to get the plans, power, and armament of their most modern ships, if he knows them, so that your gang, Dunark, can build us one like them; because the next boat that tackles us will be warned and we won't be able to take it by surprise. We won't stand a chance in the *Skylark*. With a ship like theirs, however, we can run-or we can fight, if we have to. Any other ideas, fellows?"

As neither Crane nor Dunark had any other suggestions to offer, Seaton brought out the mechanical educator, watching the creature's eyes narrowly. As he placed one headset over that motionless head the captive sneered in pure contempt, but when the case was opened and the array of tubes and transformers was revealed, that expression disappeared; and when he added a super-power stage by cutting in a heavy-duty transformer and a five-kilowatt transmitting tube, Seaton thought that he saw an instantaneously suppressed flicker of doubt or fear.

"That headset thing was child's play to him, but he doesn't like the looks of this other stuff at all. I don't blame him a bit—I wouldn't like to be on the receiving end of this hook-up myself. I'm going to put him on the recorder and on the visualizer," Seaton continued as he connected spools of wire and tape, lamps, and lenses in an intricate system and donned a headset. "I'd hate to have much of that brain in my own skull-afraid I'd bite myself. I'm just going to look on, and when I see anything I want, I'll grab it and put it into my own brain. I'm starting off easy, not using the big tube."

He closed several switches, lights flashed, and the wires and tapes began to feed through the magnets.

"Well, I've got his language, folks, he seemed to want me to have it. It's got a lot of stuff in it that I can't understand yet, though, so guess I'll give him some English."

He changed several connections and the captive spoke, in a profoundly deep bass voice.

"You may as well discontinue your attempt, for you will gain no information from me. That machine of yours was out of date with us thousands of years ago."

"Save your breath or talk sense," said Seaton, coldly. "I gave you English so that you can give me the information I want. You already know what it is. When you get ready to talk, say so, or throw it on the screen of your own accord. If you don't, I'll put on enough voltage to burn your brain out. Remember, I can read your dead brain as well as though it were alive, but I want your thoughts, as well as your knowledge, and I'm going to have them. If you give them voluntarily, I will tinker up a lifeboat that you can navigate back to your own world and let you go; if you resist I intend getting them anyway and you shall not leave this vessel alive. You may take your choice."

"You are childish, and that machine is impotent against my will. I could have defied it a hundred years ago, when I was barely a grown man. Know you, American, that we supermen of the Fenachrone are as far above any of the other and lesser breeds of beings who spawn in their millions in their countless myriads of races upon the numberless planets of the Universe as you are above the inert metal from which this, your ship, was built. The Universe is ours, and in due course we shall take it-just as in due course I shall take this vessel. Do your worst; I shall not speak." The creature's eyes flamed, hurling a wave of hypnotic command through Seaton's eyes and deep into his brain. Seaton's very senses reeled for an instant under the impact of that awful mental force; but after a short, intensely bitter struggle he threw off the spell.

"That was close, fellow, but you didn't quite ring the bell," he said grimly, staring directly into those unholy eyes. "I may rate pretty low mentally, but I can't be hypnotized into turning you loose. Also I can give you cards and spades in certain other lines which I am about to demonstrate. Being superman didn't keep the rest of your men from going out in my ray, and being a superman isn't going to save your brain. I am not depending upon my intellectual or mental force—I've got an ace in the hole in the shape of five thousand volts to apply to the most delicate centers of your brain. Start giving me what I want, and start quick, or I'll tear it out of you."

The giant did not answer, merely glared defiance and bitter hate.

"Take it, then!" Seaton snapped, and cut in the super-power stage and began turning dials and knobs, exploring that strange mind for the particular area in which he was most interested. He soon found it, and cut in the visualizer-the stereographic device, in parallel with Solon's own brain recorder, which projected a three-dimensional picture into the "viewing-area" or dark space of the cabinet. Crane and Dunark, tense and silent, looked on in strained suspense as, minute after minute, the silent battle of wills raged. Upon one side was a horrible and gigantic brain, of undreamed of power; upon the other side a strong man, fighting for all that life holds dear, wielding against that monstrous and frightful brain a weapon wrought of high-tension electricity, applied with all the skill that earthly and Osnomian science could devise.

Seaton crouched over the amplifier, his jaw set and every muscle taut, his eyes leaping from one meter to another, his right hand slowly turning up the potentiometer which was driving more and ever more of the searing, torturing output of his super-power tube into that stubborn brain. The captive was standing utterly rigid, eyes closed, every sense and faculty mustered to resist that cruelly penetrant attack upon the very innermost recesses of his mind. Crane and Dunark scarcely breathed as the three-dimensional picture in the visualizer varied from a blank to the hazy outlines of a giant space-cruiser. It faded out as the unknown exerted himself to withstand that poignant inquisition, only to come back in, clearer than before, as Seaton advanced the potentiometer still farther. Finally, flesh and blood could no longer resist that lethal probe and the picture became sharp and clear. It showed the captain-for he was no less an officer than the commander of the vessel-at a great council table, seated, together with many other officers, upon very low, enormously strong metal stools. They were receiving orders from their Emperor; orders plainly understood by Crane and the Osnomian alike, for thought needs no translation.

"Gentlemen of the Navy," the ruler spoke solemnly, "Our preliminary expedition, returned some time ago, achieved its every aim, and we are now ready to begin fulfilling our destiny, the Conquest of the Universe. This Galaxy comes first. Our base of operations will be the largest planet of that group of brilliant green suns, for they can be seen from any point in the Galaxy and are almost in the exact center of it. Our astronomers," here the captain's thoughts shifted briefly to an observatory far out in space for perfect seeing, and portrayed a reflecting telescope with a mirror five miles in diameter, capable of penetrating unimaginable myriads of light-years into space, "have tabulated all the suns, planets, and satellites belonging to this Galaxy, and each of you has been given a complete chart and assigned a certain area which he is to explore. Remember, gentlemen, that this first major expedition is to be purely one of exploration; the one of conquest will set out after you have returned with complete information. You will each report by torpedo every tenth of the year. We do not anticipate any serious difficulty, as we are of course the highest type of life in the Universe; nevertheless, in the unlikely event of trouble, report it. We shall do the rest. In conclusion, I warn you again-let no people know that we exist. Make no conquests, and destroy all who by any chance may see you. Gentlemen, go with power."

The captain embarked in a small airboat and was shot to his vessel. He took his station at an immense control board and the warship shot off instantly, with unthinkable velocity, and with not the slightest physical shock.

At this point Seaton made the captain take them all over the ship. They noted its construction, its power-plant, its controls-every minute detail of structure, operation, and maintenance was taken from the captain's mind and was both recorded and visualized.

The journey seemed to be a very long one, but finally the cluster of green suns became visible and the Fenachrone began to explore the solar systems in the area assigned to that particular vessel. Hardly had the survey started, however, when the two globular space-cruisers were detected and located. The captain stopped the ship briefly, then attacked. They watched the attack, and saw the destruction of the *Kondal*. They looked on while the captain read the brain of one of Dunark's crew, gleaning from it all the facts concerning the two space-ships, and thought with him that the two absentees from the *Kondal* would drift back in a few hours, and would be disposed of in due course. They learned that these things were automatically impressed upon the torpedo next to issue, as was every detail of everything that happened in and around the vessel. They watched him impress a thought of his own upon the record—"the inhabitants of planet three of sun six four seven three Pilarone show unusual development and may cause trouble, as they have already brought knowledge of the metal of power and of the impenetrable shield to the Central System, which is to be our base. Recommend volatilization of this planet by vessel sent on special mission." They saw the raying of the *Skylark*. They sensed him issue commands:

"Ray it for a time; he will probably open the shield for a moment, as the other one did," then, after a time skipped over by the mind under examination. "Cease raying-no use wasting power. He must open eventually, as he runs out of power. Stand by and destroy him when he opens."

The scene shifted. The captain was asleep and was awakened by an alarm gong-only to find himself floating in a mass of wreckage. Making his way to the fragment of his vessel containing the torpedo port, he released the messenger, which flew, with ever-increasing velocity, back to the capital city of the Fenachrone, carrying with it a record of everything that had happened.

"That's what I want," thought Seaton. "Those torpedoes went home, fast. I want to know how far they have to go and how long it'll take them to get there. You know what distance a parsec is, since it is purely a mathematical concept; and you must have a watch or some similar instrument with which we can translate your years into ours. I don't want to have to kill you, fellow, and if you'll give up even now I'll spare you. I'll get it anyway, you know-and you also know that a few hundred volts more will kill you."

They saw the thought received, and saw its answer: "You shall learn no more. This is the most important of all, and I shall hold it to disintegration and beyond."

Seaton advanced the potentiometer still farther, and the brain picture waxed and waned, strengthened and faded. Finally, however, it was revealed by flashes that the torpedo had about a hundred and fifty-five thousand parsecs to go and that it would take two-tenths of a year to make the journey; that the warships which would come in answer to the message were as fast as the torpedo; that he did indeed have in his suit a watch —a device of seven dials, each turning ten times as fast as its successor; and that one turn of the slowest dial measured one year of his time. Seaton instantly threw off his headset and opened the power switch.

"Grab a stopwatch quick, Mart!" he called, as he leaped to the discarded vacuum suit and searched out the peculiar timepiece. They noted the exact time consumed by one complete revolution of one of the dials, and calculated rapidly.

"Better than I thought!" exclaimed Seaton. "That makes his year about four hundred ten of our days. That gives us eighty-two days before the torpedo gets there-longer than I'd dared hope. We've got to fight, too, not run. They figure on getting the *Skylark*, then volatilizing our world. Well, we can take time enough to grab off an absolutely complete record of this guy's brain. We'll need it for what's coming, and I'm going to get it, if I have to kill him to do it."

He resumed his place at the educator, turned on the power, and a shadow passed over his face.

"Poor devil, he's conked out-couldn't stand the gaff," he remarked, half-regretfully. "However that makes it easy to get what we want, and we'd have had to kill him anyway, I guess-Bad as it is, I'd hate to bump him off in cold blood."

He threaded new spools into the machine, and for three hours, mile after mile of tape sped between the magnets as Seaton explored every recess of that monstrous, yet stupendous brain.

"Well, that's that," he declared finally, as, the last bit of information gleaned and recorded upon the flying tape, he removed the body of the Fenachrone captain into space and rayed it out of existence. "Now what to do?"

"How can we get this salt to Osnome?" asked Dunark whose thoughts were never far from that store of the precious chemical. "You are already crowded, and Sitar and I will crowd you still more. You have no room for additional cargo, and yet much valuable time would be lost in going to Osnome for another vessel."

"Yes, and we've got to get a lot of 'X', too. Guess we'll have to take time to get another vessel. I'd like to drag in the pieces of that ship, too-his instruments and a lot of the parts could be used."

"Why not do it all at once?" suggested Crane. "We can start that whole mass toward Osnome by drawing it behind us until such a velocity has been attained that it will reach there at the desired time. We could then go to 'X,' and overtake this material near the green system."

"Right you are, ace-that's a sound idea. But say, Dunark, it wouldn't be good technique for you to eat our food for any length of time. While we're figuring this out you'd better hop over there and bring over enough to last you two until we get you home. Give it to Shiro-after a couple of lessons, you'll find he'll be as good as any of your cooks."

Faster and faster the *Skylark* flew, pulling behind her the mass of wreckage, held by every available attractor. When the calculated velocity had been attained, the attractors were shut off and the vessel darted away toward that planet, still in the Carboniferous Age, which possessed at least one solid ledge of metallic "X," the rarest of all earthly metals. As the automatic controls held the cruiser upon her course, the six wanderers sat long in discussion as to what should be done, what could be done, to avert the threatened destruction of all the civilization of the Galaxy except the monstrous and unspeakable culture of the Fenachrone. Nearing their destination, Seaton rose to his feet.

"Well, folks, it's like this. We've got our backs to the wall. Dunark has troubles of his own-if the Third Planet doesn't get him the Fenachrone will, and the Third Planet is the more pressing danger. That lets him out. We've got nearly six months before the Fenachrone can get back here...."

"But how can they possibly find us here, or wherever we'll be by that time, Dick?" asked Dorothy. "The battle was a long way from here."

"With that much start they probably couldn't find us," Seaton replied soberly. "It's the world I'm thinking about. They've got to be stopped, and stopped cold-and we've got only six months to do it in....Osnome's got the best tools and the fastest workmen I know of...." his voice died away in thought.

"That sort of thing is in your department, Dick."

Crane was calm and judicial as always. "I will, of course, do anything I can. But you probably have a plan of campaign already laid out?"

"After a fashion. We've got to find out how to work through this zone of force or we're sunk without a trace. Even with rays, screens, and ships equal to theirs, we couldn't keep them from sending a vessel to destroy the earth; and they'd probably get us too, eventually. They've got a lot of stuff we don't know about, of course, since I took only one man's mind. While he was a very able man, he didn't know all that all the rest of them do, any more than any one man has all the earthly science known. Absolutely our only chance is to control that zone-it's the only thing they haven't got. Of course, it may be impossible, but I won't believe that, until I've exhausted a lot of possibilities. Dunark, can you spare a crew to build us a duplicate of that Fenachrone ship, besides those you are going to build for yourself?"

"Certainly. I will be only too glad to do so."

"Well, then, while Dunark is doing that, I suggest that we go to this Third Planet, abduct a few of their leading scientists, and read their minds. Then do the same, visiting every other highly advanced planet we can locate. There is a good chance that, by combining the best points of the warfares of many worlds, we can evolve something that will enable us to turn back these invaders."

"Why not send a copper torpedo to destroy their entire planet?" suggested Dunark.

"Wouldn't work. Their detecting screens would locate it a thousand million miles off in space, and they would ray it. With a zone of force that would get through their screens, that would be the first thing I'd do. You see, every thought comes back to that zone. We've got to get through it some way."

The course alarm sounded, and they saw that a planet lay directly in their path. It was "X," and enough negative acceleration was applied to make an easy landing possible.

"Isn't it going to be a long, slow job, chopping off two tons of that metal and fighting away those terrible animals besides?" asked Margaret.

"It'll take about a millionth of a second, Peg. I'm going to bite it off with the zone, just as I took that bite out of our field. The rotation of the planet will throw us away from the surface, then we'll release the zone and drag our prey off with us. See?"

The *Skylark* descended rapidly toward that well-remembered ledge of metal to which the object compass had led them.

"This is exactly where we landed before," Margaret commented in surprise, and Dorothy added:

"Yes, and there's that horrible tree that ate the dinosaur or whatever it was. I thought you blew it up for me, Dick?"

"I did, Dottie-blew it into atoms. Must be a good location for carnivorous trees-and they must grow awfully fast, too. As to its being the same place, Peg-sure it is. That's what object compasses are for."

Everything appeared as it had been at the time of their first visit. The rank Carboniferous vegetation, intensely, vividly green, was motionless in the still, hot, heavy air; the living nightmares inhabiting that primitive world were lying in the cooler depths of the jungle, sheltered from the torrid rays of that strange and fervent sun.

"How about it, Dot? Want to see some of your little friends again? If you do, I'll give them a shot and bring them out."

"Heavens, no! I saw them once-if I never see them again, that will be twenty minutes too soon!"

"All right-we'll grab us a piece of this ledge and beat it."

Seaton lowered the vessel to the ledge, focussed the main anchoring attractor upon it, and threw on the zone of force. Almost immediately he released the zone, pointed the bar parallel to the compass bearing upon Osnome, and slowly applied the power.

"How much did you take, anyway?" asked Dunark in amazement. "It looks bigger than the *Skylark*!"

"It is; considerably bigger. Thought we might as well take enough while we're here, so I set the zone for a seventy-five-foot radius. It's probably of the order of magnitude of half a million tons, since the stuff weighs more than half a ton to the cubic foot. However, we can handle it as easily as we could a smaller bite, and that much mass will help us hold that other stuff together when we catch up with it."

The voyage to Osnome was uneventful. They overtook the wreckage, true to schedule, as they were approaching the green system, and attached it to the mass of metal behind them by means of attractors.

"Where'll we land this junk, Dunark?" asked Seaton, as Osnome grew large beneath them.

"We'll hold this lump of metal and the fragment of the ship carrying the salt; and we'll be able to hold some of the most important of the other stuff. But a lot of it is bound to get away from us-and the Lord help anybody who's under it when it comes down! You might yell for help-and say, you might ask somebody to have that astronomical data ready for us as soon as we land."

"The parade ground will be empty now, so we will land there," Dunark replied. "We should be able to land everything in a field of that size, I should think." He touched the sender at his belt, and in the general code notified the city of their arrival and warned everyone to keep away from the parade ground. He then sent several messages in the official code, concluding by asking that one or two space-ships come out and help lower the burden to the ground. As the peculiar, pulsating chatter of the Osnomian telegraph died out, Seaton called for help.

"Come here, you two, and grab some of these attractors. I need about twelve hands to keep this plunder in the straight and narrow path."

The course had been carefully laid, with allowance for the various velocities and forces involved, to follow the easiest path to the Kondalian parade ground. The hemisphere of "X" and the fragment of the *Kondal* which bore the salt were held immovably in place by the main attractor and one auxiliary; and many other auxiliaries held sections of the Fenachrone vessel. However, the resistance of the air seriously affected the trajectory of many of the irregularly shaped smaller masses of metal, and all three men were kept busy flicking attractors right and left; capturing those strays which threatened to veer off into the streets or upon the buildings of the Kondalian capital city, and shifting from one piece to another so that none should fall freely. Two sister-ships of the *Kondal* appeared as if by magic in answer to Dunark's call, and their attractors aided greatly in handling the unruly collection of wreckage. A few of the smaller sections and a shower of debris fell clear, however, in spite of all efforts, and their approach was heralded by a meteoric display unprecedented in that world of continuous daylight.

As the three vessels with their cumbersome convoy dropped down into the lower atmosphere, the guns of the city roared a welcome; banners and pennons waved; the air became riotous with color from hundreds of projectors and odorous with a bewildering variety of scents; while all around them played numberless aircraft of all descriptions and sizes. The space below them was carefully avoided, but on all sides and above them the air was so full that it seemed marvelous that no collision occurred. Tiny one-man helicopters, little more than single chairs flying about; beautiful pleasure-planes, soaring and wheeling; immense multiplane liners and giant helicopter freighters-everything in the air found occasion to fly as near as possible to the Skylark in order to dip their flags in salute to Dunark, their Kofedix, and to Seaton, the wearer of the seven disks-their revered Overlord.

Finally the freight was landed without serious mishap and the *Skylark* leaped to the landing dock upon the palace roof, where the royal family and many nobles were waiting, in full panoply of glittering harness. Dunark and Sitar disembarked and the four others stepped out and stood at attention as Seaton addressed Roban, the Karfedix.

"Sir, we greet you, but we cannot stop, even for a moment. You know that only the most urgent necessity would make us forego the pleasure of a brief rest beneath your roof-the Kofedix will presently give you the measure of that dire need. We shall endeavor to return soon. Greetings, and, for a time, farewell."

"Overlord, we greet you, and trust that soon we may entertain you and profit from your companionship. For what you have done, we thank you. May the great First Cause smile upon you until your return. Farewell."

CHAPTER VI

The Peace Conference

"Here's a chart of the green system, Mart, with all the motions and the rest of the dope that they've been able to get. How'd it be for you to navigate us over to the third planet of the fourteenth sun?"

"While you build a Fenachrone super-generator?"

"Right, the first time. Your deducer is hitting on all eight, as usual. That big ray is hot stuff, and their ray-screen is something to write home about, too."

"How can their rays be any hotter than ours, Dick?" Dorothy asked curiously. "I thought you said we had the very last word in rays."

"I thought we had, but those birds we met back there spoke a couple of later words. Their rays work on an entirely different system than the one we use. They generate an extremely short carrier wave, like the Millikan cosmic ray, by recombining some of the electrons and protons of their disintegrating metal, and upon this wave they impose a pure heat frequency of terrific power. The Millikan rays will penetrate anything except a special ray screen or a zone of force, and carry with them-somewhat as radio frequencies carry sound frequencies-the heat rays, which volatilize anything they touch. Their ray screens are a lot better than ours, too-they generate the entire spectrum. It's a sweet system and when we revamp ours so as to be just like it, we'll be able to talk turkey to those folks on the third planet."

"How long will it take you to build it?" asked Crane, who, dexterously turning the pages of "Vega's Handbuch" was calculating their course.

"A day or so-maybe less. I've got all the stuff and with my Osnomian tools it won't take long. If you find you'll get there before I get done, you'll have to loaf a while-kill a little time."

"Are you going to connect the power plant to operate on the entire vessel and all its contents?"

"No-can't do it without redesigning the whole thing and that's hardly worth while for the short time we'll use this old bus."

Building those generators would have been a long and difficult task for a corps of earthly mechanics and electricians, but to Seaton it was merely a job. The "shop" had been enlarged and had been filled to capacity with Osnomian machinery; machine tools that were capable of performing automatically and with the utmost precision and speed any conceivable mechanical operation. He put a dozen of them to work, and before the vessel reached its destination, the new offensive and defensive weapons had been installed and thoroughly tested. He had added a third screen-generator, so that now, in addition to the four-foot hull of arenak and the repellers, warding off any material projectile, the Skylark was also protected by an outer, an intermediate, and an inner ray-screen; each driven by the super-power of a four-hundred-pound bar and each covering the entire spectrum-capable of neutralizing any dangerous frequency known to those master-scientists, the Fenachrone.

As the *Skylark* approached the planet, Seaton swung number six visiplate upon it, and directed their flight toward a great army base. Darting down upon it, he snatched an officer into the airlock, closed the door, and leaped back into space. He brought the captive into the control room pinioned by auxiliary attractors, and relieved him of his weapons. He then rapidly read his mind, encountering no noticeable resistance, released the attractors, and addressed him in his own language.

"Please be seated, lieutenant," Seaton said courteously, motioning him to one of the seats. "We come in peace. Please pardon my discourtesy in handling you, but it was necessary in order to learn your language and thus to get in touch with your commanding officer."

The officer, overcome with astonishment that he had not been killed instantly, sank into the seat indicated, without a reply, and Seaton went on:

"Please be kind enough to signal your commanding officer that we are coming down at once, for a peace conference. By the way, I can read your signals, and will send them myself if necessary."

The stranger worked an instrument attached to his harness briefly, and the *Skylark* descended slowly toward the fortress.

"I know, of course, that your vessels will attack," Seaton remarked, as he noted a crafty gleam in the eyes of the officer. "I intend to let them use all their power for a time, to prove to them the impotence of their weapons. After that, I shall tell you what to say to them."

"Do you think this is altogether safe, Dick?" asked Crane as they saw a fleet of gigantic airships soaring upward to meet them.

"Nothing sure but death and taxes," returned Seaton cheerfully, "but don't forget that we've got Fenachrone armament now, instead of Osnomian. I'm betting that they can't begin to drive their rays through even our outer screen. And even if our outer screen should begin to go into the violet — I don't think it will even go cherry-red — out goes our zone of force and we automatically go up where no possible airship can reach. Since their only space-ships are rocket driven, and of practically no maneuverability, they stand a big chance of getting to us. Anyway, we must get in touch with them, to find out if they know anything we don't, and this is the only way I know of to do it. Besides, I want to head Dunark off from wrecking this world. They're exactly the same kind of folks he is, you notice, and I don't like civil war. Any suggestions? Keep an eye on that bird, then, Mart, and we'll go down."

The *Skylark* dropped down into the midst of the fleet, which instantly turned against her the full force of their giant guns and their immense ray batteries. Seaton held the *Skylark* motionless, staring into his visiplate, his right hand grasping the zone-switch.

"The outer screen isn't even getting warm!" he exulted after a moment. The repellers were hurling the shells back long before they reached even the outer screen, and they were exploding harmlessly in the air. The full power of the ray-generators, too, which had been so destructive to the Osnomian defenses, were only sufficient to bring the outer screen to a dull red glow. After fifteen minutes of passive acceptance of all the airships could do, Seaton spoke to the captive.

"Sir, please signal the commanding officer of vessel seven-two-four that I am going to cut it in two in the middle. Have him remove all men in that part of the ship to the ends, and have parachutes in readiness, as I do not wish to cause any loss of life."

The signal was sent, and, as the officer was already daunted by the fact that their utmost efforts could not even make the strangers' screens radiate, it was obeyed. Seaton then threw on the frightful power of the Fenachrone super-generators. The defensive screens of the doomed warship flashed once — a sparkling, coruscating display of incandescent brilliance-and in the same instant went down. Simultaneously the entire midsection of the vessel exploded into light and disappeared; completely volatilized.

"Sir, please signal the entire fleet to cease action, and to follow me down. If they do not do so, I will destroy the rest of them."

The *Skylark* dropped to the ground, followed by the fleet of warships, who settled in a ring about her-inactive, but ready.

"Will you please loan me your sending instrument, sir?" Seaton asked. "From this point on I can carry on negotiations better direct than through you."

The lieutenant found his voice as he surrendered the instrument.

"Sir, are you the Overlord of Osnome, of whom we have heard? We had supposed that one was a mythical character, but you must be he-no one else would spare lives that he could take, and the Overlord is the only being reputed to have a skin the color of yours."

"Yes, lieutenant, I am the Overlord-and I have decided to become the Overlord of the entire green system, as well as of Osnome."

He then sent out a call to the commander-in-chief of all the armies of the planet, informing him that he was coming to visit him at once, and the *Skylark* tore through the air to the capital city. No sooner had the earthly vessel alighted upon the palace grounds than she was surrounded by a ring of warships who, however, made no offensive move. Seaton again used the telegraph.

"Commander-in-Chief of the armed forces of the planet Urvania; greetings from the Overlord of this solar system. I invite you to come into my vessel, unarmed and alone, for a conference. I come in peace and, peace or war as you decide, no harm shall come to you, until after you have returned to your own command. Think well before you reply."

"If I refuse?"

"I shall destroy one of the vessels surrounding me, and shall continue to destroy them, one every ten seconds, until you agree to come. If you still do not agree. I shall destroy all the armed forces upon this planet, then destroy all your people who are at present upon Osnome. I wish to avoid bloodshed and destruction, but I can and I will do as I have said."

"I will come."

The general came out upon the field unarmed, escorted by a company of soldiers. A hundred feet from the vessel he halted the guards and came on alone, erect and soldierly. Seaton met him at the door and invited him to be seated.

"What can you have to say to me?" the general demanded, disregarding the invitation.

"Many things. First, let me say that you are not only a brave man; you are a wise general-your visit to me proves it."

"It is a sign of weakness, but I believed when I heard those reports, and still believe, that a refusal would have resulted in a heavy loss of our men," was the General's reply.

"It would have," said Seaton. "I repeat that your act was not weakness, but wisdom. The second thing I have to say is that I had not planned on taking any active part in the management of things, either upon Osnome or upon this planet, until I learned of a catastrophe that is threatening all the civilization in this Galaxy-thus threatening my own distant world as well as those of this solar system. Third, only by superior force can I make either your race or the Osnomians listen to reason sufficiently to unite against a common foe. You have been reared in unreasoning hatred for so many generations that your minds are warped. For that reason I have assumed control of this entire system, and shall give you your choice between co-operating with us or being rendered incapable of molesting us while our attention is occupied by this threatened invasion."

"We will have no traffic with the enemy whatever." said the general. "This is final."

"You just think so. Here is a mathematical statement of what is going to happen to your world, unless I intervene." He handed the general a drawing of Dunark's plan and described it in detail. "That is the answer of the Osnomians to your invasion of their planet. I do not want this world destroyed, but if you refuse to make common cause with us against a common foe, it may be necessary. Have you forces at your command sufficient to frustrate this plan?"

"No; but I cannot really believe that such a deflection of celestial bodies is possible. Possible or not, you realize that I could not yield to empty threats."

"Of course not," said Seaton, "but you were wise enough to refuse to sacrifice a few ships and men in a useless struggle against my overwhelming armament, therefore you are certainly wise enough to refuse to sacrifice your entire race. However, before you come to any definite conclusion, I will show you what threatens the Galaxy."

He handed the other a headset and ran through the section of the record showing the plans of the invaders. He then ran a few sections showing the irresistible power at the command of the Fenachrone.

"That is what awaits us all unless we combine against them."

"What are your requirements?" the general asked.

"I request immediate withdrawal of all your armed forces now upon Osnome and full cooperation with me in this coming war against the invaders. In return, I will give you the secrets I have just given the Osnomians-the power and the offensive and defensive weapons of this vessel."

"The Osnomians are now building vessels such as this one?" asked the general.

"They are building vessels a hundred times the size of this one, with the same armament."

"For myself, I would agree to your terms. However, the word of the Emperor is law."

"I understand," replied Seaton. "Would you be willing to seek an immediate audience with him? I would suggest that both you and he accompany me, and we shall hold a peace conference with the Osnomian Emperor and Commander-in-Chief upon this vessel. We shall be gone less than a day."

"I shall do so at once."

"You may accompany your general, lieutenant. Again I ask pardon for my necessary rudeness."

As the Urvanian officers hurried toward the palace, the other Terrestrials, who had been listening in from another room, entered.

"It sounded as though you convinced him, Dick; but that language is nothing like Kondalian. Why don't you teach it to us? Teach it to Shiro, too, so he can cook for, and talk to, our distinguished guests intelligently, if they're going back with us."

As he connected up the educator, Seaton explained what had happened, and concluded:

"I want to stop this civil war, keep Dunark from destroying this planet, preserve Osnome for Osnomians, and make them all co-operate with us against the Fenachrone. That's one tall order, since these folks haven't the remotest notion of anything except killing."

A company of soldiers approached, and Dorothy got up hastily.

"Stick around, folks. We can all talk to them."

"I believe that it would be better for you to be alone," Crane decided, after a moment's thought. "They are used to autocratic power, and can understand nothing but one-man control. The girls and I will keep out of it."

"That might be better at that," and Seaton went to the door to welcome the guests. Seaton instructed them to lie flat, and put on all the acceleration they could bear. It was not long until they were back in Kondal, where Roban, the Karfedix, and Tarnan, the Karbix, accepted Seaton's invitation and entered the Skylark, unarmed. Back out in space, the vessel stationary, Seaton introduced the emperors and commanders-in-chief to each other-introductions which were acknowledged almost imperceptibly. He then gave each a headset, and ran the complete record of the Fenachrone brain.

"Stop!" shouted Roban, after only a moment. "Would you, the Overlord of Osnome, reveal such secrets as this to the arch-enemies of Osnome?"

"I would. I have taken over the Overlordship of the entire green system for the duration of this emergency, and I do not want two of its planets engaged in civil war."

The record finished, Seaton tried for some time to bring the four green warriors to his way of thinking, but in vain. Roban and Tarnan remained contemptuous. They would have thrown themselves upon him, but for the knowledge that no fifty unarmed men of the green race could have overcome his strength-to them supernatural. The two Urvanians were equally obdurate. This soft earth-being had given them everything; they had given him nothing and would give him nothing. Finally Seaton rose to his full height and stared at them in turn, wrath and determination blazing in his eyes.

"I have brought you four together, here in a neutral vessel in neutral space, to bring about peace between you. I have shown you the benefits to be derived from the peaceful pursuit of science, knowledge, and power, instead of continuing this utter economic waste of continual war. You all close your senses to reason. You of Osnome accuse me of being an ingrate and a traitor; you of Urvania consider me a soft-headed, sentimental weakling, who may safely be disregarded-all because I think the welfare of the numberless peoples of the Universe more important than your narrow-minded, stubborn, selfish vanity. Think what you please. If brute force is your only logic, know now that I can, and will, use brute force. Here are the seven disks," and he placed the bracelet upon Roban's knee.

"If you four leaders are short-sighted enough to place your petty enmity before the good of all civilization, I am done with you forever. I have deliberately given Urvanians precisely the same information that I have given the Osnomians-no more and no less. I have given neither of you all that I know, and I shall know much more than I do now, before the time of the conquest shall have arrived. Unless you four men, here and now, renounce this war and agree to a perpetual peace between your worlds, I shall leave you to your mutual destruction. You do not yet realize the power of the weapons I have given you. When you do realize it, you will know that mutual destruction is inevitable if you continue this internecine war. I shall continue upon other worlds my search for the one secret standing between me and a complete mastery of power. That I shall find that secret I am confident; and, having found it, I shall, without your aid, destroy the Fenachrone.

"You have several times remarked with sneers that you are not to be swayed by empty threats. What I am about to say is no empty threat-it is a most solemn promise, given by one who has both the will and the power to fulfill his every given word. Now listen carefully to this, my final utterance. If you continue this warfare and if the victor should not be utterly destroyed in its course, I swear as I stand here, by the great First Cause, that I shall myself wipe out every trace of the surviving nation as soon as the Fenachrone shall have been obliterated. Work with each other and me and we all may live-fight on and both your nations, to the last person, will most certainly die. Decide now which it is to be. I have spoken."

Roban took up the bracelet and clasped it again about Seaton's arm, saying, "You are more than ever our Overlord. You are wiser than are we, and stronger. Issue your commands and they shall be obeyed."

"Why did not you say those things first, Overlord?" asked the Urvanian emperor, as he saluted and smiled. "We could not in honor submit to a weakling, no matter what the fate in store. Having convinced us of your strength, there can be no disgrace in fighting beneath your screens. An armlet of seven symbols shall be cast and ready for you when you next visit us. Roban of Osnome, you are my brother."

The two emperors saluted each other and stared eye to eye for a long moment, and Seaton knew that the perpetual peace had been signed. Then all four spoke, in unison:

"Overlord, we await your commands."

"Dunark of Osnome is already informed as to what Osnome is to do. Say to him that it will not be necessary for him to build the vessel for me; the Urvanians will do that. Urvan of Urvania, you will accompany Roban to Osnome, where you two will order instant cessation of hostilities. Osnome has many ships of this type, and upon some of them you will return your every soldier and engine of war to your own planet. As soon as possible you will build for me a vessel like that of the Fenachrone, except that it shall be ten times as large, in every dimension, and except that every instrument, control, and weapon is to be left out."

"Left out? It shall be so built-but of what use will it be?"

"The empty spaces shall be filled after I have returned from my quest. You will build this vessel of dagal. You will also instruct the Osnomian commander in the manufacture of that metal, which is so much more resistant than their arenak."

"But, Overlord, we have...."

"I have just brought immense stores of the precious chemical and of the metal of power to Osnome. They will share it with you. I also advise you to build for yourselves many ships like those of the Fenachrone, with which to do battle with the invaders, in case I should fail in my quest. You will, of course, see to it that there will be a corps of your most efficient mechanics and artisans within call at all times in case I should return and have sudden need for them."

"All these things shall be done."

The conference ended, the four nobles were quickly landed upon Osnome and once more the *Skylark* traveled out into her element, the total vacuum and absolute zero of the outer void, with Crane at the controls.

"You certainly sounded savage, Dick. I almost thought you really meant it!" Dorothy chuckled.

"I did mean it, Dot. Those fellows are mighty keen on detecting bluffs. If I hadn't meant it, and if they hadn't known that I meant it, I'd never have got away with it."

"But you *couldn't* have meant it, Dick! You wouldn't have destroyed the Osnomians, surely-you know you wouldn't."

"No, but I would have destroyed what was left of the Urvanians, and all five of us knew exactly how it would have turned out and exactly what I would have done about it-that's why they all pulled in their horns."

"I don't know what would have happened," interjected Margaret. "What would have?"

"With this new stuff the Urvanians would have wiped the Osnomians out. They are an older race, and so much better in science and mechanics that the Osnomians wouldn't have stood much chance, and knew it. Incidentally, that's why I'm having them build our new ship. They'll put a lot of stuff into it that Dunark's men would miss-maybe some stuff that even the Fenachrone haven't got. However, though it might seem that the Urvanians had all the best of it, Urvan knew that I had something up my sleeve besides my bare arm-and he knew that I'd clean up what there was left of his race if they polished off the Osnomians."

"What a frightful chance you were taking, Dick!" gasped Dorothy.

"You have to be hard to handle those folks-and believe me, I was a forty-minute egg right then. They have such a peculiar mental and moral slant that we can hardly understand them at all. This idea of co-operation is so new to them that it actually dazed all four of them even to consider it."

"Do you suppose they will fight, anyway?" asked Crane.

"Absolutely not. Both nations have an inflexible code of honor, such as it is, and lying is against both codes. That's one thing I like about them —I'm sort of honest myself, and with either of these races you need nothing signed or guaranteed."

"What next, Dick?"

"Now the real trouble begins. Mart, oil up the massive old intellect. Have you found the answer to the problem?"

"What problem?" asked Dorothy. "You didn't tell us anything about a problem."

"No, I told Mart. I want the best physicist in this entire solar system-and since there are only one hundred and twenty-five planets around these seventeen suns, it should be simple to yon phenomenal brain. In fact, I expect to hear him say 'elementary, my dear Watson, elementary'!"

"Hardly that, Dick, but I have found out a few things. There are some eighty planets which are probably habitable for beings like us. Other things being equal, it seems reasonable to assume that the older the sun, the longer its planets have been habitable, and therefore the older and more intelligent the life...."

"'Ha! ha! It was elementary,' says Sherlock." Seaton interrupted. "You're heading directly at that largest, oldest, and most intelligent planet, then, I take it, where I can catch me my physicist?"

"Not directly at it, no. I am heading for the place where it will be when we reach it. That is elementary."

"Ouch! That got to me, Mart, right where I live. I'll be good."

"But you are getting ahead of me, Dick-it is not as simple as you have assumed from what I have said so far. The Osnomian astronomers have done wonders in the short time they have had, but their data, particularly on the planets of the outer suns, is as yet necessarily very incomplete. Since the furthermost outer sun is probably the oldest, it is the one in which we are most interested. It has seven planets, four of which are probably habitable, as far as temperature and atmosphere are concerned. However, nothing exact is yet known of their masses, motions, or places. Therefore I have laid our course to intercept the closest one to us, as nearly as I can from what meager data we have. If it should prove to be inhabited by intelligent beings, they can probably give us more exact information concerning their neighboring planets. That is the best I can do."

"That's a darn fine best, old top-narrowing down to four from a hundred and twenty-five. Well, until we get there, what to do? Let's sing us a song, to keep our fearless quartette in good voice."

"Before you do anything," said Margaret seriously, "I would like to know if you really think there is a chance of defeating those monsters."

"In all seriousness, I do. In fact, I am quite confident of it. If we had two years, I know that we could lick them cold; and by stepping on the gas I believe we can get the dope in less than the six months we have to work in."

"I know that you are serious, Dick. Now you know that I do not want to discourage any one, but I can see small basis for optimism," Crane spoke slowly and thoughtfully. "I hope that you will be able to control the zone of force-but you are not studying it yourself. You seem to be certain that somewhere in this system there is a race who already knows all about it. I would like to know your reasons for thinking that such a race exists."

"They may not be upon this system; they may have been outsiders, as we are-but I have reasons for believing them to be natives of this system, since they were green. You are as familiar with Osnomian mythology as I am-you girls in particular have read Osnomian legends to Osnomian children for hours. Also identically the same legends prevail upon Urvania. I read them in that lieutenant's brain-in fact, I looked for them. You also know that every folk-legend has some basis, however tenuous, in fact. Now, Dottie, tell about the battle of the gods, when Osnome was a pup."

"The gods came down from the sky," Dorothy recited. "They were green, as were men. They wore invisible armor of polished metal, which appeared and disappeared. They stayed inside the armor and fought outside it with swords and lances of fire. Men who fought against them cut them through and through with swords, and they struck the men with lances of flame so that they were stunned. So the gods fought in days long gone and vanished in their invisible armor, and — —"

"That's enough," interrupted Seaton. "The little red-haired girl has her lesson perfectly. Get it, Mart?"

"No, I cannot say that I do."

"Why, it doesn't even make sense!" exclaimed Margaret.

"All right, I'll elucidate. Listen!" and Seaton's voice grew tense with earnestness. "Visitors came down out of space. They were green. They wore zones of force, which they flashed on and off. They stayed inside the zones and projected their images outside, and used rays *through the zones*. Men who fought against the images cut them through and through with swords, but could not harm them since they were not actual substance; and the images directed rays against the men so that they were stunned. So the visitors fought in days long gone, and vanished in their zones of force. How does that sound?"

"You have the most stupendous imagination the world has ever seen-but there may be some slight basis of fact there, after all," said Crane, slowly.

"I'm convinced of it, for one reason in particular. Notice that it says specifically that the visitors stunned the natives. Now that thought is absolutely foreign to all Osnomian nature-when they strike they kill, and always have. Now if that myth has come down through so many generations without having that 'stunned' changed to 'killed', I'm willing to bet a few weeks of time that the rest of it came down fairly straight, too. Of course, what they had may not have been the zone of force as we know it, but it must have been a ray of some kind-and believe me, that was one educated ray. Somebody sure had something, even 'way back in those days. And if they had anything at all back there, they must know a lot by now. That's why I want to look 'em up."

"But suppose they want to kill us off at sight?" objected Dorothy. "They might be able to do it, mightn't they?"

"Sure, but they probably wouldn't want to-any more than you would step on an ant who asked you to help him move a twig. That's about how much ahead of us they probably are. Of course, we struck a pure mentality once, who came darn near dematerializing us entirely, but I'm betting that these folks haven't got that far along yet. By the way, I've got a hunch about those pure intellectuals."

"Oh, tell us about it!" laughed Margaret. "Your hunches are the world's greatest brainstorms!"

"Well, I pumped out and rejeweled the compass we put on that funny planet-as a last resort, I thought we might maybe visit them and ask that bozo we had the argument with to help us out. I think he-or it-would show us everything about the zone of force we want to know. I don't think that we'd be dematerialized, either, because the situation would give him something more to think about for another thousand cycles; and thinking seemed to be his main object in life. However, to get back to the subject, I found that even with the new power of the compass the entire planet was still out of reach. Unless they've dematerialized it, that means about ten billion light-years as an absolute minimum. Think about that for a minute!...I've just got a kind of a hunch that maybe they don't belong in this Galaxy at all-that they might be from some other Galaxy, planet and all; just riding around on it, as we are riding in the *Skylark*. Is the idea conceivable to a sane mind, or not?"

"Not!" decided Dorothy, promptly. "We'd better go to bed. One more such idea, in progression with the last two you've had, would certainly give you a compound fracture of the skull. 'Night, Cranes."

CHAPTER VII

DuQuesne's Voyage

Far from our solar system a cigar-shaped space-car slackened its terrific acceleration to a point at which human beings could walk, and two men got up, exercised vigorously to restore the circulation to their numbed bodies, and went into the galley to prepare their meal-the first since leaving the Earth some eight hours or more before.

Because of the long and arduous journey he had decided upon, DuQuesne had had to abandon his custom of working alone, and had studied all the available men with great care before selecting his companion and relief pilot. He finally had chosen "Baby Doll" Loring-so called because of his curly yellow hair, his pink and white complexion, his guileless blue eyes, his slight form of rather less than medium height. But never did outward attributes more belie the inner man! The yellow curls covered a brain agile, keen, and hard; the girlish complexion neither paled nor reddened under stress; the wide blue eyes had glanced along the barrels of so many lethal weapons, that in various localities the noose yawned for him; the slender body was built of rawhide and whalebone, and responded instantly to the dictates of that ruthless brain. Under the protection of Steel he flourished, and in return for that protection he performed, quietly and with neatness and despatch, such odd jobs as were in his line, with which he was commissioned.

When they were seated at an excellent breakfast of ham and eggs, buttered toast, and strong, aromatic coffee, DuQuesne broke the long silence.

"Do you want to know where we are?"

"I'd say we were a long way from home, by the way this elevator of yours has been climbing all night."

"We are a good many million miles from the Earth, and we are getting farther away at a rate that would have to be measured in millions of miles per second." DuQuesne, watching the other narrowly as he made this startling announcement and remembering the effect of a similar one upon Perkins, saw with approval that the coffee-cup in midair did not pause or waver in its course. Loring noted the bouquet of his beverage and took an appreciative sip before he replied.

"You certainly can make coffee, Doctor; and good coffee is nine-tenths of a good breakfast. As to where we are-that's all right with me. I can stand it if you can."

"Don't you want to know where we're going, and why?"

"I've been thinking about that. Before we started I didn't want to know anything, because what a man doesn't know he can't be accused of spilling in case of a leak. Now that we are on our way, though, maybe I should know enough about things to act intelligently, if something unforeseen should develop. If you'd rather keep it dark and give me orders when necessary, that's all right with me, too. It's your party, you know."

"I brought you along because one man can't stay on duty twenty-four hours a day, continuously. Since you are in as deep as you can get, and since this trip is dangerous, you should know everything there is to know. You are one of the higher-ups now, anyway: and we understand each other thoroughly, I believe?"

"I believe so."

Back in the bow control-room DuQuesne applied more power, but not enough to render movement impossible.

"You don't have to drive her as hard all the way, then, as you did last night?"

"No, I'm out of range of Seaton's instrument now, and we don't have to kill ourselves. High acceleration is punishment for anyone and we must keep ourselves fit. To begin with, I suppose that you are curious about that object-compass?"

"That and other things."

"An object-compass is a needle of specially-treated copper, so activated that it points always toward one certain object, after being once set upon it. Seaton undoubtedly has one upon me; but, sensitive as they are, they can't hold on a mass as small as a man at this distance. That was why we left at midnight, after he had gone to bed-so that we'd be out of range before he woke up. I wanted to lose him, as he might interfere if he knew where I was going. Now I'll go back to the beginning and tell you the whole story."

Tersely, but vividly, he recounted the tale of the interstellar cruise, the voyage of the *Skylark of Space*. When he had finished, Loring smoked for a few minutes in silence.

"There's a lot of stuff there that's hard to understand all at once. Do you mind if I ask a few foolish questions, to get things straightened out in my mind?"

"Go ahead-ask as many as you want to. It is hard to understand a lot of that Osnomian stuff—a man can't get it all at once."

"Osnome is so far away-how are you going to find it?"

"With one of the object-compasses I mentioned. I had planned on navigating from notes I took on the trip back to the Earth, but it wasn't necessary. They tried to keep me from finding out anything, but I learned all about the compasses, built a few of them in their own shop, and set one on Osnome. I had it, among other things, in my pocket when I landed. In fact, the control of that explosive copper bullet is the only thing they had that I wasn't able to get-and I'll get that on this trip."

"What is that arenak armor they're wearing?"

"Arenak is a synthetic metal, almost perfectly transparent. It has practically the same refractive index as air, therefore it is, to all intents and purposes, invisible. It's about five hundred times as strong as chrome-vanadium steel, and even when you've got it to the yield-point, it doesn't break, but stretches out and snaps back, like rubber, with the strength unimpaired. It's the most wonderful thing I saw on the whole trip. They make complete suits of it. Of course they aren't very comfortable, but since they are only a tenth of an inch they can be worn."

"And a tenth of an inch of that stuff will stop a steel-nosed machine-gun bullet?"

"Stop it! A tenth of an inch of arenak is harder to pierce than fifty inches of our hardest, toughest armor steel. A sixteenth-inch armor-piercing projectile couldn't get through it. It's hard to believe, but nevertheless it's a fact. The only way to kill Seaton with a gun would be to use one heavy enough so that the shock of the impact would kill him-and it wouldn't surprise me a bit if he had his armor anchored with an attractor against that very contingency. Even if he hasn't, you can imagine the chance of getting action against him with a gun of that size."

"Yes, I've heard that he is fast."

"That doesn't tell half of it. You know that I'm handy with a gun myself?"

"You're faster than I am, and that's saying something. You're chain lightning."

"Well, Seaton is at least that much faster than I am. You've never seen him work—I have. On that Osnomian dock he shot twice before I started, and shot twice to my once from then on. I must have been shooting a quarter of a second after he had his side all cleaned up. To make it worse I missed once with my left hand-he didn't. There's absolutely no use tackling Richard Seaton without an Osnomian ray-generator or something better; but, as you know, Brookings always has been and always will be a fool. He won't believe anything new until after he has actually been shown. Well, I imagine he will be shown plenty by this evening."

"Well, I'll never tackle him with heat. How does he get that way?"

"He's naturally fast, and has practiced sleight-of-hand work ever since he was a kid. He's one of the best amateur magicians in the country, and I will say that his ability along that line has come in handy for him more than once."

"I see where you're right in wanting to get something, since we have only ordinary weapons and they have all that stuff. This trip is to get a little something for ourselves, I take it?"

"Exactly, and you know enough now to understand what we are out here to get for ourselves. You have guessed that we are headed for Osnome?"

"I suspected it. However, if you were going only to Osnome, you would have gone alone; so I also suspect that that's only half of it. I have no idea what it is, but you've got something else on your mind."

"You're right—I knew you were keen. When I was on Osnome I found out something that only four other men-all-dead-ever knew. There is a race of men far ahead of the Osnomians in science, particularly in warfare. They live a long way beyond Osnome. It is my plan to steal an Osnomian airship and mount all its ray screens, generators, guns, and everything else, upon this ship, or else convert their vessel into a space-ship. Instead of using their ordinary power, however, we will do as Seaton did, and use intra-atomic power, which is practically infinite. Then we'll have everything Seaton's got, but that isn't enough. I want enough more than he's got to wipe him out. Therefore, after we get a ship armed to suit us, we'll visit this strange planet and either come to terms with them or else steal a ship from them. Then we'll have their stuff and that of the Osnomians, as well as our own. Seaton won't last long after that."

"Do you mind if I ask how you got that dope?"

"Not at all. Except when right with Seaton I could do pretty much as I pleased, and I used to take long walks for exercise. The Osnomians tired very easily, being so weak, and because of the light gravity of the planet, I had to do a lot of work or walking to keep in any kind of condition at all. I learned Kondalian quickly, and got so friendly with the guards, that pretty soon they quit trying to keep me in sight, but waited at the edge of the palace grounds until I came back and joined them.

"Well, on one trip I was fifteen miles or so from the city when an airship crashed down in a woods about half a mile from me. It was in an uninhabited district and nobody else saw it. I went over to investigate, thinking probably I could find out something useful. It had the whole front end cut or broken off, and that made me curious, because no imaginable fall will break an arenak hull. I walked in through the hole and saw that it was one of their fighting tenders— a combination warship and repair shop, with all of the stuff in it that I've been telling you about. The generators were mostly burned out and the propelling and lifting motors were out of commission. I prowled around, getting acquainted with it, and found a lot of useful instruments and, best of all, one of Dunark's new mechanical educators, with complete instructions for its use. Also, I found three bodies, and thought I'd try it out...."

"Just a minute. Only three bodies on a warship? And what good could a mechanical educator do you if the men were all dead?"

"Three is all I found then, but there was another one. Three men and a captain compose an Osnomian crew for any ordinary vessel. Everything is automatic, you know. As for the men being dead, that doesn't make any difference-you can read their brains just the same, if they haven't been dead too long. However, when I tried to read theirs, I found only blanks-their brains had been destroyed so that nobody could read them. That did look funny, so I ransacked the ship from truck to keelson, and finally found another body, wearing an air-helmet, in a sort of closet off the control room. I put the educator on it...."

"This is getting good. It sounds like a page of the old 'Arabian Nights' that I used to read when I was a boy. You know, it really isn't surprising that Brookings didn't believe a lot of this stuff."

"As I have said, a lot of it is hard to understand, but I'm going to show it to you-all that, and more."

"Oh, I believe it, all right. After riding in this boat and looking out of the windows, I'll believe anything. Reading a dead man's brain is steep, though."

"I'll let you do it after we get there. I don't understand exactly how it works, myself, but I know how to operate one. Well, I found out that this man's brain was in good shape, and I got a shock when I read it. Here's what he had been through. They had been flying very high on their way to the front when their ship was seized by an invisible force and thrown upward. He must have thought faster than the others, because he put on an air-helmet and dived into this locker where he hid under a pile of gear, fixing things so that he could see out through the transparent arenak of the wall. No sooner was he hidden that the front end of the ship went up in a blaze of light, in spite of their ray screens going full blast. They were up so high by that time that when the bow was burned off the other three fainted from lack of air. Then their generators went out, and pretty soon two peculiar-looking strangers entered. They were wearing vacuum suits and were very short and stocky, giving the impression of enormous strength. They brought an educator of their own with them and read the brains of the three men. Then they dropped the ship a few thousand feet and revived the three with a drink of something out of a flask."

"Must have been different from the kind handled by most booties I know, then. The stuff we've been getting lately would make a man more unconscious than ever."

"Some powerful drug, probably, but the Osnomian didn't know anything about it. After the men were revived, the strangers, apparently from sheer cruelty and love of torturing their victims, informed them in the Osnomian language that they were from another world, on the far edge of the Galaxy. They even told them, knowing that the Osnomians knew nothing of astronomy, exactly where they were from. Then they went on to say that they wanted the entire green system for themselves, and that in something like two years of our time they were going to wipe out all the present inhabitants of the system and take it over, as a base for further operations. After that they amused themselves by describing exactly the kinds of death and destruction they were going to use. They described most of it in great detail. It's too involved to tell you about now, but they've got rays, generators, and screens that even the Osnomians never heard of. And of course they've got intra-atomic energy the same as we have. After telling them all this and watching them suffer, they put a machine on their heads and they dropped dead. That's probably what disintegrated their brains. Then they looked the ship over rather casually, as though they didn't see anything they were interested in; crippled the motors; and went away. The vessel was then released, and crashed. This man, of course, was killed by the fall. I buried the men—I didn't want anybody else reading that brain-hid some of the stuff I wanted most, and camouflaged the ship so that I'm fairly sure that it's there yet. I decided then to make this trip."

"I see." Loring's mind was grappling with these new and strange facts. "That news is staggering, Doctor. Think of it. Everybody thinks our own world is everything there is!"

"Our world is simply a grain of dust in the Universe. Most people know it, academically, but very few ever give the fact any actual consideration. But now that you've had a little time to get used to the idea of there being other worlds, and some of them as far ahead of us in science as we are ahead of the monkeys, what do you think of it?"

"I agree with you, that we've got their stuff," said Loring. "However, it occurs to me as a possibility that they may have so much stuff that we won't be able to make the approach. However, if the Osnomian fittings we're going to get are as good as you say they are, I think that two such men as you and I can get at least a lunch while any other crew, no matter who they are, are getting a square meal."

"I like your style, Loring. You and I will have the world eating out of our hands shortly after we get back. As far as actual procedure over there is concerned, of course, I haven't made any definite plans. We'll have to size up the situation after we get there before we can know exactly what we'll have to do. However, we are not coming back empty-handed."

"You said something, Chief!" and the two men, so startlingly unlike physically, but so alike inwardly, shook hands in token of their mutual dedication to a single purpose.

Loring was then instructed in the simple navigation of the ship of space, and thereafter the two men took their regular shifts at the controls. In due time they approached Osnome, and DuQuesne studied the planet carefully through a telescope before he ventured down into the atmosphere.

"This half of it used to be Mardonale. I suppose it's all Kondal now. No, there's a war on down there yet-at least, there's a disturbance of some kind, and on this planet that means war."

"What are you looking for, exactly?" asked Loring, who was also examining the terrain with a telescope.

"They've got some spherical space-ships, like Seaton's. I know they had one, and they've probably built more of them since that time. Their airships can't touch us, but those ball-shaped cruisers would be pure poison for us, the way we are fixed now. Can you see any of them?"

"Not yet. Too far away to make out details. They're certainly having a hot time down there, though, in that one spot."

They dropped lower, toward the stronghold which was being so stubbornly defended by the inhabitants of the third planet of the fourteenth sun, and so savagely attacked by the Kondalian forces.

"There, we can see what they're doing now," and DuQuesne anchored the vessel with an attractor. "I want to see if they've got many of those space-ships in action, and you will want to see what war is like, when it is fought by people, who have been making war steadily for ten thousand years."

Poised at the limit of clear visibility, the two men studied the incessant battle being waged beneath them. They saw not one, but fully a thousand of the globular craft high in the air and grouped in a great circle around an immense fortification upon the ground below. They saw no airships in the line of battle, but noticed that many such vessels were flying to and from the front, apparently carrying supplies. The fortress was an immense dome of some glassy, transparent material, partially covered with slag, through which they saw that the central space was occupied by orderly groups of barracks, and that round the circumference were arranged gigantic generators, projectors, and other machinery at whose purposes they could not even guess. From the base of the dome a twenty-mile-wide apron of the same glassy substance spread over the ground, and above this apron and around the dome were thrown the mighty defensive ray-screens, visible now and then in scintillating violet splendor as one of the copper-driven Kondalian projectors sought in vain for an opening. But the Earth-men saw with surprise that the main attack was not being directed at the dome; that only an occasional ray was thrown against it in order to make the defenders keep their screens up continuously. The edge of the apron was bearing the brunt of that vicious and never-ceasing attack, and most concerned the desperate defense.

For miles beyond that edge, and as deep under it as frightful rays and enormous charges of explosive copper could penetrate, the ground was one seething, flaming volcano of molten and incandescent lava; lava constantly being volatilized by the unimaginable heat of those rays and being hurled for miles in all directions by the inconceivable power of those explosive copper projectiles-the heaviest projectiles that could be used without endangering the planet itself-being directed under the exposed edge of that unbreakable apron, which was in actuality anchored to the solid core of the planet itself; lava flowing into and filling up the vast craters caused by the explosions. The attack seemed fiercest at certain points, perhaps a quarter of a mile apart around the circle, and after a time the watchers perceived that at those points, under the edge of the apron, in that indescribable inferno of boiling lava, destructive rays, and disintegrating copper, there were enemy machines at work. These machines were strengthening the protecting apron and extending it, very slowly, but ever wider and ever deeper as the ground under it and before it was volatilized or hurled away by the awful forces of the Kondalian attack. So much destruction had already been wrought that the edge of the apron and its molten moat were already fully a mile below the normal level of that cratered, torn, and tortured plain.

Now and then one of the mechanical moles would cease its labors, overcome by the concentrated fury of destruction centered upon it. Its shattered remnants would be withdrawn and shortly, repaired or replaced, it would be back at work. But it was not the defenders who had suffered most heavily. The fortress was literally ringed about with the shattered remnants of airships, and the riddled hulls of more than a few of those mighty globular cruisers of the void bore mute testimony to the deadliness and efficiency of the warfare of the invaders.

Even as they watched, one of the spheres, unable for some reason to maintain its screens or overcome by the awful forces playing upon it, flared from white into and through the violet and was hurled upward as though shot from the mouth of some Brobdingnagian howitzer. A door opened, and from its flaming interior four figures leaped out into the air, followed by a puff of orange-colored smoke. At the first sign of trouble, the ship next it in line leaped in front of it and the four figures floated gently to the ground, supported by friendly attractors and protected from enemy rays by the bulk and by the screens of the rescuing vessel. Two great airships soared upward from back of the lines and hauled the disabled vessel to the ground by means of their powerful attractors. The two observers saw with amazement that after brief attention from an ant-like ground-crew, the original four men climbed back into their warship and she again shot into the fray, apparently as good as ever.

"What do you know about that!" exclaimed DuQuesne. "That gives me an idea, Loring. They must get to them that way fairly often, to judge by the teamwork they use when it does happen. How about waiting until they disable another one like that, and then grabbing it while its in the air, deserted and unable to fight back? One of those ships is worth a thousand of this one, even if we had everything known to the Osnomians."

"That's a real idea-those boats certainly are brutes for punishment," agreed Loring, and as both men again settled down to watch the battle, he went on: "So this is war out this way? You're right. Seaton, with half this stuff, could whip the combined armies and navies of the world. I don't blame Brookings much, though, at that-nobody could believe half of this unless they could actually see it, as we are doing."

"I can't understand it," DuQuesne frowned as he considered the situation. "The attackers are Kondalians, all right-those ships are developments of the *Skylark* —but I don't get that fort at all. Wonder if it can be the strangers already? Don't think so-they aren't due for a couple of years yet, and I don't think the Kondalians could stand against them a minute. It must be what is left of Mardonale, although I never heard of anything like that. Probably it is some new invention they dug up at the last minute. That's it, I guess," and his brow cleared. "It couldn't be anything else."

They waited long for the incident to be repeated, and finally their patience was rewarded. When the next vessel was disabled and hurled upward by the concentration of enemy forces, DuQuesne darted down, seized it with his most powerful attractor, and whisked it away into space at such a velocity that to the eyes of the Kordalians it simply disappeared. He took the disabled warship far out into space and allowed it to cool off for a long time before deciding that it was safe to board it. Through the transparent walls they could see no sign of life, and DuQuesne donned a vacuum suit and stepped into the airlock. As Loring held the steel vessel close to the stranger, DuQuesne leaped lightly through the open door into the interior. Shutting the door, he opened an auxiliary air-tank, adjusting the gauge to one atmosphere as he did so. The pressure normal, he divested himself of the suit and made a thorough examination of the vessel. He then signaled Loring to follow him, and soon both ships were over Kondal, so high as to be invisible from the ground. Plunging the vessel like a bullet towards the grove in which he had left the Kondalian airship, he slowed abruptly just in time to make a safe landing. As he stepped out upon Osnomian soil, Loring landed the Earthly ship hardly less skillfully.

"This saves us a lot of trouble, Loring. This is undoubtedly one of the finest space-ships of the Universe, and just about ready for anything."

"How did they get to it?"

"One of the screen generators apparently weakened a trifle, probably from weeks of continuous use. That let some of the rays come through; everything got hot, and the crew had to jump or roast. Nothing is hurt, though, as the ship was thrown up and out of range before the arenak melted at all. The copper repellers are gone, of course, and most of the bars that were in use are melted down, but there was enough of the main bar left to drive the ship and we can replace the melted stuff easily enough. Nothing else was hurt, as there's absolutely nothing in the structure of these vessels that can be burned. Even the insulation in the coils and generators has a melting-point higher than that of porcelain. And not all the copper was melted, either. Some of these storerooms are lined with two feet of insulation and are piled full of bars and explosive ammunition."

"What was the smoke we saw, then?"

"That was their food-supply. It's cooked to an ash, and their water was all boiled away through the safety-valves. Those rays certainly can put out a lot of heat in a second or two!"

"Can the two of us put on those copper repeller-bands? This ship must be seventy-five feet in diameter."

"Yes, it's a lot bigger than the *Skylark* was. It's one of their latest models, or it wouldn't have been on the front line. As to banding on the repellers-that's easy. That airship is half full of metal-working machinery that can do everything but talk. I know how to use most of it, from seeing it in use, and we can figure out the rest."

In that unfrequented spot there was little danger of detection from the air. And none whatsoever of detection from the ground-of ground-travel upon Osnome there is none. Nevertheless, the two men camouflaged the vessels so that they were visible only to keen and direct scrutiny, and drove their task through to completion on the shortest possible time. The copper repellers were banded on, and much additional machinery was installed in the already well-equipped shop. This done, they transferred to their warship food, water, bedding, instruments, and everything else they needed or wanted from their own ship and from the disabled Kondalian airship. They made a last tour of inspection to be sure they had overlooked nothing useful, then embarked.

"Think anybody will find those ships? They could get a good line on what we've done."

"Probably, eventually, Loring, so we'd better destroy them. We'd better take a short hop first, though, to test everything out. Since you're not familiar with the controls of a ship of this type, you need practise. Shoot us up around that moon over there and bring us back to this spot."

"She's a sweet-handling boat-easy like a bicycle," declared Loring as he brought the vessel lightly to a landing upon their return. "We can burn the old one up now. We'll never need her again, any more than a snake needs his last year's skin."

"She's good, all right. Those two hulks must be put out of existence, but we shouldn't do it here. The rays would set the woods afire, and the metal would condense all around. We don't want to leave any tracks, so we'd better pull them out into space to destroy them. We could turn them loose, and as you've never worked a ray, it'll be good practice for you. Also, I want you to see for yourself just what our best armour-plate amounts to compared with arenak."

When they towed the two vessels far out into space, Loring put into practise the instruction he had received from DuQuesne concerning the complex armament of their vessel. He swung the beam-projector upon the Kondalian airship, pressed the connectors of the softener ray, the heat ray, and the induction ray, and threw the master switch. Almost instantly the entire hull became blinding white, but it was several seconds before the extremely refractory material began to volatilize. Though the metal was less than an inch think, it retained its shape and strength stubbornly, and only slowly did it disappear in flaming, flaring gusts of incandescent gas.

"There, you've seen what an inch of arenak is like," said DuQuesne when the destruction was complete. "Now shine it on that sixty-inch chrome-vanadium armor hull of our old bus and see what happens."

Loring did so. As the beam touched it, the steel disappeared in one flare of radiance-as he swung the projector in one flashing arc from the stem to the stern there was nothing left. Loring, swinging the beam, whistled in amazement.

"Wow! What a difference! And this ship of ours has a skin of arenak six feet thick!"

"Yes. Now you understand why I didn't want to argue with anybody out here as long as we were in our steel ship."

"I understand, all right; but I can't understand the power of these rays. Suppose I had had all twenty of them on instead of only three?"

"In that case, I think that we could have whipped even the short, thick strangers."

"You and me both. But say, every ship's got to have a name. This new one of ours is such a sweet, harmless, inoffensive little thing, we'd better name her the *Violet*, hadn't we?"

DuQuesne started the *Violet* off in the direction of the solar system occupied by the warlike strangers, but he did not hurry. He and Loring practiced incessantly for days at the controls, darting here and there, putting on terrific acceleration until the indicators showed a velocity of hundreds of thousand of miles per second, then reversing the acceleration until the velocity was zero. They studied the controls and alarm system until each knew perfectly every instrument, every tiny light, and the tone of each bell. They practiced with the rays, singly and in combination, with the visiplates, and with the many levers and dials, until each was so familiar with the complex installation that his handling of every control had become automatic. Not until then did DuQuesne give the word to start out in earnest toward their goal, at an unthinkable distance.

They had not been under way long when an alarm bell sounded its warning and a brilliant green light began flashing upon the board.

"Hm...m," DuQuesne frowned as he reversed the bar. "Outside intra-atomic energy detector. Somebody's using power out here. Direction, about dead ahead-straight down. Let's see if we can see anything."

He swung number six, the telescopic visiplate, into connection. After what seemed to them a long time they saw a sudden sharp flash, apparently an immense distance ahead, and simultaneously three more alarm bells rang and three colored lights flashed briefly.

"Somebody got quite a jolt then. Three rays in action at once for three or four seconds," reported DuQuesne, as he applied still more negative acceleration.

"I'd like to know what this is all about!" he exclaimed after a time, as they saw a subdued glow, which lasted a minute or two. As the warning light was flashing more and more slowly and with diminishing intensity, the *Violet* was once more put upon her course. As she proceeded, however, the warnings of the liberation of intra-atomic energy grew stronger and stronger, and both men scanned their path intensely for a sight of the source of the disturbance, while their velocity was cut to only a few hundred miles an hour. Suddenly the indicator swerved and pointed behind them, showing that they had passed the object, whatever it was. DuQuesne instantly applied power and snapped on a small searchlight.

"If it's so small that we couldn't see it when we passed it, it's nothing to be afraid of. We'll be able to find it with a light."

After some search, they saw an object floating in space-apparently a vacuum suit!

"Shall one of us get in the airlock, or shall we bring it in with an attractor?" asked Loring.

"An attractor, by all means. Two or three of them, in fact, to spread-eagle whatever it is. Never take any chances. It's probably an Osnomian, but you never can tell. It may be one of those other people. We know they were around here a few weeks ago, and they're the only ones I know of that have intra-atomic power besides us and the Osnomians."

"That's no Osnomian," he continued, as the stranger was drawn into the airlock. "He's big enough around for four Osnomians, and very short. We'll take no chances at all with that fellow."

The captive was brought into the control room pinioned head, hand, and foot with attractors and repellers, before DuQuesne approached him. He then read the temperature and pressure of the stranger's air-supply, and allowed the surplus air to escape slowly before removing the stranger's suit and revealing one of the Fenachrone-eyes closed, unconscious or dead.

DuQuesne leaped for the educator and handed Loring a headset.

"Put this on quick. He may be only unconscious, and we might not be able to get a thing from him if he were awake."

Loring donned the headset, still staring at the monstrous form with amazement, not unmixed with awe, while DuQuesne, paying no attention to anything except the knowledge he was seeking, manipulated the controls of the instrument. His first quest was for the weapons and armament of the vessel. In this he was disappointed, as he learned that the stranger was one of the navigating engineers, and as such, had no detailed knowledge of the matters of prime importance to the inquisitor. He did have a complete knowledge of the marvelous Fenachrone propulsion system, however, and this DuQuesne carefully transferred to his own brain. He then rapidly explored other regions of that fearsome organ of thought.

As the gigantic and inhuman brain was spread before them, DuQuesne and Loring read not only the language, customs, and culture of the Fenachrone, but all their plans for the future, as well as the events of the past. Plainly in his mind they perceived how he had been cast adrift in the emptiness of the void. They saw the Fenachrone cruiser lying in wait for the two globular vessels. Looking through an extraordinarily powerful telescope with the eyes of their prisoner, they saw them approach, all unsuspecting. DuQuesne recognized all five persons in the *Skylark* and Dunark and Sitar in the *Kondal*; such was that unearthly optical instrument and so clear was the impression upon the mind before him. They saw the attack and the battle. They saw the *Skylark* throw off her zone of force and attack; saw this one survivor standing directly in line with a huge projector-spring, and saw the spring severed by the zone. The free end, under its thousands of pounds of tension, had struck the being upon the side of the head, and the force of the blow, only partially blocked by the heavy helmet, had hurled him out through the yawning gap in the wall and hundreds of miles out into space.

Suddenly the clear view of the brain of the Fenachrone became blurred and meaningless and the flow of knowledge ceased-the prisoner had regained consciousness and was trying with all his gigantic strength to break from those intangible bonds that held him. So powerful were the forces upon him, however, that only a few twitching muscles gave evidence that he was struggling at all. Glancing about him he recognized the attractors and repellers bearing upon him, ceased his efforts to escape, and hurled the full power of his baleful gaze into the black eyes so close to his own. But DuQuesne's mind, always under perfect control and now amply reenforced by a considerable proportion of the stranger's own knowledge and power, did not waver under the force of even that hypnotic glare.

"It is useless, as you observe," he said coldly, in the stranger's own tongue, and sneered. "You are perfectly helpless. Unlike you of the Fenachrone, however, men of my race do not always kill strangers at sight, merely because they are strangers. I will spare your life, if you can give me anything of enough value to me to make extra time and trouble worth while."

"You read my mind while I could not resist your childish efforts. I will have no traffic whatever with you who have destroyed my vessel. If you have mentality enough to understand any portion of my mind-which I doubt-you already know the fate in store for you. Do with me what you will." This from the stranger.

DuQuesne pondered long before he replied; considering whether it was to his advantage to inform this stranger of the facts. Finally he decided.

"Sir, neither I nor this vessel had anything to do with the destruction of your warship. Our detectors discovered you floating in empty space; we stopped and rescued you from death. We have seen nothing else, save what we saw pictured in your own brain. I know that, in common with all of your race, you possess neither conscience nor honor, as we understand the terms. An automatic liar by instinct and training whenever you think lies will best serve your purpose, you may yet have intelligence enough to recognize simple truth when you hear it. You already have observed that we are of the same race as those who destroyed your vessel, and have assumed that we are with them. In that you are wrong. It is true that I am acquainted with those others, but they are my enemies. I am here to kill them, not to aid them. You have already helped me in one way —I know as much as does my enemy concerning the impenetrable shield of force. If I will return you unharmed to your own planet, will you assist me in stealing one of your ships of space, so that I may destroy that Earth-vessel?"

The Fenachrone, paying no attention to DuQuesne's barbed comments concerning his honor and veracity, did not hesitate an instant in his reply.

"I will not. We supermen of the Fenachrone will allow no vessel of ours, with its secrets unknown to any others of the Universe, to fall into the hands of any of the lesser breeds of men."

"Well, you didn't try to lie that time, anyway," said DuQuesne, "but think a minute. Seaton, my enemy, already has one of your vessels-don't think he is too much of a fool to put it back together and to learn its every secret. Then, too, remember that I have your mind, and can get along without you; even though I am willing to admit that you could be of enough help to me so that I would save your life in exchange for that help. Also remember that, superman though you may be, your mentality cannot cope with the forces I have bearing upon you. Neither will your being a superman enable your body to retain life after I have pushed you through yonder door, dressed as you are in a silken tunic."

"I have the normal love of life," was the reply, "but some things cannot be done, even with life at stake. Stealing a vessel of the Fenachrone is one of those things. I can, however, do this much-if you will return me to my own planet, you two shall be received as guests aboard one of our vessels and shall be allowed to witness the vengeance of the Fenachrone upon your enemy. Then you shall be returned to your vessel and allowed to depart unharmed."

"Now you are lying by rote—I know just what you'd do," said DuQuesne. "Get that idea out of your head right now. The attractors now holding you will not be released until after you have told all. Then, and then only, will we try to discover a way of returning you to your own world safely, and yet in a manner which will in no way jeopardize my own safety. Incidentally, I warn you that the first sign of an attempt to play false with me in any way will mean your instant death."

The prisoner remained silent, analyzing every feature of the situation, and DuQuesne continued, coldly:

"Here's something else for you to think about. If you are unwilling to help us, what is to prevent me from killing you, and then hunting up Seaton and making peace with him for the duration of this forthcoming war? With the fragments of your vessel, which he has; with my knowledge of your mind, reenforced by your own dead brain; and with the vast resources of all the planets of the green system; there is no doubt that the plans of the Fenachrone will be seriously interfered with. Myriads of your race will certainly lose their lives, and it is quite possible that your entire race would be destroyed. Understand that I care nothing for the green system. You are welcome to it if you do as I ask. If you do not, I shall warn them and help them simply to protect my world, which is now my own personal property."

"In return for our armament and equipment, you promise not to warn the green system against us? The death of your enemy takes first place in your mind?" The stranger spoke thoughtfully. "In that I understand your viewpoint thoroughly. But, after I have remodeled your power-plant into ours and have piloted you to our planet, what assurance have I that you will liberate me, as you have said?"

"None whatever—I have made and am asking no promises, since I cannot expect you to trust me, any more than I can trust you. Enough of this argument! I am master here, and I am dictating terms. We can get along without you. Therefore you must decide quickly whether you would rather die suddenly and surely, here in space and right now, or help us as I demand and live until you get back home-enjoying meanwhile your life and whatever chance you think you may have of being liberated within the atmosphere of your own planet."

"Just a minute, Chief!" Loring said, in English, his back to the prisoner. "Wouldn't we gain more by killing him and going back to Seaton and the green system, as you suggested?"

"No." DuQuesne also turned away, to shield his features from the mind-reading gaze of the Fenachrone. "That was pure bluff. I don't want to get within a million miles of Seaton until after we have the armament of this fellow's ships. I couldn't make peace with Seaton now, even if I wanted to-and I haven't the slightest intention of trying. I intend killing him on sight. Here's what we're going to do. First, we'll get what we came after. Then we'll find the *Skylark* and blow her clear out of space, and take over the pieces of that Fenachrone ship. After that we'll head for the green system, and with their own stuff and what we'll give them, they'll be able to give those fiends a hot reception. By the time they finally destroy the Osnomians-if they do-we'll have the world ready for them." He turned to the Fenachrone. "What is your decision?"

"I submit, in the hope that you will keep your promise, since there is no alternative but death," and the awful creature, still loosely held by the attractors and carefully watched by DuQuesne and Loring, fairly tore into the task of rebuilding the Osnomian power-plant into the space-annihilating drive of the Fenachrone-for he well knew one fact that DuQuesne's hurried inspection had failed to glean from the labyrinthine intricacies of that fearsome brain: that once within the detector screens of that distant solar system these Earth-beings would be utterly helpless before the forces which would inevitably be turned upon them. Also, he realized that time was precious, and resolved to drive the *Violet* so unmercifully that she would overtake that fleeing torpedo, now many hours upon its way-the torpedo bearing news, for the first time in Fenachrone history, of the overwhelming defeat and capture of one of its mighty engines of interstellar war.

In a very short time, considering the complexity of the undertaking, the conversion of the power-plant was done and the repellers, already supposed the ultimate in protection, were reenforced by a ten-thousand-pound mass of activated copper, effective for untold millions of miles. Their monstrous pilot then set the bar and advanced both levers of the dual power control out to the extreme limit of their travel.

There was no sense of motion or of acceleration, since the new system of propulsion acted upon every molecule of matter within the radius of activity of the bar, which had been set to include the entire hull. The passengers felt only the utter lack of all weight and the other peculiar sensations with which they were already familiar, as each had had previous experience of free motion in space. But in spite of the lack of apparent motion, the *Violet* was now leaping through the unfathomable depths of interstellar space with the unthinkable speed of five times the velocity of light!

CHAPTER VIII

The Porpoise-Men of Dasor

"How long do you figure it's going to take us to get there, Mart?" Seaton asked from a corner, where he was bending over his apparatus-table.

"About three days at this acceleration. I set it at what I thought the safe maximum for the girls. Should we increase it?"

"Probably not-three days isn't bad. Anyway, to save even one day we'd have to more than double the acceleration, and none of us could do anything, so we'd better let it ride. How're you making it, Peg?"

"I'm getting used to weighing a ton now. My knees buckled only once this morning from my forgetting to watch them when I tried to walk. Don't let me interfere, though! if I am slowing us down, I'll go to bed and stay there!"

"It'd hardly pay," said Seaton. "We can use the time to good advantage. Look here, Mart — I've been looking over this stuff I got out of their ship and here's something I know you'll eat up. They refer to it as a chart, but it's three-dimensional and almost incredible. I can't say that I understand it, but I get an awful kick out of looking at it. I've been studying it a couple of hours, and haven't started yet. I haven't found our solar system, the green one, or their own. It's too heavy to move around now, because of the acceleration we're using-come on over here and give it a look."

The "chart" was a strip of some parchment-like material, or film, apparently miles in length, wound upon reels at each end of the machine. One section of the film was always under the viewing mechanism-an optical system projecting an undistorted image into a visiplate plate somewhat similar to their own-and at the touch of a lever, a small atomic motor turned the reels and moved the film through the projector.

It was not an ordinary star-chart: it was three-dimensional, ultra-stereoscopic. The eye did not perceive a flat surface, but beheld an actual, extremely narrow wedge of space as seen from the center of the galaxy. Each of the closer stars was seen in its true position in space and in its true perspective, and each was clearly identified by number. In the background were faint stars and nebulous masses of light, too distant to be resolved into separate stars — a true representation of the actual sky. As both men stared, fascinated, into the visiplate, Seaton touched the lever and they apparently traveled directly along the center line of that ever-widening wedge. As they proceeded, the nearer stars grew brighter and larger, soon becoming suns, with their planets and then the satellites of the planets plainly visible, and finally passing out of the picture behind the observers. The fainter stars became bright, grew into suns and solar systems, and were passed in turn. The chart unrolled, and the nebulous masses of light were approached, became composed of faint stars, which developed as had the others, and were passed.

Finally, when the picture filled the entire visiplate, they arrived at the outermost edge of the galaxy. No more stars were visible: they saw empty space stretching for inconceivably vast distances before them. But beyond that indescribable and incomprehensible vacuum they saw faint lenticular bodies of light, which were also named, and which each man knew to be other galaxies, charted and named by the almost unlimited power of the Fenachrone astronomers, but not as yet explored. As the magic scroll unrolled still farther, they found themselves back in the center of the galaxy, starting outward in the wedge adjacent to the one which they had just traversed. Seaton cut off the motor and wiped his forehead.

"Wouldn't that break you off at the ankles, Mart? Did you ever conceive the possibility of such a thing?"

"It would, and I did not. There are literally miles and miles of film in each of those reels, and I see that there is a magazine full of reels in the cabinet. There must be an index or a master-chart."

"Yeah, there's a book in this slot here," said Seaton, "but we don't know any of their names or numbers-wait a minute! How did he report our Earth on that torpedo? Planet number three of sun six four something Pilarone, wasn't it? I'll get the record."

"Six four seven three Pilarone, it was."

"Pilarone ... let's see...." Seaton studied the index volume. "Reel twenty, scene fifty-one, I'd translate it."

They found the reel, and "scene fifty-one" did indeed show that section of space in which our solar system is. Seaton stopped the chart when star six four seven three was at its closest range, and there was our sun; with its nine planets and their many satellites accurately shown and correctly described.

"They know their stuff, all right-you've got to hand it to 'em. I've been straightening out that brain record-cutting out the hazy stretches and getting his knowledge straightened out so we can use it, and there's a lot of this kind of stuff in the record you can get. Suppose that you can figure out exactly where he comes from with this dope and with his brain record?"

"Certainly. I may be able to get more complete information upon the green system than the Osnomians have, which will be very useful indeed. You are right—I am intensely interested in this material, and if you do not care particularly about studying it any more at this time, I believe that I should begin to study it now."

"Hop to it. I'm going to study that record some more. No human brain can take it all, I'm afraid, especially all at once, but I'm going to kinda peck around the edges and get me some dope that I want pretty badly. We got a lot of stuff from that wampus."

About sixty hours out, Dorothy, who had been observing the planet through number six visiplate, called Seaton away from the Fenachrone brain-record, upon which he was still concentrating.

"Come here a minute, Dickie! Haven't you got that knowledge all packed away in your skull yet?"

"I'll say I haven't. That bird's brain would make a dozen of mine, and it was loaded until the scuppers were awash. I'm just nibbling around the edges yet."

"I've always heard that the capacity of even the human brain was almost infinite. Isn't that true?" asked Margaret.

"Maybe it is, if the knowledge were built up gradually over generations. I think maybe I can get most of this stuff into my peanut brain so I can use it, but it's going to be an awful job."

"Is their brain really as far ahead of ours as I gathered from what I saw of it?" asked Crane.

"It sure is," replied Seaton, "as far as knowledge and intelligence are concerned, but they have nothing else in common with us. They don't belong to the genus 'homo' at all, really. Instead of having a common ancestor with the anthropoids, as they say we had, they evolved from a genus which combined the worst traits of the cat tribe and the carnivorous lizards-the most savage and bloodthirsty branches of the animal kingdom-and instead of getting better as they went along, they got worse, in that respect at least. But they sure do know something. When you get a month or so to spare, you want to put on this harness and grab his knowledge, being very careful to steer clear of his mental traits and so on. Then, when we get back to the Earth, we'll simply tear it apart and rebuild it. You'll know what I mean when you get this stuff transplanted into your own skull. But to cut out the lecture, what's on your mind, Dottie Dimple?"

"This planet Martin picked out is all wet, literally. The visibility is fine-very few clouds-but this whole half of it is solid ocean. If there are any islands, even, they're mighty small."

All four looked into the receiver. With the great magnification employed, the planet almost filled the visiplate. There were a few fleecy wisps of cloud, but the entire surface upon which they gazed was one sheet of the now familiar deep and glorious blue peculiar to the waters of that cuprous solar system, with no markings whatever.

"What d'you make of it, Mart? That's water all right-copper-sulphate solution, just like the Osnomian and Urvanian oceans-and nothing else visible. How big would an island have to be for us to see it from here?"

"So much depends upon the contour and nature of the island, that it is hard to say. If it were low and heavily covered with their green-blue vegetation, we might not be able to see even a rather large one, whereas if it were hilly and bare, we could probably see one only a few miles in diameter."

"Well, one good thing, anyway, we're approaching it from the central sun, and almost in line with their own sun, so it's daylight all over it. As it turns and as we get closer, we'll see what we can see. Better take turns watching it, hadn't we?" asked Seaton.

It was decided, and while the *Skylark* was still some distance away, several small islands became visible, and the period of rotation of the planet was determined to be in the neighborhood of fifty hours. Margaret, then at the controls, picked out the largest island visible and directed the bar toward it. As they dropped down close to their objective, they found that the air was of the same composition as that of Osnome, but had a pressure of seventy-eight centimeters of mercury, and that the surface gravity of the planet was ninety-five hundredths that of the Earth.

"Fine business!" exulted Seaton. "Just about like home, but I don't see much of any place to land without getting wet, do you? Those reflectors are probably solar generators, and they cover the whole island except for that lagoon right under us."

The island, perhaps ten miles long and half that in width, was entirely covered with great parabolic reflectors, arranged so closely together that little could be seen between them. Each reflector apparently focussed upon an object in the center, a helix which seemed to writhe luridly in that flaming focus, glowing with a nacreous, opalescent green light.

"Well, nothing much to see there—let's go down," remarked Seaton as he shot the *Skylark* over to the edge of the island and down to the surface of the water. But here again nothing was to be seen of the land itself. The wall was one vertical plate of seamless metal, supporting huge metal guides, between which floated metal pontoons. From these gigantic floats metal girders and trusses went through slots in the wall into the darkness of the interior. Close scrutiny revealed that the large floats were rising steadily, although very slowly; while smaller floats bobbed up and down upon each passing wave.

"Solar generators, tide-motors, and wave-motors, all at once!" ejaculated Seaton. *"Some* power-plant! Folks, I'm going to take a look at that if I have to drill in with a ray!"

They circumnavigated the island without revealing any door or other opening-the entire thirty miles was one stupendous battery of the generators. Back at the starting point, the *Skylark* hopped over the structure and down to the surface of the small central lagoon previously noticed. Close to the water, it was seen that there was plenty of room for the vessel to move about beneath the roof of reflectors, and that the island was one solid stand of tide-motors. At one end of the lagoon was an open metal structure, the only building visible, and Seaton brought the space-cruiser up to it and through the huge opening-for door there was none. The interior of the room was lighted by long, tubular lights running around in front of the walls, which were veritable switchboards. Row after row and tier upon tier stood the instruments, plainly electrical meters of enormous capacity and equally plainly in full operation, but no wiring or bus-bar could be seen. Before each row of instruments there was a narrow walk, with steps leading down into the water of the lagoon. Every part of the great room was plainly visible, and not a living being was even watching that vast instrument-board.

"What do you make of it, Dick?" asked Crane, slowly.

"No wiring-tight beam transmission. The Fenachrone do it with two matched-frequency separable units. Millions and millions of kilowatts there, if I'm any judge. Absolutely automatic too, or else — —" Seaton's voice died away.

"Or else what?" asked Dorothy.

"Just a hunch. I wouldn't wonder if — —"

"Hold it, Dicky! Remember I had to put you to bed after that last hunch you had!"

"Here it is, anyway. Mart, what would be the logical line of evolution when the planet has become so old that all the land has been eroded to a level below that of the ocean? You picked us out an old one, all right-so old that there's no land left. Would a highly civilized people revert to fish? That seems like a backward move to me, but what other answer is possible?"

"Probably not to true fishes-although they might easily develop some fish-like traits. I do not believe, however, that they would go back to gills or to cold blood."

"What *are* you two saying?" interrupted Margaret. "Do you mean to say that you think *fish* live here instead of people, and that *fish* did all this?" as she waved her hand at the complicated machinery about them.

"Not fish exactly, no." Crane paused in thought. "Merely a people who have adjusted themselves to their environment through conscious or natural selection. We had a talk about this very thing in our first trip, shortly after I met you. Remember? I commented on the fact that there must be life throughout the Universe, much of it that we could not understand; and you replied that there would be no reason to suppose them awful because incomprehensible. That may be the case here."

"Well, I'm going to find out," declared Seaton, as he appeared with a box full of coils, tubes, and other apparatus.

"How?" asked Dorothy, curiously.

"Fix me up a detector and follow up one of those beams. Find its frequency and direction, first, you know, then pick it up outside and follow it to where it's going. It'll go through anything, of course, but I can trap off enough of it to follow it, even if it's tight enough to choke itself," said Seaton.

"That's one thing I got from that brain record."

He worked deftly and rapidly, and soon was rewarded by a flaring crimson color in his detector when it was located in one certain position in front of one of the meters. Noting the bearing on the great circles, he then moved the *Skylark* along that exact line, over the reflectors, and out beyond the island, where he allowed the vessel to settle directly downwards.

"Now folks, if I've done this just right, we'll get a red flash directly."

As he spoke the detector again burst into crimson light, and he set the bar into the line and applied a little power, keeping the light at its reddest while the other three looked on in fascinated interest.

"This beam is on something that's moving, Mart-can't take my eyes off it for a second or I'll lose it entirely. See where we're going, will you?"

"We are about to strike the water," replied Crane quietly.

"The water!" exclaimed Margaret.

"Fair enough-why not?"

"Oh, that's right —I forgot that the *Skylark* is as good a submarine as she is an airship."

Crane pointed number six visiplate directly into the line of flight and started into the dark water.

"Mow deep are we, Mart?" asked Seaton after a time.

"Only about a hundred feet, and we do not seem to be getting any deeper."

"That's good. Afraid this beam might be going to a station on the other side of the planet-through the ground. If so, we'd have had to go back and trace another. We can follow it any distance under water, but not through rock. Need a light?"

"Not unless we go deeper."

For two hours Seaton held the detector upon that tight beam of energy, traveling at a hundred miles an hour, the highest speed he could use and still hold the beam.

"I'd like to be up above watching us. I bet we're making the water boil behind us," remarked Dorothy.

"Yeah, we're kicking up quite a wake, I guess. It sure takes power to drive the old can through this wetness."

"Slow down!" commanded Crane. "I see a submarine ahead. I thought it might be a whale at first, but it is a boat and it is what we are aiming for. You are constantly swinging with it, keeping it exactly in the line."

"O.K." Seaton reduced the power and swung the visiplate over in front of him, whereupon the detector lamp went out. "It's a relief to follow something I can see, instead of trying to guess which way that beam's going to wiggle next. Lead on, Macduff—I'm right on your tail!"

The *Skylark* fell in behind the submersible craft, close enough to keep it plainly visible in the telescopic visiplate. Finally the stranger stopped and rose to the surface between two rows of submerged pontoons which, row upon row, extended in every direction as far as the telescope could reach.

"Well, Dot, we're where we're going, wherever that is."

"What do you suppose it is? It looks like a floating isleport, like what it told about in that wild-story magazine you read so much."

"Maybe-but if so they can't be fish," answered Seaton. "Let's go —I want to look it over," and water flew in all directions as the *Skylark* burst out of the ocean and leaped into the air far above what was in truth a floating city.

Rectangular in shape, it appeared to be about six miles long and four wide. It was roofed with solar generators like those covering the island just visited, but the machines were not spaced quite so closely together, and there were numerous open lagoons. The water around the entire city was covered with wave-motors. From their great height the visitors could see an occasional submarine moving slowly under the city, and frequently small surface craft dashed across the lagoons. As they watched, a seaplane with short, thick wings curved like those of a gull, rose from one of the lagoons and shot away over the water.

"Quite a place," remarked Seaton as he swung a visiplate upon one of the lagoons. "Submarines, speedboats, and fast seaplanes. Fish or not, they're not so slow. I'm going to grab off one of those folks and see how much they know. Wonder if they're peaceable or warlike?"

"They look peaceable, but you know the proverb," Crane cautioned his impetuous friend.

"Yes, and I'm going to be timid like a mice," Seaton returned as the *Skylark* dropped rapidly toward a lagoon near the edge of the island.

"You ought to put that in a gag book, Dick," Dorothy chuckled. "You forget all about being timid until an hour afterwards."

"Watch me, Red-top! If they even point a finger at us, I'm going to run a million miles a minute."

No hostile demonstration was made as they dropped lower and lower, however, and Seaton, with one hand upon the switch actuating the zone of force, slowly lowered the vessel down past the reflectors and to the surface of the water. Through the visiplate he saw the crowd of people coming toward them-some swimming in the lagoon, some walking along narrow runways. They seemed to be of all sizes, and unarmed.

"I believe they're perfectly peaceable, and just curious, Mart. I've already got the repellers on close range-believe I'll cut them off altogether."

"How about the ray-screens?"

"All three full out. They don't interfere with anything solid, though, and won't hurt anything. They'll stop any ray attack and this arenak hull will stop anything else we are apt to get there. Watch this board, will you, and I'll see if I can't negotiate with them."

Seaton opened the door. As he did so, a number of the smaller beings dived headlong into the water, and a submarine rose quietly to the surface less than fifty feet away with a peculiar tubular weapon and a huge ray-generator trained upon the *Skylark*. Seaton stood motionless, his right hand raised in the universal sign of peace, his left holding at his hip an automatic pistol charged with X-plosive shells-while Crane, at the controls, had the Fenachrone super-generator in line, and his hand lay upon the switch, whose closing would volatize the submarine and cut an incandescent path of destruction through the city lengthwise.

After a moment of inaction, a hatch opened, a man stepped out upon the deck of the submarine, and the two tried to converse, but with no success. Seaton then brought out the mechanical educator, held it up for the other's inspection, and waved an invitation to come aboard. Instantly the other dived, and came to the surface immediately below Seaton, who assisted him into the *Skylark*. Tall and heavy as Seaton was, the stranger was half a head taller and almost twice as heavy. His thick skin was of the characteristic Osnomian green and his eyes were the usual black, but he had no hair whatever. His shoulders, though broad and enormously strong, were very sloping, and his powerful arms were little more than half as long as would have been expected had they belonged to a human being of his size. The hands and feet were very large and very broad, and the fingers and toes were heavily webbed. His high domed forehead appeared even higher because of the total lack of hair, otherwise his features were regular and well-proportioned. He carried himself easily and gracefully, and yet with the dignity of one accustomed to command as he stepped into the control room and saluted gravely the three other Earth-beings. He glanced quickly around the room, and showed unmistakable pleasure as he saw the power-plant of the cruiser of space. Languages were soon exchanged and the stranger spoke, in a bass voice vastly deeper than Seaton's own.

"In the name of our city and planet—I may say in the name of our solar system, for you are very evidently from one other than our green system—I greet you. I would offer you refreshment, as is our custom, but I fear that your chemistry is but ill adapted to our customary fare. If there be aught in which we can be of assistance to you, our resources are at your disposal-but before you leave us, I shall wish to ask from you a great gift."

"Sir, we thank you. We are in search of knowledge concerning forces which we cannot as yet control. From the power systems you employ, and from what I have learned of the composition of your suns and planets, I assume you have none of the metal of power, and it is a quantity of that element that is your greatest need?"

"Yes. Power is our only lack. We generate all we can with the materials and knowledge at our disposal, but we never have enough. Our development is hindered, our birth-rate must be held down to a minimum, many new cities which we need cannot be built and many new projects cannot be started, all for lack of power. For one gram of that metal I see plated upon that copper cylinder, of whose very existence no scientist upon Dasor has had even an inkling, we would do almost anything. In fact, if all else failed, I would be tempted to attack you, did I not know that our utmost power could not penetrate even your outer screen, and that you could volatilize the entire planet if you so desired."

"Great Cat!" In his surprise Seaton lapsed from the formal language he had been employing. "Have you figured us all out already, from a standing start?"

"We know electricity, chemistry, physics, and mathematics fairly well. You see, our race is many millions of years older than is yours."

"You're the man I've been looking for, I guess," said Seaton. "We have enough of this metal with us so that we can spare you some as well as not. But before you get it, I'll introduce you. Folks, this is Sacner Carfon, Chief of the Council of the planet Dasor. They saw us all the time, and when we headed for this, the Sixth City, he came over from the capital, or First City, in the flagship of his police fleet, to welcome us or to fight us, as we pleased. Carfon, this is Martin Crane-or say, better than introductions, put on the headsets, everybody, and get acquainted right."

Acquaintance made and the apparatus put away, Seaton went to one of the store-rooms and brought out a lump of "X," weighing about a hundred pounds.

"There's enough to build power-plants from now on. It would save time if you were to dismiss your submarine. With you to pilot us, we can take you back to the First City a lot faster than your vessel can travel."

Carfon took a miniature transmitter from a pouch under his arm and spoke briefly, then gave Seaton the course. In a few minutes, the First City was reached, and the *Skylark* descended rapidly to the surface of a lagoon at one end of the city. Short as had been the time consumed by their journey from the Sixth City, they found a curious and excited crowd awaiting them. The central portion of the lagoon was almost covered by the small surface craft, while the sides, separated from the sidewalks by the curbs, were full of swimmers. The peculiar Dasorian equivalents of whistles, bells, and gongs were making a deafening uproar, and the crowd was

197

yelling and cheering in much the same fashion as do earthly crowds upon similar occasions. Seaton stopped the *Skylark* and took his wife by the shoulder, swinging her around in front of the visiplate.

"Look at that, Dot. Talk about rapid transit! They could give the New York subway a flying start and beat them hands down!"

Dorothy looked into the visiplate and gasped. Six metal pipes, one above the other, ran above and parallel to each sidewalk-lane of water. The pipes were full of ocean water, water racing along at fully fifty miles an hour and discharging, each stream a small waterfall, into the lagoon. Each pipe was lighted in the interior, and each was full of people, heads almost touching feet, unconcernedly being borne along, completely immersed in that mad current. As the passenger saw daylight and felt the stream begin to drop, he righted himself, apparently selecting an objective point, and rode the current down into the ocean. A few quick strokes, and he was either at the surface or upon one of the flights of stairs leading up to the platform. Many of the travelers did not even move as they left the orifice. If they happened to be on their backs, they entered the ocean backward and did not bother about righting themselves or about selecting a destination until they were many feet below the surface.

"Good heavens, Dick! They'll kill themselves or drown!"

"Not these birds. Notice their skins? They've got a hide like a walrus, and a terrific layer of subcutaneous fat. Even their heads are protected that way-you could hardly hit one of them enough with a baseball bat to hurt him. And as for drowning-they can out-swim a fish, and can stay under water almost an hour without coming up for air. Even one of those youngsters can swim the full length of the city without taking a breath."

"How do you get that velocity of flow, Carfon?" asked Crane.

"By means of pumps. These channels run all over the city, and the amount of water running in each tube and the number of tubes in use are regulated automatically by the amount of traffic. When any section of tube is empty of people, no water flows through it. This was necessary in order to save power. At each intersection there are four stand pipes and automatic swim-counters that regulate the volume of water and the number of tubes in use. This is ordinarily a quiet pool, as it is in a residence section, and this channel-our channels correspond to your streets, you know-has only six tubes each way. If you will look on the other side of the channel, you will see the intake end of the tubes going down-town."

Seaton swung the visiplate around and they saw six rapidly-moving stairways, each crowded with people, leading from the ocean level up to the top of a tall metal tower. As the passengers reached the top of the flight they were catapulted head-first into the chamber leading to the tube below.

"Well, that is some system for handling people!" exclaimed Seaton. "What's the capacity of the system?"

"When running full pressure, six tubes will handle five thousand people a minute. It is only very rarely, on such occasions as this, that they are ever loaded to capacity. Some of the channels in the middle of the city have as many as twenty tubes, so that it is always possible to go from one end of the city to the other in less than ten minutes."

"Don't they ever jam?" asked Dorothy curiously. "I've been lost more than once in the New York subway, and been in some perfectly frightful jams, too-and they weren't moving ten thousand people a minute either."

"No jams ever have occurred. The tubes are perfectly smooth and well-lighted, and all turns and intersections are rounded. The controlling machines allow only so many persons to enter any tube-if more should try to enter than can be carried comfortably, the surplus passengers are slid off down a chute to the swim-ways, or sidewalks, and may either wait a while or swim to the next intersection."

"That looks like quite a jam down there now." Seaton pointed to the receiving pool, which was now one solid mass except for the space kept clear by the six mighty streams of humanity-laden water.

"If the newcomers can't find room to come to the surface they'll swim over to some other pool." Carfon shrugged indifferently. "My residence is the fifth cubicle on the right side of this channel. Our custom demands that you accept the hospitality of my home, if only for a moment and only for a beaker of distilled water. Any ordinary visitor could be received in my office, but you must enter my home."

Seaton steered the *Skylark* carefully, surrounded as she was by a tightly packed crowd of swimmers, to the indicated dwelling, and anchored her so that one of the doors was close to a flight of steps leading from the corner of the building down into the water. Carfon stepped out, opened the door of his house, and preceded his guests within. The room was large and square, and built of a synthetic, non-corroding metal, as was the entire city. The walls were tastefully decorated with striking geometrical designs in many-colored metal, and upon the floor was a softly woven rug. Three doors leading into other rooms could be seen, and strange pieces of furniture stood here and there. In the center of the floor-space was a circular opening some four feet in diameter, and there, only a few inches below the level of the floor, was the surface of the ocean.

Carfon introduced his guests to his wife —a feminine replica of himself, although she was not of quite such heroic proportions.

"I don't suppose that Seven is far away, is he?" Carfon asked of the woman.

"Probably he is outside, near the flying ball. If he has not been touching it ever since it came down, it is only because someone stronger than he pushed him aside. You know how boys are," turning to Dorothy with a smile as she spoke, "boy nature is probably universal."

"Pardon my curiosity, but why 'Seven'?" asked Dorothy, as she returned the smile.

"He is the two thousand three hundred and forty-seventh Sacner Carfon in direct male line of descent," she explained. "But perhaps Six has not explained these things to you. Our population must not be allowed to increase, therefore each couple can have only two children. It is customary for the boy to be born first, and is given the name of his father. The girl is younger, and is given her mother's name."

"That will now be changed," said Carfon feelingly. "These visitors have given us the secret of power, and we shall be able to build new cities and populate Dasor as she should he populated."

"Really? — —" She checked herself, but a flame leaped to her eyes, and her voice was none too steady as she addressed the visitors. "For that we Dasorians thank you more than words can express. Perhaps you strangers do not know what it means to want a dozen children with every fiber of your being and to be allowed to have only two-we do, all too well —I will call Seven."

She pressed a button, and up out of the opening in the middle of the floor there shot a half-grown boy, swimming so rapidly that he scarcely touched the coaming as he came to his feet. He glanced at the four visitors, then ran up to Seaton and Crane.

"Please, sirs, may I ride, just a little short ride, in your vessel before you go away?" This was said in their language.

"Seven!" boomed Carfon sternly, and the exuberant youth subsided.

"Pardon me, sirs, but I was so excited — —"

"All right, son, no harm done at all. You bet you'll have a ride in the *Skylark* if your parents will let you." He turned to Carfon. "I'm not so far beyond that stage myself that I'm not in sympathy with him. Neither are you, unless I'm badly mistaken."

"I am very glad that you feel as you do. He would be delighted to accompany us down to the office, and it will be something to remember all the rest of his life."

"You have a little girl, too?" Dorothy asked the woman.

"Yes-would you like to see her? She is asleep now," and without waiting for an answer, the proud Dasorian mother led the way into a bedroom —a bedroom without beds, for Dasorians sleep floating in thermostatically controlled tanks, buoyed up in water of the temperature they like best, in a fashion that no Earthly springs and mattresses can approach. In a small tank in a corner reposed a baby, apparently about a year old, over whom Dorothy and Margaret made the usual feminine ceremony of delight and approbation.

Back in the living room, after an animated conversation in which much information was exchanged concerning the two planets and their races of peoples, Carfon drew six metal goblets of distilled water and passed them around. Standing in a circle, the six touched goblets and drank.

They then embarked, and while Crane steered the *Skylark* slowly along the channel toward the offices of the Council, and while Dorothy and Margaret showed the eager Seven all over the vessel, Seaton explained to Carfon the danger that threatened the Universe, what he had done, and what he was attempting to do.

"Doctor Seaton, I wish to apologize to you," the Dasorian said when Seaton had done. "Since you are evidently still land animals, I had supposed you of inferior intelligence. It is true that your younger civilization is deficient in certain respects, but you have shown a depth of vision, a sheer power of imagination and grasp, that no member of our older civilization could approach. I believe that you are right in your conclusions. We have no such rays nor forces upon this planet, and never have had; but the sixth planet of our own sun has. Less than fifty of your years ago, when I was but a small boy, such a projection visited my father. It offered to 'rescue' us from our watery planet, and to show us how to build rocket-ships to move us to Three, which is half land, inhabited by lower animals."

"And he didn't accept?"

"Certainly not. Then as now our sole lack was power, and the strangers did not show us how to increase our supply. Perhaps they had more power than we, perhaps, because of the difficulty of communication, our want was not made clear to them. But, of course, we did not want to move to Three, and we had already had rocket-ships for hundreds of generations. We have never been able to reach Six with them, but we visited Three long ago; and every one who went there came back as soon as he could. We detest land. It is hard, barren, unfriendly. We have everything, here upon Dasor. Food is plentiful, synthetic or natural, as we prefer. Our watery planet supplies our every need and wish, with one exception; and now that we are assured of power, even that one exception vanishes, and Dasor becomes a very Paradise. We can now lead our natural lives, work and play to our fullest capacity-we would not trade our world for all the rest of the Universe."

"I never thought of it in that way, but you're right, at that," Seaton conceded. "You are ideally suited to your environment. But how do I get to planet Six? Its distance is terrific, even as cosmic distances go. You won't have any night until Dasor swings outside the orbit of your sun, and until then Six will be invisible, even to our most powerful telescope."

"I do not know, myself," answered Carfon, "but I will send out a call for the chief astronomer. He will meet us, and give you a chart and the exact course."

At the office, the earthly visitors were welcomed formally by the Council-the nine men in control of the entire planet. The ceremony over and their course carefully plotted, Carfon stood at the door of the *Skylark* a moment before it closed.

"We thank you with all force, Earthmen, for what you have done for us this day. Please remember, and believe that this is no idle word-if we can assist you in any way in this conflict which is to come, the resources of this planet are at your disposal. We join Osnome and the other planets of this system in declaring you, Doctor Seaton, our Overlord."

CHAPTER IX

The Welcome to Norlamin

The *Skylark* was now days upon her way toward the sixth planet, Seaton gave the visiplates and the instrument board his customary careful scrutiny and rejoined the others.

"Still talking about the human fish, Dottie Dimple?" he asked, as he stoked his villainous pipe. "Peculiar tribe of porpoises, but I'm strong for 'em. They're the most like our own kind of folks, as far as ideas go, of anybody we've seen yet-in fact, they're more like us than a lot of human beings we all know."

"I like them immensely——"

"You couldn't like 'em any other way, their size——"

"Terrible, Dick, terrible! Easy as I am, I can't stand for any such joke as that was going to be. But really, I think they're just perfectly fine, in spite of their being so funny-looking. Mrs. Carfon is just simply sweet, even if she does look like a walrus, and that cute little seal of a baby was just too perfectly cunning for words. That boy Seven is keen as mustard, too."

"He should be," put in Crane, dryly. "He probably has as much intelligence now as any one of us."

"Do you think so?" asked Margaret. "He acted like any other boy, but he did seem to understand things remarkably well."

"He would-they're 'way ahead of us in most things." Seaton glanced at the two women quizzically and turned to Crane. "And as for their being bald, this was one time, Mart, when those two phenomenal heads of hair our two little girl-friends are so proud of didn't make any kind of hit at all. They probably regard that black thatch of Peg's and Dot's auburn mop as relics of a barbarous and prehistoric age-about as we would regard the hirsute hide of a Neanderthal man."

"That may be so, too," Dorothy replied, unconcernedly, "but we aren't planning on living there, so why worry about it? I like them, anyway, and I believe that they like us."

"They acted that way. But say, Mart, if that planet is so old that all their land area has been eroded away, how come they've got so much water left? And they've got quite an atmosphere, too."

"The air-pressure," said Crane, "while greater than that now obtaining upon Earth, was probably of the order of magnitude of three meters of mercury, originally. As to the erosion, they might have had more water to begin with than our Earth had."

"Yeah, that'd account for it, all right," said Dorothy.

"There's one thing I want to ask you two scientists," Margaret said. "Everywhere we've gone, except on that one world that Dick thinks is a wandering planet, we've found the intelligent life quite remarkably like human beings. How do you account for that?"

"There, Mart, is one for the massive old bean to concentrate on," challenged Seaton: then, as Crane considered the question in silence for some time he went on: "I'll answer it myself, then, by asking another. Why not? Why shouldn't they be? Remember, man is the highest form of earthly life-at least, in our own opinion and as far as we know. In our wanderings, we have picked out planets quite similar to our own in point of atmosphere and temperature and, within narrow limits, of mass as well. It stands to reason that under such similarity of conditions, there would be a certain similarity of results. How about it, Mart? Reasonable?"

"It seems plausible, in a way," conceded Crane, "but it probably is not universally true."

"Sure not-couldn't be, hardly. No doubt we could find a lot of worlds inhabited by all kinds of intelligent things-freaks that we can't even begin to imagine now-but they probably would be occupying planets entirely different from ours in some essential feature of atmosphere, temperature, or mass."

"But the Fenachrone world is entirely different," Dorothy argued, "and they're more or less human-they're bipeds, anyway, with recognizable features. I've been studying that record with you, you know, and their world has so much more mass than ours that their gravitation is simply frightful!"

"That much difference is comparatively slight, not a real fundamental difference. I meant a hundred or so times either way-greater or less. And even their gravitation has modified their structure a lot-suppose it had been fifty times as great as it is? What would they have been like? Also, their atmosphere is very similar to ours in composition, and their temperature is bearable. It is my opinion that atmosphere and temperature have more to do with evolution than anything else, and that the mass of the planet runs a poor third."

"You may be right," admitted Crane, "but it seems to me that you are arguing from insufficient premises."

"Sure I am-almost no premises at all. I would be just about as well justified in deducing the structure of a range of mountains from a superficial study of three pebbles picked up in a creek near them. However, we can get an idea some time, when we have a lot of time."

"How?"

"Remember that planet we struck on the first trip, that had an atmosphere composed mostly of gaseous chlorin? In our ignorance we assumed that life there was impossible, and didn't stop. Well, it may be just as well that we didn't. If we go back there, protected as we are with our rays and stuff, it wouldn't surprise me a bit to find life there, and lots of it-and I've got a hunch that it'll be a form of life that'd make your grandfather's whiskers curl right up into a ball!"

"You do get the weirdest ideas, Dick!" protested Dorothy. "I hope you aren't planning on exploring it, just to prove your point?"

"Never thought of it before. Can't do it now, anyway-got our hands full already. However, after we get this Fenachrone mess cleaned up we'll have to do just that little thing, won't we, Mart? As that intellectual guy said while he was insisting upon dematerializing us, 'Science demands it.'"

"By all means. We should be in a position to make contributions to science in fields as yet untouched. Most assuredly we shall investigate those points."

"Then they'll go alone, won't they, Peggy?"

"Absolutely! We've seen some pretty middling horrible things already, and if these two men of ours call the frightful things we have seen normal, and are planning on deliberately hunting up things that even they will consider monstrous, you and I most certainly shall stay at home!"

"Yeah? You say it easy. Bounce back, Peg, you've struck a rubber fence! Rufus, you red-headed little fraud, you know you wouldn't let me go to the corner store after a can of tobacco without insisting on tagging along!"

"You're a...." began Dorothy hotly, but broke off in amazement and gasped, "For Heaven's sake, what was that?"

"What was what? It missed me."

"It went right through you! It was a kind of funny little cloud, like smoke or something. It came right through the ceiling like a flash-went right through you and on down through the floor. There it comes back again!"

Before their staring eyes a vague, nebulous something moved rapidly upward through the floor and passed upward through the ceiling. Dorothy leaped to Seaton's side and he put his arm around her reassuringly.

"'Sall right folks —I know what that thing is."

"Well, shoot it, quick!" Dorothy implored.

"It's one of those projections from where we're heading for, trying to get our range; and it's the most welcome sight these weary old eyes have rested upon for full many a long and dreary moon. They've probably located us from our power-plant rays. We're an awful long ways off yet, though, and going like a streak of greased lightning, so they're having trouble in holding us. They're friendly, we already know that-they probably want to talk to us. It'd make it easier for them if we'd shut off our power and drift at constant velocity, but we'd use up valuable time and throw our calculations all out of whack. We'll let them try to match our acceleration If they can do that, they're good."

The apparition reappeared, oscillating back and forth irregularly-passing through the arenak walls, through the furniture and the instrument boards, and even through the mighty powerplant itself, as though nothing were there. Eventually, however, it remained stationary a foot or so above the floor of the control-room. Then it began to increase in density until apparently a man stood before them. His skin, like that of all the inhabitants of the planets of the green suns, was green. He was tall and well-proportioned when judged by Earthly standards, except for his head, which was overly large, and which was particularly massive above the eyes and backward from the ears. He was evidently of great age, for what little of his face was visible was seamed and wrinkled, and his long, thick mane of hair and his square-cut, yard-long beard were a dazzling white, only faintly tinged with green.

While not in any sense transparent, nor even translucent, it was evident that the apparition before them was not composed of flesh and blood. He looked at each of the four Earth-beings intensely for a moment, then pointed toward the table upon which stood the mechanical educator, and Seaton placed it in front of the peculiar visitor. As Seaton donned a headset and handed one to the stranger, the latter stared at him, impressing upon his consciousness that he was to be given a knowledge of English. Seaton pressed the lever, receiving as he did so a sensation of an unbroken calm, a serenity profound and untroubled, and the projection spoke.

"Dr. Seaton, Mr. Crane, and ladies-welcome to Norlamin, the planet toward which you are now flying. We have been awaiting you for more than five thousand years of your time. It has been a mathematical certainty-it has been graven upon the very Sphere itself-that in time someone would come to us from without this system, bringing a portion, however small, of Rovolon-of the metal of power, of which there is not even the most minute trace in our entire solar system. For more than five thousand years our instruments have been set to detect the vibrations which would herald the advent of the user of that metal. Now you have come, and I perceive that you have vast stores of it. Being yourselves seekers after truth, you will share it with us gladly as we will instruct you in many things you wish to know. Allow me to operate the educator —I would gaze into your minds and reveal my own to your sight. But first I must tell you that your machine is too rudimentary to work at all well, and with your permission I shall make certain minor alterations."

Seaton nodded permission, and from the eyes and from the hands of the figure there leaped visible streams of force, which seized the transformers, coils and tubes, and reformed and reconnected them, under Seaton's bulging eyes, into an entirely different mechanism.

"Oh, I see!" he gasped. "Say, what are you anyway?"

"Pardon me; in my eagerness I became forgetful. I am Orlon, the First of Astronomy of Norlamin, in my observatory upon the surface of the planet. This that you see is simply my projection, composed of forces for which you have no name in your language. You can cut it off, if you wish, with your ray-screens, which even I can see are of a surprisingly high order of efficiency. There, this educator will now work very well. Please put on the remodeled headsets, all four of you."

They did so, and the rays of force moved levers, switches, and dials as positively as human hands could have moved them, and with infinitely greater speed and precision. As the dials moved, each brain received clearly and plainly a knowledge of the customs, language, and manners of the inhabitants of Norlamin. Each mind became suffused with a vast, immeasurable peace, calm power, and a depth and breadth of mental vision theretofore undreamed of. Looking deep into his mind they sensed a quiet, placid certainty, beheld power and knowledge to them illimitable, perceived depths of wisdom to them unfathomable.

Then from his mind into theirs there flowed smoothly a mighty stream of comprehension of cosmic phenomena. They hazily saw infinitely small units grouped into planetary formations to form practically dimensionless particles. These particles in turn grouped to form slightly larger ones, and after a long succession of such grouping they knew that the comparatively gigantic aggregates which then held their attention were in reality electrons and protons, the smallest units recognized by Earthly science. They clearly understood the combination of these electrons and protons into atoms. They perceived plainly the way in which atoms build up molecules, and comprehended the molecular structure of matter. In mathematical thoughts, only dimly grasped even by Seaton and Crane, were laid before them the fundamental laws of physics, of electricity, of gravitation, and of chemistry. They saw globular aggregations of matter, the suns and their planets, comprising solar systems; saw solar systems, in accordance with those immutable laws, grouped into galaxies, galaxies in turn-here the flow was suddenly shut off as though a valve had been closed, and the astronomer spoke.

"Pardon me. Your brains should be stored only with the material you desire most and can use to the best advantage, for your mental capacity is even more limited than my own. Please understand that I speak in no derogatory sense; it is only that your race has many thousands of generations to go before your minds should be stored with knowledge indiscriminately. We ourselves have not yet reached that stage, and we are perhaps millions of years older than you. And yet," he continued musingly, "I envy you. Knowledge is, of course, relative, and I can know *so* little! Time and space have yielded not an iota of their mystery to our most penetrant minds. And whether we delve baffled into the unknown smallness of the small, or whether we peer, blind and helpless, into the unknown largeness of the large, it is the same-infinity is comprehensible only to the Infinite One: the all-shaping Force directing and controlling the Universe and the unknowable Sphere. The more we know, the vaster the virgin fields of investigation open to us, and the more infinitesimal becomes our knowledge. But I am perhaps keeping you from more important activities. As you approach Norlamin more nearly, I shall guide you to my observatory. I am glad indeed that it is in my lifetime that you have come to us, and I await anxiously the opportunity of greeting you in the flesh. The years remaining to me of this cycle of existence are few, and I had almost ceased hoping to witness your coming."

The projection vanished instantaneously, and the four stared at each other in an incredulous daze of astonishment. Seaton finally broke the stunned silence. "Well, I'll be kicked to death by little red spiders!" he ejaculated. "Mart, did you see what I saw, or did I get tight on something without knowing it? That sure burned me up-it breaks me right off at the ankles, just to think of it!"

Crane walked to the educator in silence. He examined it, felt the changed coils and transformers, and gently shook the new insulating base of the great power-tube. Still in silence he turned his back, walked around the instrument board, read the meters, then went back and again inspected the educator.

"It was real, and not a higher development of hypnotism, as at first I thought it must be," he reported seriously. "Hypnotism, if sufficiently advanced, might have affected us in that fashion, even to teaching us all a strange language, but by no possibility could it have had such an effect upon copper, steel, bakelite, and glass. It was certainly real, and while I cannot begin to understand it, I will say that your imagination has certainly vindicated itself. A race of beings, who can do such things as that, can do almost anything-you have been right, from the start."

"Then you can beat those horrible Fenachrone, after all!" cried Dorothy, and threw herself into her husband's arms.

"Do you remember, Dick, that I hailed you once as Columbus at San Salvador?" asked Margaret unsteadily from Crane's encircling arm. "What could a man be called who from the sheer depths of his imagination called forth the means of saving from destruction all the civilization of millions of entire worlds?"

"Don't talk that way, please, folks," Seaton was plainly very uncomfortable. He blushed intensely, the burning red tide rising in waves up to his hair as he wriggled in embarrassment, like any schoolboy. "Mart's done most of it, anyway, you know; and even at that, we ain't out of the woods yet, by forty-seven rows of apple trees."

"You will admit, will you not, that we can see our way out of the woods, at least, and that you yourself feel rather relieved?" asked Crane.

"I think we'll be able to pull their corks now, all right, after we get some dope. It's a cinch they've either got the stuff we need or know how to get it-and if that zone is impenetrable, I'll bet they'll be able to dope out something just as good. Relieved? That doesn't half tell it, guy—I feel as if I had just pitched off the Old Man of the Sea who's been sitting on my neck! What say you girls get your fiddle and guitar and we'll sing us a little song? I feel kind of relieved-they had me worried some-it's the first time I've felt like singing since we cut that warship up."

Dorothy brought out her "fiddle"—the magnificent Stradivarius, formerly Crane's, which he had given her-Margaret her guitar, and they sang one rollicking number after another. Though by no means a Metropolitan Opera quartette, their voices were all better than mediocre, and they had sung together so much that they harmonized readily.

"Why don't you play us some real music, Dottie?" asked Margaret, after a time. "You haven't practiced for ages."

"I haven't felt like playing lately, but I do now," and Dorothy stood up and swept the bow over the strings. Doctor of Music in violin, an accomplished musician, playing upon one of the finest instruments the world has ever known, she was lifted out of herself by relief from the dread of the Fenachrone invasion and that splendid violin expressed every subtle nuance of her thought.

She played rhapsodies and paeans, and solos by the great masters. She played vivacious dances, then "Traumerei" and "Liebestraum." At last she swept into the immortal "Meditation," and as the last note died away Seaton held out his arms.

"You're a blinding flash and a deafening report, Dottie Dimple, and I love you," he declared-and his eyes and his arms spoke volumes that his light utterance had left unsaid.

Norlamin close enough so that its image almost filled number six visiplate, the four wanderers studied it with interest. Partially obscured by clouds and with its polar regions two glaring caps of snow-they would be green in a few months, when the planet would swing inside the orbit of its sun around the vast central luminary of that complex solar system-it made a magnificent picture. They saw sparkling blue oceans and huge green continents of unfamiliar outlines. So terrific was the velocity of the space-cruiser, that the image grew larger as they watched it, and soon the field of vision could not contain the image of the whole disk.

"Well, I expect Orlon'll be showing up pretty quick now," remarked Seaton; and it was not long until the projection appeared in the air of the control room.

"Hail, Terrestrials!" he greeted them. "With your permission, I shall direct your flight."

Permission granted, the figure floated across the room to the board and the rays of force centered the visiplate, changed the direction of the bar a trifle, decreased slightly their negative acceleration, and directed a stream of force upon the steering mechanism.

"We shall alight upon the grounds of my observatory upon Norlamin in seven thousand four hundred twenty-eight seconds," he announced presently. "The observatory will be upon the dark side of Norlamin when we arrive, but I have a force operating upon the steering mechanism which will guide the vessel along the required curved path. I shall remain with you until we land, and we may converse upon any topic of most interest to you."

"We've got a topic of interest, all right. That's what we came out here for. But it would take too long to tell you about it—I'll show you!"

He brought out the magnetic brain record, threaded it into the machine and handed the astronomer a head-set. Orlon put it on, touched the lever, and for an hour there was unbroken silence as the monstrous brain of the menace was studied by the equally capable intellect of the Norlaminian scientist. There was no pause in the motion of the magnetic tape, no repetition-Orlon's brain absorbed the information as fast as it could be sent, and understood that frightful mind in every particular.

As the end of the tape was reached and the awful record ended, a shadow passed over Orlon's face.

205

"Truly a depraved evolution-it is sad to contemplate such a perversion of a really excellent brain. They have power, even as you have, and they have the will to destroy, which is a thing that I cannot understand. However, if it is graven upon the Sphere that we are to pass, it means only that upon the next plane we shall continue our searches-let us hope with better tools and with greater understanding than we now possess."

"'Smatter?" snapped Seaton gravely. "Going to take it lying down, without putting up any fight at all?"

"What can we do? Violence is contrary to our very natures. No man of Norlamin could offer any but passive resistance."

"You can do a lot if you will. Put on that headset again and get my plan, offering any suggestions your far abler brain may suggest."

As the human scientist poured his plan of battle into the brain of the astronomer, Orlon's face cleared.

"It is graven upon the Sphere that the Fenachrone shall pass," he said finally. "What you ask of us we can do. I have only a general knowledge of rays, as they are not in the province of the Orlon family; but the student Rovol, of the family Rovol of Rays, has all present knowledge of such phenomena. Tomorrow I will bring you together, and I have little doubt that he will be able, with the help of your metal of power, to solve your problem."

"I don't quite understand what you said about a whole family studying one subject, and yet having only one student in it," said Dorothy, in perplexity.

"A little explanation is perhaps necessary," replied Orlon. "First, you must know that every man of Norlamin is a student, and most of us are students of science. With us, 'labor' means mental effort, that is, study. We perform no physical or manual labor save for exercise, as all our mechanical work is done by forces. This state of things having endured for many thousands of years, it long ago became evident that specialization was necessary in order to avoid duplication of effort and to insure complete coverage of the field. Soon afterward, it was discovered that very little progress was being made in any branch, because so much was known that it took practically a lifetime to review that which had already been accomplished, even in a narrow and highly specialized field. Many points were studied for years before it was discovered that the identical work had been done before, and either forgotten or overlooked. To remedy this condition the mechanical educator had to be developed. Once it was perfected a new system was begun. One man was assigned to each small subdivision of scientific endeavor, to study it intensively. When he became old, each man chose a successor-usually a son-and transferred his own knowledge to the younger student. He also made a complete record of his own brain, in much the same way as you have recorded the brain of the Fenachrone upon your metallic tape. These records are all stored in a great central library, as permanent references.

"All these things being true, now a young person may need only finish an elementary education-just enough to learn to think, which takes only about twenty-five or thirty years-and then he is ready to begin actual work. When that time comes, he receives in one day all the knowledge of his specialty which has been accumulated by his predecessors during many thousands of years of intensive study."

"Whew!" Seaton whistled, "no wonder you folks know something! With that start, I believe I might know something myself! As an astronomer, you may be interested in this star-chart and stuff-or do you know all about that already?"

"No, the Fenachrone are far ahead of us in that subject, because of their observatories out in open space and because of their gigantic reflectors, which cannot be used through any atmosphere. We are further hampered in having darkness for only a few hours at a time and only in the winter, when our planet is outside the orbit of our sun around the great central sun of our entire system. However, with the Rovolon you have brought us, we shall have real observatories far out in space; and for that I personally will be indebted to you more than I can ever express. As for the chart, I hope to have the pleasure of examining it while you are conferring with Rovol of Rays."

"How many families are working on rays-just one?"

"One upon each kind of ray. That is, each of the ray families knows a great deal about all kinds of vibrations of the ether, but is specializing upon one narrow field. Take, for instance, the rays you are most interested in; those able to penetrate a zone of force. From my own very slight and general knowledge I know that it would of necessity be a ray of the fifth order. These rays are very new-they have been under investigation only a few hundred years-and the Rovol is the only student who would be at all well informed upon them. Shall I explain the orders of rays more fully than I did by means of the educator?"

"Please. You assumed that we knew more than we do, so a little explanation would help."

"All ordinary vibrations-that is, all molecular and material ones, such as light, heat, electricity, radio, and the like-were arbitrarily called waves of the first order; in order to distinguish them from waves of the second order, which are given off by particles of the second order, which you know as protons and electrons, in their combination to form atoms. Your scientist Millikan discovered these rays for you, and in your language they are known as Millikan, or Cosmic, rays.

"Some time later, when sub-electrons were identified the rays given off by their combination into electrons, or by the disruption of electrons, were called rays of the third order. These rays are most interesting and most useful; in fact, they do all our mechanical work. They as a class are called protelectricity, and bear the same relation to ordinary electricity that electricity does to torque-both are pure energy, and they are inter-convertible. Unlike electricity, however, it may be converted into many different forms by fields of force, in a way comparable to that in which white light is resolved into colors by a prism-or rather, more like the way alternating current is changed to direct current by a motor-generator set, with attendant changes in properties. There is a complete spectrum of more than five hundred factors, each as different from the others as red is different from green.

"Continuing farther, particles of the fourth order give rays of the fourth order; those of the fifth, rays of the fifth order. Fourth-order rays have been investigated quite thoroughly, but only mathematically and theoretically, as they are of excessively short wave-length and are capable of being generated only by the breaking down of matter itself into the corresponding particles. However, it has been shown that they are quite similar to protelectricity in their general behavior. Thus, the power that propels your space-vessel, your attractors, your repellers, your object-compass, your zone of force-all these things are simply a few of the many hundreds of wave-bands of the fourth order, all of which you doubtless would have worked out for yourselves in time. Very little is known, even in theory, of the rays of the fifth order, although they have been shown to exist."

"For a man having no knowledge, you seem to know a lot about rays. How about the fifth order-is that as far as they go?"

"My knowledge is slight and very general; only such as I must have in order to understand my own subject. The fifth order certainly is not the end-it is probably scarcely a beginning. We think now that the orders extend to infinite smallness, just as the galaxies are grouped into larger aggregations, which are probably in their turn only tiny units in a scheme infinitely large.

"Over six thousand years ago the last third order rays were worked out; and certain peculiarities in their behavior led the then Rovol to suspect the existence of the fourth order. Successive generations of the Rovol proved their existence, determined the conditions of their liberation, and found that this metal of power was the only catalyst able to decompose matter and thus liberate the rays. This metal, which was called Rovolon after the Rovol, was first described upon theoretical grounds and later was found, by spectroscopy, in certain stars, notably in one star only eight light-years away, but not even the most infinitesimal trace of it exists in our entire solar system. Since these discoveries, the many Rovol have been perfecting the theory of the fourth order, beginning that of the fifth, and waiting for your coming. The present Rovol, like myself and many others whose work is almost at a standstill, is waiting with all-consuming interest to greet you, as soon as the *Skylark* can be landed upon our planet."

"Neither your rocket-ships nor your projections could get you any Rovolon?"

"No. Every hundred years or so someone develops a new type of rocket that he thinks may stand a slight chance of making the journey, but not one of these venturesome youths has as yet returned. Either that sun has no planets or else the rocket-ships have failed. Our projections are useless, as they can be driven only a very short distance upon our present carrier wave. With a carrier of the fifth order we could drive a projection to any point in the galaxy, since its velocity would be millions of times that of light and the power necessary reduced accordingly-but as I have said before, such waves cannot be generated without metal Rovolon."

"I hate to break this up—I'd like to listen to you talk for a week-but we're going to land pretty quick, and it looks as though we were going to land pretty hard."

"We will land soon, but not hard," replied Orlon confidently, and the landing was as he had foretold. The *Skylark* was falling with an ever-decreasing velocity, but so fast was the descent that it seemed to the watchers as though they must crash through the roof of the huge brilliantly lighted building upon which they were dropping and bury themselves many feet in the ground beneath it. But they did not strike the observatory. So incredibly accurate were the calculations of the Norlaminian astronomer and so inhumanly precise were the controls he had set upon their bar, that, as they touched the ground after barely clearing the domed roof and he shut off their power, the passengers felt only a sudden decrease in acceleration, like that following the coming to rest of a rapidly moving elevator, after it has completed a downward journey.

"I shall join you in person very shortly," Orlon said, and the projection vanished.

"Well, we're here, folks, on another new world. Not quite as thrilling as the first one was, is it?" and Seaton stepped toward the door.

"How about the air composition, density, gravity, temperature, and so on?" asked Crane. "Perhaps we should make a few tests."

"Didn't you get that on the educator? Thought you did. Gravity a little less than seven-tenths. Air composition, same as Osnome and Dasor. Pressure, half-way between Earth and Osnome. Temperature, like Osnome most of the time, but fairly comfortable in the winter. Snow now at the poles, but this observatory is only ten degrees from the equator. They don't wear clothes enough to flag a hand-car with here, either, except when they have to. Let's go!"

He opened the door and the four travelers stepped out upon a close-cropped lawn—a turf whose blue-green softness would shame an Oriental rug. The landscape was illuminated by a soft and mellow, yet intense green light which emanated from no visible source. As they paused and glanced about them, they saw that the *Skylark* had alighted in the exact center of a circular enclosure a hundred yards in diameter, walled by row upon row of shrubbery, statuary, and fountains, all bathed in ever-changing billows of light. At only one point was the circle broken. There the walls did not come together, but continued on to border a lane leading up to the massive structure of cream-and-green marble, topped by its enormous, glassy dome-the observatory of Orlon.

"Welcome to Norlamin, Terrestrials," the deep, calm voice of the astronomer greeted them, and Orlon in the flesh shook hands cordially in the American fashion with each of them in turn, and placed around each neck a crystal chain from which depended a small Norlaminian chronometer-radiophone. Behind him there stood four other old men.

"These men are already acquainted with each of you, but you do not as yet know them. I present Fodan, Chief of the Five of Norlamin. Rovol, about whom you know. Astron, the First of Energy. Satrazon, the First of Chemistry."

Orlon fell in beside Seaton and the party turned toward the observatory. As they walked along the Earth-people stared, held by the unearthly beauty of the grounds. The hedge of shrubbery, from ten to twenty feet high, and which shut out all sight of everything outside it, was one mass of vivid green and flaring crimson leaves; each leaf and twig groomed meticulously into its precise place in a fantastic geometrical scheme. Just inside this boundary there stood a ring of statues of heroic size. Some of them were single figures of men and women; some were busts; some were groups in natural or allegorical poses-all were done with consummate skill and feeling. Between the statues there were fountains, magnificent bronze and glass groups of the strange aquatic denizens of this strange planet, bathed in geometrically shaped sprays, screens, and columns of water. Winding around between the statues and the fountains there was a moving, scintillating wall, and upon the waters and upon the wall there played torrents of color, cataracts of harmoniously blended light. Reds, blues, yellows, greens-every color of their peculiar green spectrum and every conceivable combination of those colors writhed and flamed in ineffable splendor upon those deep and living screens of falling water and upon that shimmering wall.

As they entered the lane, Seaton saw with amazement that what he had supposed a wall, now close at hand, was not a wall at all. It was composed of myriads of individual sparkling jewels, of every known color, for the most part self-luminous; and each gem, apparently entirely unsupported, was dashing in and out and along among its fellows, weaving and darting here and there, flying at headlong speed along an extremely tortuous, but evidently carefully calculated course.

"What can that be, anyway, Dick?" whispered Dorothy, and Seaton turned to his guide.

"Pardon my curiosity, Orlon, but would you mind explaining the why of that moving wall? We don't get it."

"Not at all. This garden has been the private retreat of the family of Orlon for many thousands of years, and women of our house have been beautifying it since its inception. You may have observed that the statuary is very old. No such work has been done for ages. Modern art has developed along the lines of color and motion, hence the lighting effects and the tapestry wall. Each gem is held upon the end of a minute pencil of force, and all the pencils are controlled by a machine which has a key for every jewel in the wall."

Crane, the methodical, stared at the innumerable flashing jewels and asked, "It must have taken a prodigious amount of time to complete such an undertaking?"

"It is far from complete; in fact, it is scarcely begun. It was started only about four hundred years ago."

"*Four hundred years!*" exclaimed Dorothy. "Do you live that long? How long will it take to finish it, and what will it be like when it is done?"

"No, none of us live longer than about one hundred and sixty years-at about that age most of us decide to pass. When this tapestry wall is finished, it will not be simply form and color, as it is now. It will be a portrayal of the history of Norlamin from the first cooling of the planet. It will, in all probability, require thousands of years for its completion. You see, time is of little importance to us, and workmanship is everything. My companion will continue working upon it until we decide to pass; my son's companion may continue it. In any event, many generations of the women of the Orlon will work upon it until it is complete. When it is done, it will be a thing of beauty as long as Norlamin shall endure."

"But suppose that your son's wife isn't that kind of an artist? Suppose she should want to do music or painting or something else?" asked Dorothy, curiously.

"That is quite possible; for, fortunately, our art is not yet entirely intellectual, as is our music. There are many unfinished artistic projects in the house of Orlon, and if the companion of my son should not find one to her liking, she will be at liberty to continue anything else she may have begun, or to start an entirely new project of her own."

"You have a family, then?" asked Margaret, "I'm afraid I didn't understand things very well when you gave them to us over the educator."

"I sent things too fast for you, not knowing that your educator was new to you; a thing with which you were not thoroughly familiar. I will therefore explain some things in language, since you are not familiar with the mechanism of thought transference. The Five, a self-perpetuating body, do what governing is necessary for the entire planet. Their decrees are founded upon self-evident truth, and are therefore the law. Population is regulated according to the needs of the planet, and since much work is now in progress, an increase in population was recommended by the Five. My companion and I therefore had three children, instead of the customary two. By lot it fell to us to have two boys and one girl. One of the boys will assume my duties when I pass; the other will take over a part of some branch of science that has grown too complex for one man to handle as a specialist should. In fact, he has already chosen his specialty and been accepted for it-he is to be the nine hundred and sixty-seventh of Chemistry, the student of the asymmetric carbon atom, which will thus be his specialty from this time henceforth.

"It was learned long ago that the most perfect children were born of parents in the full prime of mental life, that is, at one hundred years of age. Therefore, with us each generation covers one hundred years. The first twenty-five years of a child's life are spent at home with his parents, during which time he acquires his elementary education in the common schools. Then boys and girls alike move to the Country of Youth, where they spend another twenty-five years. There they develop their brains and initiative by conducting any researches they choose. Most of us, at that age, solve all the riddles of the Universe, only to discover later that our solutions have been fallacious. However, much really excellent work is done in the Country of Youth, primarily because of the new and unprejudiced viewpoints of the virgin minds there at work. In that country also each finds his life's companion, the one necessary to round out mere existence into a perfection of living that no person, man or woman, can ever know alone. I need not speak to you of the wonders of love or of the completion and fullness of life that it brings, for all four of you, children though you are, know love in full measure.

"At fifty years of age the man, now mentally mature, is recalled to his family home, as his father's brain is now losing some of its vigor and keenness. The father then turns over his work to the son by means of the educator-and when the weight of the accumulated knowledge of a hundred thousand generations of research is impressed upon the son's brain, his play is over."

"What does the father do then?"

"Having made his brain record, about which I have told you, he and his companion-for she has in similar fashion turned over her work to her successor-retire to the Country of Age, where they rest and relax after their century of effort. They do whatever they care to do, for as long as they please to do it. Finally, after assuring themselves that all is well with the children, they decide that they are ready for the Change. Then, side by side as they have labored, they pass."

Now at the door of the observatory, Dorothy paused and shrank back against Seaton, her eyes widening as she stared at Orlon.

"No, daughter, why should we fear the Change?" he answered her unspoken question, calm serenity in every inflection of his quiet voice. "The life-principle is unknowable to the finite mind, as is the All-Controlling Force. But even though we know nothing of the sublime goal toward which it is tending, any person ripe for the Change can, and of course does, liberate the life-principle so that its progress may be unimpeded."

In a spacious room of the observatory, in which the Terrestrials and their Norlaminian hosts had been long engaged in study and discussion, Seaton finally rose and extended a hand toward his wife.

"Well, that's that, then, Orlon, I guess. We've been thirty hours without sleep, and for us that's a long time. I'm getting so dopey I can't think a lick. We'd better go back to the *Skylark* and turn in, and after we've slept nine hours or so I'll go over to Rovol's laboratory and Crane'll come back here to you."

"You need not return to your vessel," said Orlon. "I know that its somewhat cramped quarters have become irksome. Apartments have been prepared here for you. We shall have a meal here together, and then we shall retire, to meet again tomorrow."

As he spoke, a tray laden with appetizing dishes appeared in the air in front of each person. As Seaton resumed his seat the tray followed him, remaining always in the most convenient position.

Crane glanced at Seaton questioningly, and Satrazon, the First of Chemistry, answered his thought before he could voice it.

"The food before you, unlike that which is before us of Norlamin, is wholesome for you. It contains no copper, no arsenic, no heavy metals-in short, nothing in the least harmful to your chemistry. It is balanced as to carbohydrates, proteins, fats and sugars, and contains the due proportion of each of the various accessory nutritional factors. You will also find the flavors are agreeable to each of you."

"Synthetic, eh? You've got us analyzed," Seaton stated, rather than asked, as with knife and fork he attacked the thick, rare, and beautifully broiled steak which, with its mushrooms and other delicate trimmings, lay upon his rigid although unsupported tray-noticing as he did so that the Norlaminians ate with tools entirely different from those they had supplied to their Earthly guests.

"Entirely synthetic," Satrazon made answer, "except for the sodium chloride necessary. As you already know, sodium and chlorin are very rare throughout our system, therefore the force upon the food-supply took from your vessel the amount of salt required for the formula. We have been unable to synthesize atoms, for the same reason that the labors of so many others have been hindered-because of the lack of Rovolon. Now, however, my science shall progress as it should; and for that I join with my fellow scientists in giving you thanks for the service you have rendered us."

"We thank you instead," replied Seaton, "for the service we have been able to do you is slight indeed compared to what you are giving us in return. But it seems that you speak quite impersonally of the force upon the food supply. Did you yourself direct the preparation of these meats and vegetables?"

"Oh, no. I merely analyzed your tissues, surveyed the food-supplies you carried, discovered your individual preferences, and set up the necessary integrals in the mechanism. The forces did the rest, and will continue to do so as long as you remain upon this planet."

"Fruit salad always my favorite dish," Dorothy said, after a couple of bites, "and this one is just too perfectly divine! It doesn't taste like any other fruit I ever ate, either —I think it must be the same ambrosia that the old pagan gods used to eat."

"If all you did was to set up the integrals, how do you know what you are going to have for the next meal?" asked Crane.

"We have no idea what the form, flavor, or consistency of any dish will be," was the surprising answer. "We know only that the flavor will be agreeable and that it will agree with the form and consistency of the substance, and that the composition will be well-balanced chemically. You see, all the details of flavor, form, texture, and so on are controlled by a device something like one of your kaleidoscopes. The integrals render impossible any unwholesome, unpleasant, or unbalanced combination of any nature, and everything else is left to the mechanism, which operates upon pure chance."

"Some system, I'd rise to remark," and Seaton, with the others, resumed his vigorous attack upon the long-delayed supper.

The meal over, the Earthly visitors were shown to their rooms, and fell into a deep, dreamless sleep.

CHAPTER X

Norlaminian Science

Breakfast over, Seaton watched intently as his tray, laden with empty containers, floated away from him and disappeared into an opening in the wall.

"How do you do it, Orlon?" he asked, curiously. "I can hardly believe it, even after seeing it done."

"Each tray is carried upon the end of a beam or rod of force, and supported rigidly by it. Since the beam is tuned to the individual wave of the instrument you wear upon your chest, your tray is, of course, placed in front of you, at a predetermined distance, as soon as the sending force is actuated. When you have finished your meal, the beam is shortened. Thus the tray is drawn back to the food laboratory, where other forces cleanse and sterilize the various utensils and place them in readiness for the next meal. It would be an easy matter to have this same mechanism place your meals before you wherever you may go upon this planet, provided only that a clear path can be plotted from the laboratory to your person."

"Thanks, but it wouldn't pay. No telling where we'd be. Besides, we'd better eat in the *Skylark* most of the time, to keep our cook good-natured. Well, I see Rovol's got his boat here for me, so guess I'd better turn up a few r. p. m. Coming along, Dot, or have you got something else on your mind?"

"I'm going to leave you for a while. I can't really understand even a radio, and just thinking about those funny, complicated rays and things you are going after makes me dizzy in the head. Mrs. Orlon is going to take us over to the Country of Youth-she says Margaret and I can play around with her daughter and her bunch and have a good time while you scientists are doing your stuff."

"All right. 'Bye till tonight," and Seaton stepped out into the grounds, where the First of Rays was waiting.

The flier was a torpedo-shaped craft of some transparent, glassy material, completely enclosed except for one circular opening or doorway. From the midsection, which was about five feet in diameter and provided with heavily-cushioned seats capable of carrying four passengers in comfort, the hull tapered down smoothly to a needle point at each end. As Seaton entered and settled himself into the cushions, Rovol touched a lever. Instantly a transparent door slid across the opening, locking itself into position flush with the surface of the hull, and the flier darted into the air and away. For a few minutes there was silence, as Seaton studied the terrain beneath them. Fields or cities there were none; the land was covered with dense forests and vast meadows, with here and there great buildings surrounded by gracious, park-like areas. Rovol finally broke the silence.

"I understand your problem, I believe, since Orlon has transferred to me all the thoughts he had from you. With the aid of the Rovolon you have brought us, I am confident that we shall be able to work out a satisfactory solution of the various problems involved. It will take us some few minutes to traverse the distance to my laboratory, and if there are any matters upon which your mind is not quite clear, I shall try to clarify them."

"That's letting me down easy," Seaton grinned, "but you don't need to be afraid of hurting my feelings—I know just exactly how ignorant and dumb I am compared to you. There's a lot of things I don't get at all. First, and nearest, this airboat. It has no power-plant at all. I assume that it, like so many other things hereabouts, is riding on the end of a rod of force?"

"Exactly. The beam is generated and maintained in my laboratory. All that is here in the flier is a small sender, for remote control."

"How do you obtain your power?" asked Seaton. "Solar generators and tide motors? I know that all your work is done by protelectricity, but Orlon did not inform us as to the sources."

"We have not used such inefficient generators for many thousands of years. Long ago it was shown by research that these rays were constantly being generated in abundance in outer space, and that they could be collected upon spherical condensers and transmitted without loss to the surface of the planet by means of matched and synchronized crystals. Several millions of these condensers have been built and thrown out to become tiny satellites of Norlamin."

"How did you get them far enough out?"

"The first ones were forced out to the required distance upon beams of force produced by the conversion of electricity, which was in turn produced from turbines, solar motors, and tide motors. With a few of them out, however, it was easy to obtain sufficient power to send out more; and now, whenever one of us requires more power than he has at his disposal, he merely sends out such additional collectors as he needs."

"Now about those fifth-order rays, which will penetrate a zone of force. I am told that they are not ether waves at all?"

"They are not ether waves. The fourth order rays, of which the theory has been completely worked out, are the shortest vibrations that can be propagated through the ether; for the ether itself is not a continuous medium. We do not know its nature exactly, but it is an actual substance, and is composed of discrete particles of the fourth order. Now the zone of force, which is itself a fourth-order phenomenon, sets up a condition of stasis in the particles composing the ether. These particles are relatively so coarse, that rays and particles of the fifth order will pass through the fixed zone without retardation. Therefore, if there is anything between the particles of the ether-this matter is being debated hotly among us at the present time-it must be a sub-ether, if I may use that term. We have never been able to investigate any of these things experimentally, not even such a coarse aggregation as is the ether; but now, having Rovolon, it will not be many thousands of years until we shall have extended our knowledge many orders farther, in both directions."

"Just how will Rovolon help you?"

"It will enable us to generate a force of the ninth magnitude-that much power is necessary to set up what you have so aptly named a zone of force-and will give us a source of fourth, fifth, and probably higher orders of rays which, if they are generated in space at all, are beyond our present reach. The zone of force is necessary to shield certain items of equipment from ether vibrations; as any such vibration inside the controlling fields of force renders observation or control of the higher orders of rays impossible."

"Hm ... m, I see —I'm learning something," Seaton replied cordially. "Just as the higher-powered a radio set is, the more perfect must be its shielding?"

"Yes. Just as a trace of any gas will destroy the usefulness of your most sensitive vacuum tubes, and just as imperfect shielding will allow interfering waves to enter sensitive electrical apparatus-in that same fashion will even the slightest ether vibration interfere with the operation of the extremely sensitive fields and lenses of force which must be used in controlling forces of the higher orders."

"You haven't tested the theory of the fourth order yet, have you?"

"No, but that is unnecessary. The theory of the fourth order is not really theory at all-it is mathematical fact. Although we have never been able to generate them, we know exactly the forces you use in your ship of space, and we can tell you of some thousands of others more or less similar and also highly useful forces which you have not yet discovered, but are allowing to go to waste. We know exactly what they are, how to liberate and control them, and how to use them. In fact, in the work which we are to begin today, we shall use but little ordinary power: almost all our work will be done by fourth-order forces, liberated from copper by means of the Rovolon you have given me. But here we are at my laboratory. You already know that the best way to learn is by doing, and we shall begin at once."

* * * * *

The flier alighted upon a lawn quite similar to the one before the observatory of Orlon, and the scientist led his Earthly guest through the main entrance of the imposing structure of varicolored marble and gleaming metal and into the vast, glass-lined room that was his laboratory. Great benches lined the walls, and there were hundreds of dials, meters, tubes, transformers and other instruments, whose uses Seaton could not even guess.

Rovol first donned a suit of transparent, flexible material, of a deep golden color, instructing Seaton to do the same; explaining that much of the work would be with dangerous frequencies and with high pressures, and that the suits were not only absolute insulators against electricity, heat, and sound, but were also ray-filters proof against any harmful radiations. As each helmet was equipped with radiophones, conversation was not interfered with in the least.

Rovol took up a tiny flash-pencil, and with it deftly cut off a bit of Rovolon, almost microscopic in size. This he placed upon a great block of burnished copper, and upon it played a force. As he manipulated two levers, two more beams of force flattened out the particle of metal, spread it out over the copper, and forced it into the surface of the block until the thin coating was at every point in molecular contact with the copper beneath it—a perfect job of plating, and one done in the twinkling of an eye. He then cut out a piece of the treated copper the size of a pea, and other forces rapidly built around it a structure of coils and metallic tubes. This apparatus he suspended in the air at the extremity of a small beam of force. The block of copper was next cut in two, and Rovol's fingers moved rapidly over the keys of a machine which resembled slightly an overgrown and exceedingly complicated book-keeping machine. Streams and pencils of force flashed and crackled, and Seaton saw raw materials transformed into a complete power-plant, in its center the two-hundred-pound lump of plated copper, where an instant before there had been only empty space upon the massive metal bench. Rovol's hands moved rapidly from keys to dials and back, and suddenly a zone of force, as large as a basketball appeared around the apparatus poised in the air.

"But it'll fly off and we can't stop it with anything," Seaton protested, and it did indeed dart rapidly upward.

The old man shook his head as he manipulated still more controls, and Seaton gasped as nine stupendous beams of force hurled themselves upon that brilliant spherical mirror of pure energy, seized it in mid-flight, and shaped it resistlessly, under his bulging eyes, into a complex geometrical figure of precisely the desired form.

Lurid violet light filled the room, and Seaton turned towards the bar. That two-hundred-pound mass of copper was shrinking visibly, second by second, so vast were the forces being drawn from it, and the searing, blinding light would have been intolerable but for the protective color-filters of his helmet. Tremendous flashes of lightning ripped and tore from the relief-points of the bench to the ground-rods, which flared at blue-white temperature under the incessant impacts. Knowing that this corona-loss was but an infinitesimal fraction of the power being used, Seaton's very mind staggered as he strove to understand the magnitude of the forces at work upon that stubborn sphere of energy.

The aged scientist used no tools whatever, as we understand the term. His laboratory was a power-house; at his command were the stupendous forces of a battery of planetoid accumulators, and added to these were the fourth-order, ninth-magnitude forces of the disintegrating copper bar. Electricity, protelectricity, and fourth-order rays, under millions upon millions of kilovolts of pressure, leaped to do the bidding of that wonderful brain, stored with the accumulated knowledge of countless thousands of years of scientific research. Watching the ancient physicist work, Seaton compared himself to a schoolboy mixing chemicals indiscriminately and ignorantly, with no knowledge whatever of their properties, occasionally obtaining a reaction by pure chance. Whereas he had worked with intra-atomic energy schoolboy fashion, the master craftsman before him knew every reagent, every reaction, and worked with known and thoroughly familiar agencies to bring about his exactly predetermined ends-just as calmly certain of the results as Seaton himself would have been in his own laboratory, mixing equivalent quantities of solutions of barium chloride and of sulphuric acid to obtain a precipitate of barium sulphate.

Hour after hour Rovol labored on, oblivious to the passage of time in his zeal of accomplishment, the while carefully instructing Seaton, who watched every step with intense interest and did everything possible for him to do. Bit by bit a towering structure arose in the middle of the laboratory. A metal foundation supported a massive compound bearing, which in turn carried a tubular network of latticed metal, mounted like an immense telescope. Near the upper, outer end of this openwork tube a group of nine forces held the field of force rigidly in place in its axis; at the lower extremity were mounted seats for two operators and the control panels necessary for the operation of the intricate system of forces and motors which would actuate and control that gigantic projector. Immense hour and declination circles could be read by optical systems from the operators' seats-circles fully forty feet in diameter, graduated with incredible delicacy and accuracy into decimal fractions of seconds of arc, and each driven by variable-speed motors through gear-trains and connections having no backlash whatever.

While Rovol was working upon one of the last instruments to be installed upon the controlling panel a mellow note sounded throughout the building, and he immediately ceased his labors and opened the master-switches of his power plants.

"You have done well, youngster," he congratulated his helper, as he began to take off his protective covering, "Without your aid I could not have accomplished nearly this much during one period of labor. The periods of exercise and of relaxation are at hand-let us return to the house of Orlon, where we all shall gather to relax and to refresh ourselves for the labors of tomorrow."

"But it's almost done!" protested Seaton. "Let's finish it up and shoot a little juice through it, just to try it out."

"There speaks the rashness and impatience of youth," rejoined the scientist, calmly removing the younger man's suit and leading him out to the waiting airboat. "I read in your mind that you are often guilty of laboring continuously until your brain loses its keen edge. Learn now, once and for all, that such conduct is worse than foolish-it is criminal. We have labored the full period. Laboring for more than that length of time without recuperation results in a loss of power which, if persisted in, wreaks permanent injury to the mind; and by it you gain nothing. We have more than ample time to do that which must be done-the fifth-order projector shall be completed before the warning torpedo shall have reached the planet of the Fenachrone-therefore over-exertion is unwarranted. As for testing, know now that only mechanisms built by bunglers require testing. Properly built machines work properly."

"But I'd have liked to see it work just once, anyway," lamented Seaton as the small airship tore through the air on its way back to the observatory.

"You must cultivate calmness, my son, and the art of relaxation. With those qualities your race can easily double its present span of useful life. Physical exercise to maintain the bodily tissues at their best, and mental relaxation following mental toil-these things are the secrets of a long and productive life. Why attempt to do more than can be accomplished efficiently? There is always tomorrow. I am more interested in that which we are now building than you can possibly be, since many generations of the Rovol have anticipated its construction; yet I realize that in the interest of our welfare and for the progress of civilization, today's labors must not be prolonged beyond today's period of work. Furthermore, you yourself realize that there is no optimum point at which any task may be interrupted. Short of final completion of any project, one point is the same as any other. Had we continued, we would have wished to continue still farther, and so on without end."

"You're probably right, at that," the impetuous chemist conceded, as their craft came to earth before the observatory.

Crane and Orlon were already in the common room, as were the scientists Seaton already knew, as well as a group of women and children still strangers to the Terrestrials. In a few minutes Orlon's companion, a dignified, white-haired woman, entered; accompanied by Dorothy,

Margaret, and a laughing, boisterous group of men and women from the Country of Youth. Introductions over, Seaton turned to Crane.

"How's every little thing, Mart?"

"Very well indeed. We are building an observatory in space-or rather, Orlon is building it and I am doing what little I can to help him. In a few days we shall be able to locate the system of the Fenachrone. How is your work progressing?"

"Smoother than a kitten's ear. Got the fourth-order projector about done. We're going to project a fourth-order force out to grab us some dense material, a pretty close approach to pure neutronium. There's nothing dense enough around here, even in the core of the central sun, so we're going out to a white dwarf star-one a good deal like the companion star to Sirius in Canis Major-get some material of the proper density from its core, and convert our sender into a fifth-order machine. Then we can really get busy-go places and do things."

"Neutronium? Pure mass?" queried Crane, "I have been under the impression that it does not exist. Of what use can such a substance be to you?"

"Can't get pure neutronium, of course-couldn't use it if we could. What we need and are going to get is a material of about two and a half million specific gravity. Got to have it for lenses and controls for the fifth-order forces. Those rays go right through anything less dense without measurable refraction. But I see Rovol's giving me a nasty look. He's my boss on this job, and I imagine this kind of talk's barred during the period of relaxation, as being work. That so, chief?"

"You know that it is barred, you incorrigible young cub!" answered Rovol, with a smile.

"All right, boss; one more little infraction and I'll shut up like a clam. I'd like to know what the girls have been doing."

"We've been having a wonderful time!" Dorothy declared. "We've been designing fabrics and ornaments and jewels and things. Wait 'til you see 'em!"

"Fine! All right, Orlon, it's your party-what to do?"

"This is the time of exercise. We have many forms, most of which are unfamiliar to you. You all swim, however, and as that is one of the best of exercises, I suggest that we all swim."

"Lead us to it!" Seaton exclaimed, then his voice changed abruptly. "Wait a minute —I don't know about our swimming in copper sulphate solution."

"We swim in fresh water as often as in salt, and the pool is now filled with distilled water."

The Terrestrials quickly donned their bathing suits and all went through the observatory and down a winding path, bordered with the peculiarly beautiful scarlet and green shrubbery, to the "pool" —an artificial lake covering a hundred acres, its polished metal bottom and sides strikingly decorated with jewels and glittering tiles in tasteful yet contrasting inlaid designs. Any desired depth of water was available and plainly marked, from the fenced-off shallows where the smallest children splashed to the forty feet of liquid crystal which received the diver who cared to try his skill from one of the many spring-boards, flying rings, and catapults which rose high into the air a short distance away from the entrance.

Orlon and the others of the older generation plunged into the water without ado and struck out for the other shore, using a fast double-overarm stroke. Swimming in a wide circle they came out upon the apparatus and went through a series of methodical dives and gymnastic performances. It was evident that they swam, as Orlon had intimated, for exercise. To them, exercise was a necessary form of labor-labor which they performed thoroughly and well-but nothing to call forth the whole-souled enthusiasm they displayed in their chosen fields of mental effort.

The visitors from the Country of Youth, however, locked arms and sprang to surround the four Terrestrials, crying, "Let's do a group dive!"

"I don't believe that I can swim well enough to enjoy what's coming," whispered Margaret to Crane, and they slipped into the pool and turned around to watch. Seaton and Dorothy, both strong swimmers, locked arms and laughed as they were encircled by the green phalanx and swept out to the end of a dock-like structure and upon a catapult.

"Hold tight, everybody!" someone yelled, and interlaced, straining arms and legs held the green and white bodies in one motionless group as a gigantic force hurled them fifty feet into the air and out over the deepest part of the pool. There was a mighty splash and a miniature tidal wave as that mass of humanity struck the water. Many feet they went down before the cordon was broken and the individual units came to the surface. Then pandemonium reigned. Vigorous informal games, having to do with floating and sinking balls and effigies: pushball, in which the players never seemed to know, or to care, upon which side they were playing; water-fights and ducking contests.... A green mermaid, having felt the incredible power of Seaton's arms as he tossed her lightly away from a goal he was temporarily defending, put both her small hands around his biceps wonderingly, amazed at a strength unknown and impossible upon her world; then playfully tried to push him under. Failing, she called for help.

"He's needed a good ducking for ages!" Dorothy cried, and she and several other girls threw themselves upon him. Over and around him the lithe forms flashed, while the rest of the young people splashed water impartially over all the combatants and cheered them on. In the midst of the battle the signal sounded to end the period of exercise.

"Saved by the bell," Seaton laughed as, thoroughly ducked and almost half drowned, he was allowed to swim ashore.

When all had returned to the common room of the observatory and had seated themselves, Orlon took out his miniature ray-projector, no larger than a fountain pen, and flashed it briefly upon one of the hundreds of button-like lenses upon the wall. Instantly each chair converted itself into a form-fitting divan, inviting complete repose.

"I believe that you of Earth would perhaps enjoy some of our music during this, the period of relaxation and repose-it is so different from your own," Orlon remarked, as he again manipulated his tiny force-tube.

Every light was extinguished and there was felt a profoundly deep vibration—a note so low as to be palpable rather than audible; and simultaneously the utter darkness was relieved by a tinge of red so dark as to be barely perceptible, while a peculiar somber fragrance pervaded the atmosphere. The music rapidly ran the gamut to the limit of audibility and, in the same tempo, the lights traversed the visible spectrum and disappeared. Then came a crashing chord and a vivid flare of blended light; ushering in an indescribable symphony of sound and color, accompanied by a slower succession of shifting, blending odors.

The quality of tone was now that of a gigantic orchestra, now that of a full brass band, now that of a single unknown instrument-as though the composer had had at his command every overtone capable of being produced by any possible instrument, and with them had woven a veritable tapestry of melody upon an incredibly complex loom of sound. As went the harmony, so the play of light accompanied it. Neither music nor illumination came from any apparent source; they simply pervaded the entire room. When the music was fast-and certain passages were of a rapidity impossible for any human fingers to attain-the lights flashed in vivid, tiny pencils, intersecting each other in sharply drawn, brilliant figures, which changed with dizzying speed; when the tempo was slow, the beams were soft and broad, blending into each other to form sinuous, indefinite, writhing patterns, whose very vagueness was infinitely soothing.

"What do you think of it, Mrs. Seaton?" Orlon asked.

"Marvelous!" breathed Dorothy, awed. "I never imagined anything like it. I can't begin to tell you how much I like it. I never dreamed of such absolute perfection of execution, and the way the lighting accompanies the theme is just too perfectly wonderful for words! It was incredibly brilliant."

"Brilliant-yes. Perfectly executed-yes. But I notice that you say nothing of depth of feeling or of emotional appeal." Dorothy blushed uncomfortably and started to say something, but Orlon silenced her and continued: "You need not apologize. I had a reason for speaking as I did, for in you I recognize a real musician, and our music is indeed entirely soulless. That is the result of our ancient civilization. We are so old that our music is purely intellectual, entirely mechanical, instead of emotional. It is perfect, but, like most of our other arts, it is almost completely without feeling."

"But your statues are wonderful!"

"As I told you, those statues were made myriads of years ago. At that time we also had real music, but, unlike statuary, music at that time could not be preserved for posterity. That is another thing you have given us. Attend!"

At one end of the room, as upon a three-dimensional screen, the four Terrestrials saw themselves seated in the control-room of the *Skylark*. They saw and heard Margaret take up her guitar, and strike four sonorous chords in "A." Then, as if they had been there in person, they heard themselves sing "The Bull-Frog" and all the other songs they had sung, far off in space. They heard Margaret suggest that Dorothy play some "real music," and heard Seaton's comments upon the quartette.

"In that, youngster, you were entirely wrong," said Orlon, stopping the reproduction for a moment. "The entire planet was listening to you very attentively-we were enjoying it as no music has been enjoyed for thousands of years."

"The whole planet!" gasped Margaret. "Were you broadcasting it? How could you?"

"Easy," grinned Seaton. "They can do most anything with these rays of theirs."

"When you have time, in some period of labor, we would appreciate it very much if you four would sing for us again, would give us more of your vast store of youthful music, for we can now preserve it exactly as it is sung. But much as we enjoyed the quartette, Mrs. Seaton, it was your work upon the violin that took us by storm. Beginning with tomorrow, my companion intends to have you spend as many periods as you will, playing for our records. We shall now have your music."

"If you like it so well, wouldn't you rather I'd play you something I hadn't played before?"

"That is labor. We could not...."

"Piffle!" Dorothy interrupted. "Don't you see that I could really play right now, with somebody to listen, who really enjoys music; whereas, if I tried to play in front of a record, I'd be perfectly mechanical?"

"At-a-girl, Dot! I'll get your fiddle."

"Keep your seat, son," instructed Orlon, as the case containing the Stradivarius appeared before Dorothy, borne by a pencil of force. "While that temperament is incomprehensible to every one of us, it is undoubtedly true that the artistic mind does work in that manner. We listen."

Dorothy swept into "The Melody in F," and as the poignantly beautiful strains poured forth from that wonderful violin, she knew that she had her audience with her. Though so intellectual that they themselves were incapable of producing music of real depth of feeling, they could understand and could enjoy such music with an appreciation impossible to a people of lesser mental attainments; and their profound enjoyment of her playing, burned into her mind by the telepathic, almost hypnotic power of the Norlaminian mentality, raised her to heights of power she had never before attained. Playing as one inspired, she went through one tremendous solo after another-holding her listeners spellbound, urged on by their intense feeling to carry them further and ever further into the realm of pure emotional harmony. The bell which ordinarily signaled the end of the period of relaxation did not sound; for the first time in thousands of years the planet of Norlamin deserted its rigid schedule of life-to listen to one Earth-woman, pouring out her very soul upon her incomparable violin.

The final note of "Memories" died away in a diminuendo wail, and the musician almost collapsed into Seaton's arms. The profound silence, more impressive far than any possible applause, was soon broken by Dorothy.

"There —I'm all right now, Dick. I was about out of control for a minute. I wish they could have had that on a recorder —I'll never be able to play like that again if I live to be a thousand years old."

"It is on record, daughter. Every note and every inflection is preserved, precisely as you played it," Orlon assured her. "That is our only excuse for allowing you to continue as you did, almost to the point of exhaustion. While we cannot really understand an artistic mind of the peculiar type to which yours belongs, yet we realized that each time you play you are doing something that no one, not even yourself, can ever do again in precisely the same subtle fashion. Therefore we allowed, in fact encouraged, you to go on as long as that creative impulse should endure-not merely for our pleasure in hearing it, great though that pleasure was, but in the hope that our workers in music could, by a careful analysis of your product, determine quantitatively the exact vibrations or overtones which make the difference between emotional and intellectual music."

CHAPTER XI

Into a Sun

As Rovol and Seaton approached the physics laboratory at the beginning of the period of labor, another small airboat occupied by one man drew up beside them and followed them to the ground. The stranger, another white-bearded ancient, greeted Rovol cordially and was introduced to Seaton as "Caslor, the First of Mechanism."

"Truly, this is a high point in the course of Norlaminian science, my young friend," Caslor acknowledged the introduction smilingly. "You have enabled us to put into practice many things which our ancestors studied in theory for many a wearisome cycle of time." Turning to Rovol, he went on: "I understand that you require a particularly precise directional mechanism? I know well that it must indeed be one of exceeding precision and delicacy, for the controls you yourself have built are able to hold upon any point, however moving, within the limits of our immediate solar system."

"We require controls a million times as delicate as any I have constructed," said Rovol, "therefore I have called your surpassing skill into co-operation. It is senseless for me to attempt a task in which I would be doomed to failure. We intend to send out a fifth-order projection, something none of our ancestors ever even dreamed of, which, with its inconceivable velocity of propagation, will enable us to explore any region in the galaxy as quickly as we now visit our closest sister planet. Knowing the dimensions of this, our galaxy, you can readily understand the exact degree of precision required to hold upon a point at its outermost edge."

"Truly, a problem worthy of any man's brain," Caslor replied after a moment's thought. "Those small circles," pointing to the forty-foot hour and declination circles which Seaton had thought the ultimate in precise measurement of angular magnitudes, "are of course useless. I shall have to construct large and accurate circles, and in order to produce the slow and fast motions of the required nature, without creep, slip, play, or backlash, I shall require a pure torque, capable of being increased by infinitesimal increments.... Pure torque."

He thought deeply for a time, then went on: "No gear-train or chain mechanism can be built of sufficient tightness, since in any mechanism there is some freedom of motion, however slight, and for this purpose the director must have no freedom of motion whatever. We must have a pure torque-and the only possible force answering our requirements is the four hundred sixty-seventh band of the fourth order. I shall therefore be compelled to develop that band. The director must, of course, have a full equatorial mounting, with circles some two hundred and fifty feet in diameter. Must your projector tube be longer than that, for correct design?"

"That length will be ample."

"The mounting must be capable of rotation through the full circle of arc in either plane, and must be driven in precisely the motion required to neutralize the motion of our planet, which, as you know, is somewhat irregular. Additional fast and slow motions must, of course, be provided to rotate the mechanism upon each graduated circle at the will of the operator. It is my idea to make the outer supporting tube quite large, so that you will have full freedom with your inner, or projector tube proper. It seems to me that dimensions X37 B42 J867 would perhaps be as good as any."

"Perfectly satisfactory. You have the apparatus well in mind."

"These things will consume some time. How soon will you require this mechanism?" asked Caslor.

"We also have much to do. Two periods of labor, let us say: or, if you require them, three."

"It is well. Two periods will be ample time: I was afraid that you might need it today, and the work cannot be accomplished in one period of labor. The mounting will, of course, be prepared in the Area of Experiment. Farewell."

"You aren't going to build the final projector here, then?" Seaton asked as Caslor's flier disappeared.

"We shall build it here, then transport it to the Area, where its dirigible housing will be ready to receive it. All mechanisms of that type are set up there. Not only is the location convenient to all interested, but there are to be found all necessary tools, equipment and material. Also, and not least important for such long-range work as we contemplate, the entire Area of Experiment is anchored immovably to the solid crust of the planet, so that there can be not even the slightest vibration to affect the direction of our beams of force, which must, of course, be very long."

He closed the master switches of his power-plants and the two resumed work where they had left off. The control panel was soon finished. Rovol then plated an immense cylinder of copper and placed it in the power-plant. He next set up an entirely new system of refractory relief-points and installed additional ground-rods, sealed through the floor and extending deep into the ground below, explaining as he worked.

"You see, son, we must lose one one-thousandth of one per cent of our total energy, and provision must be made for its dissipation in order to avoid destruction of the laboratory. These air-gap resistances are the simplest means of disposing of the wasted power."

"I get you-but say, how about disposing of it when we get the thing in a ship out in space? We picked up pretty heavy charges in the *Skylark* —so heavy that I had to hold up several times in the ionized layer of an atmosphere while they faded-and this outfit will burn up tons of copper where the old ones used ounces."

"In the projected space-vessel we shall install converters to utilize all the energy, so that there will be no loss whatever. Since such converters must be designed and built especially for each installation, and since they require a high degree of precision, it is not worth while to construct them for a purely temporary mechanism, such as this one."

The walls of the laboratory were opened, ventilating blowers were built, and refrigerating coils were set up everywhere, even in the tubular structure and behind the visiplates. After assuring themselves that everything combustible had been removed, the two scientists put on under their helmets, goggles whose protecting lenses could be built up to any desired thickness. Rovol then threw a switch, and a hemisphere of flaming golden radiance surrounded the laboratory and extended for miles upon all sides.

"I get most of the stuff you've pulled so far, but why such a light?" asked Seaton.

"As a warning. This entire area will be filled with dangerous frequencies, and that light is a warning for all uninsulated persons to give our theater of operations a wide berth."

"I see. What next?"

"All that remains to be done is to take our lens-material and go," replied Rovol, as he took from a cupboard the largest faidon that Seaton had ever seen.

"Oh, that's what you're going to use! You know, I've been wondering about that stuff. I took one back with me to the Earth to experiment on. I gave it everything I could think of and couldn't touch it. I couldn't even make it change its temperature. What is it, anyway?"

"It is not matter at all, in the ordinary sense of the word. It is almost pure crystallized energy. You have, of course, noticed that it looks transparent, but that it is not. You cannot see into its substance a millionth of a micron-the illusion of transparency being purely a surface phenomenon, and peculiar to this one form of substance. I have told you that the ether is a fourth-order substance-this also is a fourth-order substance, but it is crystalline, whereas the ether is probably fluid and amorphous. You might call this faidon crystallized ether without being far wrong."

"But it should weigh tons, and it is hardly heavier than air-or no, wait a minute. Gravitation is also a fourth-order phenomenon, so it might not weigh anything at all-but it would have terrific mass-or would it, not having protons? Crystallized ether would displace fluid ether, so it might —I'll give up! It's too deep for me!" said Seaton.

"Its theory is abstruse, and I cannot explain it to you any more fully than I have, until after we have given you a knowledge of the fourth and fifth orders. Pure fourth-order material would be without weight and without mass; but these crystals as they are found are not absolutely pure. In crystallizing from the magma, they entrapped sufficient numbers of particles of the higher orders to give them the characteristics which you have observed. The impurities, however, are not sufficient in quantity to offer a point of attack to any ordinary reagent."

"But how could such material possibly be formed?"

"It could be formed only in some such gigantic cosmic body as this, our green system, formed incalculable ages ago, when all the mass comprising it existed as one colossal sun. Picture for yourself the condition in the center of that sun. It has attained the theoretical maximum of temperature-some seventy million of your centigrade degrees-the electrons have been stripped from the protons until the entire central core is one solid ball of neutronium and can be compressed no more without destruction of the protons themselves. Still the pressure increases. The temperature, already at the theoretical maximum, can no longer increase. What happens?"

"Disruption."

"Precisely. And just at the instant of disruption, during the very instant of generation of the frightful forces that are to hurl suns, planets and satellites millions of miles out into space-in that instant of time, as a result of those unimaginable temperatures and pressures, the faidon comes into being. It can be formed only by the absolute maximum of temperature and at a pressure which can exist only momentarily, even in the largest conceivable masses."

"Then how can you make a lens of it? It must be impossible to work it in any way."

"It cannot be worked in any ordinary way, but we shall take this crystal into the depths of that white dwarf star, into a region in which obtain pressures and temperatures only less than those giving it birth. There we shall play forces upon it which, under those conditions, will be able to work it quite readily."

"Hm —m —m. I want to see that! Let's go!"

They seated themselves at the panels, and Rovol began to manipulate keys, levers and dials. Instantly a complex structure of visible force-rods, beams and flat areas of flaming scarlet energy-appeared at the end of the tubular, telescope-like network.

"Why red?"

"Merely to render them visible. One cannot work well with invisible tools, hence I have imposed a colored light frequency upon the invisible frequencies of the forces. We will have an assortment of colors if you prefer," and as he spoke each ray assumed a different color, so that the end of the projector was almost lost beneath a riot of color.

The structure of force, which Seaton knew was the secondary projector, swung around as if sentient, and a lurid green ray extended itself, picked up the faidon, and lengthened out, hurling the jewel a thousand yards out through the open side of the laboratory. Rovol moved more controls and the structure again righted itself, swinging back into perfect alignment with the tube and carrying the faidon upon its extremity, a thousand yards beyond the roof of the laboratory.

"We are now ready to start our projection. Be sure your suit and goggles are perfectly tight. We must see what we are doing, so the light-rays must be heterodyned upon our carrier wave. Therefore the laboratory and all its neighborhood will be flooded with dangerous frequencies from the sun we are to visit, as well as with those from our own generators."

"O. K., chief! All tight here. You say it's ten light-years to that star. How long's it going to take us to get there?"

"About ten minutes. We could travel that far in less than ten seconds but for the fact that we must take the faidon with us. Slight as is its mass, it will require much energy in its acceleration. Our projections, of course, have no mass, and will require only the energy of propagation."

Rovol flicked a finger, a massive pair of plunger switches shot into their sockets, and Seaton, seated at his board and staring into his visiplate, was astounded to find that he apparently possessed a dual personality. He *knew* that he was seated motionless in the operator's chair in the base of the rigidly anchored primary projector, and by taking his eyes away from the visiplate before him, he could see that nothing in the laboratory had changed, except that the pyrotechnic display from the power-bar was of unusual intensity. Yet, looking into the visiplate, he was out in space *in person*, hurtling through space at a pace beside which the best effort of the *Skylark* seemed the veriest crawl. Swinging his controls to look backward, he gasped as he saw, so stupendous was their velocity, that the green system was only barely discernible as a faint green star!

Again looking forward, it seemed as though a fierce white star had separated from the immovable firmament and was now so close to the structure of force in which he was riding that it was already showing a disk perceptible to the unaided eye. A few moments more and the violet-white splendor became so intense that the watchers began to build up, layer by layer, the protective goggles before their eyes. As they approached still closer, falling with their unthinkable velocity into that incandescent inferno, a sight was revealed to their eyes such as man had never before been privileged to gaze upon. They were falling into a white dwarf star, could see everything visible during such an unheard-of journey, and would live to remember what they had seen! They saw the magnificent spectacle of solar prominences shooting hundreds of thousands of miles into space, and directly in their path they saw an immense sunspot, a combined volcanic eruption and cyclonic storm in a gaseous-liquid medium of blinding incandescence.

"Better dodge that spot, hadn't we, ace? Mightn't it be generating interfering fourth-order frequencies?" cried Seaton.

"It is undoubtedly generating fourth-order rays, but nothing can interfere with us, since we are controlling every component of our beam from Norlamin."

Seaton gripped his hand-rail violently and involuntarily drew himself together into the smallest possible compass as, with their awful speed unchecked, they plunged through that flaming, incandescent photosphere and on, straight down, into the unexplored, unimaginable interior of that frightful and searing orb. Through the protecting goggles, now a full four inches of that peculiar, golden, shielding metal, Seaton could see the structure of force in which he was, and could also see the faidon-in outline, as transparent diamonds are visible in equally transparent water. Their apparent motion slowed rapidly and the material about them thickened and became more and more opaque. The faidon drew back toward them until it was actually touching the projector, and eddy currents and striae became visible in the mass about them as their progress grew slower and slower.

"'Smatter? Something gone screwy?" demanded Seaton.

"Not at all, everything is working perfectly. The substance is now so dense that it is becoming opaque to rays of the fourth order, so that we are now partially displacing the medium instead of moving through it without friction. At the point where we can barely see to work; that is, when the fourth-order rays will be so retarded that they can no longer carry the heterodyned light waves without complete distortion, we shall stop automatically, as the material at that depth will have the required density to refract the fifth-order rays to the correct degree."

"How can our foundations stand it?" asked Seaton. "This stuff must be a hundred times as dense as platinum already, and we must he pushing a horrible load in going through it."

"We are exerting no force whatever upon our foundations nor upon Norlamin. The force is transmitted without loss from the power-plant in our laboratory to this secondary projector here inside the star, where it is liberated in the correct band to pull us through the mass, using all the mass ahead of us as anchorage. When we wish to return, we shall simply change the pull into a push. Ah! we are now at a standstill-now comes the most important moment of the entire project!"

All apparent motion had ceased, and Seaton could see only dimly the outlines of the faidon, now directly before his eyes. The structure of force slowly warped around until its front portion held the faidon as in a vise. Rovol pressed a lever and behind them, in the laboratory, four enormous plunger switches drove home. A plane of pure energy, flaming radiantly even in the indescribable incandescence of the core of that seething star, bisected the faidon neatly, and ten gigantic beams, five upon each half of the jewel, rapidly molded two sections of a geometrically-perfect hollow lens. The two sections were then brought together by the closing of the jaws of the mighty vise, their edges in exact alignment. Instantly the plane and the beams of energy became transformed into two terrific opposing tubes of force-vibrant, glowing tubes, whose edges in contact coincided with the almost invisible seam between the two halves of the lens.

Like a welding arc raised to the *nth* power these two immeasurable and irresistible forces met exactly in opposition—a meeting of such incredible violence that seismic disturbances occurred throughout the entire mass of that dense, violet-white star. Sunspots of unprecedented size appeared, prominences erupted to hundreds of times their normal distances, and although the two scientists deep in the core of the tormented star were unaware of what was happening upon its surface, convulsion after Titanic convulsion wracked the mighty globe, and enormous masses of molten and gaseous material were riven from it and hurled far out into space-masses which would in time become planets of that youthful and turbulent luminary.

Seaton felt his air-supply grow hot. Suddenly it became icy cold, and knowing that Rovol had energized the refrigerator system, Seaton turned away from the fascinating welding operation for a quick look around the laboratory. As he did so, he realized Rovol's vast knowledge and understood the reason for the new system of relief-points and ground-rods, as well as the necessity for the all-embracing scheme of refrigeration.

Even through the practically opaque goggles he could see that the laboratory was one mass of genuine lightning. Not only from the relief-points, but from every metallic corner and protuberance the pent-up losses from the disintegrating bar were hurling themselves upon the flaring, blue-white, rapidly-volatilizing ground-rods; and the very air of the room, renewed second by second though it was by the powerful blowers, was beginning to take on the pearly luster of the highly-ionized corona. The bar was plainly visible, a scintillating demon of pure violet radiance, and a momentary spasm of fear seized him as he saw how rapidly that great mass of copper was shrinking-fear that their power would be exhausted with their task still uncompleted.

But the calculations of the aged physicist had been accurate. The lens was completed with some hundreds of pounds of copper to spare, and that geometrical form, with its precious content of semi-neutronium, was following the secondary projector back toward the green system. Rovol left his seat, discarded his armor, and signaled Seaton to do the same.

"I've got to hand it to you, ace-you sure are a blinding flash and a deafening report!" Seaton exclaimed, writhing out of his insulating suit. "I feel as though I'd been pulled half-way through a knot-hole and riveted over on both ends! How big a lens did you make, anyway? Looked as though it would hold a couple of liters; maybe three."

"Its contents are almost exactly three liters."

"Hm—m—m. Seven and a half million kilograms-say eight thousand tons. *Some* mass, I'd say, to put into a gallon jug. Of course, being inside the faidon, it won't have any weight, but it'll have all its full quota of inertia. That's why you're taking so long to bring it in, of course."

"Yes. The projector will now bring it here into the laboratory without any further attention from us. The period of labor is about to end, and tomorrow we shall find the lens awaiting us when we arrive to begin work."

"How about cooling it off? It had a temperature of something like forty million degree centigrade before you started working on it; and when you got done with it, it was hot."

"You're forgetting again, son. Remember that the hot, dense material is entirely enclosed in an envelope impervious to all vibrations longer than those of the fifth order. You could put your hand upon it now, without receiving any sensation either of heat, or of cold."

"Yeah, that's right, too. I noticed that I could take a faidon right out of an electric arc and it wouldn't even be warm. I couldn't explain why it was, but I see now. So that stuff inside that lens will always stay as hot as it is right now! Zowie! Here's hoping she never explodes! Well, there's the bell-for once in my life, I'm all ready to quit when the whistle blows," and arm in arm the young Terrestrial chemist and the aged Norlaminian physicist strolled out to their waiting airboat.

CHAPTER XII

Flying Visits-Via Projection

"Well, what to do?" asked Seaton as he and Rovol entered the laboratory, "Tear down this fourth-order projector and tackle the big job? I see the lens is here, on schedule, so we can hop right into it."

"We shall have further use for this mechanism. We shall need at least one more lens of this dense material, and other scientists also may have need of one or two. Then, too, the new projector must be so large that it cannot be erected in this room."

As he spoke, Rovol seated himself at his control-desk and ran his fingers lightly over the keys. The entire wall of the laboratory disappeared, hundreds of beams of force darted here and there, seizing and working raw materials, and in the portal there grew up, to Seaton's amazement, a keyboard and panel installation such as the Earth-man, in his wildest moments, had never imagined. Bank upon bank of typewriter-like keys; row upon row of keys, pedals, and stops resembling somewhat those of the console of a gigantic pipe-organ; panel upon panel of meters, switches, and dials-all arranged about two deeply-cushioned chairs and within reach of their occupants.

"Whew! That looks like the combined mince-pie nightmares of a whole flock of linotype operators, pipe-organists, and hard-boiled radio hams!" exclaimed Seaton when the installation was complete. "Now that you've got it, what are you going to do with it?"

"There is not a control system in Norlamin adequate for the task we face, since the problem of the projection of rays of the fifth order has heretofore been of only academic interest. Therefore it becomes necessary to construct such a control. This mechanism will, I am confident, have a sufficiently wide range of application to perform any operation we shall require of it."

"It sure looks as though it could do almost anything, provided the man behind it knows how to play a tune on it-but if that rumble seat is for me, you'd better count me out right now. I followed you for about fifteen seconds, then lost you completely; and now I'm sunk without a trace," said Seaton.

"That is, of course, true, and is a point I was careless enough to overlook." Rovol thought for a moment, then got up, crossed the room to his control desk, and continued, "We shall dismantle the machine and rebuild it at once."

"Oh no-too much work!" protested Seaton, "You've got it about done, haven't you?"

"It is hardly started. Two hundred thousand bands of force must be linked to it, each in its proper place, and it is necessary that you should understand thoroughly every detail of this entire projector," Rovol answered.

"Why? I'm not ashamed to admit that I haven't got brains enough to understand a thing like that."

"You have sufficient brain capacity; it is merely undeveloped. There are two reasons why you must be as familiar with the operation of this mechanism as you are with the operation of one of your Earthly automobiles. The first is that a similar control is to be installed in your new space-vessel, since by its use you can attain a perfection of handling impossible by any other system. The second, and more important reason, is that neither I nor any other man of Norlamin could compel himself, by any force of will, to direct a ray that would take away the life of any fellow-man."

While Rovol was speaking, he reversed his rays, and soon the component parts of the new control had been disassembled and piled in orderly array about the room.

"Hm —m —m. Never thought of that. It's right too," mused Seaton. "How're you going to get it into my thick skull-with an educator?"

"Exactly," and Rovol sent a beam of force after his highly developed educational mechanism. Dials and electrodes were adjusted, connections were established, and the beams and pencils of force began to reconstruct the great central controlling device. But this time, instead of being merely a bewildered spectator, Seaton was an active participant in the work. As each key and meter was wrought and mounted, there were indelibly impressed upon his brain the exact reason for and function of the part, and later, when the control itself was finished and the seemingly interminable task of connecting it up to the output force-bands of the transformers had begun, he had a complete understanding of everything with which he was working, and understood all the means by which the ends he had so long desired were to be attained. For to the ancient scientist the tasks he was then performing were the merest routine, to be performed in reflex fashion, and he devoted most of his attention to transferring from his own brain to that of his young assistant as much of his stupendous knowledge as the smaller brain of the Terrestrial was capable of absorbing. More and more rapidly as the work progressed the mighty flood of knowledge poured into Seaton's mind. After an hour or so, when enough connections had been made so that automatic forces could be so directed as to finish the job, Rovol and Seaton left the laboratory and went into the living room. As they walked, the educator accompanied them, borne upon its beam of force.

"Your brain is behaving very nicely indeed," said Rovol, "much better than I would have thought possible from its size. In fact, it may be possible for me to transfer to you all the knowledge I have which might be of use to you. That is why I took you away from the laboratory. What do you think of the idea?"

"Our psychologists have always maintained that none of us ever uses more than a minute fraction of the actual capacity of his brain," Seaton replied after a moment's thought. "If you think you can give me even a percentage of your knowledge without killing me, go to it—I'm for it, strong!"

"Knowing that you would be, I have already requested Drasnik, the First of Psychology, to come here, and he has just arrived," answered Rovol. And as he spoke, that personage entered the room.

When the facts had been set before him, the psychologist nodded his head

"That is quite possible," he said with enthusiasm, "and I will be only too glad to assist in such an operation."

"But listen!" protested Seaton, "You'll probably change my whole personality! Rovol's brain is three times the size of mine."

"Tut-tut—nothing of the kind," Drasnik reproved him. "As you have said, you are using only a minute portion of the active mass of your brain. The same thing is true with us-many millions of cycles would have to pass before we would be able to fill the brains we now have."

"Then why are your brains so large?"

"Merely a provision of Nature that no possible accession of knowledge shall find her storehouse too small," replied Drasnik, positively. "Ready?"

All three donned the headsets and a wave of mental force swept into Seaton's mind, a wave of such power that the Terrestrial's every sense wilted under the impact. He did not faint, he did not lose consciousness-he simply lost all control of every nerve and fiber as his entire brain passed into the control of the immense mentality of the First of Psychology and became a purely receptive, plastic medium upon which to impress the knowledge of the aged physicist.

Hour after hour the transfer continued, Seaton lying limp as though lifeless, the two Norlaminians tense and rigid, every faculty concentrated upon the ignorant, virgin brain exposed to their gaze. Finally the operation was complete and Seaton, released from the weird, hypnotic grip of that stupendous mind, gasped, shook himself, and writhed to his feet.

"Great Cat!" he exclaimed, his eyes wide with astonishment. "I wouldn't have believed there was as much to know in the entire Universe as I know right now, and I know it as well as I ever knew elementary algebra. Thanks, fellows, a million times-but say, did you leave any open spaces for more? In one way, I seem to know less than I did before, there's so much more to find out. Can I learn anything more, or did you fill me up to capacity?"

The psychologist, who had been listening to the exuberant youth with undisguised pleasure, spoke calmly.

"The mere fact that you appreciate your comparative ignorance shows that you are still capable of learning. Your capacity to learn is greater than it ever was before, even though the waste space has been reduced. Much to our surprise, Rovol and I gave you all of his knowledge that would be of any use to you, and some of my own, and still theoretically you can add to it more than nine times the total of your present knowledge."

The psychologist departed, and Rovol and Seaton returned to the laboratory, where the forces were still merrily at work. There was nothing that could be done to hasten the connecting, and it was late in the following period of labor before they could begin the actual construction of the projector. Once started, however, it progressed with amazing rapidity. Now understanding the system, it did not seem strange to Seaton that he should merely actuate a certain combination of forces when he desired a certain operation performed; nor did it seem unusual or worthy of comment that one flick of his finger over that switchboard would send a force a distance of hundreds of miles to a factory where other forces were busily at work, to seize a hundred anglebars of transparent purple metal that were to form the backbone of the fifth-order projector. Nor did it seem peculiar that the same force, with no further instruction, should bring these hundred bars back to him, in a high loop through the atmosphere; should deposit them gently in a convenient space near the site of operations; and then should disappear as though it had never existed! With such tools as that, it was a matter of only a few hours before the projector was done —a task that would have required years of planning and building upon Earth.

Two hundred and fifty feet it towered above their heads, a tubular network of braced and latticed bars of purple metal, fifty feet in diameter at the base and tapering smoothly to a diameter of about ten feet at the top. Built of a metal thousands of times as strong and hard as steel, it was not cumbersome in appearance, and yet was strong enough to be absolutely rigid. Ten enormous supporting forces held the lens of neutronium immovable in the exact center of the upper end; at intervals down the shaft similar forces held variously-shaped lenses and prisms formed from zones of force; in the center of the bottom or floor of the towering structure was the double controlling system, with a universal visiplate facing each operator.

"Well, Rovol, that's that," remarked Seaton as the last connection was made. "What say we hop in and give the baby a ride over to the Area of Experiment? Caslor must have the mounting done, and we've got time enough left in this period to try her out."

"In a moment. I am setting the fourth-order projector to go out to the dwarf star after an additional supply of neutronium."

Seaton, knowing from the data of their first journey, that the controls could be so set as to duplicate their feat in every particular without supervision, stepped into his seat in the new controller, pressed a key, and spoke.

"Hi, Dottie, what's on your mind?"

"Nothing much," Dorothy's clear voice answered. "Got it done and can I see it?"

"Sure-sit tight and I'll send a boat after you."

As he spoke, Rovol's flier darted into the air and away; and in two minutes it returned, slowing abruptly as it landed. Dorothy stepped out, radiant, and returned Seaton's enthusiastic caresses with equal fervor before she spoke.

"Lover, I'm afraid you violated all known speed laws getting me over here. Aren't you afraid of getting pinched?"

"Nope-not here. Besides, I didn't want to keep Rovol waiting-we're all ready to go. Hop in here with me, this left-hand control's mine."

Rovol entered the tube, took his place, and waved his hand. Seaton's hands swept over the keys and the whole gigantic structure wafted into the air. Still upright, it was borne upon immense rods of force toward the Area of Experiment, which was soon reached. Covered as the Area was with fantastic equipment, there was no doubt as to their destination, for in plain sight, dominating all the lesser instruments, there rose a stupendous telescopic mounting, with an enormous hollow tube of metallic lattice-work which could be intended for nothing else than their projector. Approaching it carefully, Seaton deftly guided the projector lengthwise into that hollow receptacle and anchored it in the exact optical axis. Flashing beams of force made short work of welding the two tubes together immovably with angles and lattices of the same purple metal, the terminals of the variable-speed motors were attached to the controllers, and everything was in readiness for the first trial.

"What special instructions do we need to run it, if any?" Seaton asked of the First of Mechanism, who had lifted himself up into the projector.

"Very little. This motor governs the hour motion, that one the right ascension. The potentiometers regulate the degree of vernier action-any ratio is possible, from direct drive up to more than a hundred million complete revolutions of that graduated dial to give you one second of arc."

"Plenty fine, I'd say. Thanks a lot, ace. Whither away, Rovol-any choice?"

"Anywhere you please, son, since this is merely a try-out."

"O. K. We'll hop over and tell Dunark hello."

The tube swung around into line with that distant planet and Seaton stepped down hard, upon a pedal. Instantly they seemed infinite myriads of miles out in space, the green system barely visible as a faint green star behind them.

"Wow, that ray's fast!" exclaimed the pilot, ruefully. "I overshot about a thousand light years. We'll try again, with considerably less power," and he rearranged and reset the dials and meters before him. Adjustment after adjustment and many reductions in power had to be made before the projection ceased leaping millions of miles at a touch, but finally the operators became familiar with the new technique and the ray became manageable. Soon they were hovering above what had been Mardonal, and saw that all signs of warfare had disappeared. Slowly turning the controls, Seaton flashed the projection over the girdling Osnomian sea and guided it through the impregnable metal walls of the palace into the throne room of Roban, where they saw the Emperor, Tarnan the Karbix, and Dunark in close conference.

"Well, here we are," remarked Seaton. "Now we'll put on a little visibility and give the natives a treat."

"Sh-sh," whispered Dorothy, "they'll hear you, Dick-we're intruding shamefully."

"No, they won't hear us, because I haven't heterodyned the audio in on the wave yet. And as for intruding, that's exactly what we came over here for."

He imposed the audio system upon the inconceivably high frequency of their carrier wave and spoke in the Osnomian tongue.

"Greetings, Roban, Dunark, and Tarnan, from Seaton." All three jumped to their feet, amazed, staring about the empty room as Seaton went on, "I am not here in person. I am simply sending you my projection. Just a moment and I will put on a little visibility."

He brought more forces into play, and solid images of force appeared in the great hall; images of the three occupants of the controller. Introductions and greetings over, Seaton spoke briefly and to the point.

"We've got everything we came after-much more than I had any idea we could get. You need have no more fear of the Fenachrone-we have found a science superior to theirs. But much remains to be done, and we have none too much time; therefore I have come to you with certain requests."

"The Overlord has but to command," replied Roban.

"Not command, since we are all working together for a common cause. In the name of that cause, Dunark, I ask you to come to me at once, accompanied by Tarnan and any others you may select. You will be piloted by a ray which we shall set upon your controls. Upon your way here you will visit the First City of Dasor, another planet, where you will pick up Sacner Carfon, who will be awaiting you there."

"As you direct, so it shall be," and Seaton flashed the projector to the neighboring planet of Urvania. There he found that the gigantic space-cruiser he had ordered had been completed, and requested Urvan and his commander-in-chief to tow it to Norlamin, piloted by a ray. He then jumped to Dasor, there interviewing Carfon and being assured of the full co-operation of the porpoise-men.

"Well, that's that, folks," said Seaton as he shut off the power. "We can't do much more for a few days, until the gang gets here for the council of war. How'd it be, Rovol, for me to practice with this outfit while you are finishing up the odds and ends you want to clean up? You might suggest to Orlon, too, that it'd be a good deed for him to pilot those folks over here."

As Rovol wafted himself to the ground from their lofty station, Crane and Margaret appeared and were lifted up to the place formerly occupied by the physicist.

"How's tricks, Mart? I hear you're quite an astronomer?" said Seaton.

"Yes, thanks to Orlon and the First of Psychology. He seemed quite interested in increasing our Earthly knowledge. I certainly know much more than I had ever hoped to know of anything."

"Yeah, you can pilot us to the Fenachrone system now without any trouble. You also absorbed some ethnology and kindred sciences. What d'you think-with Dunark and Urvan, do we know enough to go ahead or should we take a chance on holding things up while we get acquainted with some of the other peoples of these planets of the green system?"

"Delay is dangerous, as our time is already short," Crane replied after a time. "We know enough, I believe; and furthermore, any additional assistance is problematical; in fact, it is more than doubtful. The Norlaminians have surveyed the system rather thoroughly, and no other planet seems to have inhabitants who have even approached the development attained here."

"Right-that's the way I dope it, exactly. We'll wait until the gang assembles, then go over the top. In the meantime, I called you over to take a ride in this projector-it's a darb. I'd like to shoot for the Fenachrone system first, but I don't quite dare to."

"Don't *dare* to? You?" scoffed Margaret. "How come?"

"Cancel the 'dare'—change it to 'prefer not to.' Why? Because while they can't work through a zone of force, some of their real scientists-and they have lots of them, not like the bull-headed soldier we captured-may well be able to detect a fifth-order ray-even if they can't work with them intelligently-and if they detected our ray, it'd put them on guard."

"You are exactly right, Dick," agreed Crane. "And there speaks the Norlaminian physicist, and not my old and reckless playmate Richard Seaton."

"Oh, I don't know—I told you I was getting timid as a mouse. But let's not sit here twiddling our thumbs-let's go places and do things. Whither away? I want a destination a good ways off, not something in our own back yard."

"Go back home, of course, stupe," put in Dorothy, "do you have to be told every little thing?"

"Sure-never thought of that," and Seaton, after a moment's rapid mental arithmetic, swung the great tube around, rapidly adjusted a few dials, and stepped down upon a pedal. There was a fleeting instant of unthinkable velocity; then they found themselves poised somewhere in space.

"Well, wonder how far I missed it on my first shot?" Seaton's crisp voice broke the stunned silence. "Guess that's our sun, over to the left, ain't it, Mart?"

"Yes. You were about right for distance, and within a few tenths of a light-year laterally. That is fairly close, I should have said."

"Rotten, for these controls. Except for the effect of relative proper motions, which I can't calculate yet for lack of data. I should be able to hit a gnat right in the left eye at this range-and the difference in proper motions couldn't have thrown me off more than a few hundred feet. Nope, I was too anxious-hurried too much on the settings of the slow verniers. I'll snap back and try it again."

He adjusted the verniers very carefully, and again threw on the power. Again there was the sensation of the barest perceptible moment of unimaginable speed, and they were in the air some fifty feet above the ground of Crane Field, almost above the testing shed. Seaton rapidly adjusted the variable-speed motors until they were perfectly stationary, relative to the surface of the earth.

"You are improving," commended Crane.

"Yeah-that's more like it. Guess maybe I can learn in time to shoot this gun. Well, let's go down."

They dropped through the roof into the laboratory where Maxwell, now in charge of the place, was watching a reaction and occasionally taking notes.

"Hi, Max! Seaton speaking, on a television. Got your range?"

"Exactly, Chief, apparently. I can hear you perfectly, but can't see anything," Maxwell stared about the empty laboratory.

"You will in a minute. I knew I had you, but didn't want to scare you out of a year's growth," and Seaton thickened the image until they were plainly visible.

"Please call Mr. Vaneman on the phone and tell him you're in touch with us," directed Seaton as soon as greetings had been exchanged. "Better yet, after you've broken it to them gently, Dot can talk to them, then we'll go over and see 'em."

The connection established, Dorothy's image floated up to the telephone and apparently spoke.

"Mother? This is the weirdest thing you ever imagined. We're not really here at all you know-we're actually here in Norlamin-no, I mean Dick's just sending a kind of a talking picture of us to see you on earth here....Oh, no, I don't know anything about it-it's like a talkie sent by radio, only worse, because I am saying this myself right now, without any rehearsal or anything...we didn't want to burst in on you without warning, because you'd be sure to think you were seeing actual ghosts, and we're not dead the least bit...we're having the most perfectly gorgeous time you ever imagined....Oh, I'm so excited I can't explain anything, even if I knew anything about it to explain. We'll all four of us be over there in about a second and tell you all about it. 'Bye!"

Indeed, it was even less than a second-Mrs. Vaneman was still in the act of hanging up the receiver when the image materialized in the living room of Dorothy's girlhood home.

"Hello, mother and dad," Seaton's voice was cheerful but matter-of-fact. "I'll thicken this up so you can see us better in a minute. But don't think that we are flesh and blood. You'll see simply three-dimensional talking pictures of ourselves, transmitted by radio."

For a long time Mr. and Mrs. Vaneman chatted with the four visitors from so far away in space, while Seaton gloried in the working of that marvelous projector.

"Well, our time's about up," Seaton finally ended the visit. "The quitting-whistle's going to blow in five minutes, and they don't like overtime work here where we are. We'll drop in and see you again maybe, sometime before we come back."

"Do you know yet when you are coming back?" asked Mrs. Vaneman.

"Not an idea in the world, mother, any more than we had when we started. But we're getting along fine, having the time of our lives, and are learning a lot besides. So-long!" and Seaton clicked off the power.

As they descended from the projector and walked toward the waiting airboat, Seaton fell in beside Rovol.

"You know they've got our new cruiser built of dagal, and are bringing it over here. Dagal's good stuff, but it isn't as good as your purple metal, inoson, which is the theoretical ultimate in strength possible for any material possessing molecular structure. Why wouldn't it be a sound idea to flash it into inoson when it gets here?"

"That would be an excellent idea, and we shall do so. It also has occurred to me that Caslor of Mechanism, Astron of Energy, Satrazon of Chemistry, myself, and one of two others, should collaborate in installing a very complete fifth-order projector in the new *Skylark*, as well as any other equipment which may seem desirable. The security of the Universe may depend upon the abilities and qualities of you Terrestrials and your vessel, and therefore *nothing* should be left undone which it is possible for us to do."

"You chirped something then, old scout-thanks. You might do that, while I attend to such preliminaries as wiping out the Fenachrone fleet."

In due time the reinforcements from the other planets arrived, and the mammoth space-cruiser attracted attention even before it landed, so enormous was she in comparison with the tiny vessels having her in tow. Resting upon the ground, it seemed absurd that such a structure could possibly move under her own power. For two miles that enormous mass of metal extended over the country-side, and while it was very narrow for its length, still its fifteen hundred feet of diameter dwarfed everything near by. But Rovol and his aged co-workers smiled happily as they saw it, erected their keyboards, and set to work with a will.

Meanwhile a group had gathered about a conference table —a group such as had never before been seen together upon any world. There was Fodan, the ancient Chief of the Five of Norlamin, huge-headed, with his leonine mane and flowing beard of white. There were Dunark and Tarnan of Osnome and Urvan of Urvania-smooth-faced and keen, utterly implacable and ruthless in war. There was Sacner Carfon Twenty Three Forty Six, the immense, porpoise-like, hairless Dasorian. There were Seaton and Crane, representatives of our own Earthly civilization.

Seaton opened the meeting by handing each man a headset and running a reel showing the plans of the Fenachrone; not only as he had secured them from the captain of the marauding vessel, but also everything the First of Psychology had deduced from his own study of that inhuman brain. He then removed the reel and gave them the tentative plans of battle. Headsets removed, he threw the meeting open for discussion-and discussion there was in plenty. Each man had ideas, which were thrown upon the table and studied, for the most part calmly and dispassionately. The conference continued until only one point was left, upon which argument waxed so hot that everyone seemed shouting at once.

"Order!" commanded Seaton, banging his fist upon the table. "Osnome and Urvania wish to strike without warning, Norlamin and Dasor insist upon a formal declaration of war. Earth has the deciding vote. Mart, how do we vote on this?"

"I vote for formal warning, for two reasons, one of which I believe will convince even Dunark. First, because it is the fair thing to do-which reason is, of course, the one actuating the Nor-laminians, but which would not be considered by Osnome, nor even remotely understood by the Fenachrone. Second, I am certain that the Fenachrone will merely be enraged by the warning and will defy us. Then what will they do? You have already said that you have been able to locate only a few of their exploring warships. As soon as we declare war upon them they will almost certainly send out torpedoes to every one of their ships of war. We can then follow the torpedoes with our rays, and thus will be enabled to find and to destroy their vessels."

"That settles that," declared the chairman as a shout of agreement arose. "We shall now adjourn to the projector and send the warning. I have a ray upon the torpedo, announcing the destruction by us of their vessel, and that torpedo will arrive at its destination in less than an hour. It seems to me that we should make our announcement immediately after their ruler has received the news of their first defeat."

In the projector, where they were joined by Rovol, Orlon, and several others of the various "Firsts" of Norlamin, they flashed out to the flying torpedo, and Seaton grinned at Crane as their fifth-order carrier beam went through the far-flung detector screens of the Fenachrone without setting up the slightest reaction. In the wake of that speeding messenger they flew through a warm, foggy, dense atmosphere, through a receiving trap in the wall of a gigantic conical structure, and on into the telegraph room. They saw the operator remove spools of tape from the torpedo and attach them to a magnetic sender-heard him speak.

"Pardon, your majesty-we have just received a first-degree emergency torpedo from flagship Y427W of fleet 42. In readiness."

"Put it on, here in the council chamber," a deep voice snapped.

"If he's broadcasting it, we're in for a spell of hunting," Seaton remarked. "Nope, he's putting it on a tight beam-that's fine, we can chase it up," and with a narrow detector beam he traced the invisible transmission beam into the council room.

"S'funny. This place seems awfully familiar —I'd swear I'd seen it before, lots of times-seems like I've been in it, more than once," Seaton remarked, puzzled, as he looked around the somber room, with its dull, paneled metal walls covered with charts, maps, screens, and speakers; and with its low, massive furniture. "Oh, sure, I'm familiar with it from studying the brain of that Fenachrone captain. Well, while His Nibs is absorbing the bad news, we'll go over this once more. You, Carfon, having the biggest voice of any of us ever heard uttering intelligible language, are to give the speech. You know about what to say. When I say 'go ahead' do your stuff. Now, everybody else, listen. While he's talking I've got to have audio waves heterodyned both ways in the circuit, and they'll be able to hear any noise any of us make-so all of us except Carfon want to keep absolutely quiet, no matter what happens or what we see. As soon as he's done I'll cut off the audio sending and say something to let you all know we're off the air. Got it?"

"One point has occurred to me about handling the warning," boomed Carfon. "If it should be delivered from apparently empty air, directly at those we wish to address, it would give the enemy an insight into our methods, which might be undesirable."

"H—m—m. Never thought of that ... it sure would, and it would be undesirable," agreed Seaton. "Let's see ... we can get away from that by broadcasting it. They have a very complete system of speakers, but no matter how many private-band speakers a man may have, he always has one on the general wave, which is used for very important announcements of wide interest. I'll broadcast you on that wave, so that every general-wave speaker on the planet will be energized. That way, it'll look as if we're shooting from a distance. You might talk accordingly."

"If we have a minute more, there's something I would like to ask," Dunark broke the ensuing silence. "Here we are, seeing everything that is happening there. Walls, planets, even suns, do not bar our vision, because of the fifth-order carrier wave. I understand that, partially. But how can we see anything there? I always thought that I knew something about rays, but I see that I do not. The light-rays must be released, or deheterodyned, close to the object viewed, with nothing opaque to light intervening. They must then be reflected from the object seen, must be gathered together, again heterodyned upon the fifth-order carrier, and retransmitted back to us. And there is neither receiver nor transmitter at the other end. How can you do all that from our end?"

"We don't," Seaton assured him. "At the other end there are all the things you mentioned, and a lot more besides. Our secondary projector out there is composed of forces, visible or invisible, as we please. Part of those forces comprise the receiving, viewing, and sending instruments. They are not material, it is true, but they are nevertheless fully as actual, and far more efficient, than any other system of radio, television, or telephone in existence anywhere else. It is force, you know, that makes radio or television work-the actual copper, insulation, and other matter serve only to guide and to control the various forces employed. The Norlaminian scientists have found out how to direct and control pure forces without using the cumbersome and hindering material substance...."

He broke off as the record from the torpedo stopped suddenly and the operator's voice came through a speaker.

"General Fenimol! Scoutship K3296, patrolling the detector zone, wishes to give you an urgent emergency report. I told them that you were in council with the Emperor, and they instructed me to interrupt it, no matter how important the council may be. They have on board a survivor of the Y427W, and have captured and killed two men of the same race as those who destroyed our vessel. They say that you will want their report without an instant's delay."

"We do!" barked the general, at a sign from his ruler. "Put it on here. Run the rest of the torpedo report immediately afterward."

In the projector, Seaton stared at Crane a moment, then a light of understanding spread over his features.

"DuQuesne, of course —I'll bet a hat no other Terrestrial is this far from home. I can't help feeling sorry for the poor devil-he's a darn good man gone wrong-but we'd have had to kill him ourselves before we got done with him; so it's probably as well they got him. Pin your ears back, everybody, and watch close-we want to get this, all of it."

CHAPTER XIII

The Declaration of War

The capital city of the Fenachrone lay in a jungle plain surrounded by towering hills. A perfect circle of immense diameter, its buildings of uniform height, of identical design, and constructed of the same dull gray, translucent metal, were arranged in concentric circles, like the annular rings seen upon the stump of a tree. Between each ring of buildings and the one next inside it there were lagoons, lawns and groves-lagoons of tepid, sullenly-steaming water; lawns which were veritable carpets of lush, rank rushes and of dank mosses; groves of palms, gigantic ferns, bamboos, and numerous tropical growths unknown to Earthly botany. At the very edge of the city began jungle unrelieved and primeval; the impenetrable, unconquerable jungle, possible only to such meteorological conditions as obtained there. Wind there was none, nor sunshine. Only occasionally was the sun of that reeking world visible through the omnipresent fog, a pale, wan disk; always the atmosphere was one of oppressive, hot, humid vapor. In the exact center of the city rose an immense structure, a terraced cone of buildings, as though immense disks of smaller and smaller diameter had been piled one upon the other. In these apartments dwelt the nobility and the high officials of the Fenachrone. In the highest disk of all, invisible always from the surface of the planet because of the all-enshrouding mist, were the apartments of the Emperor of that monstrous race.

Seated upon low, heavily-built metal stools about the great table in the council-room were Fenor, Emperor of the Fenachrone; Fenimol, his General-in-Command, and the full Council of Eleven of the planet. Being projected in the air before them was a three-dimensional moving, talking picture-the report of the sole survivor of the warship that had attacked the *Skylark II*. In exact accordance with the facts as the engineer knew them, the details of the battle and complete information concerning the conquerors were shown. As vividly as though the scene were being re-enacted before their eyes they saw the captive revive in the *Violet*, and heard the conversation between the engineer, DuQuesne, and Loring.

In the *Violet* they sped for days and weeks, with ever-mounting velocity, toward the system of the Fenachrone. Finally, power reversed, they approached it, saw the planet looming large, and passed within the detector screen.

DuQuesne tightened the controls of the attractors, which had never been entirely released from their prisoner, thus again pinning the Fenachrone helplessly against the wall.

"Just to be sure you don't try to start something," he explained coldly. "You have done well so far, but I'll run things myself from now on, so that you can't steer us into a trap. Now tell me exactly how to go about getting one of your vessels. After we get it, I'll see about letting you go."

"Fools, you are too late! You would have been too late, even had you killed me out there in space and had fled at your utmost acceleration. Did you but know it, you are as dead, even now-our patrol is upon you!"

DuQuesne whirled, snarling, and his automatic and that of Loring were leaping out when an awful acceleration threw them flat upon the floor, a magnetic force snatched away their weapons, and a heat-ray reduced them to two small piles of gray ash. Immediately thereafter a beam of force from the patrolling cruiser neutralized the retractors bearing upon the captive, and he was transferred to the rescuing vessel.

The emergency report ended, and with a brief "Torpedo message from flagship Y427W resumed at point of interruption," the report from the ill-fated vessel continued the story of its own destruction, but added little in the already complete knowledge of the disaster.

Fenor of the Fenachrone leaped up from the table, his terrible, flame-shot eyes glaring venomously-teetering in Berserk rage upon his block-like legs-but he did not for one second take his full attention from the report until it had been completed. Then he seized the nearest object, which happened to be his chair, and with all his enormous strength hurled it across the floor, where it lay, a tattered, twisted, shapeless mass of metal.

"Thus shall we treat the entire race of the accursed beings who have done this!" he stormed, his heavy voice reverberating throughout the room. "Torture, dismemberment and annihilation to every...."

"Fenor of the Fenachrone!" a tremendous voice, a full octave lower than Fenor's own terrific bass, and of ear-shattering volume and timbre in that dense atmosphere boomed from the general-wave speaker, its deafening roar drowning out Fenor's raging voice and every other lesser sound.

"Fenor of the Fenachrone! I know that you hear, for every general-wave speaker upon your reeking planet is voicing my words. Listen well, for this warning shall not be repeated. I am speaking by and with the authority of the Overlord of the Green System, which you know as the Central System of this, our Galaxy. Upon some of our many planets there are those who wished to destroy you without warning and out of hand, but the Overlord has ruled that you may continue to live provided you heed these, his commands, which he has instructed me to lay upon you.

"You must forthwith abandon forever your vainglorious and senseless scheme of universal conquest. You must immediately withdraw your every vessel to within the boundaries of your solar system, and you must keep them there henceforth.

"You are allowed five minutes to decide whether or not you will obey these commands. If no answer has been received at the end of the calculated time the Overlord will know that you have defied him, and your entire race shall perish utterly. Well he knows that your very existence is an affront to all real civilization, but he holds that even such vileness incarnate, as are the Fenachrone, may perchance have some obscure place in the Great Scheme of Things, and he will not destroy you if you are content to remain in your proper place, upon your own dank and steaming world. Through me, the two thousand three hundred and forty-sixth Sacner Carfon of Dasor, the Overlord has given you your first, last and only warning. Heed its every word, or consider it the formal declaration of a war of utter and complete extinction!"

The awful voice ceased and pandemonium reigned in the council hall. Obeying a common impulse, each Fenachrone leaped to his feet, raised his huge arms aloft, and roared out rage and defiance. Fenor snapped a command, and the others fell silent as he began howling out orders.

"Operator! Send recall torpedoes instantly to every outlying vessel!" He scuttled over to one of the private-band speakers. "X-794-PW! Radio general call for all vessels above E blank E to concentrate on battle stations! Throw out full-power defensive screens, and send the full series of detector screens out to the limit! Guards and patrols on invasion plan XB-218!"

"The immediate steps are taken, gentlemen!" He turned to the Council, his rage unabated. "Never before have we supermen of the Fenachrone been so insulted and so belittled! That upstart Overlord will regret that warning to the instant of his death, which shall be exquisitely postponed. All you of the Council know your duties in such a time as this-you are excused to perform them. General Fenimol, you will stay with me-we shall consider together such other details as require attention."

After the others had left the room Fenor turned to the general.

"Have you any immediate suggestions?"

"I would suggest sending at once for Ravindau, the Chief of the Laboratories of Science. He certainly heard the warning, and may be able to cast some light upon how it could have been sent, and from what point it came."

The Emperor spoke into another sender, and soon the scientist entered, carrying in his hand a small instrument upon which a blue light blazed.

"Do not talk here, there is grave danger of being overheard by that self-styled Overlord," he directed tersely, and led the way into a ray-proof compartment of his private laboratory, several floors below.

"It may interest you to know that you have sealed the doom of our planet and of all the Fenachrone upon it," Ravindau spoke savagely.

"Dare you speak thus to me, your sovereign?" roared Fenor.

"I dare so," replied the other, coldly. "When all the civilization of a planet has been given to destruction by the unreasoning stupidity and insatiable rapacity of its royalty, allegiance to such royalty is at an end. SIT DOWN!" he thundered as Fenor sprang to his feet. "You are no longer in your throne-room, surrounded by servile guards and by automatic rays. You are in MY laboratory, and by a movement of my finger I can hurl you into eternity!"

The general, aware now that the warning was of much more serious import than he had suspected, broke into the acrimonious debate.

"Never mind questions of royalty!" he snapped. "The safety of the race is paramount. Am I to understand that the situation is really grave?"

"It is worse than grave-it is desperate. The only hope for even ultimate triumph is for as many of us as possible to flee instantly clear out of the Galaxy, in the hope that we may escape the certain destruction to be dealt out to us by the Overlord of the Green System."

"You speak folly, surely," returned Fenimol. "Our science is-must be-superior to any other in the Universe?"

"So thought I until this warning came in and I had an opportunity to study it. Then I knew that we are opposed by a science immeasurably higher than our own."

"Such vermin as those two whom one of our smallest scouts captured without a battle, vessel and all? In what respects is their science even comparable to ours?"

"Not those vermin, no. The one who calls himself the Overlord. That one is our master. He can penetrate the impenetrable shield of force and can operate mechanisms of pure force behind it; he can heterodyne, transmit, and use the infra-rays, of whose very existence we were in doubt until recently! While that warning was being delivered he was, in all probability, watching you and listening to you, face to face. You in your ignorance supposed his warning borne by the ether, and thought therefore he must be close to this system. He is very probably at home in the Central System, and is at this moment preparing the forces he intends to hurl against us."

The Emperor fell back into his seat, all his pomposity gone, but the general stiffened eagerly and went straight to the point.

"How do you know these things?"

"Largely by deduction. We of the school of science have cautioned you repeatedly to postpone the Day of Conquest until we should have mastered the secrets of sub-rays and of infra-rays. Unheeding, you of war have gone ahead with your plans, while we of science have continued to study. We know a little of the sub-rays, which we use every day, and practically nothing of the infra-rays. Some time ago I developed a detector for infra-rays, which come to us from outer space in small quantities and which are also liberated by our power-plants. It has been regarded as a scientific curiosity only, but this day it proved of real value. This instrument in my hand is such a detector. At normal impacts of infra-rays its light is blue, as you see it now. Some time before the warning sounded it turned a brilliant red, indicating that an intense source of infra-rays was operating in the neighborhood. By plotting lines of force I located the source as being in the air of the council hall, almost directly above the table of state. Therefore the carrier wave must have come through our whole system of screens without so much as giving an alarm. That fact alone proves it to have been an infra-ray. Furthermore, it carried through those screens and released in the council room a system of forces of great complexity, as is shown by their ability to broadcast from those pure forces without material aid a modulated wave in the exact frequency required to energize our general speakers.

"As soon as I perceived these facts I threw about the council room a screen of force entirely impervious to anything longer than ultra-rays. The warning continued, and I then knew that our fears were only too well grounded-that there is in this Galaxy somewhere a race vastly superior to ours in science and that our destruction is a matter of hours, perhaps of minutes."

"Are these ultra-rays, then, of such a dangerous character?" asked the general. "I had supposed them to be of such infinitely high frequency that they could be of no practical use whatever,"

"I have been trying for years to learn something of their nature, but beyond working out a method for their detection and a method of possible analysis that may or may not succeed I can do nothing with them. It is perfectly evident, however, that they lie below the level of the ether, and therefore have a velocity of propagation infinitely greater than that of light. You may see for yourself, then, that to a science able to guide and control them, to make them act as carrier waves for any other desired frequency-to do all of which the Overlord has this day shown himself capable-they should theoretically afford weapons before which our every defense would be precisely as efficacious as so much vacuum. Think a moment! You know that we know nothing fundamental concerning even our servants, the sub-rays. If we really knew them we could utilize them in thousands of ways as yet unknown to us. We work with the merest handful of forces, empirically, while it is practically certain that the enemy has at his command the entire spectrum, visible and invisible, embracing untold thousands of bands of unknown but terrific potentiality."

"But he spoke of a calculated time necessary before our answer could be received. They must, then, be using vibrations in the ether."

"Not necessarily-not even probably. Would we ourselves reveal unnecessarily to an enemy the possession of such rays? Do not be childish. No, Fenimol, and you, Fenor of the Fenachrone, instant and headlong flight is our only hope of present salvation and of ultimate triumph-flight to a far distant Galaxy, since upon no point in this one shall we be safe from the infra-beams of that self-styled Overlord."

"You snivelling coward! You pusillanimous bookworm!" Fenor had regained his customary spirit as the scientist explained upon what grounds his fears were based. "Upon such a tenuous fabric of evidence would you have such a people as ours turn tail like beaten hounds? Because, forsooth, you detect a peculiar vibration in the air, will you have it that we are to be invaded and destroyed forthwith by a race of supernatural ability? Bah! Your calamity-howling clan has delayed the Day of Conquest from year to year —I more than half believe that you yourself or some other treacherous poltroon of your ignominious breed prepared and sent that warning, in a weak and rat-brained attempt to frighten us into again postponing the Day of Conquest! Know now, spineless weakling, that the time is ripe, and that the Fenachrone in their might are about to strike. But you, foul traducer of your emperor, shall die the death of the cur you are!" The hand within his tunic moved and a vibrator burst into operation.

"Coward I may be, and pusillanimous, and other things as well," the scientist replied stonily, "but, unlike you, I am not a fool. These walls, this very atmosphere, are fields of force that will transmit no rays directed by you. You weak-minded scion of a depraved and obscene house-arrogant, overbearing, rapacious, ignorant-your brain is too feeble to realize that you are clutching at the Universe hundreds of years before the time has come. You by your overweening pride and folly have doomed our beloved planet-the most perfect planet in the Galaxy in its grateful warmth and wonderful dampness and fogginess-and our entire race to certain destruction. Therefore you, fool and dolt that you are, shall die-for too long already have you ruled." He flicked a finger and the body of the monarch shuddered as though an intolerable current of electricity had traversed it, collapsed and lay still.

"It was necessary to destroy this that was our ruler," Ravindau explained to the general. "I have long known that you are not in favor of such precipitate action in the Conquest: hence all this talking upon my part. You know that I hold the honor of Fenachrone dear, and that all my plans are for the ultimate triumph of our race?"

"Yes, and I begin to suspect that those plans have not been made since the warning was received."

"My plans have been made for many years; and ever since an immediate Conquest was decided upon I have been assembling and organizing the means to put them into effect. I would have left this planet in any event shortly after the departure of the grand fleet upon its final expedition—Fenor's senseless defiance of the Overlord has only made it necessary for me to expedite my leave-taking."

"What do you intend to do?"

"I have a vessel twice as large as the largest warship Fenor boasted; completely provisioned, armed, and powered for a cruise of one hundred years at high acceleration. It is hidden in a remote fastness of the jungle. I am placing in that vessel a group of the finest, brainiest, most highly advanced and intelligent of our men and women, with their children. We shall journey at our highest speed to a certain distant Galaxy, where we shall seek out a planet similar in atmosphere, temperature, and mass to the one upon which we now dwell. There we shall multiply and continue our studies; and from that planet, in that day when we shall have attained sufficient knowledge, there shall descend upon the Central System of this Galaxy the vengeance of the Fenachrone. That vengeance will be all the sweeter for the fact that it shall have been delayed."

"But how about libraries, apparatus and equipment? Suppose that we do not live long enough to perect that knowledge? And with only one vessel and a handful of men we could not cope with that accursed Overlord and his navies of the void."

"Libraries are aboard, so are much apparatus and equipment. What we cannot take with us we can build. As for the knowledge I mentioned, it may not be attained in your lifetime nor in mine. But the racial memory of the Fenachrone is long, as you know; and even if the necessary problems are not solved until our descendants are sufficiently numerous to populate an entire planet, yet will those descendants wreak the vengeance of the Fenachrone upon the races of that hated one, the Overlord, before they go on with the Conquest of the Universe. Many questions will arise, of course; but they shall be solved. Enough! Time passes rapidly, and all too long have I talked. I am using this time upon you because in my organization there is no soldier, and the Fenachrone of the future will need your great knowledge of warfare. Are you going with us?"

"Yes."

"Very well." Ravindau led the general through a door and into an airboat lying upon the terrace outside the laboratory. "Drive us at speed to your home, where we shall pick up your family."

Fenimol took the controls and laid a ray to his home —a ray serving a double purpose. It held the vessel upon its predetermined course through that thick and sticky fog and also rendered collision impossible, since any two of these controller rays repelled each other to such a degree that no two vessels could take paths which would bring them together. Some such provision had been found necessary ages ago, for all Fenachrone craft were provided with the same space-annihilating drive, to which any comprehensible distance was but a journey of a few moments, and at that frightful velocity collision meant annihilation.

"I understand that you could not take any one of the military into your confidence until you were ready to put your plans into effect," the general conceded. "How long will it take you to get ready to leave? You have said that haste is imperative, and I therefore assume that you have already warned the other members of the expedition."

"I flashed the emergency signal before I joined you and Fenor in the council room. Each man of the organization has received that signal, wherever he may have been, and by this time most of them, with their families, are on the way to the hidden cruiser. We shall leave this planet in fifteen minutes from now at most —I dare not stay an instant longer than is absolutely necessary."

The members of the general's family were bundled, amazed, into the airboat, which immediately flew along a ray laid by Ravindau to the secret rendezvous.

In a remote and desolate part of the planet, concealed in the depths of the towering jungle growth, a mammoth space-cruiser was receiving her complement of passengers. Airboats, flying at their terrific velocity through the heavy, steaming fog as closely-spaced as their controller rays would permit, flashed signals along their guiding beams, dove into the apparently impenetrable jungle, and added their passengers to the throng pouring into the great vessel.

As the minute of departure drew near, the feeling of tension aboard the cruiser increased and vigilance was raised to the maximum. None of the passengers had been allowed senders of any description, and now even the hair-line beams guiding the airboats were cut off, and received only when the proper code signal was heard. The doors were shut, no one was allowed outside, and everything was held in readiness for instant flight at the least alarm. Finally a scientist and his family arrived from the opposite side of the planet-the last members of the organization-and, twenty-seven minutes after Ravindau had flashed his signal, the prow of that mighty space-ship reared toward the perpendicular, poising its massive length at the predetermined angle. There it halted momentarily, then disappeared utterly, only a vast column of tortured and shattered vegetation, torn from the ground and carried for miles upward into the air by the vacuum of its wake, remaining to indicate the path taken by the flying projectile.

Hour after hour the Fenachrone vessel bored on, with its frightful and ever-increasing velocity, through the ever-thinning stars, but it was not until the last star had been passed, until everything before them was entirely devoid of light, and until the Galaxy behind them began to take on a well-defined lenticular aspect, that Ravindau would consent to leave the controls and to seek his hard-earned rest.

Day after day and week after week went by, and the Fenachrone vessel still held the rate of motion with which she had started out. Ravindau and Fenimol sat in the control cabin, staring out through the visiplates, abstracted. There was no need of staring, and they were not really looking, for there was nothing at which to look. Outside the transparent metal hull of that monster of the trackless void, there was nothing visible. The Galaxy of which our Earth is an infinitesimal mote, the Galaxy which former astronomers considered the Universe, was so far behind that its immeasurable diameter was too small to affect the vision of the unaided eye. Other Galaxies lay at even greater distances away on either side. The Galaxy toward which they were making their stupendous flight was as yet untold millions of light-years distant. Nothing was visible-before their gaze stretched an infinity of emptiness. No stars, no nebulæ, no meteoric matter, nor even the smallest particle of cosmic dust-absolutely empty space. Absolute vacuum and absolute zero. Absolute nothingness—a concept intrinsically impossible for the most highly trained human mind to grasp.

Conscienceless and heartless monstrosities though they both were, by heredity and training, the immensity of the appalling lack of anything tangible oppressed them. Ravindau was stern and serious, Fenimol moody. Finally the latter spoke.

"It would be endurable if we knew what had happened, or if we ever could know definitely, one way or the other, whether all this was necessary."

"We shall know, general, definitely. I am certain in my own mind, but after a time, when we have settled upon our new home and when the Overlord shall have relaxed his vigilance, you shall come back to the solar system of the Fenachrone in this vessel or a similar one. I know what you shall find-but the trip shall be made, and you shall yourself see what was once our home planet, a seething sun, second only in brilliance to the parent sun about which she shall still be revolving."

"Are we safe, even now-what of possible pursuit?" asked Fenimol, and the monstrous, flame-shot wells of black that were Ravindau's eyes almost emitted tangible fires as he made reply:

"We are far from safe, but we grow stronger minute by minute. Fifty of the greatest minds our world has ever known have been working from the moment of our departure upon a line of investigation suggested to me by certain things my instruments recorded during the visit of the self-styled Overlord. I cannot say anything yet: even to you-except that the Day of Conquest may not be so far in the future as we have supposed."

CHAPTER XIV

Interstellar Extermination

"I hate to leave this meeting-it's great stuff" remarked Seaton as he flashed down to the torpedo room at Fenor's command to send recall messages to all outlying vessels, "but this machine isn't designed to let me be in more than two places at once. Wish it were-maybe after this fracas is over we'll be able to incorporate something like that into it."

The chief operator touched a lever and the chair upon which he sat, with all its control panels, slid rapidly across the floor toward an apparently blank wall. As he reached it, a port opened a metal scroll appeared, containing the numbers and last reported positions of all Fenachrone vessels outside the detector zone, and a vast magazine of torpedoes came up through the floor, with an automatic loader to place a torpedo under the operator's hand the instant its predecessor had been launched.

"Get Peg here quick, Mart-we need a stenographer. Till she gets here, see what you can do in getting those first numbers before they roll off the end of the scroll. No, hold it-as you were! I've got controls enough to put the whole thing on a recorder, so we can study it at our leisure."

Haste was indeed necessary for the operator worked with uncanny quickness of hand. One fleeting glance at the scroll, a lightning adjustment of dials in the torpedo, a touch upon a tiny button, and a messenger was upon its way. But quick as he was, Seaton's flying fingers kept up with him, and before each torpedo disappeared through the ether gate there was fastened upon it a fifth-order tracer ray that would never leave it until the force had been disconnected at the gigantic control board of the Norlaminian projector. One flying minute passed during which seventy torpedoes had been launched, before Seaton spoke.

"Wonder how many ships they've got out, anyway? Didn't get any idea from the brain-record. Anyway, Rovol, it might be a sound idea for you to install me some more tracer rays on this board, I've got only a couple of hundred, and that may not be enough-and I've got both hands full."

Rovol seated himself beside the younger man, like one organist joining another at the console of a tremendous organ. Seaton's nimble fingers would flash here and there, depressing keys and manipulating controls until he had exactly the required combination of forces centered upon the torpedo next to issue. He then would press a tiny switch and upon a panel full of red-topped, numbered plungers; the one next in series would drive home, transferring to itself the assembled beam and releasing the keys for the assembly of other forces. Rovol's fingers were also flying, but the forces he directed were seizing and shaping material, as well as other forces. The Norlaminian physicist, set up one integral, stepped upon a pedal, and a new red-topped stop precisely like the others and numbered in order, appeared as though by magic upon the panel at Seaton's left hand. Rovol then leaned back in his seat-but the red-topped stops continued to appear, at the rate of exactly seventy per minute, upon the panel, which increased in width sufficiently to accommodate another row as soon as a row was completed.

Rovol bent a quizzical glance upon the younger scientist, who blushed a fiery red, rapidly set up another integral, then also leaned back in his place, while his face burned deeper than before.

"That is better, son. Never forget that it is a waste of energy to do the same thing twice with your hands and that if you know precisely what is to be done, you need not do it with your hands at all. Forces are tireless, and they neither slip nor make mistakes."

"Thanks, Rovol—I'll bet this lesson will make it stick in my mind, too."

"You are not thoroughly accustomed to using all your knowledge as yet. That will come with practice, however, and in a few weeks you will be as thoroughly at home with forces as I am."

"Hope so, Chief, but it looks like a tall order to me."

Finally the last torpedo was dispatched, the tube closed, and Seaton moved the projection back up into the council chamber, finding it empty.

"Well, the conference is over-besides, we've got more important fish to fry. War has been declared, on both sides, and we've got to get busy. They've got nine hundred and six vessels out, and every one of them has got to go to Davy Jones' locker before we can sleep sound of nights. My first job'll have to be untangling those nine oh six forces, getting lines on each one of them, and seeing if I can project straight enough to find the ships before the torpedoes overtake them. Mart, you and Orlon, the astronomer, had better dope out the last reported positions of each of those vessels, so we'll know about where to hunt for them. Rovol, you might send out a detector screen a few light years in diameter, to be sure none of them slips a fast one over on us. By starting it right here and expanding it gradually, you can be sure that no Fenachrone is inside it. Then we'll find a hunk of copper on that planet somewhere, plate it with some of their own 'X' metal, and blow them into Kingdom Come."

"May I venture a suggestion?" asked Drasnik, the First of Psychology.

"Absolutely-nothing you've said so far has been idle chatter."

"You know, of course, that there are real scientists among the Fenachrone; and you yourself have suggested that while they cannot penetrate the zone of force nor use fifth-order rays, yet they might know about them in theory, might even be able to know when they were being used-detect them, in other words. Let us assume that such a scientist did detect your rays while you were there a short time ago. What would he do?"

"Search me....I bite, what would he do?"

"He might do any one of several things, but if I read their nature aright, such a one would gather up a few men and women-as many as he could-and migrate to another planet. For he would of course grasp instantly the fact that you had used fifth-order rays as carrier waves, and would be able to deduce your ability to destroy. He would also realize that in the brief time allowed him, he could not hope to learn to control those unknown forces; and with his terribly savage and vengeful nature and intense pride of race, he would take every possible step both to perpetuate his race and to obtain revenge. Am I right?"

Seaton swung to his controls savagely, and manipulated dials and keys rapidly.

"Right as rain, Drasnik. There —I've thrown around them a fifth-order detector screen, that they can't possibly neutralize. Anything that goes out through it will have a tracer slapped onto it. But say, it's been half an hour since war was declared-suppose we're too late? Maybe some of them have got away already, and if one couple of 'em has beat us to it, we'll have the whole thing to do over again a thousand years or so from now. You've got the massive intellect, Drasnik. What can we do about it? We can't throw a detector screen all over the Galaxy."

"I would suggest that since you have now guarded against further exodus, it is necessary to destroy the planet for a time. Rovol and his co-workers have the other projector nearly done. Let them project me to the world of the Fenachrone, where I shall conduct a thorough mental investigation. By the time you have taken care of the raiding vessels, I believe that I shall have been able to learn everything we need to know."

"Fine-hop to it, and may there be lots of bubbles in your think-tank. Anybody else know of any other loop-holes I've left open?"

No other suggestions were made, and each man bent to his particular task. Crane at the starchart of the Galaxy and Orlon at the Fenachrone operator's dispatching scroll rapidly worked out the approximate positions of the Fenachrone vessels, and marked them with tiny green lights in a vast model of the Galaxy which they had already caused forces to erect in the air of the projector's base. It was soon learned that a few of the ships were exploring quite close to their home system; so close that the torpedoes, with their unthinkable acceleration, would reach them within a few hours. Ascertaining the stop-number of the tracer ray upon the torpedo which should first reach its destination, Seaton followed it from the stop upon his panel out to the flying messenger. Now moving with a velocity many times that of light, it was, of course, invisible to direct vision; but to the light waves heterodyned upon the fifth-order projector rays, it was as plainly visible as though it were stationary. Lining up the path of the projectile accurately, he then projected himself forward in that exact line, with a flat detector-screen thrown out for half a light year upon each side of him. Setting the controls, he flashed ahead, the detector stopping him the instant that the invisible barrier encountered the power-plant of the exploring raider. An oscillator sounded a shrill and rising note, and Seaton slowly shifted his controls until he stood in the control room of the enemy vessel.

The Fenachrone ship, a thousand feet long and more than a hundred feet in diameter, was tearing through space toward a brilliant blue-white star. Her crew were at battle stations, her navigating officers peering intently into the operating visiplates, all oblivious to the fact that a stranger stood in their very midst.

"Well, here's the first one, gang," said Seaton, "I hate like sin to do this-it's altogether too much like pushing baby chickens into a creek to suit me, but it's a dirty job that's got to be done."

As one man, Orlon and the other remaining Norlaminians leaped out of the projector and floated to the ground below.

"I expected that," remarked Seaton. "They can't even think of a thing like this without getting the blue willies—I don't blame them much, at that. How about you, Carfon? You can be excused if you like."

"I want to watch those forces at work. I do not enjoy destruction, but like you, I can make myself endure it."

Dunark, the fierce and bloodthirsty Osnomian prince, leaped to his feet, his eyes flashing.

"That's one thing I never could get about you, Dick!" he exclaimed in English. "How a man with your brains can be so soft-so sloppily sentimental, gets clear past me. You remind me of a bowl of mush-you wade around in slush clear to your ears. Faugh! It's their lives or ours! Tell me what button to push and I'll be only too glad to push it. I wanted to blow up Urvania and you wouldn't let me; I haven't killed an enemy for ages, and that's my trade. Cut out the sob-sister act and for Cat's sake, let's get busy!"

"'At-a-boy, Dunark! That's tellin' 'im! But it's all right with me—I'll be glad to let you do it. When I say 'shoot' throw in that plunger there-number sixty-three."

Seaton manipulated controls until two electrodes of force were clamped in place, one at either end of the huge power-bar of the enemy vessel; adjusted rheostats and forces to send a disintegrating current through that massive copper cylinder, and gave the word. Dunark threw in the switch with a vicious thrust, as though it were an actual sword which he was thrusting through the vitals of one of the awesome crew, and the very Universe exploded around them-exploded into one mad, searing coruscation of blinding, dazzling light as the gigantic cylinder of copper resolved itself instantaneously into the pure energy from which its metal originally had come into being.

Seaton and Dunark staggered back from the visiplates, blinded by the intolerable glare of light, and even Crane, working at his model of the galaxy, blinked at the intensity of the radiation. Many minutes passed before the two men could see through their tortured eyes.

"Zowie! That was fierce!" exclaimed Seaton, when a slowly-returning perception of things other than dizzy spirals and balls of flame assured him that his eyesight was not permanently gone. "It's nothing but my own fool carelessness, too. I should have known that with all the light frequencies in heterodyne for visibility, enough of that same stuff would leak through to make strong medicine on these visiplates-for I knew that that bar weighed a hundred tons and would liberate energy enough to volatilize our Earth and blow the by-products clear to Arcturus. How're you coming, Dunark? See anything yet?"

"Coming along O. K. now, I guess-but I thought for a few minutes I'd been bloody well jobbed."

"I'll do better next time. I'll cut out the visible spectrum before the flash, and convert and reconvert the infra-red. That'll let us see what happens, without the direct effect of the glare-won't burn our eyes out. What's my force number on the next nearest one, Mart?"

"Twenty-nine."

Seaton fastened a detector ray upon stop twenty-nine of the tracer-ray panel and followed its beam of force out to the torpedo hastening upon its way toward the next doomed cruiser. Flashing ahead in its line as he had done before, he located the vessel and clamped the electrodes of force upon the prodigious driving bar. Again, as Dunark drove home the detonating switch, there was a frightful explosion and a wild glare of frenzied incandescence far out in that desolate region of interstellar space; but this time the eyes behind the visiplates were not torn by the high frequencies, everything that happened was plainly visible. One instant, there was an immense space-cruiser boring on through the void upon its horrid mission, with its full complement of the hellish Fenachrone performing their routine tasks. The next instant there was a flash of light extending for thousands upon untold thousands of miles in every direction. That flare of light vanished as rapidly as it had appeared-instantaneously-and throughout the entire neighborhood of the place where the Fenachrone cruiser had been, there was nothing. Not a plate nor a girder, not a fragment, not the most minute particle nor droplet of disrupted metal nor of condensed vapor. So terrific, so incredibly and incomprehensibly vast were the forces liberated by that mass of copper in its instantaneous decomposition, that every atom of substance in that great vessel had gone with the power-bar —had been resolved into radiations which would at some distant time and in some far-off solitude unite with other radiations, again to form matter, and thus obey Nature's immutable cyclic law.

Thus vessel after vessel was destroyed of that haughty fleet which until now had never suffered a reverse and a little green light in the galactic model winked out and flashed back in rosy pink as each menace was removed. In a few hours the space surrounding the system of the Fenachrone was clear; then progress slackened as it became harder and harder to locate each vessel as the distance between it and its torpedo increased. Time after time Seaton would stab forward with his detector screen extended to its utmost possible spread, upon the most carefully plotted prolongation of the line of the torpedo's flight, only to have the projection flash far beyond the vessel's furthest possible position without a reaction from the far-flung screen. Then he would go back to the torpedo, make a minute alteration in his line, and again flash forward, only to miss it again. Finally, after thirty fruitless attempts to bring his detector screen into contact with the nearest Fenachrone ship, he gave up the attempt, rammed his battered, reeking briar full of the rank blend that was his favorite smoke, and strode up and down the floor of the projector base-his eyes unseeing, his hands jammed deep into his pockets, his jaw thrust forward, clamped upon the stem of his pipe, emitting dense, blue clouds of strangling vapor.

"The maestro is thinking, I perceive," remarked Dorothy, sweetly, entering the projector from an airboat. "You must all be blind, I guess-you no hear the bell blow, what? I've come after you-it's time to eat!"

"'At-a-girl, Dot-never miss the eats! Thanks," and Seaton put his problem away, with perceptible effort.

"This is going to be a job, Mart," he went back to it as soon as they were seated in the airboat, flying toward "home." "I can nail them, with an increasing shift in azimuth, up to about thirty thousand light-years, but after that it gets awfully hard to get the right shift, and up around a hundred thousand it seems to be darn near impossible-gets to be pure guesswork. It can't be the controls, because they can hold a point rigidly at five hundred thousand. Of course, we've got a pretty short back-line to sight on, but the shift is more than a hundred times as great as the possible error in backsight could account for, and there's apparently nothing either regular or systematic about it that I can figure out. But....I don't know....Space is curved in the fourth dimension, of course....I wonder if...hm —m —m." He fell silent and Crane made a rapid signal to Dorothy, who was opening her mouth to say something. She shut it, feeling ridiculous, and nothing was said until they had disembarked at their destination.

"Did you solve the puzzle, Dickie?"

"Don't think so-got myself in deeper than ever, I'm afraid," he answered, then went on, thinking aloud rather than addressing any one in particular:

"Space is curved in the fourth dimension, and fifth-order rays, with their velocity, may not follow the same path in that dimension that light does-in fact, they do not. If that path is to be plotted it requires the solution of five simultaneous equations, each complete and general, and each of the fifth degree, and also an exponential series with the unknown in the final exponent, before the fourth-dimensional concept can be derived ... hm —m —m. No use-we've struck something that not even Norlaminian theory can handle."

"You surprise me." Crane said. "I supposed that they had everything worked out."

"Not on fifth-order stuff-it's new, you know. It begins to look as though we'd have to stick around until every one of those torpedoes gets somewhere near its mother-ship. Hate to do it, too-it'll take six months, at least, to reach the vessels clear across the Galaxy. I'll put it up to the gang at dinner-guess they'll let me talk business a couple of minutes overtime, especially after they find out what I've got to say."

He explained the phenomenon to an interested group of white-bearded scientists as they ate. Rovol, to Seaton's surprise, was elated and enthusiastic.

"Wonderful, my boy!" he breathed. "Marvelous! A perfect subject for years after year of deepest study and the most profound thought. Perfect!"

"But what can we *do* about it?" asked Seaton, exasperated. "We don't want to hang around here twiddling our thumbs for a year waiting for those torpedoes to get to wherever they're going!"

"We can do nothing but wait and study. That problem is one of splendid difficulty, as you yourself realize. Its solution may well be a matter of lifetimes instead of years. But what is a year, more or less? You can destroy the Fenachrone eventually, so be content."

"But content is just exactly what I'm *not*!" declared Seaton, emphatically. "I want to do it, and do it *now*!"

"Perhaps I might volunteer a suggestion," said Caslor, diffidently; and as both Rovol and Seaton looked at him in surprise he went on: "Do not misunderstand me. I do not mean concerning the mathematical problem in discussion, about which I am entirely ignorant. But has it occurred to you that those torpedoes are not intelligent entities, acting upon their own volition and steering themselves as a result of their own ordered mental processes? No, they are mechanisms, in my own province, and I venture to say with the utmost confidence that they are guided to their destinations by streamers of force of some nature, emanating from the vessels upon whose tracks they are."

"'Nobody Holme' is right!" exclaimed Seaton, tapping his temple with an admonitory forefinger. "'Sright, ace —I thought maybe I'd quit using my head for nothing but a hatrack now, but I guess that's all it's good for, yet. Thanks a lot for the idea-that gives me something I can get my teeth into, and now that Rovol's got a problem to work on for the next century or so, everybody's happy."

"How does that help matters?" asked Crane in wonder. "Of course it is not surprising that no lines of force were visible, but I thought that your detectors screens would have found them if any such guiding beams had been present."

"The ordinary bands, if of sufficient power, yes. But there are many possible tracer rays not reactive to a screen such as I was using. It was very light and weak, designed for terrific velocity and for instantaneous automatic arrest when in contact with the enormous forces of a power bar. It wouldn't react at all to the minute energy of the kind of beams they'd be most likely to use for that work. Caslor's certainly right. They're steering their torpedoes with tracer rays of almost infinitesimal power, amplified in the torpedoes themselves-that's the way I'd do it myself. It may take a little while to rig up the apparatus, but we'll get it-and then we'll run those birds ragged-so fast that their ankles'll catch fire-and won't need the fourth-dimensional correction after all."

When the bell announced the beginning of the following period of labor, Seaton and his co-workers were in the Area of Experiment waiting, and the work was soon under way.

"How are you going about this, Dick?" asked Crane.

"Going to examine the nose of one of those torpedoes first, and see what it actually works on. Then build me a tracer detector that'll pick it up at high velocity. Beats the band, doesn't it, that neither Rovol nor I, who should have thought of it first, ever did see anything as plain as that? That those things are following a ray?"

"That is easily explained, and is no more than natural. Both of you were not only devoting all your thoughts to the curvature of space, but were also too close to the problem-like the man in the woods, who cannot see the forest because of the trees."

"Yeah, may be something in that, too. Plain enough, when Caslor showed it to us," said Seaton.

While he was talking, Seaton had projected himself into the torpedo he had lined up so many times the previous day. With the automatic motions set to hold him stationary in the tiny instrument compartment of the craft, now traveling at a velocity many times that of light, he set to work. A glance located the detector mechanism, a set of short-wave coils and amplifiers, and a brief study made plain to him the principles underlying the directional loop finders and the controls which guided the flying shell along the path of the tracer ray. He then built a detector structure of pure force immediately in front of the torpedo, and varied the frequency of his own apparatus until a meter upon one of the panels before his eyes informed him that his detector was in perfect resonance with the frequency of the tracer ray. He then moved ahead of the torpedo, along the guiding ray.

"Guiding it, eh?" Dunark congratulated him.

"Kinda. My directors out there aren't quite so hot, though. I'm a trifle shy on control somewhere, so much so that if I put on anywhere near full velocity, I lose the ray. Think I can clear that up with a little experimenting, though."

He fingered controls lightly, depressed a few more keys, and set one vernier, already at a ratio of a million to one, down to ten million. He then stepped up his velocity, and found that the guides worked well up to a speed much greater than any ever reached by Fenachrone vessels or torpedoes, but failed utterly to hold the ray at anything approaching the full velocity possible to his fifth-order projector. After hours and days of work and study-in the course of which hundreds of the Fenachrone vessels were destroyed-after employing all the resources of his mind, now stored with the knowledge of rays accumulated by hundreds of generations of highly-trained research specialists in rays, he became convinced that it was an inherent impossibility to trace any ether wave with the velocity he desired.

"Can't be done, I guess, Mart," he confessed, ruefully. "You see, it works fine up to a certain point; but beyond that, nothing doing. I've just found out why-and in so doing, I think I've made a contribution to science. At velocities well below that of light, light-waves are shifted a minute amount, you know. At the velocity of light, and up to a velocity not even approached by the Fenachrone vessels on their longest trips, the distortion is still not serious-no matter how fast we want to travel in the *Skylark*, I think I can guarantee that we will still be able to see things. That is to be expected from the generally-accepted idea that the apparent velocity of any ether vibration is independent of the velocity of either source or receiver. However, that relationship fails at velocities far below that of fifth-order rays. At only a very small fraction of that speed the tracers I am following are so badly distorted that they disappear altogether, and I have to distort them backwards. That wouldn't be too bad, but when I get up to about one per cent of the velocity I want to use, I can't calculate a force that will operate to distort them back into recognizable wave-forms. That's another problem for Rovol to chew on, for another hundred years."

"That will, of course, slow up the work of clearing the Galaxy of the Fenachrone, but at the same time I see nothing about which to be alarmed," Crane replied. "You are working very much faster than you could have done by waiting for the torpedoes to arrive. The present condition is very satisfactory, I should say," and he waved his hand at the galactic model, in nearly three-fourths of whose volume the green lights had been replaced by pink ones.

"Yeah, pretty fair as far as that goes-we'll clean up in ten days or so-but I hate to be licked. Well, I might as well quit sobbing and get busy!"

In due time the nine hundred and sixth Fenachrone vessel was checked off on the model, and the two Terrestrials went in search of Drasnik, whom they found in his study, summing up and analyzing a mass of data, facts, and ideas which were being projected in the air around him.

"Well, our first job's done," Seaton stated. "What do you know that you feel like passing around?"

"My investigation is practically complete," replied the First of Psychology, gravely. "I have explored many Fenachrone minds, and without exception I have found them chambers of horror of a kind unimaginable to one of us. However, you are not interested in their psychology, but in facts bearing upon your problem. While such facts were scarce, I did discover a few interesting items. I spied upon them in public and in their most private haunts. I analyzed them individually and collectively, and from the few known facts and from the great deal of guesswork and conjecture there available to me, I have formulated a theory. I shall first give you the known facts. Their scientists cannot direct nor control any ray not propagated through ether, but they can detect one such frequency or band of frequencies which they call 'infra-rays' and which are probably the fifth-order rays, since they lie in the first level below the ether. The detector proper is a type of lamp, which gives a blue light at the ordinary intensity of such rays as would come from space or from an ordinary power plant, but gives a red light under strong excitation."

"Uh-huh, I get that O. K.," said Seaton. "Rovol's great-great-great-grandfather had 'em —I know all about 'em," Seaton encouraged Drasnik, who had paused, with a questioning glance. "I know exactly how and why such a detector works. We gave 'em an alarm, all right. Even though we were working on a tight beam from here to there, our secondary projector there was radiating enough to affect every such detector within a thousand miles."

Drasnik continued: "Another significant fact is that a great many persons —I learned of some five hundred, and there were probably many more-have disappeared without explanation and without leaving a trace; and it seems that they disappeared very shortly after our communication was delivered. One of these was Fenor, the Emperor. His family remain, however, and his son is not only ruling in his stead, but is carrying out his father's policies. The other disappearances are all alike and are peculiar in certain respects. First, every man who vanished belonged to the Party of Postponement-the minority party of the Fenachrone, who believe that the time for the Conquest has not yet come. Second, every one of them was a leader in thought in some field of usefulness, and every such field is represented by at least one disappearance-even the army, as General Fenimol, the Commander-in-Chief, and his whole family, are among the absentees. Third, and most remarkable, each such disappearance included an entire family, clear down to children and grand-children, however young. Another fact is that the Fenachrone Department of Navigation keeps a very close check upon all vessels, particularly vessels capable of navigating outer space. Every vessel built must be registered, and its location is always known from its individual tracer ray. No Fenachrone vessel is missing."

"I also sifted a mass of gossip and conjecture, some of which may bear upon the subject. One belief is that all the persons were put to death by Fenor's secret service, and that the Emperor was assassinated in revenge. The most widespread belief, however, is that they have fled. Some hold that they are in hiding in some remote shelter in the jungle, arguing that the rigid registration of all vessels renders a journey of any great length impossible and that the detector screens would have given warning of any vessel leaving the planet. Others think that persons as powerful as Fenimol and Ravindau could have built any vessel they chose with neither the knowledge nor consent of the Department of Navigation, or that they could have stolen a Navy vessel, destroying its records; and that Ravindau certainly could have so neutralized the screens that they would have given no alarm. These believe that the absent ones have migrated to some other solar system or to some other planet of the same sun. One old general loudly gave it as his opinion that the cowardly traitors had probably fled clear out of the Galaxy, and that it would be a good thing to send the rest of the Party of Postponement after them. There, in brief, are the salient points of my investigation in so far as it concerns your immediate problem."

"A good many straws pointing this way and that," commented Seaton. "However, we know that the 'postponers' are just as rabid on the idea of conquering the Universe as the others are-only they are a lot more cautious and won't take even a gambler's chance of a defeat. But you've formed a theory-what is it, Drasnik?"

"From my analysis of these facts and conjectures, in conjunction with certain purely psychological indices which we need not take time to go into now, I am certain that they have left their solar system, probably in an immense vessel built a long time ago and held in readiness for just such an emergency. I am not certain of their destination, but it is my opinion that they have left this Galaxy, and are planning upon starting anew upon some suitable planet in some other Galaxy, from which, at some future date, the Conquest of the Universe shall proceed as it was originally planned."

"Great balls of fire!" blurted Seaton. "They couldn't —not in a million years!" He thought a moment, then continued more slowly: "But they could-and, with their dispositions, they probably would. You're one hundred per cent. right, Drasnik. We've got a real job of hunting on our hands now. So-long, and thanks a lot."

Back in the projector Seaton prowled about in brown abstraction, his villainous pipe poisoning the circumambient air, while Crane sat, quiet and self-possessed as always, waiting for the nimble brain of his friend to find a way over, around, or through the obstacle confronting them.

"Got it, Mart!" Seaton yelled, darting to the board and setting up one integral after another. "If they did leave the planet in a ship, we'll be able to watch them go-and we'll see what they did, anyway, no matter what it was!"

"How? They've been gone almost a month already," protested Crane.

"We know within half an hour the exact time of their departure. We'll simply go out the distance light has traveled since that time, gather in the rays given off, amplify them a few billion times, and take a look at whatever went on."

"But we have no idea of what region of the planet to study, or whether it was night or day at the point of departure when they left."

"We'll get the council room, and trace events from there. Day or night makes no difference-we'll have to use infra-red anyway, because of the fog, and that's almost as good at night as in the daytime. There is no such thing as absolute darkness upon any planet, anyway, and we've got power enough to make anything visible that happened there, night or day. Mart, I've got power enough here to see and to photograph the actual construction of the pyramids of Egypt in that same way-and they were built thousands of years ago!"

"Heavens, what astounding possibilities!" breathed Crane. "Why, you could...."

"Yeah, I could do a lot of things," Seaton interrupted him rudely, "but right now we've got other fish to fry. I've just got the city we visited, at about the time we were there. General Fenimol, who disappeared, must be in the council room down here right now. I'll retard our projection, so that time will apparently pass more quickly, and we'll duck down there and see what actually did happen. I can heterodyne, combine, and recombine just as though we were watching the actual scene-it's more complicated, of course, since I have to follow it and amplify it too, but it works out all right."

"This is unbelievable, Dick. Think of actually seeing something that really happened in the past!"

"Yeah, it's kinda strong, all right. As Dot would say, it's just too perfectly darn outrageous. But we're doing it, ain't we? I know just how, and why. When we get some time I'll shoot the method into your brain. Well, here we are!"

Peering into the visiplates, the two men were poised above the immense central cone of the capital city of the Fenachrone. Viewing with infra-red light as they were, the fog presented no obstacle and the indescribable beauty of the city of concentric rings and the wonderfully luxuriant jungle growth were clearly visible. They plunged down into the council chamber, and saw Fenor, Ravindau, and Fenimol deep in conversation.

"With all the other feats of skill and sorcery you have accomplished, why don't you reconstruct their speech, also?" asked Crane, with a challenging glance.

"Well, old Doubting Thomas, it might not be absolutely impossible, at that. It would mean two projectors, however, due to the difference in speed of sound-waves and light-waves. Theoretically, sound-waves also extend to an infinite distance, but I don't believe that any possible detector and amplifier could reconstruct a voice more than an hour or so after it had spoken. It might, though-we'll have to try it some time, and see. You're fairly good at lip-reading, as I remember it. Get as much of it as you can, will you?"

As though they were watching the scene itself as it happened-which, in a sense, they were-they saw everything that had occurred. They saw Fenor die, saw the general's family board the airboat, saw the orderly embarkation of Ravindau's organization. Finally they saw the stupendous take-off of the first inter-galactic cruiser, and with that take-off, Seaton went into action. Faster and faster he drove that fifth-order beam along the track of the fugitive, until a speed was attained beyond which his detecting converters could not hold the ether-rays they were following. For many minutes Seaton stared intently into the visiplate, plotting lines and calculating forces, then he swung around to Crane.

"Well, Mart, noble old bean, solving the disappearances was easier than I thought it would be; but the situation as regards wiping out the last of the Fenachrone is getting no better, fast."

"I glean from the instruments that they are heading straight out into space away from the Galaxy, and I assume that they are using their utmost acceleration?"

"I'll say they're traveling! They're out in absolute space, you know, with nothing in the way and with no intention of reversing their power or slowing down-they must've had absolute top acceleration on every minute since they left. Anyway, they're so far out already that I couldn't hold even a detector on them, let alone a force that I can control. Well, let's snap into it, fellow-on our way!"

"Just a minute, Dick. Take it easy, what are your plans?"

"Plans! Why worry about plans? Blow up that planet before any more of 'em get away, and then chase that boat clear to Andromeda, if necessary. Let's go!"

"Calm down and be reasonable-you are getting hysterical again. They have a maximum acceleration of five times the velocity of light. So have we, exactly, since we adopted their own drive. Now if our acceleration is the same as theirs, and they have a month's start, how long will it take us to catch them?"

"Right again. Mart —I sure was going off half-cocked again," Seaton conceded ruefully, after a moment's thought. "They'd always be going a million or so times as fast as we would be, and getting further ahead of us in geometrical ratio. What's your idea?"

"I agree with you that the time has come to destroy the planet of Fenachrone. As for pursuing that vessel through intergalactic space, that is your problem. You must figure out some method of increasing our acceleration. Highly efficient as is this system of propulsion, it seems to me that the knowledge of the Norlaminians should be able to improve it in some detail. Even a slight increase in acceleration would enable us to overtake them eventually."

"Hm —m —m." Seaton, no longer impetuous, was thinking deeply. "How far are we apt to have to go?"

"Until we get close enough to them to use your rays-say half a million light-years."

"But surely they'll stop, some time?"

"Of course, but not necessarily for many years. They are powered and provisioned for a hundred years, you remember, and are going to 'a distant galaxy.' Such a one as Ravindau would not have specified a *distant* Galaxy idly, and the very closest Galaxies are so far away that even the Fenachrone astronomers, with their reflecting mirrors five miles in diameter, could form only the very roughest approximations of the true distances."

"Our astronomers are all wet in their guesses, then?"

"Their estimates are, without exception, far below the true values. They are not even of the correct order of magnitude.'"

"Well, then, let's mop up on that planet. Then we'll go places and do things."

Seaton had already located the magazines in which the power bars of the Fenachrone war-vessels were stored, and it was a short task to erect a secondary projector of force in the Fenachrone atmosphere. Working out of that projector, beams of force seized one of the immense cylinders of plated copper and at Seaton's direction transported it rapidly to one of the poles of the planet, where electrodes of force were clamped upon it. In a similar fashion seventeen more of the frightful bombs were placed, equidistant over the surface of the world of the Fenachrone, so that when they were simultaneously exploded, the downward forces would be certain to meet sufficient resistance to assure complete demolition of the entire globe. Everything in readiness, Seaton's hand went to the plunger switch and closed upon it. Then, his face white and wet, he dropped his hand.

"No use, Mart—I can't do it. It pulls my cork. I know darn well you can't either—I'll yell for help."

"Have you got it on the infra-red?" asked Dunark calmly, as he shot up into the projector in reply to Seaton's call. "I want to see this, all of it."

"It's on-you're welcome to it," and, as the Terrestrials turned away, the whole projector base was illuminated by a flare of intense, though subdued light. For several minutes Dunark stared into the visiplate, savage satisfaction in every line of his fierce green face as he surveyed the havoc wrought by those eighteen enormous charges of incredible explosive.

"A nice job of clean-up, Dick," the Osnomian prince reported, turning away from the visiplate. "It made a sun of it-the original sun is now quite a splendid double star. Everything was volatized, clear out, far beyond their outermost screen."

"It had to be done, of course-it was either them or else all the rest of the Universe," Season said, jerkily. "However, even that fact doesn't make it go down easy. Well, we're done with this projector. From now on it's strictly up to us and *Skylark Three*. Let's beat it over there and see if they've got her done yet-they were due to finish up today, you know."

It was a silent group who embarked in the little airboat. Half way to their destination, however, Seaton came out of his blue mood with a yell.

"Mart, I've got it! We can give the *Lark* a lot more acceleration than they are getting-and won't need the assistance of all the minds of Norlamin, either."

"How?"

"By using one of the very heavy metals for fuel. The intensity of the power liberated is a function of atomic weight, or atomic number, and density; but the fact of liberation depends upon atomic configuration—a fact which you and I figured out long ago. However, our figuring didn't go far enough-it couldn't: we didn't know anything then. Copper happens to be the most efficient of the few metals which can be decomposed at all under ordinary excitation-that is, by using an ordinary coil, such as we and the Fenachrone both use. But by using special exciters, sending out all the orders of rays necessary to initiate the disruptive processes, we can use any metal we want to. Osnome has unlimited quantities of the heaviest metals, including radium and uranium. Of course we can't use radium and live-but we can and will use uranium, and that will give us something like four times the acceleration possible with copper. Dunark, what say you snap over there and smelt us a cubic mile of uranium? No-hold it—I'll put a flock of forces on the job. They'll do it quicker, and I'll make 'em deliver the goods. They'll deliver 'em fast, too, believe us-we'll see to that with a ten-ton bar. The uranium bars'll be ready to load tomorrow, and we'll have enough power to chase those birds all the rest of our lives!"

Returning to the projector, Seaton actuated the complex system of forces required for the smelting and transportation of the enormous amount of metal necessary, and as the three men again boarded their aerial conveyance, the power-bar in the projector behind them flared into violet incandescence under the load already put upon it by the new uranium mine in distant Osnome.

The *Skylark* lay stretched out over two miles of country, exactly as they had last seen her, but now, instead of being water-white, the ten-thousand-foot cruiser of the void was one jointless, seamless structure of sparkling, transparent, purple inoson. Entering one of the open doors, they stepped into an elevator and were whisked upward into the control room, in which a dozen of the aged, white-bearded students of Norlamin were grouped about a banked and tiered mass of keyboards, which Seaton knew must be the operating mechanism of the extraordinarily complete fifth-order projector he had been promised.

"Ah, youngsters, you are just in time. Everything is complete and we are just about to begin loading."

"Sorry, Rovol, but we'll have to make a couple of changes-have to rebuild the exciter or build another one," and Seaton rapidly related what they had learned, and what they had decided to do.

"Of course, uranium is a much more efficient source of power," agreed Rovol, "and you are to be congratulated for thinking of it. It perhaps would not have occurred to one of us, since the heavy metals of that highly efficient group are very rare here. Building a new exciter for uranium is a simple task, and the converters for the corona-loss will, of course, require no change, since their action depends only upon the frequency of the emitted losses, not upon their magnitude."

"Hadn't you suspected that some of the Fenachrone might be going to lead us a life-long chase?" asked Dunark curiously.

"We have not given the matter a thought, my son," the Chief of the Five made answer. "As your years increase, you will learn not to anticipate trouble and worry. Had we thought and worried over the matter before the time had arrived, you will note that it would have been pain wasted, for our young friend Seaton has avoided that difficulty in a truly scholarly fashion."

"All set, then, Rovol?" asked Seaton, when the forces flying from the projector had built the compound exciter which would make possible the disruption of the atoms of uranium. "The metal, enough of it to fill all the spare space in the hull, will be here tomorrow. You might give Crane and me the method of operating this projector, which I see is vastly more complex even than the one in the Area of Experiment."

"It is the most complete thing ever seen upon Norlamin," replied Rovol with a smile. "Each of us installed everything in it that he could conceive of ever being of the slightest use, and since our combined knowledge covers a large field, the projector is accordingly quite comprehensive."

Multiple headsets were donned, and from each of the Norlaminian brains there poured into the minds of the two Terrestrials a complete and minute knowledge of every possible application of the stupendous force-control banked in all its massed intricacy before them.

"Well, that's some outfit!" exulted Seaton in pleased astonishment as the instructions were concluded. "It can do anything but lay an egg-and I'm not a darn bit sure that we couldn't make it do that! Well, let's call the girls and show them around this thing that's going to be their home for quite a while."

While they were waiting, Dunark led Seaton aside.

"Dick, will you need me on this trip?" he asked. "Of course I knew there was something on your mind when you didn't send me home when you let Urvan, Carfon and the others go back."

"No, we're going it alone-unless you want to come along. I did want you to stick around until I got to a good chance to talk to you alone-now will be a good a time as any. You and I have traded brains, and besides, we've been through quite a lot of grief together, here and there—I want to apologize to you for not passing along to you all this stuff I've been getting here. In fact, I really wish I didn't have to have it myself. Get me?"

"Got you? I'm 'way ahead of you! Don't want it, not any part of it-that's why I've stayed away from any chance of learning any of it, and the one reason why I am going back home instead of going with you. I have just brains enough to realize that neither I nor any other man of my race should have it. By the time we grow up to it naturally we shall be able to handle it, but not until then."

The two brain brothers grasped hands strongly, and Dunark continued in a lighter vein: "It takes all kinds of people to make a world, you know-and all kinds of races, except the Fenachrone, to make a Universe. With Mardonale gone, the evolution of Osnome shall progress rapidly, and while we may not reach the Ultimate Goal, I have learned enough from you already to speed up our progress considerably."

"Well, that's that. Had to get it off my chest, although I knew you'd get the idea all right. Here are the girls-Sitar too. We'll show 'em around."

Seaton's first thought was for the very brain of the ship-the precious lens of neutronium in its thin envelope of the eternal jewel-without which the beam of fifth-order rays could not be directed. He found it a quarter of a mile back from the needle-sharp prow, exactly in the longitudinal axis of the hull, protected from any possible damage by bulkhead after massive bulkhead of impregnable inoson. Satisfied upon that point, he went in search of the others, who were exploring their vast new space-ship.

Huge as she was, there was no waste space-her design was as compact as that of a fine radio set. The living quarters were grouped closely about the central compartment, which housed the power plants, the many ray generators and projectors, and the myriads of controls of the marvelous mechanism for the projection and direction of fifth-order rays. Several large compartments were devoted to the machinery which automatically serviced the vessel-refrigerators, heaters, generators and purifiers for water and air, and the numberless other mechanisms which would make the cruiser a comfortable and secure home, as well as an invincible battleship, in the heatless, lightless, airless, matterless waste of illimitable, inter-galactic space. Many compartments were for the storage of food-supplies, and these were even then being filled by forces under the able direction of the first of Chemistry.

"All the comforts of home, even to the labels," Seaton grinned, as he read "Dole No. 1" upon cans of pineapple which had never been within thousands of light-years of the Hawaiian Islands, and saw quarter after quarter of fresh meat going into the freezer room from a planet upon which no animal other than man had existed for many thousands of years. Nearly all of the remaining millions of cubic feet of space were for the storage of uranium for power, a few rooms already having been filled with ingot inoson for repairs. Between the many bulkheads that divided the ship into numberless airtight sections, and between the many concentric skins of purple metal that rendered the vessel space-worthy and sound, even though slabs many feet thick were to be shown off in any direction-in every nook and cranny could be stored the metal to keep those voracious generators full-fed, no matter how long or how severe the demand for power. Every room was connected through a series of tubular tunnels, along which force-propelled cars or elevators slid smoothly-tubes whose walls fell together into air-tight seals at any point, in case of a rupture.

As they made their way back to the great control-room room of the vessel, they saw something that because of its small size and clear transparency they had not previously seen. Below that room, not too near the outer skin, in a specially-built spherical launching space, there was *Skylark Two*, completely equipped and ready for an interstellar journey on her own account!

"Why, hello, little stranger!" Margaret called. "Rovol, that was a kind thought on your part. Home wouldn't quite be home without our old *Skylark*, would it, Martin?"

"A practical thought, as well as a kind one," Crane responded. "We undoubtedly will have occasion to visit places altogether too small for the really enormous bulk of this vessel."

"Yes, and whoever heard of a sea-going ship without a small boat?" put in irrepressible Dorothy. "She's just too perfectly kippy for words, sitting up there, isn't she?"

CHAPTER XV

The Extra-Galactic Duel

Loaded until her outer skin almost bulged with tightly packed bars of uranium and equipped to meet any emergency of which the combined efforts of the mightiest intellects of Norlamin could foresee even the slightest possibility, *Skylark Three* lay quiescent. Quiescent, but surcharged with power, she seemed to Seaton's tense mind to share his own eagerness to be off; seemed to be motionlessly straining at her neutral controls in a futile endeavor to leave that unnatural and unpleasant environment of atmosphere and of material substance, to soar outward into absolute zero of temperature and pressure, into the pure and undefiled ether which was her natural and familiar medium.

The five human beings were grouped near an open door of their cruiser; before them were the ancient scientists, who for so many days had been laboring with them in their attempt to crush the monstrous race which was threatening the Universe. With the elders were the Terrestrials' many friends from the Country of Youth, and surrounding the immense vessel in a throng covering an area to be measured only in square miles were massed myriads of Norlaminians. From their tasks everywhere had come the mental laborers; the Country of Youth had been left depopulated; even those who, their lifework done, had betaken themselves to the placid Nirvana of the Country of Age, returned briefly to the Country of Study to speed upon its way that stupendous Ship of Peace.

The majestic Fodan, Chief of the Five, was concluding his address:

"And may the Unknowable Force direct your minor forces to a successful conclusion of your task. If, upon the other hand, it should by some unforeseen chance be graven upon the Sphere that you are to pass in this supreme venture, you may pass in all tranquillity, for the massed intellect of our entire race is here supporting me in my solemn affirmation that the Fenachrone shall not be allowed to prevail. In the name of all Norlamin, I bid you farewell."

Crane spoke briefly in reply and the little group of Earthly wanderers stepped into the elevator. As they sped upward toward the control room, door after door shot into place behind them, establishing a manifold seal. Seaton's hand played over the controls and the great cruiser of the void tilted slowly upward until its narrow prow pointed almost directly into the zenith. Then, very slowly at first, the unimaginable mass of the vessel floated lightly upward, with a slowly increasing velocity. Faster and faster she flew-out beyond measurable atmosphere, out beyond the outermost limits of the green system. Finally, in interstellar space, Seaton threw out super-powered detector and repelling screens, anchored himself at the driving console with a force, set the power control at "molecular" so that the propulsive force affected alike every molecule of the vessel and its contents, and, all sense of weight and acceleration lost, he threw in the plunger switch which released every iota of the theoretically possible power of the driving mass of uranium.

Staring intently into the visiplate, he corrected their course from time to time by minute fractions of a second of arc; then, satisfied at last, he set the automatic forces which would guide them, temporarily out of their course, around any obstacles, such as the uncounted thousands of solar systems lying in or near their path. He then removed the restraining forces from his body and legs, and with a small pencil of force wafted himself over to Crane and the two women.

"Well, bunch," he stated, matter-of-fact, "we're on our way. We'll be this way for some time, so we might as well get used to it. Any little thing you want to talk over?"

"How long will it take us to catch 'em?" asked Dorothy "Traveling this way isn't half as much fun as it is when you let us have some weight to hold us down."

"Hard to tell exactly, Dottie. If we had precisely four times their acceleration and had started from the same place, we would of course overtake them in just the number of days they had the start of us, since the distance covered at any constant positive acceleration is proportional to the square of the time elapsed. However, there are several complicating factors in the actual situation. We started out not only twenty-nine days behind them, but also a matter of five hundred thousand light-years of distance. It will take us quite a while to get to their starting-point. I can't tell even that very close, as we will probably have to reduce this acceleration before we get out of the Galaxy, in order to give detectors and repellers time to act on stars and other loose impediments. Powerful as those screens are and fast as they work, there is a limit to the velocity we can use here in this crowded Galaxy. Outside it, in free space, of course we can open her up again. Then, too, our acceleration is not exactly four times theirs, only three point nine one eight six. On the other hand, we don't have to catch them to go to work on them. We can operate very nicely at five thousand light-centuries. So there you are-it'll probably be somewhere between thirty-nine and forty-one days, but it may be a day or so more or less."

"How do you know they are using copper?" asked Margaret. "Maybe their scientists stored up some uranium and know how to use it."

"Nope, that's out like a light. First, Mart and I saw only copper bars in their ship. Second, copper is the most efficient metal found in quantity upon their planet. Third, even if they had uranium or any metal of its class, they couldn't use it without a complete knowledge of, and ability to handle, the fourth and fifth orders of rays."

"It is your opinion, then, that destroying this last Fenachrone vessel is to prove as simple a matter as did the destruction of the others?" Crane queried, pointedly.

"Hm-m-m. Never thought about it from that angle at all, Mart.... You're still the ground-and-lofty thinker of the outfit, ain't you? Now that you mention it, though, we may find that the Last of the Mohicans ain't entirely toothless, at that. But say, Mart, how come I'm as wild and cock-eyed as I ever was? Rovol's a slow and thoughtful old codger, and with his accumulation of knowledge it looks like I'd be the same way."

"Far from it," Crane replied. "Your nature and mine remain unchanged. Temperament is a basic trait of heredity, and is neither affected nor acquired by increase of knowledge. You acquired knowledge from Rovol, Drasnik, and others, as did I—but you are still the flashing genius and I am still your balance wheel. As for Fenachrone toothlessness: now that you have considered it, what is your opinion?"

"Hard to say. They didn't know how to control the fifth order rays, or they wouldn't have run. They've got real brains, though, and they'll have something like seventy days to work on the problem. While it doesn't stand to reason that they could find out much in seventy days, still they may have had a set-up of instruments on their detectors that would have enabled them to analyze our fields and thus compute the structure of the secondary projector we used there. If so, it wouldn't take them long to find out enough to give us plenty of grief-but I don't really believe that they knew enough. I don't quite know what to think. They may be easy and they may not; but, easy or hard to get, we're loaded for bear and I'm plenty sure that we'll pull their corks."

"So am I, really, but we must consider every contingency. We know that they had at least a detector of fifth-order rays...."

"And if they did have an analytical detector," Seaton interrupted, "they'll probably slap a ray on us as soon as we stick our nose out of the Galaxy!"

"They may-and even though I do not believe that there is any probability of them actually doing it, it will be well to be armed against the possibility."

"Right, old top-we'll do that little thing!"

Uneventful days passed, and true to Seaton's calculations, the awful acceleration with which they had started out could not be maintained. A few days before the edge of the Galaxy was reached, it became necessary to cut off the molecular drive, and to proceed with an acceleration equal only to that of gravitation at the surface of the Earth. Tired of weightlessness and its attendant discomforts to everyday life, the travelers enjoyed the interlude immensely, but it was all too short-too soon the stars thinned out ahead of *"Three's"* needle prow. As soon as the way ahead of them was clear, Seaton again put on the maximum power of his terrific bars and, held securely at the console, set up a long and involved integral. Ready to transfer the blended and assembled forces to a plunger, he stayed his hand, thought a moment, and turned to Crane.

"Want some advice, Mart. I'd thought of setting up three or four courses of five-ply screen on the board—a detector screen on the outside of each course, next to it a repeller, then a full-coverage ether-ray screen, then a zone of force, and a full-coverage fifth-order ray-screen as a liner. Then, with them all set up on the board, but not out, throw out a wide detector. That detector would react upon the board at impact with anything hostile, and automatically throw out the courses it found necessary."

"That sounds like ample protection, but I am not enough of a ray-specialist to pass an opinion. Upon what point are you doubtful?"

"About leaving them on the board. The only trouble is that the reaction isn't absolutely instantaneous. Even fifth-order rays would require a millionth of a second or so to set the courses. Now if they were using ether waves, that would be lots of time to block them, but if they *should* happen to have fifth-order stuff it'd get here the same time our own detector-impulse would, and it's just barely conceivable that they might give us a nasty jolt before the defenses went out. Nope, I'm developing a cautious streak myself now, when I take time to do it. We've got lots of uranium, and I'm going to put one course out."

"You cannot put everything out, can you?"

"Not quite, but pretty nearly, I'll leave a hole in the ether screen to pass visible light-no, I won't either. You folks can see just as well, even on the direct-vision wall plates, with light heterodyned on the fifth, so we'll close all ether bands, absolutely. All we'll have to leave open will be the one extremely narrow band upon which our projector is operating, and I'll protect that with a detector screen. Also, I'm going to send out all four courses, instead of only one-then I'll *know* we're all right."

"Suppose they find our one band, narrow as it is? Of course, if that were shut off automatically by the detector, we'd be safe; but would we not be out of control?"

"Not necessarily—I see you didn't get quite all this stuff over the educator. The other projector worked that way, on one fixed band out of the nine thousand odd possible. But this one is an ultra-projector, an improvement invented at the last minute. Its carrier wave can be shifted at will from one band of the fifth order to any other one; and I'll bet a hat that's *one* thing the Fenachrone haven't got! Any other suggestions?...all right, let's get busy!"

A single light, quick-acting detector was sent out ahead of four courses of five-ply screen, then Seaton's fingers again played over the keys, fabricating a detector screen so tenuous that it would react to nothing weaker than a copper power bar in full operation and with so nearly absolute zero resistance that it could be driven at the full velocity of his ultra-projector. Then, while Crane watched the instruments closely and while Dorothy and Margaret watched the faces of their husbands with only mild interest, Seaton drove home the plunger that sent that prodigious and ever-widening fan ahead of them with a velocity unthinkable millions of times that of light. For five minutes, until that far-flung screen had gone as far as it could be thrown by the utmost power of the uranium bar, the two men stared at the unresponsive instruments, then Seaton shrugged his shoulders.

"I had a hunch," he remarked with a grin. "They didn't wait for us a second. 'I don't care for some,' says they, 'I've already had any.' They're running in a straight line, with full power on, and don't intend to stop or slow down."

"How do you know?" asked Dorothy. "By the distance? How far away are they?"

"I know, Red-Top, by what I didn't find out with that screen I just put out. It didn't reach them, and it went so far that the distance is absolutely meaningless, even expressed in parsecs. Well, a stern chase is proverbially a long chase, and I guess this one isn't going to be any exception."

Every eight hours Seaton launched his all-embracing ultra-detector, but day after day passed and the instruments remained motionless after each cast of that gigantic net. For several days the Galaxy behind them had been dwindling from a mass of stars down to a huge bright lens;

down to a small, faint lens; down to a faintly luminous patch. At the previous cast of the detector it had still been visible as a barely-perceptible point of light in the highest telescopic power of the visiplate. Now, as Dorothy and Seaton, alone in the control room, stared into that visiplate, everything was blank and black; sheer, indescribable blackness; the utter and absolute absence of everything visible or tangible.

"This is awful, Dick....It's just too darn horrible. It simply scares me pea-green!" she shuddered as she drew herself to him, and he swept both his mighty arms around her in a soul-satisfying embrace.

"'Sall right, darling. That stuff out there'd scare anybody—I'm scared purple myself. It isn't in any finite mind to understand anything infinite or absolute. There's one redeeming feature, though, cuddle-pup—we're together."

"You chirped it, lover!" Dorothy returned his caresses with all her old-time fervor and enthusiasm. "I feel lots better now. If it gets to you that way, too, I know it's perfectly normal—I was beginning to think maybe I was yellow or something...but maybe you're kidding me?" she held him off at arm's length, looking deep into his eyes: then, reassured, went back-into his arms. "Nope, you feel it, too," and her glorious auburn head found its natural resting-place in the curve of his mighty shoulder.

"Yellow!...You?" Seaton pressed his wife closer still! and laughed aloud. "Maybe-but so is picric acid; so is nitroglycerin; and so is pure gold."

"Flatterer!" Her low, entrancing chuckle bubbled over. "But you know I just revel in it. I'll kiss you for that!"

"It *is* awfully lonesome out here, without even a star to look at," she went on, after a time, then laughed again. "If the Cranes and Shiro weren't along, we'd be really 'alone at last,' wouldn't we?"

"I'll say we would! But that reminds me of something. According to my figures, we might have been able to detect the Fenachrone on the last test, but we didn't. Think I'll try 'em again before we turn in."

Once more he flung out that tenuous net of force, and as it reached the extreme limit of its travel, the needle of the micro-ammeter flickered slightly, barely moving off its zero mark.

"Whee! Whoopee!" he yelled. "Mart, we're on 'em!"

"Close?" demanded Crane, hurrying into the control room upon his beam.

"Anything but. Barely touched 'em-current something less than a thousandth of a microampere on a million to one step-up. However, it proves our ideas are O. K."

The next day—*Skylark III* was running on Eastern Standard Time, of the Terrestrial United States of America-the two mathematicians covered sheet after sheet of paper with computations and curves. After checking and rechecking the figures, Seaton shut off the power, released the molecular drive, and applied acceleration of twenty-nine point six oh two feet per second; and five human beings breathed as one a profound sigh of relief as an almost-normal force of gravitation was restored to them.

"Why the let-up?" asked Dorothy. "They're an awful long ways off yet, aren't they? Why not hurry up and catch them?"

"Because we're going infinitely faster than they are now. If we kept up full acceleration, we'd pass them so fast that we couldn't fight them at all. This way, we'll still be going a lot faster than they are when we get close to them, but not enough faster to keep us from maneuvering relatively to their vessel, if things should go that far. Guess I'll take another reading on 'em."

"I do not believe that I should," Crane suggested, thoughtfully. "After all, they may have perfected their instruments, and yet may not have detected that extremely light touch of our ray last night. If so, why put them on guard?"

"They're probably on guard, all right, without having to be put there-but it's a sound idea, anyway. Along the same line I'll release the fifth-order screens, with the fastest possible detector on guard. We're just about within reach of a light copper-driven ray right now, but it's a cinch they can't send anything heavy this far, and if they think we're overconfident, so much the better."

"There," he continued, after a few minutes at the keyboard. "All set. If they put a detector on us, I've got a force set to make a noise like a New York City fire siren. If pressed, I'd reluctantly admit that in my opinion we're carrying caution to a point ten thousand degrees below the absolute zero of sanity. I'll bet my shirt that we don't hear a yip out of them before we touch 'em off. Furthermore...."

The rest of his sentence was lost in a crescendo bellow of sound. Seaton, still at the controls, shut off the noise, studied his meters carefully, and turned around to Crane with a grin.

"You win the shirt, Mart. I'll give it to you next Wednesday, when my other one comes back from the laundry. It's a fifth-order detector ray, coming in beautifully on band forty-seven fifty, right in the middle of the order."

"Aren't you going to put a ray on 'em?" asked Dorothy in surprise.

"Nope-what's the use? I can read theirs as well as I could one of my own. Maybe they know that too-if they don't we'll let 'em think we're coming along, as innocent as Mary's little lamb, so I'll let their ray stay on us. It's too thin to carry anything, and if they thicken it up much I've got an axe set to chop it off." Seaton whistled a merry lilting refrain as his fingers played over the stops and keys.

"Why, Dick, you seem actually pleased about it." Margaret was plainly ill at ease.

"Sure am. I never did like to drown baby kittens, and it kinda goes against the grain to stab a guy in the back, when he ain't even looking, even if he is a Fenachrone. If they can fight back some I'll get mad enough to blow 'em up happy."

"But suppose they fight back too hard?"

"They can't—the worst that can possibly happen is that we can't lick them. They certainly can't lick us, because we can outrun 'em. If we can't get 'em alone, we'll beat it back to Norlamin and bring up re-enforcements."

"I am not so sure," Crane spoke slowly. "There is, I believe, a theoretical possibility that sixth-order rays exist. Would an extension of the methods of detection of fifth-order rays reveal them?"

"*Sixth*? Sweet spirits of niter! Nobody knows anything about them. However, I've had one surprise already, so maybe your suggestion isn't as crazy as it sounds. We've got three or four days yet before either side can send anything except on the sixth, so I'll find out what I can do."

He flew at the task, and for the next three days could hardly be torn from it for rest; but

"O. K., Mart," he finally announced. "They exist, all right, and I can detect 'em. Look here," and he pointed to a tiny receiver, upon which a small lamp flared in brilliant scarlet light.

"Are they sending them?"

"No, fortunately. They're coming from our bar. See, it shines blue when I put a grounded shield between it and the bar, and stays blue when I attach it to their detector ray."

"Can you direct them?"

"Not a chance in the world. That means a lifetime, probably many lifetimes, of research, unless somebody uses a fairly complete pattern of them close enough to this detector so that I can analyze it. 'Sa good deal like calculus in that respect. It took thousands of years to get it in the first place, but it's easy when somebody that already knows it shows you how it goes."

"The Fenachrone learned to direct fifth-order rays so quickly, then, by an analysis of our fifth-order projector there?"

"Our secondary projector, yes. They must have had some neutronium in stock, too-but it would have been funny if they hadn't, at that-they've had intra-atomic power for ages."

Silent and grim, he seated himself at the console, and for an hour he wove an intricate pattern of forces upon the inexhaustible supply of keys afforded by the ultra-projector before he once touched a plunger.

"What are you doing? I followed you for a few hundred steps, but could go no farther."

255

"Merely a little safety-first stuff. In case they should send any real pattern of sixth-order rays this set-up will analyze it, record the complete analysis, throw out a screen against every frequency of the pattern, throw on the molecular drive, and pull us back toward the galaxy at full acceleration, while switching the frequency of our carrier wave a thousand times a second, to keep them from shooting a hot one through our open band. It'll do it all in about a millionth of a second, too —I want to get us all back alive if possible! Hm —m. They've shut off their ray-they know we've tapped onto it. Well, war's declared now-we'll see what we can see."

Transferring the assembled beam to a plunger, he sent out a secondary projector toward the Fenachrone vessel, as fast as it could be driven, close behind a widespread detector net. He soon found the enemy cruiser, but so immense was the distance that it was impossible to hold the projection anywhere in its neighborhood. They flashed beyond it and through it and upon all sides of it, but the utmost delicacy of the controls would not permit of holding even upon the immense bulk of the vessel, to say nothing of holding upon such a relatively tiny object as the power bar. As they flashed repeatedly through the warship, they saw piecemeal and sketchily her formidable armament and the hundreds of men of her crew, each man at battle station at the controls of some frightful engine of destruction. Suddenly they were cut off as a screen closed behind them-the Earth-men felt an instant of unreasoning terror as it seemed that one-half of their peculiar dual personalities vanished utterly. Seaton laughed.

"That was a funny sensation, wasn't it? It just means that they've climbed a tree and pulled the tree up after them."

"I do not like the odds, Dick," Crane's face was grave. "They have many hundreds of men, all trained; and we are only two. Yes, only one, for I count for nothing at those controls."

"All the better, Mart. This board more than makes up the difference. They've got a lot of stuff, of course, but they haven't got anything like this control system. Their captain's got to issue orders, whereas I've got everything right under my hands. Not so uneven as they think!"

Within battle range at last, Seaton hurled his utmost concentration of direct forces, under the impact of which three courses of Fenachrone defensive screen flared through the ultra-violet and went black. There the massed direct attack was stopped-at what cost the enemy alone knew-and the Fenachrone countered instantly and in a manner totally unexpected. Through the narrow slit in the fifth-order screen through which Seaton was operating, in the bare one-thousandth of a second that it was open, so exactly synchronized and timed that the screens did not even glow as it went through the narrow opening, a gigantic beam of heterodyned force struck full upon the bow of the *Skylark*, near the sharply-pointed prow, and the stubborn metal instantly flared blinding white and exploded outward in puffs of incandescent gas under the awful power of that Titanic thrust. Through four successive skins of inoson, the theoretical ultimate of possible strength, toughness, and resistance, that frightful beam drove before the automatically-reacting detector closed the slit and the impregnable defensive screens, driven by their mighty uranium bars, flared into incandescent defense. Driven as they were, they held, and the Fenachrone, finding that particular attack useless, shut off their power.

"Wow! They sure have got something!" Seaton exclaimed in unfeigned admiration. "They sure gave us a solid kick that time! We will now take time out for repairs. Also, I'm going to cut our slit down to a width of one kilocycle, if I can possibly figure out a way of working on that narrow a band, and I'm going to step up our shifting speed to a hundred thousand. It's a good thing they built this ship of ours in a lot of layers-if that'd go through the interior we would have been punctured for fair. You might weld up those holes, Mart, while I see what I can do here."

Then Seaton noticed the women, white and trembling, upon a seat.

"'Smatter? Cheer up, kids, you ain't seen nothing yet. That was just a couple of little preliminary love-taps, like two boxers kinda feeling each other out in the first ten seconds of the first round."

"Preliminary love-taps!" repeated Dorothy, looking into Seaton's eyes and being reassured by the serene confidence she read there. "But they hit us, and hurt us badly—why, there's a hole in our *Skylark* as big as a house, and it goes through four or five layers!"

"Yes, but we're not hurt a bit. They're easily fixed, and we've lost nothing but a few tons of inoson and uranium. We've got lots of spare metal. I don't know what I did to him, any more than he knows what he did to us, but I'll bet my other shirt that he knows he's been nudged!"

Repairs completed and the changes made in the method of projection, Seaton actuated the rapidly-shifting slit and peered through it at the enemy vessel. Finding their screens still up, he directed a complete-coverage attack upon them with four bars, while with the entire massed power of the remaining generators concentrated into one frequency, he shifted that frequency up and down the spectrum, probing, probing, ever probing with that gigantic beam of intolerable energy—feeling for some crack, however slight, into which he could insert that searing sheet of concentrated destruction. Although much of the available power of the Fenachrone was perforce devoted to repelling the continuous attack of the Terrestrials, they maintained an equally continuous attack offensive, and in spite of the narrowness of the open slit and the rapidity with which that slit was changing from frequency to frequency, enough of the frightful forces came through to keep the ultra-powered defensive screens radiating far into the violet—and, the utmost power of the refrigerating system proving absolutely useless against the concentrated beams being employed, mass after mass of inoson was literally blown from the outer and secondary skins of the *Skylark* by the comparatively tiny jets of force that leaked through the momentarily open slit from time to time, as exact synchronization was accidentally obtained.

Seaton, grimly watching his instruments, glanced at Crane, who, calm but watchful at his console, was repairing the damage as fast as it was done.

"They're sending more stuff, Mart, and it's getting hotter to handle. That means they're building more projectors. We can play that game, too. They're using up their fuel reserves fast; but we're bigger than they are, carry more metal, and it's more efficient metal, too. Only one way out of it, I guess—what say we put in enough generators to smother them down by brute force, no matter how much power it takes?"

"Why don't you use some of those awful copper shells? Or aren't we close enough yet?" Dorothy's low voice came clearly, so utterly silent was that frightful combat.

"Close! We're still better than two hundred thousand light-years apart! There may have been longer-range battles than this somewhere in the Universe, but I doubt it. And as for copper, even if we could get it to them, it'd be just like so many candy kisses compared to the stuff we're both using. Dear girl, there are fields of force extending for thousands of miles from each of these vessels beside which the exact center of the biggest lightning flash you ever saw would be a dead area!"

He set up a series of integrals and, machine after machine, in a space left vacant by the rapidly-vanishing store of uranium, there appeared inside the fourth skin of the *Skylark* a row of gigantic generators, each one adding its hellish output to the already inconceivable stream of energy being directed at the foe. As that frightful flow increased by leaps and bounds, the intensity of the Fenachrone attack diminished, and finally it ceased altogether as every iota of the enemy's power became necessary for the maintenance of the defenses. Still greater grew the stream of force from the *Skylark*, and, now that the attack had ceased, Seaton opened the slit wider and stopped its shifting, in order still further to increase the efficiency of his terrible weapon. Face set in a fighting mask and eyes hard as gray iron, deeper and deeper he drove his now irresistible forces. His flying fingers were upon the keys of his console; his keen and merciless eyes were in a secondary projector near the now doomed ship of the Fenachrone, directing masterfully his terrible attack. As the output of his generators still increased, Seaton began to compress a searing hollow sphere of seething energy upon the furiously-straining defensive screens of the Fenachrone. Course after course of the heaviest possible screen was sent out, driven by massed batteries of copper now disintegrating at the rate of tons in every second, only to flare through the ultra-violet and to go down before that dreadful, that irresistible onslaught. Finally, as the inexorable sphere still contracted, the utmost efforts of the defenders could not keep their screens away from their own vessel, and simultaneously the prow and the stern of the Fenachrone cruiser was bared to that awful field of force, in which no possible substance could endure for even the most infinitesimal instant of time.

There was a sudden cessation of all resistance, and those Titanic forces, all directed inward, converged upon a point with a power behind which there was the inconceivable energy of four hundred thousand tons of uranium, being disintegrated at the highest possible rate, short of instant disruption. In that same instant of collapse, the enormous mass of power-copper in the Fenachrone cruiser and the vessel's every atom, alike of structure and contents, also exploded into pure energy at the touch of that unimaginable field of force.

In that awful moment before Seaton could shut off his power it seemed to him that space itself must be obliterated by the very concentration of the unknowable and incalculable forces there unleashed-must be swallowed up and lost in the utterly indescribable brilliance of the field of radiance driven to a distance of millions upon incandescent millions of miles from the place where the last representatives of the monstrous civilization of the Fenachrone had made their last stand against the forces of Universal Peace.

Epilogue

The three-dimensional, moving, talking, almost living picture, being shown simultaneously in all the viewing areas throughout the innumerable planets of the Galaxy, faded out and the image of an aged, white-bearded Norlaminian appeared and spoke in the Galactic language.

"As is customary, the showing of this picture has opened the celebration of our great Galactic holiday, Civilization Day. As you all know, it portrays the events leading up to and making possible the formation of the League of Civilization by a mere handful of planets. The League now embraces all of this, the First Galaxy, and is spreading rapidly throughout the Universe. Varied are the physical forms and varied are the mentalities of our almost innumerable races of beings, but in Civilization we are becoming one, since those backward people who will not co-operate with us are rendered impotent to impede our progress among the more enlightened.

"It is peculiarly fitting that the one who has just been chosen to head the Galactic Council-the first person of a race other than one of those of the Central System to prove himself able to wield justly the vast powers of that office-should be a direct descendant of two of the revered persons whose deeds of olden times we have just witnessed.

"I present to you my successor as Chief of the Galactic Council, Richard Ballinger Seaton, the fourteen hundred sixty-ninth, of Earth."

The End